THE COVER-UP

DANA GRIFFIN

Copyright © Dana H. Griffin 2012

This book is a work of fiction. Names, characters, places, and incidents either are the product of the author's imagination or are used fictitiously, and any resemblance to actual person, living or dead, business establishments, events, or locales is entirely coincidental.

Without limiting the rights under copyright reserved above, no part of this publication may be reproduced, stored in, or introduced into a retrieval system, or transmitted in any form or by any means (electronic, mechanical, photocopying, recording, or otherwise) without the prior written permission of both the copyright owner.

The scanning, uploading, and distribution of this book via the Internet or via any other means without the permission of the copyright owner is illegal and punishable by law. Please purchase only authorized electronic or printed editions, and do not participate in or encourage electronic piracy of copyrighted materials. Your support of the author's rights is appreciated.

Also By Dana Griffin

Coerced

Calamity

Blamed

For Becky

Chapter One

Monday, June 14 2:07 p.m.

Chunks of rubber as large as garbage can lids flew from the tire of the main landing gear of the Omega Airline 737.

LaGuardia Airport air traffic controller Sanchez Lopez's heart pounded as he watched the aircraft continue to accelerate for another thousand feet. Then, slots in the sides of the two jet engines opened and the nose of the airplane dipped, indicating the crew rejected the takeoff.

Sanchez looked to his right. United Airlines Flight 549 crossed the end of runway three-one and began its flare to slow its descent rate for landing. Runway four, which the Omega aircraft barreled down, intersected runway three-one. There was the potential for a collision, or the runway being contaminated from the debris from Omega's tire. He keyed his microphone. "United 549, go around. Aircraft on the runway."

Omega continued through the intersection and raced toward the end of the pavement. It appeared to be going too fast to stop on the remaining runway. The last two thousand feet was built out over Flushing Bay, with a twenty-foot drop to the water.

Sanchez curled his toes as if pressing on the brakes of the aircraft, willing it to stop. Eventually, his training kicked in. He raised his voice to get the attention of the other six controllers. "Omega 918 is going off the end of the runway."

The other controllers pivoted their heads to the end of runway four.

Sanchez confirmed visually that United 549 was in a climb, retracting its landing gear, before he spoke into his boom microphone. "United 549, fly heading three four zero. Climb and maintain five thousand feet."

He glanced back in time to see Omega slide off the end of runway four.

"Shit!" Sanchez braced himself against the counter as if he were in the airplane.

The airplane was airborne for two hundred feet, then smashed through the first set of approach-light stanchions. Parts of the engine cowling ripped away as if from an explosion. The plane continued forward, its nose canted down, for another two hundred feet before it collided with the second stanchion. The tail of the aircraft rose before slamming down, sending out a shower of water.

The 737's left wing sat on the stanchion. The right one lay in the water, canting the aircraft thirty degrees. Its nose looked as if a wrecking ball had smacked it.

Chapter Two

Monday, June 14 2:52 p.m.

Kyle Masters sat in the instructor seat of the 737 simulator, evaluating the two pilots in the captain's and first officer's seats. Kyle still marveled, after twenty-five years of being an airline pilot, that technology made flying this computer seem as real as flying the actual aircraft.

The two applicants were completing their final training requirement to become two more of Omega Airline's 5000 pilots. Kyle was one of four instructors, out of 200 at Omega, qualified to conduct the check-ride.

The two flew a category III instrument landing system autoland approach to within fifty feet of the runway. The first officer said, "Minimums."

With the exception of the thickest fog, they should have seen the runway lights. They did not today because Kyle had programmed the simulator to not show any. He leaned forward to better evaluate what they would do next.

The Captain pushed a button on the throttles. The engines increased power, and the airplane pitched up. "Going around. Flaps fifteen. Check power. Positive rate gear up. Set missed approach altitude."

Kyle smiled. If they continued flying this flawlessly, he'd see no reason not to hand them new pilot licenses with B-737 typed on them.

The phone on the back wall of the simulator rang.

In Kyle's eight years as an instructor, the phone had rung only twice. It was Omega's policy not to interrupt training unless the simulator building was on fire, or some other emergency.

Using a nonchalant voice, Kyle asked, "One of your wives calling to see how you're doing?"

Neither pilot said anything.

They must be nervous? Or was it, as his wife Karen often replied lately, he wasn't as funny as he thought? Kyle unbuckled his seatbelt and stood. "Sorry about this, guys. Continue on this heading and altitude. Relax a moment."

He lifted the phone from its cradle. "Hello." He hoped his disgust was apparent.

"Kyle, it's Morgan. Stop your check-ride and come to my office immediately."

Morgan Steele, or Morgue as some of the instructors called him because he had the humor of a dead man, was the vice president of Flight Standards and Training. He was Kyle's boss and the man in charge of pilot training for all three of Omega's fleets.

Kyle smiled with anticipation. Steele might be announcing that Kyle had been selected to be the new 737 fleet manager.

That position was responsible for the instructors and training for the fleet. The 737 position had been vacant since the former manager had been selected to head the Boeing 787 program. Omega would be the launch customer in the U.S. for the 787. Kyle and another instructor, Richard Ryan, were assistant fleet managers of the 737 and were considered top contenders for the open position.

Dread began to knot Kyle's stomach. Steele might be telling him he had been turned down for the position before announcing who had been chosen.

"Ah, sir, if it's to tell me I didn't get the fleet manager position, you can tell me now, and we won't have to disrupt these two pilots' check-ride."

"What? Oh. No, it's not that. That decision will have to wait a while." He sighed. "We've had an accident. You're going to the scene to represent the company in the investigation."

For a moment, Kyle thought he'd heard wrong. *An accident?* Then reality set in, making his hands shake. "Oh." He chastised himself for being so forward with his previous comment. "I'll be right there."

Kyle hung up. An accident! What happened? Was the crew anyone he knew? He pushed the button on the instructor's panel to lower the simulator.

"I hate to do this to you guys, but I'm being called away on an important matter and can't finish your check-ride." *Important matter?* "Call training, and they'll reschedule you."

He gathered his things. The two pilots had turned in their seats to look back at him, the disappointment evident on their faces. Twenty-two years earlier, if Kyle's final check-ride to become an Omega pilot had been cancelled, he would have been frustrated too. They had spent the last two months in training, and if they passed this check-ride, they would begin their careers as pilots for one of the premier major airlines. Both probably hadn't slept well last night, kept awake by the need to go over and over the different procedures they had learned so they didn't screw up today's test. To have it canceled seemed cruel.

After getting briefed by Steele, Kyle ran to his car. He had enough time to make the half-hour drive home, pack a bag, and hurry back to the Houston Intercontinental Airport to catch a flight to Newark.

The few details Steele provided ran through his head. It appeared the crew had rejected the takeoff and slid off the end of the runway. Passengers were being rescued. They did not know if anyone had been killed, or the extent of any injuries. They also didn't know if the crew was okay or why they had rejected the takeoff.

Omega had two thousand flights a day, and there might be one rejected takeoff a week without any mishaps. Why hadn't they stopped on the runway?

A pickup was parked in front of his multi-gabled, Craftsman home at the end of a cul-de-sac filled with similar upper-middle-income homes. Shrubs and flowers filled a trailer attached to the pickup. Karen stood on the lawn in shorts and a patterned t-shirt, a glass of iced tea in her hand. She would occasionally point, and a man would dig around a shrub to remove it.

Kyle took a deep breath as he parked, preparing himself for this exchange. The frown on Karen's face darkened his mood. *It's good to see you too.*

"What are you doing home so early?" Her tone was more accusatory than inquisitive.

When had getting off early gone from being a pleasant surprise to something suspicious? Several sharp replies came to mind. One was, *why are these men tearing out our landscaping and replacing it?* He had no idea this would be happening. Kyle assumed Rachael, one of Karen's friends, suggested she do so. It was easy for Rachael to live so extravagantly; her husband made more money than Kyle.

He wished Karen was secure enough she didn't feel the need to live up to others' standards. And he wished he didn't look down on her for lacking confidence in herself. "I have to go to LaGuardia." He motioned with his head. "Let's go inside. I'll tell you why."

She sipped her drink before following him.

When she closed the door, more firmly than he thought necessary, he said, "We've had an accident at LaGuardia, and I'm flying there to assist with the investigation."

She searched his face.

Kyle hoped the old Karen, the one who would be expecting him to be joking, would search for the telltale sign of a prank. Her narrowed eyes told him differently.

"You're the only one who can go?"

"There will be others from the company there. My knowledge of how we operate the airplane and how the crews are trained will be needed."

"What about our counseling session tonight?"

A flicker of anger made him clench his teeth. She thought an appointment with a marriage counselor more important than finding out why an airliner crashed? Then he realized that to Karen, it was. "I'll have to cancel. I'm sorry."

"You don't want our marriage to work, do you?" Her face twisted with rage. "You canceled last week's appointment when you *had* to fill in for someone who was oh so conveniently, sick."

Her doubting him raised his anger. He wished she could look at the big picture. "It might seem that way, but that's not true." He reached out to hold her, but she held her toned arms up to ward him off. "The accident happened less than an hour ago. They stopped the check-ride I was giving to send me there. If it was any other reason, I'd tell them I couldn't go. I can't say no to this. The airline is in a crisis."

"Our marriage is in crisis," she shrieked. "As usual, you're choosing your job over us."

"That's not true."

"Isn't it?"

He glanced at his watch. "I have to pack. Come to the bedroom, so we can talk."

"What's the point?" She started toward the kitchen. "You don't want to talk."

Hadn't he just asked her to?

She turned back to him. "Either you come with me tonight, or I want a divorce." Her eyes burned with determination.

Kyle's shoulders sagged, and he bowed his head. It seemed all they did now was fight. After a huge blow-up several weeks ago over Karen's constant spending, she'd made an ultimatum: they go to counseling to work out their differences or they'd separate. This was the first time either of them mentioned divorce.

"Please don't do this now. I want to work things out. When I get back from this investigation, I'll do whatever it takes."

"Screw you! It'll just be something else then. I'm through." She disappeared into the kitchen.

Kyle stood in the hall to the master bedroom and considered calling Steele and telling him he couldn't go. That would end his chance to be fleet manager. He might be fired from the training department. What a waste that would be. He'd worked hard to become an instructor and then assistant fleet manager.

Steele had hinted he might be the new fleet manager if he represented the airline well in this investigation. In a couple of years, when Steele retired, Kyle might be in line for his position. If things worked out, Kyle could end his airline career as Executive Vice President of operations, the position above Steele's and just below the CEO's. With the bump in salary and the stock options each of these positions would present him, they could retire very comfortably. Didn't Karen realize this? The way she spent money, he would have thought she would be supporting his decision to accept a job with more responsibility, like aiding in the investigation.

Chapter Three

Monday, June 14 4:41 p.m.

On the flight to Newark, Kyle tried to review the training records of the two pilots involved in the accident, but his concentration kept wandering. He spent most of the flight staring out the window with his stomach in knots, thinking about Karen's claim she wanted a divorce. He hoped she was crying out to him the only way she knew, by threatening him with the one thing she didn't want. Yet she didn't make idle threats. What would this do to Travis, their fourteen-year-old son? Kyle leaned back in his seat and closed his eyes. How had they let their marriage become so miserable?

After he checked into his room at the Marriott Hotel at LaGuardia, he turned on the TV selecting a news station before calling Steele. The picture of one of their airplanes sitting in the water, with its nose and right wing submerged like a child's discarded toy, sickened him. He'd been naive to think this only happened to other airlines and not Omega.

"I just checked into the hotel," he said to Steele after he answered. "I'll be going downstairs to the NTSB briefing in a few minutes. What've you learned?"

Steele sighed. It was the most emotion Kyle could ever remember him showing. "The captain, Brent Musgrave, died in the accident. The first officer, Cheryl Wells, is in critical condition."

Kyle plopped down in a chair and held his head in his hand. It could have been him on that flight, and Travis would be fatherless. How would the captain's family deal with this tragedy?

"She's in surgery," Steele said. "The instrument panel crushed both of her legs, and they'll have to pin them back together. She had a concussion and may have internal bleeding. Two of the four flight attendants have neck or back injuries. Ten passengers died, either from the accident or after evacuating. At last count, sixty-eight were injured, ranging from critical to minor."

Kyle mentally shook himself, pulling out of his despair. He had to find out what happened so another accident could be prevented. "Have you heard why they rejected the takeoff?"

"The tower controller claims to have seen the right landing gear tire shedding rubber on the takeoff roll. We don't know at what airspeed they rejected. We'll learn that when the First Officer can talk to us, or from the data on the FDR."

Kyle glanced at his watch while wondering how long it would take the NTSB to analyze the information on the Flight Data Recorder. "I'd better head down to the briefing. I'll call you afterward."

Reporters clogged the hall to the conference room where the NTSB would hold their briefing. The area was awash in bright light from the numerous video news crews and the constant flashing from the still photographers. Reporters shouted out questions to those that passed them. Port Authority police blocked the entrance to the room, letting only the investigation team inside.

An attractive blonde woman wearing a navy-blue pantsuit shoved a microphone into Kyle's face. "Who might you be, sir?"

Kyle ducked his head. "No comment."

"Your shirt says Omega Airlines. Is it safe to fly on your airline?"

Kyle wanted to avoid the question but knew this was a perfect opportunity to give the airline some good publicity. "Yes, it's very safe to fly on Omega. We haven't had an accident in the last ten years and are considered one of the safest airlines in the world."

Other reporters circled him with a cacophony of questions.

His mouth went dry. The heat from the blinding camera lights made his forehead sweat. "I have no more comments." He shoved his way through the crowd, keeping his head down. His heart pounded.

The reporters continued to shout questions at him. "What was the cause of the accident? What's your name? What will Omega do to prevent another accident like this one? Was the captain an unsafe pilot?"

He showed his airline ID to the police at the door. They let him through.

At the front stood several people wearing dark blue windbreakers with NTSB stenciled on them. Several wore caps with the same lettering. Throughout the room, others wore jackets with FAA, ALPA, and Boeing emblems. ALPA, the Air Line Pilots Association, always sent a team of investigators to an accident of one of their member airlines.

In a corner, the FAA huddled together, talking quietly. Occasionally, one of them would glance around the room before turning their attention back to the huddle.

Troy Kircher, Omega Airlines Newark chief pilot, talked to a woman from the NTSB. Kircher was an overweight man in his sixties with deep wrinkles on his forehead from his ever-present scowl.

Kyle approached Kircher and reined in his dislike for the man. He had a reputation for being a bully, looking to chastise pilots for any infraction.

"One of my pilots will be the first to examine the flight deck," Kircher said.

This was an unusual request, Kyle thought, unless Kircher hoped to hide something incriminating that could have contributed to the accident. Kyle doubted that was possible. The NTSB was extremely thorough. Or, he wondered, was Kircher trying to protect his image? The crew was Newark-based, and Kircher might feel it would reflect poorly on his supervision if one of his crews caused the accident.

The woman, who was short and petite, stared up at Kircher without being intimidated by the larger man's scowl. "We can't allow that."

Kircher narrowed his eyes. "Only one of my pilots will know if it's safe for other investigators to be on my aircraft."

"Mr. Kircher." The woman stepped closer. "The NTSB is in charge of this investigation. It may be *your* aircraft, but we will make the decisions from now on concerning who will and will not enter it." She took the edge out of her voice. "I'll value your knowledge of the airline's procedures, as I'll be in charge of the operational part of the investigation."

To diffuse the conflict, Kyle offered his hand to the woman. "Hi. Kyle Masters with Omega Airlines."

The challenging look on the woman's face softened. She shook Kyle's hand. "Lori Almond. I'm the assistant investigator in charge."

Kircher scowled at Kyle. "Take a seat. I'll give you an assignment in a minute."

Kyle had left Houston with the impression he would be in charge of Omega's investigation, assisting the NTSB in whatever way he could. He realized Kircher might have been given the same impression from his boss, Earl Dorsey, in the ever-present departmental turf wars at Omega.

"Thanks, but I'd rather stand. It was a long flight."

Kircher's face reddened.

Kyle tried not to smirk.

Turning back to Lori, Kircher said. "Obviously, I need to talk to your superior, then."

Lori smiled with a it-won't-do-you-any-good-expression.

This made Kyle like her.

She gestured to a middle-aged, pudgy man with red hair talking on a cell phone. "Mark Evans is the IIC. You can bring your request up with him. He'll tell you the same thing, though."

Kircher stepped over next to Evans.

Lori rolled her eyes before turning her attention to Kyle. She wore her sandy brown hair short, framing her bright eyes. Prominent cheekbones and a sharp jawline would draw men's gaze that would linger. She appeared to be in her mid-forties, but wrinkles around her mouth and eyes suggested she might be older.

"I'm sorry about that," Kyle said. "Not everyone at Omega is as arrogant."

Lori cocked her head. "So, what's this, an attempt to get on my good side, hoping we can be buddies and you can influence the course of the investigation?"

Kyle's face burned. "No, it was an apology for the way an asshole talked to you. If I can help discover why this accident happened, I'll be around to do as needed." He turned to walk away.

"Hey, Masters, I think your name was." She shrugged. "That was uncalled for. I'm sorry."

To their side, Kircher gestured wildly with a raised voice and Evans shook his head.

Gesturing with his head to Kircher, Kyle said, "He doesn't bring out the best in people."

The corners of her mouth turned up.

"Why don't we take our seats and we can get started." Evans shouted.

Twenty people who represented interested parties to the investigation sat facing the twelve NTSB investigators standing at the front of the room.

"I'm Mark Evans, the NTSB investigator in charge. You'll probably hear the other NTSB investigators refer to me as the IIC. I regret we all have to meet under these circumstances. I offer my condolences to Omega Airlines for the loss of your crew member. Assisting me in the investigation is Lori Almond, who will be my second in command."

She stood to his side.

"If I'm not available, Lori should be."

He introduced the other eleven NTSB investigators—specialists in air traffic control operations, meteorology, human performance, structures, systems, power plants, maintenance records, survival factors, aircraft performance, cockpit voice recorder and flight data recorder, and metallurgy. Evans had everyone in the room state their affiliation and job title.

A middle-aged man with a fair complexion stood. "Glenn Skaggs, FAA, office of accident investigations and prevention."

"Good to see you again, Glenn." Evans gave him a brief smile.

Several others of the FAA group identified themselves, and Evans greeted them with their first names. It was obvious they'd all worked together before.

"Pierre Chavette, with the FAA." He was a short, dark-haired man who spoke with an accent. He didn't give a title.

"I haven't seen you at an investigation before, Mr. Chavette," Evans said. "Are you new to the group?"

Chavette squirmed in his seat. "Ah, no, sir. I'm with Chicago fisdo." The acronym FSDO, pronounced fisdo by those in the airline industry, stood for the Flight Standards District Office.

Evans frowned. "Are you affiliated with Omega Airlines' operational certificate?"

"Ah, no sir. The Chicago fisdo has an interest in this accident."

"Inspector Chavette will only be with us for a day or so, and then must attend to his duties in Chicago." Skaggs looked at his notepad while he spoke.

Kyle wondered what Chavette's interest in the accident was. The FSDO that handled their certificate was in Houston.

When everyone was introduced, Evans said, "Unfortunately, there won't be much we can do tonight. We'll go to the scene and examine the runway and surrounding area. The aircraft came to rest in an unsafe position for us to board and examine it. Cranes will lift the aircraft onto dollies, and it'll be towed to a hangar." He glanced at his watch. "They should arrive soon and will work through the night. The aircraft won't be at the hangar until daybreak."

They broke up so Evans could give a press conference. Kyle remained behind to listen to the reporters' questions and learn what the NTSB already knew.

The reporters stormed into the room and stood in front of Evans.

"What was the cause of the accident?" asked the blonde reporter who had shoved the microphone in Kyle's face.

"I won't speculate on the cause. The NTSB and its partners have just begun the investigation. Until we hear the cockpit voice recording, analyze the flight data recorder, and interview the first officer, the preliminary cause will not be known."

"Did a flock of birds cause the crash?" a male reporter shouted.

Kyle shook his head. A couple of years prior, a US Airways Airbus taking off from LaGuardia flew into a flock of geese and lost power to both engines. It successfully landed in the Hudson River, and all survived.

"We don't know the reason for the accident at this time," Evans repeated. "We'll be looking into every possibility."

"It's been reported terrorists stormed the flight deck. Is there any truth to this?"

Although this question seemed ridiculous, Evans' expression didn't change. "We'll be looking into every possibility."

Kyle left the room, shaking his head at the reporters' efforts to sensationalize the story. Kircher stood off to the side, talking on his phone. He pointed a finger at Kyle and curled it several times in a *come here* gesture.

Kyle sighed and sauntered over.

Kircher finished his call. "Kyle, we need to talk."

Chapter Four

Monday, June 14 10:45 p.m.

Kyle doubted Kircher wanted to talk. In his experience, the Chief Pilot was condescending to the pilots he managed and didn't value outside opinions. Kyle stood in front of Kircher and lifted his eyebrows.

Kircher rested a hand on Kyle's shoulder.

Instead of slapping the hand away like he wanted, Kyle stared at the hand until Kircher dropped it to his side.

"I know you were told you'd be leading our investigation. You and I both know you don't have the management experience. To keep the higher-ups in Houston happy, we'll let them think you're doing so. But I'll be the lead investigator so that we don't look bad in front of the FAA and NTSB."

Kyle frowned. "You don't think I have enough management experience?"

Kircher put on what Kyle thought must be his compassionate face. "You're a good instructor. I've heard a lot of good things from my pilots about you. A real good instructor." He nodded his head. "But being an instructor hasn't prepared you to defend our airline against the assault we'll be getting from the NTSB or FAA. My years as a chief pilot make me more qualified for that role. So while we're here, you'll answer to me."

"Ah, that's a good point." Kyle raised an eyebrow. "I'm curious though, where were you when we brought the new generation 737s onboard? I don't remember you holding my hand while I had daily meetings with the FAA. They wanted every 737-qualified pilot to go through initial training like they'd never flown one. The training program I developed convinced them that wasn't necessary." Kyle put his hand on Kircher's shoulder. "But your experience must've somehow influenced me then."

Kircher's face turned crimson.

Satisfaction spread through Kyle before he narrowed his eyes. "I was told I'm leading this investigation. You'll answer to me." He stepped away.

"You better not fuck up," Kircher said. "If you do, I'll make sure Houston knows you screwed up on your own."

Kyle and the other investigators were driven down the perimeter road around the airport to the end of runway four. The van shuddered when each jet on runway three-one blasted by, only several hundred feet away. The delays must have been extensive, with LaGuardia using one runway for both takeoffs and landings instead of one for each. Runway four was closed so the investigative team could examine it and collect the shredded tire pieces.

At the end of runway four, everyone climbed out of the van and stood looking northeast at the wreckage sitting in the water. Construction lighting from the shore shone on the airplane.

The evacuation slides on the right side bobbed in the water. The left ones waved back and forth in the wind. Kyle was glad he wasn't boarding the airplane, as the dark cabin gave him an ominous shiver.

This wasn't how his beloved 737 was supposed to be resting. He kicked at the ground to bring himself out of the melancholy and examined the airplane as best he could.

The speed brakes, the six desk-sized panels on the top of each wing, had been stowed. During a rejected takeoff, they would have deployed, protruding from the top of the wing to destroy lift, giving the tires more traction to stop the aircraft. The flaps had been lowered from their takeoff position. It was an emergency procedure to lower the speed brakes and flaps to evacuate the airplane. This made it easier for passengers who evacuated out the window exits to slide off the wing. Either the captain had lived long enough to do so, or the first officer had done this.

He made a mental note to check into it. Pride rose in his chest because the crew had followed the procedure he and the other instructors had drilled into them.

Brandon Spikol, one of Omega's maintenance investigators, stood beside Kyle. "What a mess."

"Yeah. What a mess."

The roar from the generators powering the lights and the aircraft nearby made conversation without shouting difficult. In the water a short distance from the aircraft, several New York Airport Port Authority police boats kept the media and other spectators away.

"The last person off forgot to close the doors," Kyle said.

Brandon smiled. "The slides are still inflated. I'll sign'em off."

Kyle smiled at the joke. When a system on an airplane was tested by maintenance, if it passed, a mechanic signed paperwork certifying it airworthy.

Kyle's smile vanished. "I wish we could see the landing gear."

"Me too. Prior to 918's flight here from Houston, the crew had us check out number four tire. The mechanic who inspected it said it had worn through two layers of cord, but the third wasn't visible."

Number four tire was the one reported shedding rubber.

The NTSB investigators had everyone form a line across the runway, walk down it, and inspect it with flashlights. They started at the departure end, closest to the 737, and worked their way toward where it had begun its takeoff roll. The first third of the runway was coated in melted rubber from the thousands of tires that had landed on it. From his experience Kyle knew that made the runway slick and reduced the braking coefficient needed to get stopped. Was that a contributing factor?

Several hundred feet from the departure end, pieces of the disintegrated tire became visible. Each piece was photographed and marked. Measurements were taken from the end and side of the runway. The biggest pieces were found three quarters of the way from where the 737 had begun its takeoff roll. This was where the tire disintegrated. They searched the runway for something that might've punctured the tire but found nothing.

They worked their way back down the runway to the departure end, not finding anything they hadn't found the first time. Kyle stopped where the accumulation of tire pieces was the biggest and looked at the remaining runway. The distance looked short, incredibly short. Sitting ten feet higher in the cockpit and traveling better than one hundred-twenty knots would've made it seem even shorter. Why would the crew decide to reject with so little runway left? It looked suicidal to consider such a maneuver.

The cranes arrived and began setting up. It would take most of the night before they were rigged to the airplane and ready to lift it.

There was nothing for Kyle to do, so he went back to the hotel to get a few hours of sleep.

In bed, he thought about what he had learned during the briefing and seen on the runway. His thoughts drifted to Karen's threat. If he hadn't come to the accident, would their counseling session have been productive? Would they have gone to bed tonight and cuddled for the first time in months?

Kyle rolled over, pissed at himself. He hadn't called home. How could he convince her he wanted to salvage their marriage when he couldn't take a couple of minutes to let her know he had arrived safely? No doubt she thought this typical of him—which, he had to admit, it was. He'd call first thing in the morning before she took Travis to school.

Chapter Five

Tuesday, June 15 4:30 a.m.

Kyle arrived at the crash scene after his three-hour nap, dull and lethargic.

Several investigators stood together on the end of the runway, watching the crane crew complete their rigging. A short distance away, Lori Almond paced briskly with a two-way radio in her hand. Kyle could join the group of men who would be bullshitting about the cause of the accident, or he could get to know the woman in charge of the operational part of the investigation. He was Omega's expert on the 737's procedures.

As he approached, she gave him a quick once over and went back to watching the crane crew. She wore the same clothes as last night.

"Hi. Have you been here all night?"

Lori's nostrils flared, as if smelling his shower and shave. "No, I got up to see the sunrise." She looked away with eyebrows furrowed and a subtle shake of her head.

Ah, another wiseass. He hid his smile by taking a drink of coffee he had brought from the hotel.

They watched a worker stand precariously atop a wing attaching a sling that was draped around the wing to a crane hook. Lori cleared her throat. "What can you tell me about the crew of the flight?"

"The captain was Brent Musgrave."

Lori donned glasses that rested on the end of her nose, dug out a notepad, and scribbled notes.

Kyle wondered if she had recently started needing the glasses or had worn them for several years as he did. "He's been with Omega twenty-three years, and a 737 captain for ten. There's nothing unusual in his training records except six months ago he received additional training for sterile cockpit procedures."

Airline crews were forbidden to talk about anything unrelated to the flight while taxiing and flying below ten thousand feet. Because of the routine, monotonous nature of airline flying, crews became complacent, making this the most violated rule.

Lori frowned. "Why the additional training?"

"I don't know yet. I've left a message with my boss to have someone in Houston look into it. I'm guessing he had a routine line check by one of our instructors or an FAA inspector and broke the sterile cockpit rule. A routine line check is given—"

"Heh, flyboy, I'm an ATP with ten thousand hours and several type ratings. I've a master's degree in aerospace engineering. I *know* what a line check is."

He stifled his frustration. "Look." Kyle held out his arms. "I've never worked with the NTSB before. I didn't know you were so qualified or knowledgeable about our operation. Is there anything else I need to know?"

Lori turned away. "I'm sorry. I'm under a lot of pressure. This is my first time as an assistant IIC of a major airline accident. The Chairman and Evans are watching me carefully. My daughters are upset our vacation to Cape Cod next week will be canceled."

"How old are your daughters?" He asked.

"Eighteen and sixteen."

"You're old enough to have daughters that age?"

That brightened her mood. "Thanks, but the light isn't good enough to reveal the wrinkles."

Ah, so there is a jokester under that irritability. "It's good your daughters still want to go on vacation with their parents. I have a son who's fourteen. So far, he still enjoys going places with us." *Us.* He studied the wreckage, wondering if his sigh was apparent. "Won't your daughters and husband still get to go?"

"They've already gone on vacation with him and his new wife. This was to be our time together." Her voice dripped with bitterness.

He rubbed his face. *Smooth Kyle. Very smooth.* "I'm sorry. I just assumed—"

"We divorced a couple of years ago. I was really looking forward to this time before my oldest goes off to college next year. It'll be difficult to drag her away from now on."

Kyle stepped from one foot to the other. "Ah, what's it...what's it like being divorced?" He stared at the rigger, who walked precariously down the upper wing and crawled in a window exit, to avoid Lori's eye.

"The first year is hard. Eventually you get through it."

He sensed her studying him.

"Why? Are you getting divorced?"

Good question. "My wife threatened me with one before I left to come here."

"Why?"

"I had an affair with Heidi Klum."

She peered over the top of her glasses like a schoolmarm. "You wish."

He tugged the corners of his lips up, then let them fall. "I work too much. I don't make enough money. We can't seem to talk without fighting." He shrugged.

"I hope you can work it out."

Could they?

Lori stared at the airplane for several seconds. "Did you know the captain of this flight?"

"No, but I gave the first officer, Cheryl Wells, her recurrent training a year ago. She's been with Omega for eight years and a 737 FO the entire time. She's an exceptional pilot. Cheryl also is a facilitator of our Threat and Error Management course. A facilitator teaches—" When Lori raised her eyebrows, Kyle held up his hands. "Sorry, I didn't know if you knew what we taught in this course."

"So." She pointed to the wreckage. "She taught your crews how to recognize errors and correct them before something like this happened."

The irony in her words was not lost on him. "She's the last person I'd expect to be involved in an accident. There must've been extenuating circumstances for this to happen." His words tumbled out.

"What else have you learned?"

He told her about the conversation last night with Brandon, the maintenance investigator.

Lori made a note.

"They had one seat out of one hundred and seventy-four empty. I don't know yet if the empty seat was to accommodate the jump seater, or that was all the passengers they had. The webperf showed they were weight limited for the runway." He studied her a moment, wondering if she knew what a webperf was. Each airline called it something different.

"Is a webperf your weight and balance and performance data?"

"Yeah."

"So they were at the maximum weight that allowed them to accelerate to V1 and stop on the remaining runway?"

V1 was a decision speed. If the crew had a malfunction prior to this speed, they could safely reject the takeoff and stop. At V1 or after, they would continue the takeoff and handle the problem in flight. Even catastrophic events, such as an engine fire or failure, were handled in flight if it occurred at or after V1, because there might not be sufficient runway to stop after that speed.

"Yeah."

"Who was the jump seater?" Lori scribbled on her pad.

"His name was Ernest Norman. He's not an Omega Airlines' pilot. Only another airline pilot or FAA inspector is allowed to ride in the observer seat in the cockpit. I'm trying to find who he's affiliated with. Do you know which hospital the injured passengers were taken to?"

"There were several. Why?"

Kyle turned toward the skyscrapers of New York City a few miles away. "Since both pilots were injured," *or died*, he thought to himself, "I'm guessing the jump seater would be in a hospital. He'd have had a front row seat to what happened during the takeoff."

Lori nodded while scratching a note.

"We're ready to start lifting it," a voice on the two-way radio said.

"Go ahead," Evans' voice said over the radio.

Chapter Six

Tuesday, June 15 5:12 a.m.

The eastern horizon glowed orange when the right wing of the wrecked 737 rose until level with the left. The entire airplane lifted several feet above the approach light stanchions. Water ran out the open cargo compartments and dripped off the wing.

When the aircraft cleared the water and Kyle could see other views of the 737, a knot formed in his stomach. The landing gear had been sheared off. The bottom of the fuselage was dented like an empty beer can. A suitcase rested precariously on the lip of the open forward cargo compartment. The lower portion of the engine cowlings were missing. The cookie-jar-sized generator on the right engine dangled from its electrical wires. The right wing was bent up a quarter of the way from the tip. The windshields were gone, and the fuselage under them deformed inward from the airplane's collision with the approach light stanchions. The left side was damaged more than the right.

Kyle shook his head at the scope of the damage.

The airplane swung over the end of the runway and settled onto dollies.

When they began to tow the 737 to a hangar on the southeastern side of the airport, the sun was well up.

Once the wreck was parked, Omega's maintenance investigators removed panels at the tail to access the cockpit voice and flight data recorders. Two NTSB investigators watched their work.

A whistling of air escaped from the left forward evacuation slide as it was deflated. Kyle approached the group forming around the ladder leaning against the cabin door opening. Investigators from the NTSB, FAA, Boeing, and Omega stood nearby.

Evans positioned himself at the base of the ladder, blocking access. "Mr. Masters from Omega, NTSB investigator Caulk, and Almond will do the initial inspection. Mr. Masters will point out any irregularities, which will be noted. We'll photograph the cockpit and cabin, then the rest of you can do your inspection."

Kircher patted Kyle on the shoulder. "Look it over good. Let me know what you discover."

The look Kyle gave Kircher made the Chief Pilot back up a step, darkening his complexion.

Glenn Skaggs, who headed the FAA investigators, shook his head. "I must insist a member of the FAA team accompany them on this initial inspection."

Evans frowned. "You've never insisted on this before, Glenn. Why now?"

"Due to the magnitude of this accident, the FAA doesn't want any irregularities to be overlooked."

Kyle frowned. "What irregularities are you talking about? This accident wasn't any worse than others. We don't have a history of pilot or maintenance violations. Our relationship with the Houston fisdo is stellar."

Skaggs peered up into the cabin. "This accident may not appear significant to you, but it does to us." He dropped his gaze to Kyle. "Your airline killed eleven people and injured sixty-eight. That bears close scrutiny."

When put in that perspective, Kyle had to agree with him. But an American Airlines accident ten years earlier had killed all two hundred and sixty on board and five on the ground. Did the FAA consider this accident significant because it was the first major one since the U. S. Airways crash into the Hudson two years ago?

"The three of them will make their inspection, then you'll be free to make yours." Evans cocked an eyebrow at him. "We don't want evidence destroyed because someone carelessly pushed something out of place, do we?"

Skaggs flicked his hand at the airplane and walked off.

Kyle followed the two NTSB investigators up the ladder. Caulk lifted a video camera to his eye and shot the forward galley area before turning aft and shooting down the aisle.

Lori lifted the digital SLR that hung around her neck and fired off photos of the cabin.

"I wonder if the overhead bins opened during the crash, or did the passengers try to take their stuff with them while evacuating?" Kyle asked. Luggage was strewn haphazardly on the floor and seats. Jackets, books, and newspapers littered the floor.

"Probably both," Lori said. "We'll interview them and find out." She stood in the cockpit door and took numerous shots. She squatted and took many more, capturing the overhead panel where the majority of the switches were. When done, she moved out of the way so Caulk could videotape it.

When Caulk stepped back, Lori said to Kyle, "Don't touch anything, but stand in the door and let me know if you see something out of the ordinary. If you could, give us a running narration of switch position and anything that strikes you as unusual."

Kyle stood in the doorway to the flight deck. Blood covered both gray sheepskin-covered seats as if they had been dyed red. It was splattered on the overhead panel and side windows, and a puddle stained the floor under both seats. His heart pounded and his hands trembled.

The control yokes, normally attached to columns that rose out of the floor, had been cut off just above where the pilot's legs would have been. The instrument panel was crumbled in and down. The damage was more significant on the captain's side. A large portion of the instrument panel had been cut away, he assumed, to get the pilots out of their seats.

He hoped the stench was from the sea water the airplane had rested in and not from the dead or injured pilots. His stomach clenched, and he swallowed the bile that rose in his throat. How would it look for Omega's head investigator to vomit? He shook his head and studied the overhead panel. "Someone," he swallowed, "turned off the battery."

Lori rested a hand on his back. Her hip touched him as she leaned forward and held a small digital recorder next to his head.

Her touch eased his trembling. He took several deep breaths, shoving away the bloody images of the two pilots.

"Take your time." She patted him on the back. "I know it's not easy the first time you see this."

This reassured him he wasn't a wimp. "Someone put the start levers in the fuel shut-off position. The flaps handle is in the forty-degree position. That would be standard procedure for an evacuation. The QRHs are in their stowed position, so this was done by memory, or someone shoved them back into their slots after completing the evacuation checklist." Kyle was about to explain the QRH stood for quick reference handbook that held all the abnormal and emergency procedures, but he didn't want Lori to bash his head in with the tape recorder.

When she didn't ask, he continued.

"The autobrakes are selected to RTO as they should have been."

This was a position the crew would select while preparing for takeoff. If they rejected, maximum braking would be applied automatically. He recited other things he observed, all of which were in the proper position for takeoff.

"Other than the damage and blood, everything looks like it should for an evacuation."

Lori lifted her hand and backed up. "Okay, you two can step out."

Kyle climbed down the ladder, taking in large breaths of the fresh air coming in through the open hangar doors. He didn't meet anyone's eyes, fearing they'd see his pallor.

"Glenn, you and your group can enter," Lori said as she climbed down the ladder.

At the tail, a couple of NTSB personnel overseeing, the Omega maintenance investigators set the black boxes, as the media liked to call them, on Styrofoam. The orange cockpit voice recorder, or CVR, and flight data recorder each were the size of a loaf of bread.

Lori bent down and examined them. "Good. They don't look damaged." She turned to one of the NTSB investigators who had been overseeing their removal. "The FAA is standing by with one of their Gulfstreams to fly you to our lab. Call me as soon as you've retrieved the data."

"Will do," Ed Holstrom, the CVR analyst said. "If they aren't damaged, I should know something within a few hours after I get there." He looked at his watch. "It'll probably be mid-afternoon."

Kyle glanced at the time. It was eight forty-five. He walked off to the side and dialed Karen's cell phone. She should be taking Travis to school. He could ride his bike like Kyle had at his age, but Karen insisted on driving him for safety. After a few rings, his son answered. "Hi." His voice was reserved.

"Hey, buddy. How's it going?"

"All right."

"I'm sorry I didn't call last night. It got pretty hectic after I got here." Silence. Travis loved everything to do with flying and airplanes. Kyle didn't understand why he wasn't pumping him for information about the crash. "Is anything wrong?"

"Are you and Mom getting a divorce?"

The knot in Kyle's stomach returned. Either Travis had noticed the trouble between them, or Karen had told him. If she had, Kyle now knew she was serious. He clenched his fists, upset that Karen would tell Travis without him being there. "Ah, we're having some problems. I hope we can work them out. I don't want a divorce. I want to stay married."

There was silence on the phone. At fourteen, Travis was becoming wiser and more mature each day, but Kyle often denied this by talking to him as if he was still a child. "We were supposed to go to counseling last night, but I had to miss it to come here."

Travis didn't reply.

"None of this is because of anything you've done. We both love you very much. That will never, ever change."

"I'm at school. I gotta go."

There was a rustling. Karen's muffled voice said, "Have a good day. I love you." A car door closed. "I don't suppose you'll be home tonight," she said. "That means I'll have to take him to his Kung Fu lesson you were supposed to attend with him."

Kyle reeled in his anger. As much as he wanted to lash out, somehow, they had to overcome their differences. If he was more sincere, she might realize he was trying. "No. I can't get away."

"So you're dropping this in my lap. What am I supposed to do during the hour he's there?"

She wasn't making it easy. He took a deep breath to keep from blurting out the tremendous pressure he was under and closed his eyes and counted to five. "You could take a lesson, too. It's exercise." He hoped his suggestive tone would soften her.

"I get plenty every morning."

"Look, I'm sorry you have to do this, but I can't get away—" The phone went dead, and he knew it wasn't from a bad signal.

He clenched his teeth. How did they get to this place? What were they doing to Travis? He stared out the hangar doors across the airport, not noticing anything in particular.

When he lifted his phone to call Karen back, it rang. It was Steele.

Chapter Seven

Tuesday, June 15 8:52 a.m.
Kyle put his phone to his ear. "Good morning, sir."

"The jump seater is an FAA inspector," Morgan Steele said.

Kyle recalled the FAA huddled together and their desire to be the first to board the aircraft. "Nobody here seems to know that."

"I've called our POI, and he told me Ernest Norman doesn't work in the Houston office." The POI was the principal operations inspector with the FAA in the Houston FSDO who oversaw Omega Airlines' operation.

Kyle remembered Evan's confusion over the Inspector from Chicago being part of the FAA investigative team. "I think Norman is associated with the Chicago fisdo."

"I'll look into it."

When Kyle closed his eyes, the image of the blood splatter in the cockpit was emblazoned on his eyelids. "What hospital were the FO and flight attendants taken to? There's a good chance Norman's there too."

"Mount Sinai. I'll have someone call to see if he's a patient there."

"How is the first officer?" Imagining how painful it must have been for Cheryl Wells when the instrument panel had trapped her in her seat made Kyle squirm.

"She came through surgery okay. They're worried about internal bleeding."

"When can we talk to her?"

"I'll find out. When they play the recording from the CVR, I want you there."

Kyle welcomed the opportunity. He was dying to hear what had caused the accident. "Will do. I need to find out if the NTSB knows the jump seater was an FAA inspector. I don't think they do."

Kyle looked across the hangar and didn't spot Evans. Lori stood under the bent wing, examining it. He walked up beside her. "My superiors would like me there when you play the CVR."

"Once I hear it's intact, I'll be flying to D.C. in an FAA jet to hear it. I'm sure the FAA won't mind giving you a lift."

"Thank you." He paused. "Did you know the jump seater was an FAA inspector?"

"What!" Lori narrowed her eyes. She looked across the hangar and spotted Skaggs climbing down the ladder from the cabin door. She marched toward him.

The anger that molded her features couldn't be faked. Kyle was relieved he and Omega Airlines weren't the only ones unaware that an FAA inspector sat in the cockpit. He followed her around the airplane.

"Skaggs!" Lori's voice carried across the hangar. "When were you going to let us know there was an FAA inspector on board?"

Skaggs' eyes widened before he glanced around. Several people stopped and stared.

Skaggs motioned with his head. "Over here."

Lori and Kyle followed him to a corner of the hangar. They were joined by Chavette, the FAA official from Chicago.

"I wanted to tell you, Lori, as soon as I found out. I've been ordered from above to not mention it unless—" He closed his eyes briefly. "I mean, until you found out."

"Until I found out!"

Kyle was glad her anger wasn't directed at him.

Skaggs leaned close and, through clenched teeth, said, "Keep your voice down."

Kircher climbed down the ladder and noticed their huddle. He approached with a furrowed brow. "What's going on?"

Kyle told him.

Kircher's eyes bored into Kyle. "You shouldn't discuss this without me."

Skaggs looked around the hangar. "Let's find someplace more private."

He led them out of the hangar, down a hall, and to an empty office.

On the way there, Lori called Evans, who joined them.

When Skaggs closed the door, he took a deep breath before beginning. "As I was saying, Washington ordered me not to mention this until it was discovered. I know that is not the way we usually investigate an accident."

"He wasn't just on board, he sat on the jump seat," Kyle said.

Skaggs turned his face to the floor. "I know."

"Where is he? We need to talk to him," Lori said.

Evans frowned at her, as if she overrode his authority.

Skaggs swiveled his gaze to Chavette. "The inspector has gone on vacation."

Vacation? Kyle's mouth gaped. He was too dumbfounded to say anything.

"Get him back here," Evans said.

"We'll try." Chavette's French accent was very prominent. "We're not sure what his plans were. The last holiday he took, there were no phones or Internet access where he was."

"We don't care," Lori said. "Send a helicopter to pick him up. We need to hear what happened."

This time, Evans glared at her.

"Like I said, we'll try to find him if we can." Chavette shuffled his feet, not meeting anyone's eyes.

"You let an inspector who was a witness to an accident go on vacation?" Kyle knew the FAA was screwed up, but this was beyond incompetent. "What are you hiding?"

"We're not hiding anything!" Chavette said.

Kyle found his denial a little strong.

"After the accident, the inspector called me, told me he had been on board, and was leaving to take his vacation," Chavette said more civilly. "I took a statement from him and faxed it to headquarters in D.C."

"A statement? We haven't discovered why the crew rejected the takeoff, and you let a witness to the event leave?" Kyle's face warmed.

"We need a copy of his statement," Evans said.

"I'll see about getting one," Skaggs said.

"How could you let this guy go on vacation?" Lori asked, her face red.

Evans gave Lori a glance that told Kyle she was overstepping her authority. "I want him back here by tonight."

"You have no authority to tell the FAA what their employees will do!" Chavette said.

"I can't believe this!" Kircher yelled. "Un-fucking-believable!"

Kyle was surprised Kircher hadn't said anything so far. He wondered why the normally confrontational chief pilot had been quiet until now. Was he hoping Kyle would screw up so he could report this to Houston?

"Okay, let's all calm down," Skaggs said. "Mark, I'll work on getting you a copy of his statement. You can share it with Omega Airlines if you'd like."

"You're damn right he will!" Kircher bellowed.

Why does he have to be here? Kyle stared at him, pleading for him to shut up.

Evans looked at his watch. "When will I have it?"

"Ah, I don't know. They'll probably have to get approval from the Administrator. She might have to run it through legal first."

"Why?" Kyle asked. "FAA inspectors are only observers. Did this one do something to cause the accident?"

"Oh, that's preposterous!" Chavette said.

"Is it?" Kyle asked. "You've kept it secret there was an inspector on board who disappeared after the accident. Now you're giving us the runaround about reading his statement. If the situation was reversed and we hid pilots involved, you'd have the airline shut down."

"We just need to be sure the FAA is protected here," Skaggs said. "We don't want to alarm the public that a flight with an FAA inspector on board is unsafe. It'll take some time to analyze this."

The inequality in this scenario infuriated Kyle.

"The NTSB has a press briefing scheduled at noon," Evans said. "I'll expect a copy of that statement by then."

"Jesus!" Chavette said.

"Mark, you don't want to do that." Skaggs' voice rose. "As you're well aware, the FAA Administrator is the former NTSB chairman. She knows how things work in Washington. You start threatening the FAA, and she'll call in whatever favors she can. You might find yourself removed from this investigation."

"You can't shut us up so easily," Kircher said.

Oh yes, they can, Kyle thought.

"No!" Skaggs turned on Kircher, his eyes slits. "If Omega Airlines breathes a word of this to the press, we'll shut you down so fast, it'll make your head spin. When you try to begin operations afterward, we'll make it next to impossible for you."

"Okay, we're all in a bad position," Lori said. "You could get Mark and I removed from this investigation and shut down Omega. It'll eventually come out an FAA inspector was on board. Then the FAA's screwed. This inspector will be a huge asset in determining the cause of the accident. The sooner we figure that out, the quicker the public will feel it's safe to travel on Omega or any other 737. They'll know the FAA is doing everything they can to keep them safe."

She gave everyone a second to digest this. "I suggest the FAA find their inspector and release his statement to the NTSB. In the meantime, the NTSB and Omega will continue our investigation as we would without this revelation."

The exhale Skaggs let out made it seem he was relieved this wasn't going any further. Kyle knew if the FAA was backed into a corner, they would do what they thought best for them. The outcome for Omega might not be good.

"I'll be discussing this—" Kyle's hand on Kircher's shoulder and a shake of his head made the chief pilot stop talking and glare at Kyle.

"Let's all meet again at eleven thirty before the noon press briefing," Evans said.

In the hall and away from the others, Kircher stopped Kyle and pointed a finger in his face. "Don't you ever stop me from saying what I want in a meeting."

Kyle wanted to snap his finger off. "We can use this to our advantage. We need to let the FAA come forward on their own, though. They obviously screwed up and are trying to figure out what to do about it. Let's give them a day to do that. If they don't, we leak this to the ALPA investigators."

"Those assholes!"

"If they leak this, it might appear to the FAA that the pilot's union discovered this on their own. ALPA would have nothing to lose by going to the press. The FAA would have a hard time shutting us down for something the union leaked."

Kircher's face brightened. "I like that. I'm calling Dorsey and letting him know what we have come up with." He walked away, punching in a number on his phone.

What we *came up with? Asshole.*

Chapter Eight

Tuesday, June 15 10:23 a.m.

Kyle watched a forklift lower the three landing gear legs recovered from Flushing Bay to the hangar floor. The outboard tire on the right main gear was missing except for the ragged edge of the bead that sealed it to the wheel. The other three main tires had places where the rubber was melted, caused by hydroplaning.

Running his hand over the roughened and cracked deformation on the tire, Kyle wondered if the landing on the wet runway caused the worn tire to wear excessively so that it disintegrated on the takeoff roll.

Lori approached, a cell phone to her ear before she disconnected. "Can you find out if the gate agents who boarded the flight are working today?"

"Sure."

"If they are, would you accompany me to interview them? They may be more open with you there, and you can explain procedures I'm not familiar with."

"Okay." Did his one-word answers impress her?

A few phone calls later, he and Lori walked through the terminal.

"When did you find out about the FAA inspector?" She asked.

"Last week." He tried to appear serious.

She frowned.

With a subtle shake of his head, he said, "That was an attempt to be funny. Right before I told you about it."

"Have you learned anything else since then?"

"No. Hey." He held out his hands, palms up. "I'm on your side here. If I find out something, even if it'll look bad for Omega, the NTSB will be the first to know."

Her expression softened, and she looked away. "Okay. I'm not used to having vital information kept from us."

"Phew! I thought it was my deodorant."

She snickered.

"Our people in Houston are calling the New York hospitals to see if Norman is a patient. I'll let you know if we find him."

Her face brightened. "Thanks."

Gate agent Kaydrain Gognat, one of the agents who had boarded Flight 918 the day before, waited for them in the station manager's office. They introduced themselves and sat around a desk.

Of the hundreds of gate agents Kyle had encountered in his career, some stuck in his head because of their vivacious personalities. "I looked forward to seeing you when I passed through LaGuardia."

A smile came to Gognat's round, chubby face. "I remember you, too. You're one of the good ones."

Lori cocked an eyebrow.

"We have our easy-to-get-along-with Captains." Gognat's smile dropped. "And our difficult ones. Captain Masters is in the former category," she said to Lori.

"I fooled her." Kyle shrugged.

"Was Captain Musgrave, the Captain of Flight 918 yesterday, one of the good ones?" Lori asked.

"I didn't really know him."

"How was his demeanor yesterday?" Lori's phone vibrated. She looked at the caller ID, then set it aside.

"I only saw him for a moment when the flight arrived. He seemed okay then. I'll tell you this, though, after that FAA inspector boarded, the atmosphere on the flight deck seemed pretty tense. I can understand why, too. The FAA inspector was very arrogant."

"How do you mean?" Kyle asked.

"As I escorted him down to the aircraft, he looked at how I parked the passenger loading bridge against the aircraft. He said I'd better adjust it before I boarded passengers and he'd check it later."

"What was wrong with the passenger loading bridge?" Lori asked.

"It was parked just a little crooked. There was daylight between one side of the bumper and the aircraft."

"How big a gap are we talking?" Kyle asked.

"Maybe that much." Gognat held her thumb and finger an inch apart. "An infant wouldn't have been able to get their foot between it."

"What did you do?" Lori made a note.

"I adjusted it so the bumper touched along its entire length."

Lori looked up from her notepad. "Did the inspector say anything further to you afterward?"

"No."

"What about the captain or first officer?" Lori looked over the top of her glasses. "Did you have any conversations with them?"

"Only when I asked them if they were ready to close up before they pushed back."

"And that was when they seemed tense?" Lori glanced at her vibrating phone and set it aside.

"Yes."

"Explain, please, what you mean," Lori said.

"Oh, I don't know." Gognat's gaze looked over Kyle and Lori's head. "The Captain asked if I'd verified all the overhead bins were closed and all the passengers were seated. Well, that's my job. I'm not supposed to ask if he's ready to close up if that isn't done. I know it's procedure and all, but it was the way he asked me. Like he was trying to prove to the FAA he was being safe."

Kyle had seen many pilots like this. They might be lackadaisical until the FAA or an instructor was onboard, then became super meticulous.

"Anything else?" Lori asked.

"The captain seemed to check all the paperwork very carefully, then handed it to the first officer to do the same. He only said what was needed without any extraneous conversation."

"But you hadn't seen him often enough to know if he was normally this way," Lori said. "Is that correct?"

"I guess. But I've seen lots of crews with an FAA inspector onboard, and they didn't seem as nervous as this captain was."

"Okay." Lori scribbled a note. "What was the first officer's demeanor?"

"She came up here before we started boarding to buy a cup of coffee and stopped to say hello on her way back down to the aircraft. She seemed relaxed and easygoing. But when I poked my head in the cockpit just before push back, she didn't say a word. Her smile was gone. She looked tense."

Kyle's memory of the outgoing Cheryl Wells, the first officer, agreed with Gognat's. It was one of the reasons she had been selected to facilitate their Threat and Error Management course. Her engaging personality encouraged others to talk during the class.

Lori handed her one of her cards. "Thank you for your time. If you think of anything else, please give me a call or email me."

Walking away from the office, Lori asked Kyle. "You seem deep in thought."

He realized he'd gone into what Karen called Kyle's world. He rubbed his forehead. "In my position, I work with a lot of FAA inspectors. Most are good people trying to do their job the best they can. There are a few who like to throw their weight around and make things difficult."

With a shake of her head, Lori said, "Just spit it out without going all politically correct on me."

"What if this inspector had a previous run-in with Captain Musgrave? His presence on the flight deck could've made Musgrave nervous, second guessing his decisions during the takeoff roll when the tire destroyed itself. Or, he had a bad experience with an FAA inspector."

Lori cocked an eyebrow. "What makes you think this?"

"Musgrave had additional training in sterile cockpit procedures six months ago. What if this inspector was the one who instigated this retraining? He either arranged to ride on Musgrave's flight yesterday to check on him again, or just randomly took this flight and Musgrave was the captain. Or, Musgrave is now leery of FAA inspectors."

Lori gestured back to the office. "I realize the gate agent suggested the inspector made the atmosphere tense. But you said this captain had been with the airline twenty-three years. He'd have flown with numerous inspectors in that time. Airline pilots are used to being scrutinized."

Kyle considered her comment then met her eyes. "If I'm wrong, why is the FAA hiding their inspector? What if they know there was a prior incident between the captain and the inspector, and they're worried how this'll look to the public?"

Pointing a finger, Lori said, "Find out what caused Musgrave to be retrained six months ago."

"Gee, I wish I'd thought of that," he said.

Lori rolled her eyes.

Chapter Nine

Tuesday, June 15 11:22 a.m.
On the walk back to the hangar, Kyle called Steele.

He informed Kyle that the instructor who gave Captain Musgrave the additional training six months ago was flying and hadn't returned Steele's call. Nor had FAA inspector Norman been located at any New York hospital. They had expanded their search to the surrounding areas.

Kyle finished his call before Lori finished hers, which gave him the opportunity to study her discreetly. Although short, she matched his brisk pace, making him wonder if she always walked this fast, or only when the incredible pressure of a major airline accident pushed her.

The troubles in his marriage made him wonder what had ended hers. Did her fiery temper cause too many arguments, or was it something else? From what he had witnessed, she only became pissed when provoked. But some men's dominant personalities made it difficult for them to give in to a woman's feelings and desires. *Am I doing that in my marriage?*

In the office at the hangar they'd used before, Skaggs addressed Lori and Evans from the NTSB; Kyle and Kircher from Omega; and Chavette, the FAA Inspector from Chicago. "Washington needs more time to review the inspector's statement before releasing it to the NTSB." He jingled loose change in his pockets, not looking anyone in the eye.

"Why?" Lori and Evans asked together.

The glance Evans threw Lori's way showed he thought she was out of line.

"I wasn't told why," Skaggs said. "After the review of the CVR this afternoon, I'll see when it'll be released."

To Kyle, this seemed like government babble. "What's so incriminating about this statement that it can't be released?" Kyle asked.

"Inspector Chavette, you took his statement," Skaggs said. "Can you answer this?"

The brightening of Skaggs' face gave Kyle the impression Skaggs was glad to be putting Chavette on the spot.

"There's nothing incriminating." His accent was more pronounced. "This is a complicated matter the FAA needs to study."

"Is the NTSB informing the public the FAA was on board our aircraft?" Kyle asked Evans.

Evans didn't look up from reading a message on his phone. "No. We're waiting till after we've heard the CVR."

"Why?" Kyle couldn't believe Evans was caving in to the FAA's desires.

"The Chairman wants to know all the facts before the media begins speculating on the cause."

Lori stared at the floor, her face unreadable.

Kyle couldn't tell if she agreed or disagreed with this decision. It seemed the NTSB was backing off pushing the FAA, but it also made sense. If the inspector had sat quietly on the jump seat saying nothing, making the FAA appear guilty of contributing to the accident would do more harm than good. Omega's management in Houston must have realized this too, or they would have called the FAA on their bluff to shut them down if they mentioned the inspector's presence.

"One of our Gulfstreams is parked outside, waiting to fly us to D.C. to listen to the CVR after the news conference," Skaggs said.

"I need to be on that flight," Kircher said.

Lori glanced at Evans, who was engrossed with his phone. When he said nothing, she said, "It's NTSB policy to have only one individual from each investigative group present during the review of the CVR. Mr. Masters has requested to be there to represent Omega Airlines."

"I'll be taking Kyle's place," Kircher said.

How much longer will I be plagued with this asshole's presence? "We'd better let our bosses sort that out."

"Damn right we will." Kircher stormed out of the office, cell phone in hand, punching in numbers.

When the meeting broke up, Kyle passed him in the hall.

The chief pilot paced with his phone to his ear, his face red. "I'm the most qualified person to be there. Don't cave into the training department." He paused. "No sir. I didn't mean any disrespect. I think you've overlooked the fact a chief pilot should be there versus an instructor."

Kyle smiled.

Outside the hangar where the press conference would be given, he stood off to the side, hoping the reporters didn't notice the Omega Airlines logo on his shirt. He had learned last night to not speak to the media. If any approached, he would bolt for the safety of the hangar. The roar of jets on the other side of the hangar muffled the reporters' shouted questions.

Evans stood behind the podium, a dozen microphones attached to it. "Good afternoon, everyone. I'm Mark Evans from the NTSB. Unfortunately, we don't have much else to report at this time." He gave the status of the aircraft recovery and the state of the cockpit voice and flight data recorders. "The First Officer of the flight is still in intensive care and unable to answer questions. We hope she's well enough tomorrow to discuss the takeoff. I'll take a few questions."

"Why would the crew abort the takeoff?" a TV reporter asked.

"We suspect they blew a tire on their takeoff roll and attempted to stop."

"How often do airliner tires blow up?" a woman journalist asked.

Kyle snickered. Tires didn't blow up like a bomb the way the journalist was making it sound.

"Not very often. There are probably less than ten incidents a year of tire malfunctions in the entire industry."

"Is the NTSB grounding the 737 fleet to inspect their tires?" a male journalist asked.

"The NTSB does not have the authority to ground airplanes. We can recommend the FAA do so, if we feel such a justification is necessary. At this time, we have no reason to make such a suggestion. You can ask my counterpart at the FAA when I'm through if they intend to."

"Are there any plans to ground Omega Airlines 737s?" a female reporter asked.

"The NTSB is not making this recommendation."

"Aren't airliners supposed to be able to reach their takeoff speed and then have enough runway to stop?" asked a male TV reporter.

Kyle was impressed. This reporter knew more than most.

"That is a calculation the crew and their dispatcher make before every takeoff. We're not sure, at this time, why this flight was unable to stop on the available runway."

"It was reported earlier that terrorists had stormed the cockpit and caused this crash. Is the NTSB ruling this out at this time?" asked another reporter.

Kyle rolled his eyes.

"We are not ruling anything out at this time. The reports from the aircraft fire and rescue personnel did not support terrorist activity."

"Did a flock of birds cause it?" another reporter asked.

"The engines do not indicate damage caused by bird strikes. The engines will be torn down and inspected as part of our investigation. We have not ruled out the possibility the crew rejected the takeoff to avoid birds crossing their departure path. But aircraft that took off before Omega Airlines did not report any bird activity. Until we review the cockpit voice recorder and question the first officer, we haven't ruled anything out."

"Is it safe to fly on Omega Airlines?" a female reporter asked.

"At this time, the NTSB does not feel Omega Airlines is any less safe than any other airline."

This pleased Kyle.

"I'll turn the rest of the briefing over to FAA Safety Inspector Glenn Skaggs."

Skaggs took Evans' place at the microphones and adjusted one. "As of a few minutes ago, the FAA revoked First Officer Cheryl Wells' pilot certificate. If First Officer Wells wishes to become a pilot again after she recovers from the injuries she sustained in the unfortunate accident, the FAA will take the matter under consideration."

Kyle clenched his fists and let out a long sigh. *Bastards.* No one had determined the cause of the accident, but the FAA already blamed the crew. This was a knee-jerk reaction they'd taken recently whenever an aviation incident hit the news—guilty until proven innocent. Pilots weren't given the same liberties everyone else was granted.

"The FAA will continue to assist the NTSB in the investigation into this accident," Skaggs continued. "I'll take a few questions."

Kyle took a few deep breaths.

Skaggs answered several questions related to the revocation of Wells' license. The reporters weren't educated enough in aviation matters to ask how the FAA could take such drastic action without a court hearing and ruling. Kyle was tempted to ask them himself but didn't want to get on the wrong side of the FAA just yet. He needed to be an insider to the investigation. If he pissed off the FAA, he could be shut out.

Chapter Ten

Tuesday, June 15 12:17 p.m.
Kyle climbed the stairs to the FAA Gulfstream IV for the flight to D.C stopping to inspected the cockpit layout. The switches and instruments were so different than the 737, he wouldn't know how to start the jet, let alone fly it. It would be fun to try if a qualified pilot sat in one of the pilot seats.

In the cabin, the seats were plush leather with wood veneer trim on the armrests. He took one of the forward-facing double ones and buckled its belt. He stretched his legs out, something he couldn't do on an airliner. This was the way to travel.

Lori, Skaggs, and Chavette entered. If one of the FAA men sat near him and tried to engage in conversation Kyle would move to one of the other twelve seats. With the FAA indiscriminately rescinding Cheryl Wells' license, Kyle would have expressed his disapproval at this unwarranted action, even though that decision wasn't made by either of these two FAA employees.

Lori saved him by sitting beside him, talking on the phone as she buckled her seatbelt with the phone cradled on her shoulder.

It pleased him that their relationship had become so convivial.

Skaggs sat across the aisle from them, Chavette in a row ahead of them.

This added to the disdain Kyle sensed between the two FAA inspectors. Was it because of departmental differences, since each worked for a different branch, or a personality clash?

Kyle typed out an email on his phone and sent it to Steele. *Any luck finding Inspector Norman?* He would have called Steele, but did not want to alert Skaggs and Chavette they were looking for Norman. If Omega found him in a nearby hospital, Kyle worried the FAA would put a guard on Norman's door, preventing him from being accessed.

After they were airborne, Kyle reclined his seat and closed his eyes. Sleep came a moment later.

✈✈✈

The thump of the landing gear being lowered on the approach to Ronald Reagan Airport in Washington D.C. woke Kyle. Lori slept with her head on his shoulder, as if it had slid there accidently. She had drooled, wetting his shirt. If the situation was reversed, he would be embarrassed to awaken in such an intimate position. Yet, he did not shrug to move her as he would have if she were a guy or a woman he disliked.

The thirty-five-minute nap didn't replenish his lack of sleep. If anything, his lethargy pulled harder, making him wish for a soft bed.

When the aircraft touched down with a bump, Lori woke with a start. She looked around and wiped her cheek. She reached to wipe the wet spot on his shirt, but stopped, a blush blossoming on her cheeks. "Sorry."

He rubbed his face to hide his smile. "God, could I use a cup of coffee."

Lori fumbled in her purse. "There's a Starbucks on the way. I can give you a ride, if you'd like."

"Thanks."

They exited the airplane, walked through the general aviation terminal, and outside to Lori's Toyota Venza.

Chavette boarded Skaggs' SUV.

The Venza was similar in size and style to Karen's BMW X5, but cost twenty thousand dollars less. Karen wouldn't have considered driving a Toyota.

"Nice car," he said.

"Thanks. It's very practical for a single mother."

The office towers, hotels, and restaurants of Crystal City went by as they rode in silence. "You said you were a pilot. How'd you end up at the NTSB?" Kyle asked.

She glanced at him and then back at the road, making him regret how he worded his question. He probably came across as elitist thinking the NTSB was beneath him. "I was a pilot for

Continental for several years. I enjoyed the flying, but after my daughters were born, I cried every time I left home."

"Yeah, that's hard. When Travis, my son, was young, it seemed each time I returned from a trip, he'd changed. I missed his first day of school, numerous hockey games, and all those other precious moments I'll never get back."

Her silence made Kyle question if that was all she would say on the matter. Was she regretting the moments she missed, or that he had interrupted her?

But when they stopped at a light, she continued. "My husband had to deal with getting our daughters to school and their other activities like a single parent. His performance at his job suffered. I decided to put my education to work and applied to the NTSB, hoping being closer to home would make life easier."

"Sounds like a good choice." In some ways, Karen staying home and not having a career made caring for Travis so much easier. He had never needed to juggle his career to accommodate hers. Why hadn't he told her how much he appreciated her for that? *What else have I neglected to tell her?*

There had been many times he had called home to tell her his flight was late, or that he was filling in for another instructor. He had taken for granted Karen's acceptance of his erratic schedule and hours.

After stopping for coffee, they crossed the Potomac River on the Fourteenth Street Bridge and pulled into the NTSB headquarters on L'Enfant Plaza a block away. The proximity of NTSB offices to the spot where a flight had crashed into the bridge because of ice on its wings many years ago was not lost on Kyle.

Pointing back to the bridge, he said, "Your investigators didn't have far to travel for the Air Florida accident."

"No, they sure didn't."

Chapter Eleven

Tuesday, June 15 1:48 p.m.

Kyle followed Lori into the CVR lab. The room was the size of most corporate conference rooms, with twelve chairs around the oblong table.

In attendance to listen to the cockpit voice recorder was Ed Holstrom, the CVR analyst from the NTSB; Leo Brandish, an Airline Pilots Association investigator who was a pilot at Omega; and Glenn Skaggs and Pierre Chavette from the FAA. It wasn't explained why the FAA had two members of the investigative team present. Kyle wondered if Lori was privy to the information and would share it with him later.

Lori handed each of them a document. "This is a non-disclosure agreement you'll need to sign. By doing so, you agree to not divulge what was discovered from the cockpit voice recorder to anyone other than those in attendance now. Only after the surviving crewmember has heard it, and agrees to release it to the public, can you discuss it with others."

She put the signed documents in a file. "I'll need to collect everyone's cell phones and any other electronic devices you have."

These items were placed in a drawer outside the CVR audio laboratory.

"Everyone will have to stay until the review of the recording is completed." Lori took a seat beside Holstrom at the head of the table.

Kyle wished he hadn't ordered the venti coffee at Starbucks.

"The CVR on Omega's 737 is the latest generation of cockpit voice recorders," Holstrom said. "Unlike older recorders that record thirty minutes of conversation on a continuous tape, this one is a solid-state device that records one hundred and twenty minutes of conversation, and then begins recording over itself. If everyone is in agreement, I'll play only the last thirty minutes before the recording ends. This should record the preflight procedures, the taxiing to the runway, and the takeoff roll."

Chavette leaned forward. "I think we should hear the entire recording, so we can establish whether this crew performed their duties correctly." His accent pronounced.

Why, asshole, so you can attempt to justify revoking Cheryl Wells' license?

"For the initial hearing, we can learn enough in the last thirty minutes to begin figuring out what happened on the accident takeoff," Lori said. "We'll review the recording in its entirety at a later time."

Chavette's eyebrows furrowed. "Very well."

"For those not aware," Holstrom said, "the CVR picks up sound from four microphones, the captain's, the first officer's, the jump seater's, and the area microphone on the overhead panel."

Holstrom pushed a key on the computer.

A male voice came over the lab's speakers as if recorded by a distant microphone. *Be careful. This guy tried to violate me six months ago. He'll do so again if he can.* The inflection suggested he was whispering.

They heard a faint, muffled conversation for a few minutes that Kyle surmised was between FAA Inspector Norman and the flight attendants in the cabin, then a clicking and rattling. Several in the room frowned.

"That must be the jump seat being unfolded out of the wall," Kyle said.

Are you all set there? the same male voice asked. There was no reply. This same voice said, *If you're ready, I'll brief you on the emergency equipment.* It became apparent this was the Captain's voice, Brent Musgrave.

I'm familiar with the 737, a male voice said. This would be the inspector's voice, yet he sounded similar to the captain.

I need to go over this stuff with you anyway, the captain said.

For the next several minutes, he gave a thorough briefing on all the emergency equipment, its location and usage, and the sterile cockpit procedure. Kyle was proud of him. He had covered everything.

Do you have any questions? the captain asked.

No, the inspector said. There was no doubt from his tone that he was annoyed.

Several minutes of faint conversations were heard from the flight attendants, welcoming the passengers.

The captain and first officer did the initiation checklist, followed by several more minutes of silence.

Kyle couldn't help but compare the difference in the cockpit with and without an FAA Inspector. Normally, the crew would talk about their plans that night, or on their next day off, or some airline rumor they had heard. Put an inspector in the cockpit, and the atmosphere became that of a surgical waiting room.

Gate agent Gognat and the captain talked about making sure the overhead bins were closed.

A humming of an electrical component and then a tearing sound made several in the CVR lab look at Kyle.

"That must be the webperf being printed and ripped off the printer," he said.

A minute later, the first officer's voice, louder and clearer than the other voices, was heard again. *The numbers check out.*

Paper rustled. Kyle thought it was the webperf being passed to the captain.

"It appears the captain's and the jump seater's microphones aren't being picked up by the CVR." Holstrom stared at his computer with a frown.

This explained why the captain's and inspector's voices were muffled and weak compared to the first officer's clear voice. Hers was recorded by a boom microphone next to her lips. The area microphone picking up the captain's and inspector's voice was several feet from their mouths. It also captured the other noises in the cockpit.

Looks good. Kyle assumed this was the captain.

Let me see that.

Kyle assumed this was the inspector asking to look at the webperf. The tone suggested it was not a request. It was Norman's job to examine it, but most inspectors would have asked to see it.

Before push checklist, the captain said.

The first officer read the checklist, and the captain responded to her.

Push back clearance. The captain called for at the completion of the checklist.

The first officer called the air traffic ground controller and was given clearance to push back from the gate.

The captain relayed this information to the ground crew over the airplane's intercom.

No conversation took place for over a minute. They could hear the faint whine of other airplanes and the cabin safety announcement.

There's something not right on this, a male voice said. Kyle couldn't determine if it was the inspector or the captain.

What's wrong, a male voice asked. Paper rustled.

Kyle guessed Norman had discovered a problem with the webperf and made the crew figure out the discrepancy he found. It was a typical tactic some FAA inspectors used to put crews on edge.

I don't see anything. Do you, Cheryl? the captain asked.

Paper rustled as the webperf must've been passed between them, followed by silence.

You're clear to start one or two, the ramp agent said over the intercom.

Ah, standby, the captain said.

Oh, I didn't subtract for the four half-weights, the first officer said.

There were several frowns around the CVR lab.

"Children are considered half the weight of adults in weight calculations," Kyle said. "They must have had four children onboard."

A few moments later, the first officer's voice was heard. *There. I've made the adjustment. I'll make the correction in the flight management computer.* Keys clicked.

Push back complete, the ramp agent said. *The towbar is disconnected. Do you need us to stay on the headset while you start?*

Yes. Hang on for another minute or so, the captain said.

There, that's done, the first officer said.

If you notice anything else, please let us know, the captain said. *Was there anything else?*

No one said anything.

Kyle guessed Musgrave asked the inspector. He admired the captain for trying to make the inspector part of the crew so the atmosphere would be less adversarial.

They started the engines, received taxi instructions, and began taxiing to the runway.

The crew remained silent, except to acknowledge instructions from the air traffic controllers or to confirm to each other that they were turning onto the correct taxiways.

With the exception of the weight calculation, the instructor in Kyle graded the crew as performing without a flaw.

Taking this left onto bravo, the captain said.

I agree, the first officer said.

Are you sure?

Kyle guessed this was Norman questioning them.

I'll stop here. Confirm with ground the taxi instructions. This would have been the captain.

Before Wells could break into the busy frequency to talk to the ground controller, he said over the radio, *Omega 918, don't stop there. Traffic behind you. Continue taking that left onto Bravo. Continue on Bravo to the end.*

Omega 918, left on bravo and take it to the end, the first officer said.

There were several more minutes of silence except for the distant roar of the jets taking off from the runway parallel to the taxiway.

Before takeoff checklist, the captain said.

The first officer completed this with the captain acknowledging a few critical items.

They were told to contact the tower.

Omega 918, LaGuardia tower, line up and wait, the controller's Spanish-accented voice told them.

Omega 918, line up and wait, the first officer said.

After an adequate time to taxi onto the runway and line up on the runway centerline, the captain turned control of the flight over to the first officer. *Your aircraft.*

My aircraft, the first officer responded.

A moment later, the accented voice said, *Omega 918 cleared for takeoff. Fly runway heading. Wind three-six-zero at eight.*

Omega 918, cleared for takeoff, runway heading, the captain said.

The whine of the engines' acceleration increased in tempo and the nose gear thumped as it rolled over the runway centerline lights. This bumping increased in frequency as the airplane picked up speed.

Everyone in the CVR lab sat up.

Kyle leaned forward, closing his eyes, concentrating on his hearing.

Check power, the first officer said.

Power checked, the captain said.

A few moments later, the captain spoke again. *One hundred knots.*

The engine whine remained constant; the frequency of the thumping of the nose gear continued to increase.

Several seconds later, there was a loud bang as if something had hit the airplane, and the buzz of a vibration. Several more loud bangs followed in quick succession, and the buzzing intensified.

Kyle visualized the large pieces of the tire they had found on the runway slamming into the airplane.

Continue was spoken loud and clear by a male voice.

Pride welled up as Kyle heard the captain make the correct decision.

Abort, a male voice said immediately afterward. It was not spoken as distinctly.

A second later they heard it again. *Abort.* This was spoken louder.

Abort! Damn it. Abort! This was yelled.

Kyle frowned.

A second later, a male voice could be heard, loud and clear. *Reject!*

Kyle closed his eyes, dread rolling through him, knowing he had heard the fateful mistake.

The whine of engines lessened, then increased as reverse thrust was applied. *Shit* yelled out a male voice.

Kyle could not determine who said this.

For the next five seconds, the engines roared at full reverse. *Fuck. We aren't going to make it,* a male voice yelled.

Fuck, fuck, fuck!

Bill, the first officer said softly.

Less than a second later, there was a loud impact, as if someone had slammed a sledgehammer onto the table in the CVR lab.

Everyone in the room flinched.

On the recording were grunts, distant screams.

Kyle trembled as if in the airplane.

Another impact made everyone in the lab jump again. Metal ripped and bent. Glass broke. People screamed.

The recording ended.

Chapter Twelve

Tuesday, June 15 2:33 p.m.

Everyone in the cockpit voice recorder lab sat stunned and wide eyed when the recording ended.

Lori hugged herself, swiveling her seat back and forth. She was pale. Ed Holstrom, the CVR analyst, stared at his computer as if he hadn't really heard the horrifying end to the flight.

Kyle trembled and thought his emotions justified when he saw how distressed Lori and Ed were. They would have experienced recordings of numerous violent accidents in previous investigations but were still moved.

Leo Brandish, the Omega Airlines ALPA investigator, slumped in his seat, staring at his notepad on the table. Pierre Chavette, the FAA inspector from Chicago, rested his head in his hands. Glenn Skaggs, representing the FAA in the investigation, lifted his coffee cup, but stopped and set it on the table when his shaking hand threatened to spill the liquid.

When Kyle's heart rate slowed and he had replayed the last several minutes of the recording over in his head, he shot from his seat and paced. "That goddamned inspector caused this accident!"

Skaggs flinched. Chavette's eyes moved back and forth as if following the grain in the mahogany of the table.

Lori ran her hand through her hair. "We need to talk to that inspector more than ever."

Kyle continued to pace. "He's the reason eleven people are dead and sixty-eight injured. How could someone so inept work for you?"

Skaggs cleared his throat. "Before we make any *more* accusations, we need to listen to the recording again, beginning with the take-off roll."

Kyle sigh. He didn't look forward to hearing the violent end to the flight again. He plopped into his seat and picked up his pen, ready to take more notes. Listening again, they would hear little details they might have missed the first time.

Holstrom clicked his mouse a few times. The recording began.

Omega nine-eighteen, cleared for takeoff, runway heading.

A male voice Kyle assumed to be the captain's spoke.

The airplane accelerated. *Bang!*

"Stop the recording," Lori said to Holstrom. "That would have been when the tire began separating."

Chavette sat up and glared at Lori. "They should have aborted then."

"That's not Omega's FAA-approved policy," Kyle said.

Chavette turned his narrowed eyes at Kyle. "What is your policy?"

"After one-hundred knots, we reject a takeoff only for an engine failure or something that'll prevent the airplane from flying."

Chavette huffed. "Well, I... I wouldn't have approved that procedure if it had come through my office."

Lori held up her hands as if separating Kyle and Chavette. "We can settle this argument later." She nodded at Holstrom. "Play the recording, please."

Continue, a male voice spoke loud and clear.

Abort was spoken immediately afterward.

This wasn't spoken as distinctly, and Kyle couldn't determine if this voice was the same as the one that said, *continue.*

Abort! After another second came more yelling. *Abort. Damnit! Abort.*

More than a second later, but less than two, a male voice was heard. *Reject!*

Kyle raised his hand.

The recording stopped.

"That was the captain who initially said, 'Continue'," Kyle said. "We train so if any event happens on the takeoff roll, the captain will say, 'continue,' or 'reject.' Your inspector said 'abort.' Omega doesn't use that word to call for a rejected takeoff. You, Mr. Chavette, just did."

"To... to... to me it sounded like de Capitan saying abort," Chavette stammered. "He had to say it trey times to get de first officer to comply."

"It's Omega's procedure to have the captain execute a rejected takeoff," Kyle said. "If the first officer is flying, as was the case on this flight, they move the throttles up and engage the auto-throttles. The first officer then says, 'check power,' and moves his or her hand off the throttles. The captain puts his, or hers, on them so if they decide to reject, their hand is already there, ready to pull the power back to idle."

Chavette waved his hand. "Dis... dis... capitan obviously had a... had a... different procedure and couldn't get de first officer to adhere to it."

"You're wrong." Kyle shook his head. His face warmed. "After the voice says abort three times, we hear someone say reject and the sound of the rejected takeoff commencing. It was the inspector yelling abort, not the captain."

"Obviously dis capitan was not competent." Chavette's voice rose. "We heard it at de beginning of de recording. He missed dee correction for dee children, and de inspector had to point it out to him. Then he had dis non-standard takeoff procedure of having de first officer do de aborted takeoffs." Chavette's face was crimson. He waved his hands around wildly. "He...he...he initially said abort three times. When de first officer didn't do so, he remembered he was supposed to say, 'reject'."

Kyle locked his eyes on Chavette's. "You're wrong. Go fly on any Omega Airlines flight today, and you won't find a single captain having the first officer keep their hands on the throttle during the takeoff roll."

Kyle hoped Lori would give him some support. She stared at them as if watching a tennis match. Sitting beside her, Skaggs rolled his pen back and forth.

"I agree with Kyle," Brandish said. "I've never seen one of our captains let the first officer keep their hands on the throttle on the takeoff roll."

"Don't you get it?" Chavette yelled. "De pause between de last abort yelled, and de reject being spoken, is de Capitan fighting to get de first officer's hands off de throttles because she a woman and panicked."

Lori glared at Chavette. "No more sexist remarks or I'll have you removed from this investigation."

Her tone made Kyle glad she wasn't directing that warning at him.

"When de Capitan finally gets her to let go, he yells reject," Chavette said as if he hadn't heard Lori. "Only now it's too late to stop on de remaining runway."

"Bullshit." Kyle took a deep breath. "The captain wouldn't have said 'continue,' and then 'abort' three times right after it, hesitate, and then 'reject'."

"I agree," Brandish said.

"As I've pointed out, it's obviously this captain was incompetent!" Chavette said.

"You don't want to accept your inspector contributed to this accident." Kyle smacked the table with his fist. Beside him, Brandish flinched. "He felt pressure to do what the FAA wanted or suffer the consequences. At the beginning of the recording, we discovered this inspector tried to violate him six months ago. The captain must've felt he would do so again if he didn't reject."

"The inspector was doing his job." Chavette took on an unhealthy red hue.

"This inspector went out of his way to intimidate the crew. He was unreceptive to a briefing on the emergency equipment." Kyle jabbed his finger at Chavette. "Which, as you know, is required for the captain to brief. You can't consider the half-weight calculation a mistake. The webperf showed them capable of taking off with the children considered adults. Calculating them as half weights would've shown the airplane lighter. We all know those assumed weights the industry uses are a joke."

The edge of the table cut into Kyle's waist. "The captain rejected when the intimidating inspector yelled, 'Abort, abort, abort damnit abort'."

Chavette stood, knocking his chair over. "I will not stand here and let you demean de FAA dis way."

Kyle waved a hand as if dismissing Chavette. "Good! Leave! You're not helping this investigation."

Lori stood. "Everyone, calm down!"

Skaggs continued rolling his pen back and forth, seemingly oblivious to Kyle and Chavette's argument.

"Skaggs, what do you think?" Lori asked.

His chest rose and fell. "I don't know. It's hard to say. Their voices sound similar."

"I can do a voice analysis," Holstrom said. "It'll determine if the two male voices are different. It'll take a few hours."

"Yes, please do that." Lori glanced from Kyle to Chavette. "We're all tired from being up all night. Let's call it a day and meet back here tomorrow at eight. Remember the disclosure statements you signed. You cannot talk about what you heard to anyone outside of this room."

Everyone nodded.

To Skaggs, Lori said, "I urge you to find this inspector and make him available for questioning."

Skaggs nodded.

Lori stood. "I'll see everyone tomorrow."

Paper rustled as Kyle gathered his notepad and stuffed it in his computer case. "Which hotel would you recommend?"

"The Marriott in Crystal City isn't far. Let me make some phone calls, and I can drop you off on my way home."

Chapter Thirteen

Tuesday, June 15 3:40 p.m.
Kyle followed Lori to her car outside the NTSB headquarters. The late-afternoon sun made him squint after sitting in the windowless cockpit voice recorder lab.

Inside the Venza, Kyle hoped her air conditioning would cool the stifling heat that made him sweat. "Those assholes know full well what happened and don't want to admit it. They're scared shitless." He buckled his seat belt. "Skaggs knows. That's why he sat there so fascinated by his pen."

Lori said nothing as she pulled into traffic.

He raised his eyebrows. "Tell me you don't believe Chavette's bullshit."

"You forget, I work for the NTSB. I report only the facts without bias."

"Okay, Ms. NTSB, only the facts ma'am, what are, *the facts*?"

"The facts? Are you ready for them, or are you like the FAA and can't accept the truth?"

"Lay them on me."

"Your captain allowed someone to intimidate him and rejected a takeoff he shouldn't have."

Kyle slumped in his seat. "Go ahead, give it to me straight. Don't pussy foot around the truth." Regardless of what FAA Inspector Norman said or did, Musgrave had screwed up. He never should have rejected the takeoff.

Lori chuckled at his self-mocking deprecation. "I know you know that, too. You just got caught up in trying to blame someone else."

He exhaled, loud and slow. "Yeah, I did." He replayed the last minutes of the recording over in his head, wondering when it would fade away and stop haunting him. He wished he could shake the Captain. *What were you thinking?*

"Jesus, what an asshole that Chavette is." Kyle shook his head. "Doesn't he realize the purpose of the investigation is not to lay blame, but uncover how the accident happened so another can be prevented?"

"I wouldn't say he's an asshole."

Kyle frowned at her.

"I'd say he's an arrogant asshole." Her smile returned.

"That he is. Of course, my arguing with Chavette made it look like I wanted to blame them." Kyle sighed. "What's Chavette doing there, by the way? Evans seemed to know Skaggs and the other FAA investigators last night at the briefing. If Chavette isn't part of the FAA accident analysis group, what's his interest in this accident?"

"I don't know."

"Can you find out?"

She glanced at him. "What'll that prove? If the FAA wants him there, we have to allow it as long as he isn't hindering the investigation."

"I'm going to find out what his interest is. He's here for a reason. He has nothing to do with Omega's operation."

He watched a United Airlines Airbus fly down the Potomac and bank to line up with runway 19 at Reagan. Kyle loved flying that approach. When just a couple hundred feet above the ground a sharp turn to align with the runway made it one of Omega's more demanding approaches. In the distance, the Capitol dome of Congress stood above the other government buildings.

He pointed to it. "When the public hears an FAA inspector intimidated the crew into rejecting a takeoff that resulted in an accident, they'll be outraged. The FAA is supposed to make flying safer, not less so. Congress will get involved to give the appearance they have the public's safety in mind. The FAA Administrator will have to answer questions about how this happened. People at the FAA are going to lose their jobs over this. No wonder they're hiding the inspector."

Lori scrunched up her face. "So, they... what, have Norman stashed in an FAA safe house? You watch too much TV."

"He certainly isn't on vacation. No way would they allow that. Do you realize how inept they'd look if an FAA inspector is discovered being a contributing factor in an accident and they let him go on vacation before the investigation begins? That'd be worse than him contributing to the accident."

"We will eventually talk to him. They probably have him somewhere, prepping him for his interview. He could be right here in D.C."

"Right." Kyle snorted. "They probably have him in Alaska, or someplace equally as remote, doing filing in a back room. After you've written the final report on the accident, they'll promote him."

"It'll take over a year and a half for us to complete our investigation." She smirked as if what he'd said was the most absurd thing she'd ever heard. "They can't hide him that long."

"Yeah? I bet they'll try."

✈✈✈

Sticking the keycard into the hotel door lock and hearing the beep, Kyle shoved the door open to his room at the Marriott. It was like the hundreds of rooms he had stayed in during his airline career. They all began to blend in together. The navy-blue comforter on the king size bed made him want to plop on it, but he had a phone call to make. He punched in Steele's number.

"What did you find out from the CVR?" Steele asked.

Hi. Good to hear from you too. "Unfortunately, I had to sign a confidentiality statement and can't talk about it. What I can tell you is we need to find that FAA jump seater. He was a major factor in this accident."

"How so?"

Kyle weighed his options. "All I'll say is, we need to find him. He contributed to the cause of the rejected takeoff."

Steele was silent a moment. "Did he influence the crew in some way?"

Kyle sighed. "He didn't silently observe."

Steele said nothing. Kyle visualized him sitting at his desk, his head cocked, and his eyes roving the room.

"The public needs to know this," Steele finally said. "Right now, the media is portraying us as an unsafe airline. If it's known an FAA inspector was onboard who's gone missing, this'll deflect the attention away from us. I'll discuss with the other VPs and the PR group."

Kyle stopped pacing at the foot of the bed. "How's First Officer Wells? We need to talk to her and confirm what I heard on the CVR. If she gives her consent, we could release the recording to the media."

"A couple of hours ago, she was listed in stable condition. Her doctors say she might be able to answer a few questions tomorrow."

"I'll visit her as soon as I get back to LaGuardia," Kyle said. "Have you found out anything about the training Musgrave had six months ago?"

"Musgrave was line checked by an FAA inspector and forgot to turn his cell phone off. While taxiing to the runway, it rang. He brought the airplane to a stop, shut it off without answering, and continued taxiing. The inspector tried to violate him. Luckily, Musgrave filled out an FSAP report. The FAA wanted to ignore the report and violate him anyway. The only way the company could appease the FAA was to give Musgrave an hour of ground school in sterile cockpit procedures and a line check. I'm still looking into who the inspector was."

Kyle thought most FAA inspectors would have verbally reprimanded Musgrave and taken the matter no further. "The inspector who tried to violate Musgrave was Ernie Norman."

"I assume you know this from the CVR. I've called the POI, requesting information about Norman. Our calls are going to voice mail and are not being returned."

When Steele ended the call, Kyle collapsed on the bed. Sleep tugged at his eyelids. He wondered how Lori could drive home.

He closed his eyes and tried to quiet his mind but replayed the argument with Chavette over and over. Did the FAA already know how their inspector influenced the crew and was waiting to hear how apparent that was on the CVR? Skaggs and Chavette were bound by the confidentiality agreement, too. Would they tell their bosses and risk that exposure?

Chavette, no doubt, would not honor the agreement if he could protect the FAA. Was he also protecting himself?

Chapter Fourteen

Wednesday, June 16 6:30 a.m.
Kyle pulled his head out from under the shower in his room in D.C. and listened. His cell phone was ringing. He grabbed a towel and hurried into the room. A glance at the phone's screen while he dried his face revealed it was Steele. This early in the morning, it had to be bad news. It was an hour earlier in Houston.

"First officer Cheryl Wells died in the night," Steele said.

Kyle dropped onto the bed. "Oh God." He rested his head in his hand. He had taken the captain's death hard, knowing it might have been him on a bad day. But he hadn't known Musgrave. Although Kyle wasn't Cheryl's friend, he had enjoyed her vibrant personality whenever she passed through the training center. "Does her family know?"

"Her husband's been notified."

Kyle was grateful he didn't have to tell him. How would you tell a family member their loved one died from an accident that wasn't their fault? "How did she pass away? I thought she was off the critical list?"

"She went into cardiac arrest in the night. They feel she must have developed a blood clot from her injuries, or the stress taxed her heart."

Kyle sighed. "What can I do?"

"Nothing. We'll assist her husband with the funeral arrangements and arrange to fly her body home. Let me know what is determined after the voice analysis."

"Okay." Kyle disconnected and checked his phone. There were no voicemails. He had called home last night and left messages on Karen's cell and the home phone. He'd slept so deeply, he worried he might have missed her return call. Cheryl's death reminded him how short and precious life could be. He *needed* to tell Karen how much he loved her. Waking her early was not a way to patch up their marriage. He would call again later.

✈✈✈

Kyle arrived at the NTSB offices by taxi just before eight. Several black Chevrolet Suburbans had been parked haphazardly. A van marked FBI was parked near the entrance. Someone wearing a polo shirt with FBI stenciled on it leaned in through the open side door.

At the door, a man in his twenties who wore a suit stopped him. "Let's see some identification."

Kyle showed him his driver's license, as well as the NTSB visitor ID issued to him the day before.

"What's the purpose of your visit?"

"I'm to review a voice analysis of a cockpit voice recording from my airline's accident two days ago." Kyle slipped his wallet back in his pocket. "Who are you? I didn't see you here yesterday."

The man flashed FBI credentials. "I'll have to call upstairs to get approval to let you enter the building."

"Why? This wasn't needed yesterday."

The agent moved away without a word, making Kyle all the more curious.

Around the lobby, several people dressed in suits appeared to be questioning people with NTSB IDs.

The agent who'd stopped Kyle spoke into a cell phone, listened, disconnected, and motioned Kyle toward the elevator. "You'll be met when you get off."

Lori stood waiting for him when the elevator doors opened on the second floor. Her eyes were red rimmed, her mouth pursed. More people in suits stood talking on cell phones or questioning others. Yesterday, the activity in NTSB offices had been like any business office.

"Hi. What's going on?" he asked.

Lori took a deep breath and let it out quick. "Our offices were broken into last night. The CVR recording for 918 is missing."

He frowned as if she spoke gibberish. "What? How'd that happen?"

"We don't know. The FBI is looking at the security tapes from last night and questioning everyone who worked late." She turned away a moment. When she met his gaze and blinked, a tear ran down her cheek that she wiped away. "Ed Holstrom was found murdered this morning."

Kyle flinched. "The carefree, easy-going analyst? Why would anyone murder him?" He considered holding her to provide some comfort but thought that might be unprofessional. He rested his hand on her shoulder. Then his suspicions surfaced. "Is his death related to the break-in?"

"We don't know. He and his partner were found shot in Marshall Heights. It's a dangerous part of town. I don't know why he'd be there. He lives in the opposite direction. When we left yesterday, he was going to work on the voice analysis for a while, and then go home and come back early this morning."

"Do you think this had anything to do with the accident investigation?"

Her scowl told him she thought the idea preposterous.

"Well, this might make you see why I think that. The first officer died last night."

Lori put a hand to her mouth. Her eyes moved back and forth as if looking to see if he was serious.

"Her death, Holstrom's, and this." He gestured to the agents milling about. "I can't help but feel they're connected."

She shook her head. "What? The FAA has a team of hit men, killing off people and breaking into government offices? They aren't the CIA, killing enemy combatants. You need to accept your captain screwed up. There is no big conspiracy." She cast him a sharp look and walked away.

Kyle caught up to her. "Does the FAA know about the missing recording?"

"No. We'll inform them when they arrive for the eight o'clock meeting."

"They're going to love this."

She shot him a look that would have burned if she'd had lasers in her eyes.

When Brandish, Skaggs, and Chavette arrived, they met in a conference room since the CVR lab was a crime scene. Lori broke the news about the missing recording and Holstrom's death.

Kyle watched the two FAA inspectors for any sign they already knew this.

Skaggs flinched. He paled and studied the table.

The corners of Chavette's mouth turned up, before he hid the expression behind his hand and looked down. "The FAA is sorry for your loss."

He spoke in a tone as if he had read his statement aloud. But Kyle wondered if his deep dislike for the man clouded his judgment.

"Thank you," Lori said.

"Where does that leave the investigation?" Chavette asked.

"We'll continue as we were," Lori said. "If the recording is found, it will be included in the final report. Otherwise, our findings will be based on other data and witness accounts. Speaking of which, have you located Inspector Norman?"

Chavette shook his head. "No. We sent a helicopter to de cabin where he went fishing last year, and he wasn't there. We're still searching for him."

Kyle smirked. *Yeah, I bet you are.*

"When do we get a copy of the statement you took from him?" Lori asked.

Chavette shrugged. "Our superiors are still looking it over. With today's news and knowing this will affect the investigation, I'll urge them to release it soon."

Right. You'll probably tell them to destroy it.

Through this exchange, Skaggs had glanced at Kyle several times, always turning away when Kyle returned his stare.

"Do you have anything to offer, Mr. Skaggs?" Kyle asked.

Skaggs took a deep breath before speaking. "No. I'm sorry to hear about the death of your co-worker. Let me know if there is anything I can do."

His comment, Kyle judged, was heartfelt.

"Thank you," Lori said.

"I have more bad news," Kyle said. He told them about Cheryl Wells.

"The FAA is sorry for your loss, too," Chavette said in the same tone he had previously used.

Skaggs looked up. "You said she died of natural causes?"

"That's what they're thinking," Kyle said.

Skaggs slouched into his seat.

"I hope they do an autopsy," Kyle said. "If it's discovered anything irregular happened, I hope her family sues the responsible parties."

Chavette tipped his chin up to Kyle. "What are you insinuating?"

Satisfied he had rattled him, Kyle warmed to his subject. "I'm not insinuating anything. I'm hoping we can determine if her death was a result of her injuries—" He paused and met Chavette's glare. "Or from other factors."

"Why wouldn't it be from her injuries?" Chavette's face had become red. "How else would she have died?"

"Yesterday afternoon, she was reported in stable condition, but then died overnight. That leaves the last surviving crew member who could tell us what happened silenced. All we have now is the testimony of your missing inspector."

"I don't like what you are suggesting." Chavette stabbed a finger at Kyle. "De FAA had nothing to do with this accident or de first officer's death."

"So you say," Kyle said.

"Let's all calm down." Lori raised her voice to be heard above Kyle and Chavette. "Everyone's upset." She turned to Skaggs and, in conversational tone, said, "We'd like Inspector Norman's statement by the end of the day."

"You're not in charge of de investigation." Chavette pointed a finger at Lori. "That will be up to your superiors to request."

"When this meeting is over, I'll be making that request." Lori leaned forward with narrowed eyes. "I'll urge them in the strongest terms to inform the media an FAA Inspector who can't be located sat in Omega's cockpit."

"You have no authority to be making these statements." Chavette breathed rapidly.

Skaggs put a hand on Chavette's shoulder. "I'll see what I can do about getting you a copy of Inspector Norman's statement."

Chavette shrugged Skagg's hand away and pointed at Lori. "You can't blackmail de FAA into doing as you wish. We have procedures and protocol we have to adhere to. We will release Norman's statement when we have completed reviewing it."

Kyle snorted. "Or after you make one up that absolves you of any guilt."

Chavette shot to his feet. "I demand you remove him from this investigation." He pointed at Kyle. "His accusations are not helping de matter."

"It is you I may have removed," Lori said. "You seem to be the one obstructing it."

"I'll be letting my superiors know how you are treating de FAA in this matter."

"Go for it. I'll still be urging the IIC and the board members to let the media know about your missing inspector and your inability to issue us a copy of his statement."

A smile came to Kyle's face. He loved seeing Lori standing up to the belligerent official.

His smile made Chavette narrow his eyes. The red in his face deepened.

"I'll pass on your request," Skaggs said. He subtly shook his head when he glanced at Chavette.

Chavette stormed out of the room. The tension seemed to be sucked out with his departure.

"Can we get a ride back to LaGuardia, or should we find alternate transportation?" Lori asked Skaggs.

"The Gulfstream is at Reagan, standing by." He looked at his watch. "We can plan to be airborne in an hour."

✈✈✈

Lori pulled out of the NTSB parking lot.

From the passenger seat, Kyle said, "I like the way you stood up to the FAA in there."

"I was just doing my job." She squirmed in her seat. Her mouth opened and she began to say something but didn't.

"What is it?"

"You and your conspiracy theories have me second guessing what everyone is saying and how they're acting."

He was glad she was pulling her head out of the sand. "Well, you have to admit, it's pretty coincidental."

"Yes. But there could be explanations for everything." She stopped at a light.

"Such as?"

"The first officer could have died naturally." Lori faced him. "She was severely injured. Ed could have been murdered over something his partner was involved in. The break-in at our offices could have been criminals looking for something valuable. Several computers are missing."

Those were good points. But Kyle didn't believe the coincidence. "Where was the recording for 918 kept?"

"In a vault in the CVR lab."

Kyle remembered seeing a safe-like structure built into the corner of the room. "How does one get in the vault?"

"There's a cipher punch lock on the door."

"Who has the combination to the lock?"

She shook her head. "You realize the FBI has already asked me these questions."

"Humor me."

"Ed, the chairman, Evans, since he's the IIC for this investigation, and a couple other IIC's who are working other investigations." She pulled away when the light changed to green. "918 wasn't the only recording missing. There were several others in the vault that were stolen, too."

Kyle worked his mouth back and forth. The other missing recordings didn't help his theory. "They might've forced Ed to open the vault for them before he was murdered. What did the security video show?"

"I haven't seen it." She chewed on her lower lip, as if considering what he said.

"I wish I could."

Lori snorted. "I'm sure the FBI would be glad to take time from their schedule to show them to you."

He batted his eyes. "Maybe if an NTSB investigator for the accident of one of the missing recordings asked, they would."

She shook her head. "What are you going to see that trained FBI investigators didn't?"

"Okay. Okay, Miss-Voice-Of-Reason."

They rode for several blocks in silence. To break it up and so she didn't think him a nutcase stuck on his conspiracy theory, he asked, "Were your daughters glad you made it home for the night?"

A smile brightened her face until the ringing of her cell phone dissolved it. "Almond." She listened. "Sir, I've got someone in my car. Can I call you back in just a couple of minutes?"

She disconnected and chewed on her lip.

"What's the matter?" Kyle asked.
"It doesn't concern you."

Chapter Fifteen

Wednesday, June 16 9:22 a.m.

Kyle sat in the same seat on the FAA jet as he had the day before.

Lori sat away from him this time, staring out the window, not talking to the others, turning her cell phone over and over in her hand.

Did she keep her distance on purpose? He had come to enjoy their camaraderie and hoped she hadn't decided to put some space between them because of his mistrust of the FAA.

After landing in LaGuardia and parking in front of the hangar occupied by the wrecked 737, Kyle stood outside the Gulfstream, pretending to study the long, thin wing. When Lori walked down the stairs, he fell in step with her. "You okay?"

"What? Oh. Yeah. Just thinking about the investigation." The wind ruffled her short hair. "What are you doing now?"

"I'm going to the hospital to talk to our flight attendants." Kyle raised his voice over a jet taking off from the runway two hundred feet away. "See what they can tell me about the accident, the mood of the flight deck crew, and the FAA inspector. I'll see if the doctor who took care of Cheryl Wells will talk to me."

She glanced past him and stiffened.

Chavette stood at the nose of the Gulfstream, staring at them with a menacing scowl.

"Let me know what you find out." She walked around the aircraft, giving Chavette a wide berth.

Halfway to the hangar, Mark Evans approached Lori and stopped in front of her. When Kyle passed them, Evans stared down at Lori, shaking a finger at her. Another jet taking off prevented Kyle from hearing what he said, but Lori looked around the airport and occasionally threw her arms out in gesture justifying what she'd said.

✈✈✈

Philip Worden, Associate Administrator of Aviation Safety for the FAA, sat at his desk at 800 Independence Avenue in D.C. He looked up from the report he was reading when Chris Emerson, Glenn Skaggs' supervisor, walked in.

"You got a sec?"

Worden dropped his reading glasses onto his desk. "Sure. What's up?"

Emerson closed the door.

This piqued Worden's curiosity.

"Glenn Skaggs just called." Emerson sat on the edge of a chair across from Worden. "The NTSB was broken into last night and the recording for Omega 918 stolen. The NTSB CVR analyst responsible for the lab was found murdered in another part of town." Emerson fell against the backrest. "The First Officer for the flight also died in the night."

Although Emerson had spoken clearly, Worden tried to make sense of what he had said. Each event seemed separate, but Emerson gave him the impression they were linked. What were the chances of all three happening during the same night? It had to be astronomical. "Jesus. Did Skaggs say why this was done?"

Emerson shook his head. "The NTSB is just as much in the dark as we are. The FBI is at their offices, investigating the break-in."

"Okay, let's think of this logically." He looked around his office, not seeing any of it. "Why would anyone want to steal a CVR?"

"Obviously, there's damaging evidence on it."

"I agree, but what would that be? And who'd want to destroy this evidence?" Worden thought he knew the answer to his second question but felt the need to vocalize his thoughts.

"Either us, or Omega. Maybe Omega's captain aborted the takeoff against their company procedure. Since we had an inspector on the flight, they can claim he coerced the captain into aborting."

"In today's cover-your-ass environment, it'd be easy to think an airline might do that, but no airline ever has before. Airline's reputations haven't been tarnished by the stupid mistakes their flight crews have made before. So, why now?"

Emerson appeared to be giving what Worden had said some thought.

"They'd be really sticking it out there if the FBI discovers they did this. If they were going to blame us, why hasn't the media been notified of our inspector's presence? They should've been claiming he influenced their crew shortly after the accident news broke."

Emerson shrugged.

The chair squeaked as Worden rocked back and forth. "If Omega didn't steal the recording, that leaves only us to point the finger at. I can't imagine how you'd go about doing such a thing. Who here would have the resources to pull something like this off?"

Emerson seemed to study something on the front of Worden's desk.

Was he thinking about his question, or avoiding answering it? Worden continued with his line of thinking. "Let's pretend for a moment we did. Why? What would be on this recording for someone to risk their career and jail time over?"

"Skaggs is bound by the confidentiality agreement and couldn't tell me," Emerson said. "What he did say was we need to find the inspector in the jump seat." He consulted a notepad he carried. "An... Ernest Norman... and hear what he has to say."

Worden frowned. "What do you mean find? Where the hell is he?"

"Norman's missing. Supposedly, he went on vacation."

Worden's quickening heartbeat made him take a deep breath to calm down. "How could someone let this guy go on vacation?"

"That's the story his supervisor is giving Skaggs and the NTSB."

"What idiot said that?" Worden looked forward to telling this supervisor to find a new job.

"Pierre Chavette. The Chicago fisdo manager where Norman works."

Worden stood and paced behind his desk. "Does Krubsack know this?"

"Hell if I know. He's been making himself scarce."

Worden dropped into his chair, consulted a phone directory, and dialed the number of Chavette's supervisor. The call went to voice mail. "Jerry, when you get this, call me immediately before you do anything else." He didn't disguise his anger, then dialed Krubsack's cell phone and left the same message.

Stabbing off the speaker phone with his index finger, Worden wished he had used it to stab Krubsack in the ribs. "There damn well better be a good reason why I haven't been informed this asshole went missing. How can we promote aviation safety if our key witness disappears?"

A disturbing realization came to Worden. "Why hasn't the NTSB notified the media our inspector was onboard? Omega should've informed them. He would have been on their passenger manifest."

"Skaggs doesn't know who made the request, but it appears someone here requested the NTSB not mention it yet."

"Who would make such a request? It'll come out eventually; why hide it?"

Emerson's cheeks puffed out in a sigh. "I'm guessing, but I'd say the same person who told Skaggs not to mention it when he participated in the news conferences."

Worden narrowed his eyes. "Who? It'd better not be you."

"No. It was above me."

Worden sat back and studied Emerson as if he had said the most outlandish thing. "There are only three people above you who could've made that request. One of them is me. Since I didn't, that leaves the Administrator and the Deputy Administrator. Which one gave Skaggs that order?"

"Halloren."

The little prick. "Our new politically appointed Deputy Administrator doesn't know how to keep his people in the loop on decisions concerning their departments." Worden paced again. "Halloren must be worried our inspector said or did something to influence Omega's crew. How would he know this?"

"The story Chavette is giving everyone is he took a statement from Norman before he vanished. Yet, no one has seen it."

"Unless Chavette's lying, he'd have given it to Krubsack, who is either sitting on it or has gone around me to the Administrator or

Halloren." Worden tried not to be pissed off, but he found himself clenching his teeth.

"Possibly. You should also know, somehow Chavette was part of the committee that heard the CVR. Skaggs doesn't know how that was arranged, as he's always the sole FAA member of the committee. Regardless, Skaggs doesn't trust Chavette."

"Why?" The more Worden was hearing of this Chavette, the easier it would be to fire him.

"Skaggs couldn't go into specific detail without violating the confidentiality agreement. But he did tell me Chavette was belligerent and argumentative with Omega's representative after they heard the recording. This morning, Chavette seemed pleased to hear the recording was missing."

Worden shook his head. "Is Chavette only trying to protect his inspector, or is there more to this?"

Emerson held out his hands, palms up.

"What's on the CVR that would force Chavette to tarnish the reputation of the FAA this way?"

Silence from Emerson told Worden he didn't know.

"I need to go talk to our Deputy Administrator and ask why he's not keeping those responsible for this investigation in the loop."

"Consider, before you do, what you'll say to him," Emerson said.

Worden frowned.

"Would a fisdo manager from Chicago have the resources to break into the NTSB and steal a recording? And possibly murder the analyst responsible for the lab, and cause the death of the first officer if he's trying to destroy something our inspector said or did?"

Worden fell into his chair. "You think Halloren arranged this?"

"He's got the political connections to be appointed to the FAA with no aviation background. He'd know somebody who would know somebody who could pull all that off."

This was Washington, after all. Not only were there numerous government agencies capable of pulling off a break-in of another government agency, there were many private contractors qualified as well.

"I can't just sit back and let some political appointee break numerous laws while ruining the FAA's reputation." Worden took a deep breath and blew it out slow. "Does he realize the shit storm we'll be under if he orchestrated this?"

"What if Halloren didn't order it? What if the Administrator did?"

"Shit. The Administrator, being the former NTSB Chairman, probably could've requested the CVR analyst open the vault for her and then had him murdered." Worden rubbed his forehead. "Would she take such a chance?"

Emerson shrugged.

"It doesn't matter who ordered it. It never should've been thought up in the first place. Goddamnit."

Emerson cocked an eyebrow. "Regardless, do you want to know if either of them had any part in this? Are they going to tell you they did? If they do, do you want to know? You'd have to do something about it or be imprisoned. If we don't know who's involved, nothing can happen to us."

Worden ran a hand through his gray hair. "We'll look pretty inept if we say we suspected something but didn't act on our suspicions."

"If we're wrong, and neither one of them had anything to do with this, our careers are over."

Chapter Sixteen

Wednesday, June 16 9:57 a.m.

Kyle took a taxi from LaGuardia to Mount Sinai Hospital in New York City. Outside of flight attendant Sherri Logsdon's room, he paused to gather himself. He didn't know how receptive Logsdon would be. Would she be in too much pain to talk? Two pilots Kyle was responsible for training had caused the accident that put her in the hospital. She might hold some resentment toward him.

Logsdon was in her early sixties and wore a c-collar around her neck. A plastic brace covered her hospital gown from waist to shoulders. The pungent odor of antiseptic mingled with the lilies on the bedside table.

Logsdon turned from the TV and looked at him as she would a stranger. After all, Omega had ten thousand flight attendants and Kyle couldn't remember flying with her.

He kicked himself mentally for not thinking to bring some flowers of his own. "Hi. I'm Kyle Masters from the Omega pilot training department. How are you doing?" He squeezed his eyes shut, regretting asking such a ridiculous question. *She's in the hospital, stupid.*

Logsdon pointed the remote at the TV, turning it down. "I'm glad to be alive." Her voice was raspy. She cleared her throat. "I hear others weren't so lucky."

"Yeah, unfortunately. Is there anything I can do for you?"

"No."

He wasn't sure if she was being nice, or just wanted to be rid of him. "Do you feel up to a few questions about the accident? It'll help us discover what happened."

"Yeah, I guess."

Kyle opened his notebook and looked at it. "You were the lead flight attendant of four on the flight."

"Yeah."

She would've been sitting on the flight attendant jump seat at the front of the cabin. "Then Demisha Melton would have been sitting beside you."

"Yes, sir."

Kyle smiled. "You don't have to call me sir. Kyle will be fine."

She nodded—and grimaced from the effort.

Kyle scrunched up his face. "Sorry, that looked like it hurt. Then sitting on the aft jump seat would've been Luther Stoess and Laurinda Cowan."

"Yes, sir..." she subtly shook her head, "Kyle."

"Now, that wasn't so hard, was it?" He gave her a smile. "You flew to LaGuardia with the captain and first officer. How'd they seem?"

"Ah, okay. They didn't bug us like some crews."

"Did they seem to get along with each other? Was there any tension between them?"

"No. They seemed very relaxed, like they'd flown together recently."

"Did the captain have any non-standard procedures that you're aware of?"

"No." A look of concentration came to her. "In his briefing, he was thorough, but not overly so. He covered everything he was supposed to without making it monotonous."

Kyle made a note. "How'd the flight to LaGuardia go?"

"Fine. There was some turbulence on the approach, but the landing was smooth."

"What about the landing roll or the taxi to the gate? Was there anything unusual?"

"Hmmm, during the landing, it seemed we skidded a few times. You know, how the airplane will jerk like the tires are skidding. The taxi to the gate seemed normal."

Since it had been raining the day of the accident, Kyle guessed the runway was wet and the airplane had hydroplaned several times. "Did the pilots say anything about the jerking after you parked?"

"No."

"Okay. Let's talk about Flight 918. Was there an FAA jump seater on the flight?"

Logsdon scowled. "Yes. What an asshole."

Kyle smiled. "In what way?"

"He wanted to see our manuals. I know that's his job, but it was the way he asked that bugged me."

Kyle frowned. "How so?"

"He said, 'Are your manuals up to date?' and we all acknowledged they were. Then he said, 'Well I'll need to see them to be sure.' So we all showed him. He thumbed through them like he was looking for something suspicious. Luther had a recent bulletin printed off a computer folded inside his. The inspector threw it on the floor and told Luther that wasn't supposed to be there. When Luther explained he kept them there for easy reference, the inspector told him if he couldn't remember important bulletins, he should find another job."

Kyle matched her scowl. "You're right. He is an asshole. How'd he treat the pilots?"

"I got busy boarding the flight when he entered the cockpit, so I didn't see how they interacted with each other. When I handed the captain a glass of ice, just before we pushed back, his hand shook."

From what Kyle had heard on the CVR, his hand probably would've shaken too. "Was there anything unusual about the taxi out to the runway?"

"Not that I remember."

"What can you tell me about the takeoff?"

Logsdon looked across the room, not saying anything for several seconds. She wiped her eyes with the sheet of the bed, then spoke in a trembly voice. "At first it seemed normal. Then it sounded like something hit the airplane several times. The whole airplane shook. Just when the shaking and banging stopped, we rejected the takeoff. There were a couple of jerks like the pilots were stepping on the brakes hard and then letting up on them. The engines roared like they do when the pilots put them in reverse after landing." She blinked several times. Tears slid down her cheeks. "Then we hit something really hard and I hit my head on the jump seat and almost blacked out."

She wiped her face again before continuing. "Then we hit something even harder and came to a stop. I was dazed. I didn't know where I was. Then all of a sudden, I realized what had happened to us. We were sitting at an unusual angle. Like this."

She held her arms out like wings, with one higher than the other. She screwed up her face from the effort. "At first, I was surprised we were still alive, the impact had been so hard. My back and head throbbed. I wasn't sure I could stand up. People were screaming and yelling."

When she paused, Kyle took her hand and patted it. He handed her a tissue.

Logsdon wiped her eyes with it. "I knew if I didn't get out of the airplane, I might die. Demisha was yelling, 'I'm hurt! I'm hurt!' I found the PA microphone and yelled, 'Evacuate! Evacuate!'" A sob escaped her, and she turned away.

"You were very brave," Kyle said. He continued to hold her hand.

Logsdon took several deep breaths. "I unbuckled my seatbelt and struggled to stand up. The pain in my back almost made me drop to my knees. I knew if I didn't get my door open and get the passengers off the airplane, we'd all die. But the weight of my door was too much for me to push open."

Her door would've weighed more, being on the elevated side of the airplane with gravity pulling against it.

"I heard the slide on the opposite door inflate and saw Demisha had opened her door just before she fell out and landed in the water."

Kyle wasn't sure his two hundred pounds would have prevented him from being pulled out when the door on the downhill side opened and the evacuation slide inflated.

Logsdon shook her head and winced from the action of doing so. "Passengers were rushing forward and fighting to get out. One of the first-class passengers was a big guy. He must have seen me struggling with my door because he shoved me aside and opened it. The slide inflated, but went straight down, just barely touching the water. I tried to direct passengers out the other door, but a few made it by me and ended up falling out. They screamed until they hit the water. I was afraid someone might push me out."

Her voice choked with emotion, Kyle barely understood her.

She turned to Kyle and sobbed. "This wasn't like anything we'd practiced in training. I wasn't prepared for something like this."

Kyle gave her a sympathetic smile and patted her hand some more. He tried to visualize the scene, knowing his imagination wasn't close to how stressful and panicked it would have felt to be in the crash.

She blew her nose. "Eventually, Luther came forward and told me everyone was off. We looked in the cockpit," Logsdon squeezed her eyes shut. "There was so much blood. The captain had the yoke stuck in him. The instrument panel was crushed into the first officer's legs. She was crying out. Luther tried to help her out of her seat but couldn't get her free." Tears streamed down Logsdon's face. "The first officer said, 'My legs are trapped! Go! Go! Get everyone off and go!'"

Logsdon sobbed a couple of times. "Luther and I looked at each other. We didn't know what to do. I thought we might explode at any minute." She took a couple of shuddering breaths. "A rescue boat came up close to the aircraft and one of the rescue people climbed up into the aircraft and told Luther and me to get off. We slid down the slide on the right side and pulled into a boat."

"We train for something like that and think we can handle it," Kyle said in what he hoped was his most sincere voice. "It's only after we experience what you did that we know how we'll do. You should be proud of yourself."

"Thank you. I was just acting on reflex, though." She was silent a moment. "I wasn't as brave as the first officer."

Every pilot who heard of Cheryl's actions would question if they would be as brave. He couldn't imagine the overwhelming panic she had to experience at being trapped in an airplane that might catch fire and knowing she couldn't get out. "Is there anything I can do for you or your family?"

"No. Thank you, though."

"I appreciate you talking to me." Kyle laid one of his cards on a bedside table. "Call if there's anything I can do, or if you think of something I need to know that will help us figure out what happened."

He turned to leave but stopped at the door. "What happened to the FAA inspector?"

"That asshole was one of the first ones off the airplane."

Kyle scrunched up his face. "What? He didn't try to help get everyone off?"

"No! He ran out of the cockpit, carrying his briefcase, and slid down the slide on the right side without a word to anyone."

"You're kidding." *Stupid comment, Kyle.*

"No."

This inspector never ceased to amaze Kyle with his arrogance. "What happened to him after he got off the airplane?"

"I don't know."

Chapter Seventeen

Wednesday, June 16 11:16 a.m.

Several hours after meeting with Emerson, Philip Worden approached the Deputy Administrator's office.

Stewart Halloren's young assistant looked up from her computer. "He's expecting you. Go on in."

Worden wondered if this was because he had called ahead, or for some other reason. He knocked on the door as he entered the office.

Halloren's feet rested on his desk while he read a stack of papers that must have been one of the numerous reports the administration generated. "Phil, come in."

Worden sat in a chair across from him and attempted to slow his thudding heart. He hoped Emerson was wrong. "Have you heard about the break-in at the NTSB and the murder of their CVR lab analyst?"

A cocky smile came to Halloren's face. "Yes, Jerry Krubsack heard from his investigator, Chavette, and didn't sit on the information. He briefed me immediately."

Worden tried to mask his irritation over Halloren's remark; Kurbsack had gone around him. "Since you're so informed, did you know the first officer for the flight died in the night?"

Halloren pursed his lips for a moment. "Yes. It's very tragic."

"It's kind of a coincidence, don't you think? The CVR of an accident one of our inspectors was involved in is stolen about the same time the NTSB investigator responsible for it is murdered, and the only surviving crew member dies. All within hours of each other."

Halloren shrugged. "Is it a coincidence, or three related acts?"

"If someone in the FAA had anything to do with this, it could be more damaging to us than if the public knew our inspector was onboard the flight."

Halloren cocked an eyebrow. "Why would anyone at the FAA have anything to do with this? If I were to suspect someone, I'd blame Omega Airlines for the break-in and the two deaths."

Worden frowned. He was trying to dismiss the three acts as random, yet wanted to link Omega to all three. "I don't see how this would be in their favor."

"What if their investigator, what's his name, Minor or something…"

"Masters," Worden said. "Kyle Masters."

Halloren dropped his feet to the floor. "What if he violated the confidentiality agreement and told his superiors their crew was responsible for the accident and we had an inspector onboard who they could blame for their negligence? Without the CVR recording and their crew, they can claim we coerced them into aborting the takeoff." Halloren turned his hands palms up. "They can shift the blame onto us. The public will start buying tickets on Omega again without fear. By the time the NTSB finalizes their report, the public will have forgotten all about this. It's a win-win for them."

Worden did not find that theory so easy to believe.

Halloren smiled. "Oh, don't look so surprised you didn't think of this. This is why Congress appoints people like me to this position. People who've been stuck in a bureaucracy for years lose sight of the big picture."

Worden clenched his jaw and took a deep breath. "If what you suggest is true, why hasn't Omega come out in their press statements claiming this?"

The smug smile Halloren exhibited made Worden want to slap the little prick.

"Because I told Glenn Skaggs to threaten we'd shut them down if they mentioned our inspector's presence on the flight."

"Why would you do that?" Worden couldn't believe he'd be so stupid.

"How do you know it was me who came up with the idea?" Halloren cocked his head.

Did the Administrator order this?

"Obviously, the reputation of the FAA had to be protected. Until we hear all the details, I didn't want Omega blaming us for their accident."

Worden raised his eyebrows. "If they claimed that, and we shut them down, Omega would go to Congress, complaining we were taking drastic actions. If it turns out our inspector had something to do with the accident, we'll be taken before a Senate committee."

Halloren waved a hand. "Trust me, it won't get that far. Our threat so far has kept Omega quiet. I'm sure after a few days, they'll want this accident forgotten."

Worden scrutinized Halloren for a clue why that would be. "If Omega wants this behind them, why would they steal the CVR?"

Halloren shrugged. "Maybe they didn't?"

Worden could understand why Halloren was in the position he was. He would spin anything to make it sound good to whomever he talked to. "If Omega didn't steal the recording or have anything to do with the two deaths last night, there's only one other organization who might be to blame."

Twin vertical creases formed between Halloren's eyebrows. "Do you actually think someone at the FAA would do as you're suggesting?"

"Skaggs said Chavette seemed pleased when he found out the recording was missing."

Halloren's gaze shifted across his desk before he lifted it to Worden. "Do you suspect Chavette had something to do with this?"

"I don't know. There's a lot about Mr. Chavette's actions that don't make sense. Supposedly he took a statement from our inspector after the accident. I haven't seen it. Have you?"

Halloren frowned. "There's a statement to what he witnessed? No, I haven't. Get me a copy of it."

Worden shoved down the anger that rose. He wasn't Halloren's errand boy.

"Is there anything else?" Halloren asked.

"Did you know our inspector went on vacation?"

Creases lined Halloren's forehead. "Did he? How convenient. Now, if the media gets wind of his presence on the flight, he won't be hounded by them."

Worden's mouth gaped. "Well, that's a good point. But, have you thought this through? If Congress finds out we had an inspector on this flight, and then let him go on vacation before the investigation begins, we'll have a hard time explaining that."

He paused, frustrated he had to lecture his superior—who should already know what he had to say. "The FAA exists to promote aviation safety. One way to do that is investigate accidents so the cause can be identified, and training recommended that will prevent another. If our eyewitness to the accident isn't available to assist with the investigation and make recommendations, we aren't living up to our doctrine."

A thoughtful look crossed Halloren's face. "That's a good point, Phil. I can see why you'd think that. Have Krubsack get Chavette to recall this inspector from his vacation. Although by doing so, we're putting his life at risk if Omega is silencing witnesses."

"Chavette claims he can't locate the inspector."

Halloren's mouth did a quick twist before he looked down. "That's odd. Have Chavette put more effort into it." He sat back. "No, on second thought, have Krubsack look into finding our inspector. You're right, Mr. Chavette's actions seem perplexing. We need to keep an eye on him in case he's trying to cover up something."

"Do you think he's capable of pulling off last night's break-in? If so, the FBI should be informed."

Halloren shook his head, making Worden sit back, dumbfounded. "Now it is you who's not thinking this through. Alerting the FBI someone from the FAA might've stolen evidence from the NTSB will be a media nightmare we don't want. You're worried we might end up before a Senate committee? This will definitely put us there." Halloren sighed. "Before we go creating trouble for ourselves, we need to investigate this very carefully. Have Krubsack look into Chavette to see if he's hiding anything embarrassing to us. We don't need to damage the reputation of the FAA, or one of our employees, unnecessarily."

"If Krubsack's investigation reveals Mr. Chavette—" Worden lifted his eyebrows, "—or anyone else from the FAA was responsible for any of last night's events, the FBI will have to be notified. Regardless of what this does to the FAA's reputation."

Halloren turned away and looked out the window. "Let's hope that doesn't happen. If someone had the resources to pull off a break-in and two murders, I'm sure they'd do whatever it took to protect themselves." He met Worden's eyes and did not look away. "Now, if you'll excuse me, I have a plane to catch."

Chapter Eighteen

Wednesday, June 16 2:06 p.m.

Kyle's cab dropped him off at the Marriott. He hadn't taken a change of clothes to D.C. yesterday, thinking he would be back to LaGuardia by day's end. In his room, he turned on the TV and found a news station.

"Earlier," the bottle blonde newscaster said, "the NTSB held a news conference."

Kyle quickly pulled a clean polo over his head.

The screen changed to show Mark Evans, the NTSB Investigator In Charge, standing behind a podium with numerous microphones attached to it.

A reporter asked, "Does the NTSB know the cause of the accident?"

"It's still too early in the investigation to come up with a conclusive cause. It appears one of the main landing gear tires blew on takeoff and the crew elected to reject the takeoff."

"Did a review of the cockpit voice recorder say why the crew did that?" a reporter shouted.

"As I'm sure you're aware, the NTSB headquarters was broken into last night, and the recording from Omega Flight 918's CVR, as well as several others, were stolen." Evans paused. "Losing this data before we've had a chance to fully analyze it will hinder our investigation."

Kyle frowned. Why didn't he tell them about Inspector Norman being on their jump seat and what they had heard? Lori claimed she was going to request the NTSB announce that.

"Did someone from the NTSB listen to the recording before it was stolen?" another reporter asked.

Evans adjusted several of the microphones, not moving them much. "Yes, several from the investigative team listened to it, but we didn't have an opportunity to do our full analysis of the recording. Because of this, I won't speculate on what transpired."

Kyle sat on bed. *What the hell?* Evans sounded like a politician with his vague answers. He had never heard an NTSB press conference be so noncommittal.

"An accident doesn't happen because of any one reason," he continued. "Until we've had a chance to interview everyone involved with the flight and do a more thorough analysis of the aircraft, we won't know how those factors contributed to the accident."

The television showed the newscaster at the studio. "Omega Airlines could not be reached to comment."

Kyle's cell phone rang.

"Kyle, it's Lori. Where are you?"

Was he supposed to be at a meeting? Or was she anxious to hear what the flight attendants had to say? Regardless, being caught in his room made him feel he was doing something he wasn't supposed to. "I had to come to my room to get something."

"Would you come to my room?" Lori's voice was soft, sincere, almost pleading.

Was she suggesting what he thought? "Ah, Ms. Almond, all things considered, I don't think it's a good idea for me to come to—"

"What? God, you're so full of yourself." The sincerity in her voice was gone. "I need to talk to you about the investigation and don't want to be seen talking to you. Would going for a ride tarnish your reputation?"

Heat rose in Kyle's cheeks. "Okay. Okay. Calm down. It was the way you asked ... never mind. Yeah, I'll be there in fifteen minutes."

"I'll leave the door ajar. Just walk in. I don't want to take a chance that you'll be seen standing in the hall outside my room." She disconnected.

Kyle looked at his phone. What was with all the cloak-and-dagger stuff?

✈✈✈

Kyle knocked on Lori's door as he pushed it open. She paced by the window. He smiled until the scowl on her face dissolved it. "What's up?"

She stopped. "Thanks for coming. Close the door. I had no one else I could talk to about this."

"What's going on?"

She sighed. "Did you see the press conference?"

"Part of it." Kyle sat in the chair at the desk. "Why didn't Evans tell them about Norman?"

Lori dropped into a chair. "I'm not sure, but I'm guessing for the same reason I don't want to be seen talking to you."

Kyle frowned.

Lori slid to the edge of the bed. "That phone call on the way to the airport this morning was the Chairman telling me to distance myself from you and your airline and to quit antagonizing the FAA."

"Why?"

She stood and paced. "I'm not sure. The NTSB and the FAA have always worked together investigating accidents. The subject airline was always a part of the investigation. Occasionally, tempers will flare and there will be disagreements, but we always work through these."

"It would appear the FAA got to the Chairman somehow," Kyle said.

She fell back into her chair. "For once, I'm going to agree with you. The NTSB is supposed to evaluate other government agencies' effectiveness in preventing transportation accidents. From our investigation, safety recommendations can be given without political regard. It appears the Chairman is not holding up our charter to the public."

"From my point of view, which you've already pointed out is outlandish, it appears your chairman is protecting the FAA."

Lori smiled while he spoke.

"What?"

"Do you always put in a disclaimer before you get to the point?"

He held out his arms, palms up. "I'm afraid of getting my head bitten off."

Her smile fell away. "I'm sorry. I don't mean to be so harsh. You're a nice guy doing a good job. I'm glad you're on this investigation."

"Thanks. You're not so bad yourself."

Her cheeks reddened. "Thank you, I guess."

To defuse the intimacy hanging in the air, he said, "Your Chairman must have gotten to Evans too?"

"It would seem so."

"Your Chairman is setting himself up to take a fall. The FAA can't hide the fact that Norman was on that flight. He was listed on the webperf. Even if they destroy the paper copy that was on the airplane, there will be an electronic copy in our computers in Houston. There was the gate agent and the flight attendants who saw him in the cockpit. The flight attendants aren't about to forget him." He told her about his interview of flight attendant Logsdon.

Lori shook her head. "Norman was one of the first passengers off?"

Kyle nodded. "Besides you and me, there were three others who listened to Norman coercing the crew into rejecting the takeoff. They can't cover this up."

"They must know that, but are hoping they won't have to when the media's interest in it dies."

"We need to find Norman and make him come forward and tell the truth," Kyle said. "If he won't, we can leak to the media where he is."

"I can't ignore my other duties in this investigation to look for him. It might take a couple of days working full-time to find him."

"We haven't been able to locate him in a hospital in the greater New York City area," Kyle said. "He might've been treated and released, or not even injured. I'm going to talk to the fire and rescue crew and see if they remember a passenger matching Norman's description. Maybe they can tell us what became of him after he left the airplane."

Lori looked off in the distance, her eyebrows bunched together. "What?"

"I'd like to go with you. I have to interview them as part of the investigation. My NTSB credentials might get us more information than you could alone."

Kyle smiled. "Well, I don't work for you. Therefore, you have no way of knowing when and where I'll be. I'm on my way there now."

Lori smiled. "That's funny. I was too."

Chapter Nineteen

Wednesday, June 16 3:12 p.m.

Kyle stood outside LaGuardia fire and rescue, waiting for Lori to arrive. Sweat trickled down his back, either from the hot sun on this almost cloudless, mid-eighty-degree day or the tension of possibly being watched.

Would the FAA watch him, in the hopes of preventing him from exposing their inspector? If they did, and he was discovered interviewing the rescue workers, the most likely thing they would do was request the NTSB remove him from the investigation. Since it seemed the NTSB was bending to the FAA's will, they probably wouldn't hesitate to comply. Kyle would go back to training pilots and trying to get the truth out of the FAA from the sidelines. But Lori could be fired. For that reason, he decided to keep his true interest in the accident—and his interactions with Lori—as clandestine as possible.

He replayed their earlier conversation, wondering why the NTSB Chairman thought it best to withhold the presence of the FAA jump seater from the media. Naturally, Kyle thought Evans had been coerced by the FAA, but how and why? It would eventually come out. Too many people had seen Norman there. But without the CVR, or the testimonies by either pilot, it would be difficult to blame the FAA for having a part in the accident. Would the FAA silence Brandish, Lori, the two FAA inspectors, and Kyle so they wouldn't reveal what they had heard on the CVR? If they did, would it raise suspicion that something incriminating happened in the cockpit during the takeoff roll if that avenue of the investigation was not looked into further? Withholding this information would only tarnish the NTSB's esteemed reputation.

The safest thing for Kyle and Lori was to make Norman's participation in the accident known to the public. Kyle considered making an anonymous call to the media. But to be credible, he would have to reveal what he had heard on the CVR and the FAA's threat to shut down Omega. The FAA would know the most likely source of that information had been Kyle.

Unless he could attribute the leak as coming from the Chief Pilot, Kircher. This would get him out of Kyle's way. But that might make Kircher look good to Omega's management, instead of putting him in hot water. That was the last thing Kyle wanted to do.

A silver sedan pulled into the parking lot with Lori behind the wheel, a cell phone held to her ear. She parked, nodded a few times, and put the phone away while she exited the car.

No other cars followed her or parked on the street where the driver could watch her.

Was he letting his mind run wild with his suspicions and there was no big conspiracy, as Lori claimed?

A man wearing navy blue work pants and a t-shirt with Fire and Rescue stenciled over the left breast walked out of one of the four open overhead doors. Four yellow fire trucks were backed into the building. "May I help you?"

Lori held out her credentials and identified them.

"You'll need to talk to the chief." The fireman gestured to the firehouse. They followed him inside and down a hall lined with rubber boots and soiled fire coats into an office area.

Chief Roland Caudill, a broad-shouldered man in his forties, came out from behind his desk and shook their hands. He gestured to the two visitor's chairs across his desk and returned to his seat. "How can I help you folks?"

"We have some questions about the rescue of the passengers of Omega Airline's Flight 918. Okay if I record this?" Lori held up a miniature recorder.

Caudill shrugged. "Sure."

Lori stated the time, date, location, and who was in attendance. "Chief, what time were you notified of Omega 918's accident?"

"At approximately fourteen-fifteen."

Lori went on to ask how many fire trucks were dispatched, from what locations on the airport, and how long it took them to respond. What steps did they take to secure the scene? What was the state of the aircraft when they arrived, and when were rescue boats dispatched? And how many passengers had been evacuated from the airplane when they arrived?

Kyle listened, and occasionally asked a question he thought would aid in training their pilots, since his purpose for being there had nothing to do with the rescue of the passengers. Lori's questions, though, were all things the NTSB included in their report. Not only was the accident analyzed but so was the rescue operation, in order to determine ways to improve it. Kyle was impressed with her method of putting the chief at ease while she asked questions that had the potential to uncover an error he might have made.

"How many passengers needed medical care?" she asked.

"I was busy coordinating the rescue." Caudill stood and walked to his office door. "I didn't have time to pay attention to the condition of the passengers. Gillespie, get in here," he yelled into the station.

A few moments later, a guy in his early thirties walked in. "Yeah, Chief?"

"Paramedic Anthony Gillespie, this is Lori Almond from the NTSB and Kyle Masters from Omega Airlines." Caudill returned to his seat. "They have a few questions about the condition of the passengers I can't answer."

They shook hands, Gillespie coming to stand to the side of the chief's desk. Lori asked him questions about the injured passengers' care and when they were transported to hospitals.

When it seemed Lori had exhausted them with her questions, Kyle asked, "There's a missing passenger we haven't been able to locate. He was a thin man wearing a white shirt and dark pants. He might have been one of the first off the airplane."

"The FAA guy?" Gillespie asked.

Kyle tried to not let his surprise show, but his eyebrows shot up.

"Did he identify himself as one?" Lori's tone of voice suggested she was as surprised as Kyle.

"Oh, yeah. When we arrived, I noticed him trying to swim to shore with a briefcase. He swam using one arm like the other might be broken. We fished him out and examined him. It appeared he had fractured his clavicle and possibly his hip. When I tried to move his briefcase out of the way, he yelled at me and told me that it had to stay within his sight. You'd have thought he had the launch codes for nuclear weapons."

Gillespie shook his head. "We put his arm in a sling and sat him off to the side to attend to more seriously injured passengers. Except this asshole got in our faces and told us we needed to rush him to the hospital. You'd have thought he was the only injured passenger and about to die. We explained there were more seriously injured passengers that would be going before him. So, he pulled out his FAA credentials and ordered us to take him to the hospital to be treated so he could then brief his superiors.

"I thought, 'what the hell.' Maybe it was important for the FAA to know what happened." Gillespie shrugged. "We loaded him up in the in the next ambulance and sent him to St. Luke's Roosevelt."

✈✈✈

Outside the firehouse, Kyle asked, "Do you want to meet me at St. Luke's?"

Lori's chest rose and fell as she looked toward the hangar housing the wrecked airplane. "I'd better not. Besides—" Two vertical creases appeared between her eyes. "I thought your company couldn't find him in a local hospital."

"Maybe there was a clerical error, or he checked in under another name."

Lori shook her head. "It never ceases to amaze me how stupid and desperate some people can be in a crisis. Norman escaped from a wrecked airplane that might catch fire and guarded his briefcase instead of helping the other passengers. He didn't want any evidence left behind that placed him in that cockpit."

"Probably." Kyle's cell phone rang. He held up a finger as he answered it.

"This is Doctor Rangaraju. I'm returning your call." The man had a thick Indian accent.

"Yes, Doctor, thank you for calling. I'm a pilot manager for Omega Airlines that employed one of your patients, Cheryl Wells. I was wondering if I could ask some questions about her death?"

"I'm sorry. Her death was unexpected. Unfortunately, I cannot talk about her care due to doctor-patient confidentiality."

"You say her death was unexpected, why was that?"

"I am sorry. I cannot talk about that. If there's nothing else, I have patients to attend to."

"Doctor, I think she was murdered. Someone is trying to cover up their involvement in the airline accident Ms. Wells was involved in. Please, I'd like to meet with you to discuss her case."

There was silence, then Dr. Rangaraju said, "Without her husband's consent, I can't divulge any details of her care."

"Do you know if an autopsy will be performed?"

Lori scrunched up her face and mouthed, "Shit."

"No. Her husband saw no need for one."

"Do you know if her body is still at the hospital?"

"I think it was being flown to her home yesterday to be cremated."

Shit.

"If she was murdered, why have the police not spoken to me about this?" Rangaraju asked.

"I don't know. I had better discuss this with them. Thank you for your help." He disconnected the call.

"Shit, shit, shit!" Lori kicked the tire of her car. "What was I thinking? We should have ordered her body autopsied."

"You can do that?"

"Yes. I was so distracted by Ed's death and the break in, and then the chairman ordering me to distance myself from you, I forgot."

"You need to order that autopsy, before she's cremated."

Chapter Twenty

Thursday, June 17 3:56 p.m.

Morgan Steele followed Earl Dorsey, Omega Airline's Vice President of Operations, down the hall to a conference room at the Sheraton Hotel in Houston. He pulled his smart phone out of his inside jacket pocket, fiddled with the on-screen apps, and dropped it back where he had found it.

Sitting at a table was George Niemeier, the FAA Principal Operations Inspector responsible for overseeing Omega Airlines operations, and two other men.

Niemeier and the other two stood. Steele judged Niemeier's companions to be higher up in the FAA by their expensive-looking suits.

"Gentlemen." Niemeier shook hands with Steele and Dorsey. "It's my pleasure to introduce Deputy Administrator Stewart Halloren and Manager of Flight Standards Service, Jerry Krubsack."

Steele thought Halloren, someone he judged to be in his forties, used a firm handshake to signify the power of the person behind it. He'd see about that.

"Would you like coffee?" Niemeier gestured to the side table where a coffee service had been set up.

Usually, Niemeier was more to the point, making Steele question why he had chosen this moment to be so hospitable. His curiosity was also piqued as to why two of the FAA's upper echelons were present for this surreptitious meeting. He decided to play along. Without consulting Dorsey, Steele shrugged. "Coffee would be good."

Dorsey sighed before following him to the urn.

Steele wondered if Dorsey, whose rank equaled his own, was upset Steele had taken the lead by accepting this offer. Regardless, Steele fixed his coffee without a glance at Dorsey. He didn't want the FAA to feel any dissent between them.

Once seated across from the FAA, Dorsey said, "We aren't happy with your lack of cooperation over the last several days."

"That's the purpose of this meeting," Halloren said. "We'd like to apologize for that. First off, the FAA offers its condolences on the loss of your two crew members. I can only imagine what you and everyone at your airline must be going through."

Dorsey sat back. "Thank you."

Steele didn't feel as pacified. There was an agenda for this meeting, and the Deputy Administrator's remark struck Steele as an easing of what was to come.

"It's been a rough few days." Dorsey rubbed his jaw. "It would have been easier if we'd been able to get some answers from—"

Halloren held his hand up. "Mr. Dorsey, I can understand your disgruntlement. I called this meeting in the hopes we could work out some arrangements that might be beneficial to your company, as a way of making amends."

Steele leaned forward.

"We're listening," Dorsey said.

"As you are well aware, there was an FAA safety inspector onboard your aircraft at the time of the unfortunate accident." Halloren looked at both of them. "We're not here to point fingers. We have a proposition that could benefit both our organizations."

"Go on," Dorsey said.

When Dorsey glanced in Steele's direction, he nodded signaling for him to take the lead.

"We propose from this point forward you *not* mention our inspector's presence on board your aircraft during the accident takeoff. You can handle the press and any employees who know of his existence in any way you see fit, as long as you *never* acknowledge he had anything to do with the accident."

Steele furrowed his brow. For the FAA to make such a request, their inspector must have had a direct influence on the rejected takeoff. No wonder Kyle told him they needed to find this inspector.

"In exchange," Halloren continued, "we'll ease the process of approving your 787 operation."

Obviously, Steele concluded, this inspector had a detrimental influence on the crew for the FAA to make such a generous offer.

"In what way?" Dorsey asked.

"You can consider any and all procedures, maintenance programs, and approvals will be met with minimal resistance. We'll fast-track everything you bring to us within a day or so."

Steele cocked an eyebrow, incredulous at their proposal. To bring a new airplane into an airline's operation was a cumbersome process. Routes had to be approved. Procedures for how the airplane would be flown, boarded, evacuated, and maintained had to be developed, written, and approved. Each of the numerous manuals usually took several passes between the FAA and the airline before being approved.

Afterward, the FAA monitored the initial training for the crews, mechanics, and gate agents to verify they were being trained to the approved procedures. Before flying the aircraft with passengers, the FAA observed a couple of typical flights with a full complement of crew members. Once these hurdles had been overcome, the airline could put the airplane into service.

The process was more streamlined for an airplane that another airline already flew. To approve a newly certified airplane, such as the 787, with all its new technology, flying oceanic, international flights, the process was daunting.

"Will this agreement include the initial training and proving flights?" Steele asked.

Halloren glanced at Krubsack, who nodded his head.

This acknowledgement by Halloren's underling told Steele the Deputy Administrator wasn't familiar with what he was proposing if he needed approval from someone under him.

"We'll need this spelled out in writing," Dorsey said. "So there are no misunderstandings just what this offer covers."

This last sentence, Steele knew, was a softening of his request so they didn't lose this incredible deal.

"Obviously, for reasons we all are aware, we cannot do that," Halloren said. "Such a document could hinder this agreement if other parties were to discover it."

Steele gave Dorsey a subtle shake of his head.

"Without a written agreement, how do we know you'll keep your word, or exactly what the agreement covers?" Dorsey asked.

"You'll have to take our word," Halloren said. "Just as we'll have to accept your word you'll uphold your end of the bargain."

This would be Steele's cue to weigh in. "We're in a different position than you. The media's interest in this accident and its cause will die in a week or so. By the time the NTSB finishes their investigation and writes the final report a year and a half from now, the public won't even remember or care about the accident. It'll be a couple of months before we seek approval of routes and procedures. You might've changed your mind by then, after we've covered up your inspector's ineptitude."

Halloren fidgeted.

Steele hoped his satisfaction didn't show. Making the official realize they wouldn't roll over for them was quite a coup.

"Should you choose not to accept our generous offer, this accident will make us feel we need to examine Omega Airlines' operation more carefully." Krubsack folded his hands on the table.

Clearly, it was Krubsack's turn to play bad cop.

"We'll flood your airline with safety inspectors." Krubsack narrowed his eyes. "Hardly a flight will fly without an inspector on board. We'll thoroughly inspect all of your airplanes and maintenance records, looking for discrepancies. You know how cumbersome it is to operate on time when the FAA is looking over your shoulder."

Steele clinched his fist under the table. Most flights would fly normally, but some would be delayed while inspectors gave crews or mechanics a hard time about minor discrepancies. Passengers would miss important engagements, tarnishing Omega's reputation.

"When you do submit 787 materials for approval," Krubsack continued, "we'll need to take a close look at it. We're understaffed, and it's difficult to say how long it will take to review everything. An airplane with all that new technology..." He put on a thoughtful expression. "We'll have to be careful you aren't rushing to operate it when you haven't considered all the implications. We might not be so careful if the submitting airline hadn't recently had an accident and numerous violations and discrepancies."

He paused, the trace of a smirk beneath his scowl. "In the meantime, the ads you've been touting about being the first U.S.

airline to fly the 787 might not happen. United Airlines isn't far behind you in their approval process."

Steele rubbed a throbbing vein in his forehead. "You're obviously worried we'll let the media know about your inspector's contribution to the accident. I think we'll conclude this meeting and arrange a press briefing."

"Don't test us." Halloren pointed with a finger. "What Mr. Krubsack suggested will happen immediately if you turn this deal down or mention this agreement to anyone outside this room."

Steele cocked an eyebrow. "If the press is made aware of your inspector's contribution to our accident, Congress will call you into hearings."

"What will you tell the press?" Krubsack said. "There was an FAA inspector onboard your flight? We'll confirm it. That he contributed to the accident? We'll deny it. How will you prove us wrong?"

Heat rose up Steele's neck and across his cheeks. "Several other people heard the CVR."

"From what we've heard," Krubsack said, "the two NTSB investigators thought what they heard was inconclusive. Unfortunately, one of them was murdered. The other, we hear, is under a lot of stress and might have to be relieved of her duties. That leaves our two investigators who disagreed with yours."

"ALPA had one of our pilots who is a trained investigator who also listened to the recording," Steele said.

Krubsack sat back, dropping his hands in his lap. "We've heard a rumor he has a drinking problem. The FAA is very intolerant of alcohol abuse. I'm sure his recall of events on the CVR might change if he knew any investigation into his misuse of alcohol would cause him to lose his pilot license."

"We'll have your goddamn inspector's testimony when he's found!" Dorsey said.

Krubsack smirked. "Do you really think he's going to admit he had something to do with an accident that has left twelve people dead and sixty-eight injured? He'll lose his job and his pension if he does."

Steele let out a deep breath. "Why even present this offer if you have nothing to lose?"

"We'd like to avoid any difficulties either of our two organizations will have to suffer as a result of this unfortunate event," Halloren said.

Steele hated his soft, soothing tone—as if he was doing everyone a favor.

"Omega Airline has already received a black eye in the press because of this accident and will be facing lawsuits from the injured and other victims' families. We feel bad you have to suffer alone when we *might have* contributed to your situation. To ease your burden, we'd like to help you with your 787-approval process."

"We'll need to discuss this with our superiors." Dorsey stood.

Steele wasn't ready to concede the discussion, but knew he needed to calm down before he said things that might damage Omega's bargaining position further. He pushed his chair back and stood.

Halloren looked at his watch. "We'll be flying back to D.C. in thirty minutes. We'll need your answer by then. Otherwise," he said, a cocky smile on his face, "good luck with the 787 program."

✈✈✈

Steele and Dorsey walked to Steele's BMW, the most secure place to make a call without leaving the premises. Steele started the car and set the air conditioning to high, hoping it would cool his temper.

From the passenger seat, Dorsey called Earl Wagner, the Executive Vice President, putting him on speaker phone. They explained the FAA's offer—and threat.

"Motherfuckers," Wagner said. "What do you guys think?"

"We can't accept this offer," Steele said. "We'll have no proof they'll keep their promise when we begin seeking approval of the 787 program. Or, just what the deal covers."

"If we don't, we're fucked anyway!" Earl Dorsey said.

"Morgan, how much will this save us if we accept their offer?" Wagner's voice came from a distance. Steele guessed he had leaned back in his chair, away from the speaker phone, probably staring at the ceiling.

Steele ran some calculations in his head. "Fifty million dollars."

Dorsey blew out his cheeks. "Then we've got to accept their bribe. It'll cost us millions more in delays and fines with them riding our flights and inspecting our airplanes. The board of directors will go ballistic if they hear we could have saved fifty million dollars and bad press from delayed flights."

Wagner sighed. "I'm inclined to agree. Any other reservations, Morgan?"

Steele sighed. "Their inspector must have contributed to the accident or they wouldn't be making this deal. I hate to let them off without this being revealed. But we'll have a hard time proving this without the CVR. It'll be Kyle Masters' word against their three inspectors."

"I wish we knew if Leo Brandish had a drinking problem as they suggested," Dorsey said.

Steele shrugged. "I don't know him. Kyle will stand behind what he heard. If we convince the right reporters their inspector contributed to the accident, and the FAA hasn't revealed this, it could be a sensational story that will have all of them before Congress."

"But it will be Masters' word against theirs," Dorsey said. "They'll portray us as fabricating this story to spread blame for the accident. This will piss the FAA off and we'll be lucky if we ever get the 787 approved."

"And because of the accident, it will be hard to convince the Senate Commerce Committee the FAA is unnecessarily stalling the approval," Wagner said.

Steele lifted the corners of his mouth. "Well, I've got something that'll make them sign an agreement and honor it."

Chapter Twenty-One

Thursday, June 17 3:49 p.m.

Kyle walked into the Emergency Room at St. Luke's Roosevelt Hospital in New York City. Various nationalities were represented by the twenty to thirty people waiting. Some sat rocking or were held by loved ones. Others paced. The smell of disinfectant did nothing to mask the urine and body odor from decades of people waiting for emergency medical attention.

While waiting in line at the reception window, Kyle remembered the times he had visited the ER with Travis after injuries from hockey or a fall from his bike. There was also the memory of being helpless several years ago when he had landed in Seattle late one night and had a call from Karen, telling him she had taken Travis to the ER with a high fever and they wanted to admit him. Kyle couldn't make it home until the next day. He had spent a restless night worried about Travis and guilty for not being there for Karen. This scenario was familiar to many airline crews with families.

When next in line, he put on what he hoped was a worried look. Knowing how unscrupulous the FAA had been so far in the investigation he knew he would have to act the same way to get the information he wanted. Although he would lie it did not bother him knowing the FAA had been doing the same thing.

To the middle-aged woman seated at the reception desk, he said, "Hi. My uncle was on the airline that crashed a couple of days ago. We haven't heard from him since then. I was wondering if he's admitted here?"

"What's his name?"

"Ernest Norman. He goes by Ernie, though." Kyle had no idea of Norman used that first name.

The woman clicked several times with her mouse and typed. "I show him treated and released the same day."

Kyle sighed and pretended to look relieved. "Oh, thank God. Does it say what was wrong with him?"

"I can't give out that information."

Kyle glanced left and right to portray embarrassment. In a low voice, he said, "I hate to say this, but I haven't been real close to my uncle lately. You know how it is trying to raise a family with a disabled wife and maintain a job and all." He sighed heavily for dramatic effect. "I don't have his address or phone number. Do you have it there?"

The receptionist's eyebrows rose. "You said he was your uncle?"

Kyle hoped being caught in his lie didn't show. "Yes, my mother's brother."

"Wouldn't your mother have it?"

Kyle looked down, hoping this made him look uncomfortable. "My mother passed away a few months ago. My father and Uncle Ernie never got along. I doubt Dad would have it." He hoped he didn't slip and fall on any of this bullshit he was spewing.

The woman huffed and looked around. She took a pen and wrote on a piece of paper.

Kyle suppressed a grin. He was getting good at this lying thing.

A woman dressed in hospital scrubs whose name tag read Charge Nurse approached. She looked at Kyle, then the receptionist. "Who's next, Chandra?"

Chandra's eyes widened. "I'm sorry, sir. I can't help you," she said to Kyle while crumbling the piece of paper and dropping it in a waste can behind her. She picked up a clipboard and handed it to the nurse. "Next," she said to the man behind Kyle.

He walked away empty-handed.

✈✈✈

Steele and Dorsey returned to the conference room where the FAA waited. Steele maintained the scowl he had worn when they left twenty minutes ago. "Gentlemen, we accept your offer, but with one condition."

Halloren raised his eyebrows. "And that is?"

"We need something in writing assuring us you'll honor your agreement in the future."

Halloren shook his head. "As we've previously stressed, we cannot do that. You have our word we'll approve your 787 program with minimal fuss."

Steele pursed his lips before speaking. "That's what worries us. You use words like minimal. Today, it might mean approval will take a day or two. Four months from now, it could be a couple of weeks, or more. In the meantime, we've helped you cover up your inspector's egregious misconduct. We won't agree to this with just a promise."

"I'm sorry, if you insist on something in writing, we don't have a deal." Halloren gestured to his right. "Mr. Krubsack will call every FSDO in the country, ordering them to put inspectors on Omega flights. Our maintenance inspectors will swarm over your aircraft. You'd better hope everything is in order, or you'll be facing record fines and your pilots and mechanics will have violations on their records."

Steele would love to slap the confident smirk off the arrogant bastard's face. The thing that prevented him was the knowledge that Halloren's expression was about to change on its own.

Dorsey cocked an eyebrow. "When this meeting is over, we'll call a press conference and let the public know an FAA inspector contributed to the accident. To hide his involvement, you tried to bribe us."

Halloren's eyes narrowed.

"You can threaten us with this detailed inspection, but you don't have the manpower or the budget to pull this stunt off for very long," Steele said. "Eventually, the work those inspectors have put aside will cause other airlines to complain the examinations they need, or procedures awaiting approval, aren't being accomplished. They'll go to the Senate Oversight Committee, asking them to do something about it. In the meantime, you'll have racked up a bunch of overtime and travel expenses."

Halloren's nostrils flared.

Steele tried not to grin. "You'll eventually have to go to Congress and ask for money to cover this budget overrun. They'll remember us claiming one of your inspectors contributed to our accident and you tried to cover it up by bribing us before launching your aggressive examination into our operation. If they've forgotten, we'll be there to remind them."

Krubsack pushed back from the table and stood. "I guess we have nothing further to discuss. I have numerous fisdos to call. Good luck with your 787 program."

"Before you leave," Steele said, setting his phone on the table, "you might want to listen to this." He selected the app that made his phone a digital recorder, moved the slider back almost to the beginning of the file, and selected play.

Halloren's voice came over the speaker. "As you are well aware, there was an FAA safety inspector onboard your aircraft at the time of the unfortunate accident. We're not here to point fingers. We have a proposition that could benefit both our organizations."

Krubsack collapsed back into his chair, eyes wide.

They listened to Halloren explain the deal they proposed.

Steele stopped the recording. "The sound quality was better than I hoped. I'm sure the media will be able to identify your voice from speeches you've given." He directed his words at Halloren, who had paled and slumped in his chair.

"What exactly do you need this agreement to say?"

Krubsack stared at Halloren. "Sir, can I have moment?"

Halloren took the legal pad Dorsey handed him with the proposed agreement they had written in Steele's car. Halloren read it, handed it to Krubsack.

He read it, then looked at Steele and Dorsey. "Could you give us a minute, please?"

"We'll be outside," Dorsey said.

In the hall, Dorsey shot a fist in the air. "We got him."

Steele sighed. If they agreed to this, it would save Omega a lot of time and money. They would be able to hold the FAA to their end of the bargain, or could threaten to release a copy of it and the recording to the media. It would make Omega look guilty of assisting the FAA's attempt to cover up their inspector's contribution to the accident, but Steele felt they could explain this away by what the FAA threatened them with. Regardless, it would be the FAA that was before a Senate review board on the matter. Omega might suffer some fines, but would eventually come out unscathed.

Steele hated that they would assist in covering up the inspector's negligence, but the airline was a business, and sometimes they had to put principles aside.

Several minutes later, they were called back into the room.

"We reworded it slightly," Krubsack said. He didn't maintain eye contact with them. "If you agree, we'll take it back to our office, type it up, sign it, and fax it over to you to do the same. We have a couple of conditions, though."

Halloren's gaze stayed on the table.

Steele read the document, then handed it to Dorsey. "They are?"

"Kyle Masters will have to be pulled off the investigation and prohibited from ever mentioning what he's uncovered. We'll also need the gate agents and flight attendants who can put our inspector on the jump seat to not reveal he was there. If word of this agreement is leaked, we'll consider the deal void. We'll expect this document to be destroyed when your 787 program is approved."

Steele and Dorsey glanced at each other, then nodded.

Chapter Twenty-Two

Thursday, June 18 5:23 p.m.

In a taxi on the way back to LaGuardia from St. Luke's, Kyle took out his phone, held it a moment, and then selected the number for home.

After the fourth ring, Travis answered. "Hello." His voice lacked any enthusiasm.

"Hey, Buddy. How're you doing?"

"Okay."

"Did you get a bunch of homework today at school?"

"The usual."

Normally, his son would have told him the amount of homework assigned was completely unfair. Kyle sighed. "Look, Travis, Mom and I have grown apart. I don't like that we have, but I want to work out our differences. When I get back from this investigation, we'll work on that. It'll take us some time, though. I'm sorry you're the one getting caught in the middle. I love you very much and will do all I can to spare you any more pain."

Silence.

"You still there, Buddy?"

"Yeah. Do you still love Mom?"

"Yes. Very much." *Even though she's making it difficult.*

"So why are you getting a divorce?"

Because your mother seems to want it regardless of what I want, or what it'll do to you. "I think Mom thinks it's hopeless and we can't work out our problems. I wish she hadn't told you that until we had a chance to discuss this."

"Are you having an affair?"

Kyle squeezed the phone. *Is Karen trying to make me the bad guy?* He took a deep breath, hoping to breathe out some of the anger swirling around in him. "*No.* I'm not having an affair. I've not been with another woman since Mom and I married. Is that what she told you?"

Travis said nothing for a moment. Kyle could sense his unease. Should he betray his mother's trust, or discuss this with Kyle to learn the truth?

"Mom said you must love someone else or your job more than us."

Bitch. "That's not true, Travis. I like my job. I get a lot of satisfaction from it. I don't *love* it more than I do you or Mom. I'm also not in love with another woman. I work a lot, which might make her think that. I know the amount of time I'm away is hard on both of you."

"Okay."

Travis seemed done talking. Just like Kyle, Travis wasn't a big talker on the phone. "Can I talk to Mom?"

"Okay. See ya."

Travis yelled, "Mom, Dad's on the phone!"

Kyle tried to calm himself down so the first conversation he had with Karen in two days wasn't a shouting match.

"Yes," she said without warmth.

"Hi. Thanks for taking Travis to his lesson yesterday."

"Someone has to care for our son."

If she had said anything other than that, Kyle told himself he could have remained calm. Blood pounded in his ears. "Why did you tell Travis I was having an affair?"

"If you're going to raise your voice, I don't want to talk you."

Kyle took a deep breath. "Why would you tell him that?"

"You certainly haven't been yourself lately."

"So you think I'm having an affair? You know, you haven't been easy to get along with, either." Why did he let her push his buttons? He caught the taxi driver glancing at him in the mirror. He took two deep breaths, since one didn't work last time.

"That's the problem with you. You want to blame our problems on me while I stay home and pick up after you."

He was about to say, "You're welcome to get a job if you'd like," but realized she had hung up.

He finished the ride back to the Marriott staring out the window, wondering how they could resolve their problems when each conversation resulted in a fight.

At the hotel, Kyle made his way to the conference room for the first progress meeting of the investigation. Each of the different investigating teams would brief the other groups.

While listening to the NTSB meteorology investigator give a summation of the weather conditions at the time of the accident, Kyle's phone vibrated in its holster. It was Steele. Anticipating this call would be in response to the meeting with the FAA, he stepped out into the hall.

"Kyle, we need to fill the fleet manager's position, and we're offering you the position."

Satisfaction rolled through him, making him giddy. Hearing he had managed to achieve what he had been working for the last couple of years brought a smile to his face. "Ah, thank you. Thank you very much."

"You've done a great job as an assistant fleet manager, and going forward with the expansion we have planned, we need you to be an integral part of the management team that leads the airline."

"I'd like that." He pumped a fist and silently mouthed, "Yes."

"When can you return to work out the details of your contract?"

Kyle looked at his watch. "I've missed the last flight to Houston. I'll be on the first flight in the morning."

"Okay. Be thinking about what you'd like for a salary."

Think about what you'd like for a salary? Kyle assumed he would be told what the position paid. He had no idea he could request his salary. This was turning out better than he thought. "I will. Did the FAA request the position be filled as a result of the accident?"

"Not directly." Steele's words were spoken as if he was thinking about what to say. "We've been meaning to fill the position for some time. The ah ... accident was a reminder of how important it is to be proactive with our management of the airline. I doubt the accident was a result of this position being vacant. But looking forward, we need people like you helping us manage our growing airline."

Kyle frowned. Unless addressing a group of pilots, Steele wasn't prone to this management mumbo-jumbo speak. "I appreciate the confidence. Who's taking my place in the investigation?"

There was a pause, as if Steele hadn't considered this. Kyle wondered if he was reading too much into this, or was he thinking about the meeting with the FAA?

"Ah, be thinking about who you'd like to replace you there. For now, you can forget about the accident."

Kyle glowed in his new responsibility. But he couldn't forget about the accident. It happened to an airplane in the fleet he was now responsible for. The outcome of the investigation would cause them to make changes to how the airplane was operated and how they trained the crews to anticipate the accident scenario.

On a more global level, the public needed to know the crew was coerced into rejecting the takeoff. They had to find Norman and get him to tell the truth about what happened so the FAA couldn't cover up their inspector's ineptitude. The FAA would need to train other inspectors in how to observe flights without pressuring the crews into making mistakes. "Should I continue looking for the missing inspector?"

"No." This came out abruptly. "We need you to concentrate on getting up to speed on your new position. Your attendance will be mandatory for manpower planning, weekly operational, fleet standardization, and various other meetings. You'll have to learn how to be prepared for those meetings. You'll have to come up with a training plan for the new pilots we'll be hiring so we can hire the maximum amount each month. You'll also have to determine how many instructors you'll need to interview, hire, and oversee their training."

Steele spewed this stuff out like talking to someone who hadn't worked in the training department for the last several years. "We have to finalize our order with Boeing and how we want the new aircraft configured. You'll be a part of that." He paused. "The NTSB is responsible for the investigation. They can coordinate with the FAA on locating and interviewing the missing inspector."

"Okay," he said knowing his tone showed how confused he was. He knew what his duties would be. As the assistant fleet manager, Kyle occasionally sat in on meetings when the former fleet manager was unavailable. He had assisted in the other duties Steele had laid out. During his interview for the position, Kyle had laid out his plans for how he would manage the fleet. Steele's answer was excessively wordy for someone usually abrupt and to the point.

The door to the conference room opened, and members of the investigation left. Several acknowledged Kyle as they passed.

He nodded.

The only reason he could think Steele seemed not himself was the meeting with the FAA had rattled him somehow and Steele was plotting how best to deal with what was discussed. "Did the meeting with the FAA have anything to do with the 737 I need to be made aware of?" It was time to ask the questions his new position allowed him.

"Ah, well...no. It dealt with the approval process of the 787. You can put the accident investigation behind you now and concentrate on your new position. I'll see you tomorrow morning, Mr. Fleet Manager."

✈✈✈

On the flight from Houston to D.C. aboard the FAA Gulfstream, Jerry Krubsack waited for Stewart Halloren to finish a call on the airplane's satellite phone. When he had, Krubsack cleared his throat. "Do you think Omega will be able to keep their investigator quiet? From what Chavette said, he's very arrogant and outspoken."

"They'll have to, if they want us to honor our end of the agreement."

Krubsack took a moment to gather his courage. "We shouldn't have agreed to the document Omega shoved down our throats. If it's discovered, we'll go to prison."

Halloren stabbed a finger at him. "If you'd run your department properly, we wouldn't be in this mess." Venom filled Halloren's voice. "Norman should never have been hired as a safety inspector. Have you seen his record? Why wasn't he fired years ago? Jesus! What incompetency."

Krubsack's ears burned.

"And how in the hell did someone like Chavette get promoted to manager of a FSDO? He's almost as inept as Norman. How many other Normans and Chavettes work for us? I should fire everyone and bring in people who can think."

A moment passed while Halloren regained some composure. "As far as signing that document, what choice did we have? That goddamn recording changed everything. If they played that to the media, we'd have gone before the Senate Oversight Committee."

Krubsack's stomach had been in knots since the accident because of the direction the FAA had taken. "We should have been upfront from the beginning and let the NTSB know our inspector was on that flight. Trying to cover it up has made the situation worse."

Halloren shook his head. "It never ceases to amaze me how bureaucrats don't look at the big picture."

Krubsack's face warmed.

"If we'd done what you suggest, the media would've talked of nothing else for the next week. They would've asked why this FAA *safety inspector* didn't do something to prevent the accident. When the NTSB later told the media this representative from the government agency responsible for aviation safety was, in fact, the cause of the accident, Congress would convene a review board."

Halloren leaned closer to Krubsack. "Have you ever been before a Senate review board?"

Krubsack turned away from Halloren's glare.

"I didn't think so. Trust me. You don't want to sit there with five Senators staring you down, trying to assure the public they are looking out for their interests by asking pointed questions. How would you explain keeping an inept employee in your organization for as long as you have?"

Krubsack knew his answer would have made him sound clueless. He didn't know.

The FAA was such a large bureaucracy, it was impossible for him to know how each inspector who worked under him performed. He had to rely on the respected field managers. Norman's had covered up the man's incompetence.

"You can thank the Administrator and me for avoiding media scrutiny of your poorly managed department. Because I can assure you, if this had come before a Senate hearing, someone would've lost their job. Trust me. It wouldn't be the Administrator or myself."

This had been a worry of Krubsack's from the time he heard of Norman's involvement. Because of this, he had willingly done as he was told. Now, the only satisfaction he had from following along was the knowledge if the cover-up was discovered, those above him responsible for it would be unemployed as well.

Regardless of how well Halloren thought they were now protected, he should have a plan in place for other contingencies. "We need to think about how we'll handle this if Omega can't keep a lid on Masters."

"I've already had an investigator..." Halloren turned away. "Omega Airlines won't want any of this to come out now. They'll keep him in line."

"There is still that woman from the NTSB who's heard the CVR."

Halloren stared out the airplane window. "She's taken care of."

Chapter Twenty-Three

Thursday, June 17 6:17 p.m.

After Kyle's phone conversation with Steele, he re-entered the conference room. Several NTSB investigators talked on the phone or typed on laptops. Lori wasn't one of them. He hated to leave the investigation without saying goodbye. He would call her later.

In his room, he called home, hoping the news of his promotion might make Karen more receptive to staying married.

Travis answered.

"Hey, Buddy, I got great news! I got the fleet manager position." Kyle sounded as excited as Travis had recently when he called Kyle to tell him he had become a starting wingman on his hockey team.

"Good for you." The enthusiasm and words were something Karen might say.

Kyle sighed, realizing how much children pick up from their parents. Was he passing anything good on to his son?

Kyle went on as if Travis cared. "Most of my time will be spent in the office or meetings. It'll mostly be eight to five, with every weekend and holiday off. No more missed birthday celebrations or hockey games."

"Does that mean you won't get a divorce?" Life came into his voice.

"I never wanted a divorce. Since I'll be home more, I hope it'll change Mom's mind." Kyle knew he was putting all the blame of the implied divorce on Karen's shoulders when he shared fault for it. But he still stung over her telling Travis he loved his job or someone else more.

"Cool."

Hearing his son sound like himself again lifted Kyle's spirits. He hoped he could keep him that way. "Can I talk to Mom and tell her the good news?"

"She's gone to the store."

"Okay. Tell her for me and that I'll be home tomorrow night. Ask her to call me when she gets back."

"Okay."

Kyle stared at his phone and considered calling Karen's cell. Would she answer? She had hung up on him the last time they had talked. If she wanted to talk about the promotion and how this could help their marriage, she could call. He was tired of always being the one to make the effort. But she might feel the same way. To ease his conscience, he decided if she didn't call by the time he went to bed, he'd call her.

He went to the bar off the lobby and ordered a steak and beer. He was halfway through the bottle when Lori walked in, dressed in jeans and a patterned tee shirt, never looking his way. She ordered from a waitress and began reading the book she carried.

Kyle slipped off his stool and walked over to her with his beer. "Hi. What are you reading?"

She showed no sign of being glad to see him as she lifted the book so he could see the cover. *The Girl with the Dragon Tattoo.*

Kyle thought it was an appropriate book for another strong-willed, intelligent woman. "I've read that. How do you like it?"

She shrugged. "I've almost put it aside several times. It's taken me this long to get into it." She held it open in the middle.

"It starts getting really good now. I've read the sequels. They all start out slow."

She gestured to the chair across from her. "Would you like to sit down?"

"Sure, thanks."

The waitress returned with a glass of red wine and set it in front of Lori, then departed. Lori swirled, sniffed, and sipped it.

"I'll be leaving the investigation."

One of her eyebrows rose. "How come?"

"I've been promoted. I'm now the fleet manager of the 737." This brought on a wave of satisfaction that pulled a smile out of him.

Lori didn't look happy for him. "Congratulations. I assume this is something you've wanted."

Why couldn't she be more excited for him? Was she upset he was leaving her to get the FAA to come forward on her own? "Yeah, for a year or so."

She took another sip and looked anywhere but at him.

Had he misread her? He thought their time together had drawn them closer than mere acquaintances.

She thumbed the pages of her book.

"Well, I'll let you get back to your book."

She took another sip. "No, please stay. I'm leaving the investigation, too."

"Why?"

The glass went to her lips again before she spoke. "The Chairman feels I'm hindering the investigation."

Kyle scrunched up his face. "What? How?"

Regret filled her face before looking at him fully. "I told Evans I'd interviewed the fire and rescue chief. He was pissed. He claimed I was trying to run my own investigation and he wouldn't have it. Shortly after that, the Chairman called and told me I was off the investigation and to return to the office."

Kyle slumped. If he hadn't told her he was going to interview the fire and rescue personnel she might not have gone either. "What will you do now?"

She shrugged. "I'll probably continue with the study I was working on before the accident. I might be put in the rotation to investigate the next accident. More likely, they'll punish me and keep me in the office awhile." The disappointment of not seeing a major accident investigation through to its completion was etched all over her face. "I doubt I'll ever be the IIC of an accident."

"What was the subject of your study?" Would talking about something else cheer her up?

A trace of a smile touched her face before vanishing. "I was analyzing the number of accidents or incidents in which crew fatigue was a contributing factor."

"Good. I'm glad someone is looking into that. Crew fatigue is probably the biggest safety concern facing the industry."

"I know." She took another sip. "Probably that'll be taken from me, too, and I'll be assigned some minor report that won't have much significance." There was no denying the bitterness in her words.

"I'm sorry this is happening to you."

"Their loss."

"Yeah," he said. "Their loss. You were doing a good job."

The bartender came over with Kyle's salad. "Do you want to eat this here or back at the bar?"

Kyle looked at Lori.

She gestured to the table with the wave of a hand.

"Here, please," he told the bartender.

After he left, Kyle sat back, making no move to eat.

"Please eat. Mine will be here shortly."

"I can wait. I guess you'll be able to take that vacation with your daughters."

She brightened. "Yeah, I guess that's something good that'll come of this."

"It's been a few years since I've been to the Cape. Have you ever been there before?"

"Not to vacation." Lori sat up and paid more attention to him, a soft grin on her face.

"It's fun. Your daughters will like it." He shook his head. "I'm glad I'm not taking teenage daughters there. I'd be up all night worrying they'd be doing what I did when I was their age."

Lori smiled. "Why, were you one of those wild boys, constantly getting in trouble and breaking girls' hearts?"

He pretended to exhibit a cocky attitude. "Yeah, that was me."

Her smile broadened. "You're so full of shit."

Kyle pretended to look offended. "Oh, the stories I could tell of the broken hearts out there."

"Let me guess." Her expression changed as if visualizing a thought. "When you were a teenager, you worked at the local airport fueling airplanes and doing odd jobs to earn money for flying lessons. You didn't have time for girls."

He smiled. "No. That's your story, except it was boys not girls."

Lori's mouth dropped. "How'd you know?"

"I guessed. I've seen how you look at airplanes. To you, they're beautifully crafted pieces of exotic machinery. I'm guessing when you fly, you love the complexity of it all as well as the freedom and joy of moving three dimensionally. You're constantly looking down at the beauty the world beholds."

"No, that's how *you* feel about it." She smiled. "And me, too. What did you do as a teenager?"

"Summers, I worked construction jobs and thought of girls and airplanes constantly. I realized later in life why I never had a steady girlfriend. They wanted me to spend time and money on them instead of flying lessons." He frowned. "Can you believe such a thing?"

She laughed.

They talked through dinner about airplanes they had flown, their children, and books they had read, laughing often.

When they finished and were paying their bills, Kyle considered asking her if she would like another drink. The thought of enjoying this woman's company while his family was so troubled back in Houston made him feel guilty.

As if sensing his distress, Lori asked, "What'd your wife think of your promotion?"

Kyle blew out his cheeks with a sigh. He checked his phone and saw he had a good signal but no missed calls. "I don't know. Travis seemed cool with it. Karen wasn't home and hasn't called me back."

The beer bottle made a scraping noise on the table as he rolled it between his hands before asking, "Why did you get divorced?"

Lori stared off in the distance before responding. "After maternity leave, my ex-husband didn't like it when I went back to flying, and would've preferred I hadn't joined the NTSB. He's a lobbyist, and we didn't need my income. Eventually, he gave me the ultimatum, my career or him." She shrugged.

"I'm sorry. He shouldn't have done that. That's not right."

"I can't really blame him. I'm probably hard to live with." She smiled. "Besides my fierce temper you've been the recipient of—" Her smile dissolved, "I'm not your typical woman. I was the one who fixed things around the house. I might be home for months at a time and then be gone without any notice for a couple of weeks while investigating an accident."

Would he and Karen have separated years ago if she worked? Would it have helped?

"Usually it's the husband who wants a divorce. Why do you think your wife wants a one?" Lori asked.

He tipped the empty beer bottle up wishing there had been another swallow. "I'm getting a divorce because my wife is very insecure. She feels we need the big house, expensive furniture, and cars to make her life happy. So I work hard to provide these things.

Because I do, she blames our problems on my not being around." He realized he had spit this out in a bitter tone.

He slumped in his seat. "I'm not being fair, either. She's a wonderful mother and, until a few years ago, put up with all my faults."

Lori gave him a sympathetic smile.

They left the bar and together walked to the elevator. "Are your daughters better off with you divorced?" he asked.

She studied him a moment and must have found his question sincere. "I'd say for the most part, yes. I know it's hard being at one parent's every other weekend and alternating Thanksgiving and Christmas. It'll be good training for when they get married." She smiled at her attempt at humor, but the smile faded. "When we're together, we laugh and do what we want. I'm not being distracted by being a wife. Or feeling I have to be someone I'm not."

Kyle tried to imagine what this kind of life would be like for Travis if it came to that. Would he be okay, or become a troubled young man?

"My ex-husband's new wife is probably good for my daughters. She wears a lot of jewelry, makeup, and is very fashion conscious. So my daughters are getting exposure to things I couldn't show them."

The elevator stopped at her floor. Kyle stuck out his hand, "Good night, Lori. I've enjoyed our talk."

She opened up her arms and hugged him, holding him longer than a casual hug.

Initially, Kyle justified the desire to hold her as long as she wanted, hoping he could take away her hurt and disappointment of being forced off the investigation. In reality he savored having a woman want to hug him more than the brief embraces he and Karen had given each other the last several months.

"Goodbye, Kyle. Good luck."

The elevator doors shut. Goodbye seemed to have such finality to it. He wished she had simply said good luck.

Chapter Twenty-Four

Friday, June 18 4:45 p.m.

Kyle drove home after discussing his promotion with Steele, a smile plastered on his face. When he pulled off I-45 and drove down the Woodlands Parkway toward home, his smile dissolved, and a knot formed in his stomach. He had tried to call Karen when his flight from LaGuardia landed that morning, and again before driving home. Each time, his call went to voicemail.

He stopped at the grocery store near the house and bought a dozen roses before continuing home.

Pulling into the garage, he parked next to Karen's BMW. Kyle wasn't sure if he was glad or disappointed she was home. From his Honda Accord he dug out his suitcase and carried it and the flowers to the door, stopping to steel his spine before putting his hand on the knob.

Karen stepped from the kitchen and walked toward him carrying a cocktail glass with an amber liquid and ice, and a warm smile.

He wondered if she had made the scotch for him, thinking he would need it after she asked him to move out. Her demeanor was impossible to read, and he feared his marriage was over for good, despite the desire to keep his family together.

But that thought got shoved aside when he noticed the loose silk tee she wore, her nipples poking at the fabric. The top's boatneck had slid off her bare shoulder, revealing toned muscles. Gaping arm holes exposed the side swell of her breasts when she lifted her arms to hug him. Tight linen shorts finished out her outfit. He swallowed.

"Congratulations. I got your message. That's wonderful." Her arms wrapped around his neck as she leaned up and kissed him. Her tongue parted his lips, danced with his tongue.

He tasted her minty toothpaste, becoming dazed. For a fleeting moment, he thought of pushing her away and asking what was up, but found himself falling deeper into her arms. When she broke away, he clung to the zeal cursing through him.

She handed him the drink. "I hope I didn't put too much water in it. If I did, I'll make another. Are these for me?" She took the flowers and held them to her nose.

No, they're for the woman that used to live here. "...yeah. Thanks for the drink." He wondered if he sounded as confused as he felt.

She took his hand and led him into the kitchen. He ran his thumb over the back of hers, wondering if this was how the children felt as they followed the pied piper. Right now, he would follow her anywhere.

Then logic returned. The woman looked, felt, and sounded like his wife, although it had been awhile since she had dressed as provocatively. The house looked like their house, yet he couldn't help wondering if he had slipped into an alternate universe. "Where's Travis?"

"He's spending the night at his friend Steve's. I thought we'd celebrate alone."

"Great." Four days ago, when he had left to investigate the accident, he thought spending the evening alone with him was the last thing Karen would want. Had he been that wrong about her? He sipped his drink, trying to take in this change. How long did it take her to get in those shorts? He had never seen her top before. Did she buy it just for tonight?

"I thought I'd grill a steak and we'd have salads with it."

"Um...sounds good to me. What can I do to help?"

She pointed to a chair at the island. "Nothing. Sit and tell me about your week."

Karen took a bottle of vodka from a cabinet, cracked the seal, poured a shot into a cocktail glass and added cranberry juice. Other than a very occasional glass of wine, she hardly ever drank. She didn't like taking in the extra calories. The movement of her arms caused the openings in her arm holes to give him glimpses of her naked breasts.

He became hard and squirmed to get comfortable. Although he *loved* how she was dressed, he wondered if there was an ulterior motive for it. After months of fighting, he decided he didn't care.

She held her glass up and they clinked them together. "To the new fleet manager."

"Thank you."

Karen set her drink down and unwrapped the roses "I'm sorry I haven't been more talkative while you were gone. Things were a little crazy."

He sat back and folded his arms across his chest. "Oh. How so?" He tried to sound casual, but knew he had an accusatory tone. What could justify her actions over the last several days?

She snipped the ends of the stems. "Travis had a lot of homework, and Rachael's step children were giving her a hard time. I also looked into becoming a personal trainer, which took some time. I thought about calling you several times, but worried I might interrupt something important."

Karen placed the roses in a vase, filled it with water, and set it on the table. Standing beside him, she pulled his head to her chest and kissed the top of it. "Sorry. I'm sure what you were going through was pretty stressful too." Karen walked back around the island with her gaze turned away, making it difficult to read her expression.

Her excuses for not "being more talkative" were bullshit. She hadn't helped Travis with his homework in a couple of years. Rachael was one of her workout friends who was on either her second or third marriage. The spoiled brats that were her stepchildren always gave their father's younger wife a hard time. This had never occupied Karen's time before.

Kyle sipped his drink. He could point this out to her, but did he want to be right, or be happy? So often he had wanted to be right and called Karen on a flawed point of view. Usually, it was over a moot point, and all he had accomplished was to make her angrier. Maybe she realized how selfish she had been and was trying to make amends.

She glanced at him, smiled, and brought vegetables out of the refrigerator to make salads. "Enough about me. Tell me about the new job."

She was going to love this. "The salary is two hundred and fifty thousand dollars."

Karen stopped breaking apart lettuce and gawked at him. "Seriously?"

"Yeah." He smiled. "It's hard to believe, isn't it? Morgue didn't bat an eye when I asked for that amount. I wish I'd asked for more." A thought that had been bugging him returned. Why hadn't Steele tried to negotiate his salary? Had he expected to pay Kyle more? Steele also seemed distant or distracted today. What was up with that?

"Holy crap." She beamed.

"I'll also get stock options if I meet my target goals. If we cashed in the ones I received today, they'd net us twenty thousand dollars."

Karen's eyebrows approached her hairline.

"We're hanging on to them. Our stock took a hit because of the accident, but when it's no longer in the news and we start expanding as planned, it'll go up. Hopefully, by the time Travis goes to college, the options might pay for it."

She wiped her hands on a towel and came around and wrapped her arms around him. "Oh my God, I can't believe it."

"Guess all my hard work the last several years paid off." He regretted these words as soon as they left his mouth. He didn't mean to rub it in her face that he was right and she had been wrong. But, damnit, it was true.

Karen didn't seem to notice. She kissed him, long and lusciously. "Well then, we really need to celebrate."

When Kyle thought of their relationship, this was how he remembered it. They used to have conversations about their day, getting excited or upset together over something that had happened.

When he sensed Karen was going to break their embrace, he ran his hands down her back, feeling her ribs under her hard body. "I missed you." He wasn't sure if he meant this week or the last several months.

She kissed him again. "I missed you, too." She refilled their cocktails. "Let's go outside while I grill the steak."

He leaned against a column and told her about interviewing flight attendant Sherri Logsdon. Being a former flight attendant, Kyle knew Karen would be interested in hearing Logsdon's experience.

While he talked, Karen's eyebrows rose and fell. She said, "Oh my God!" several times. "I don't know what I would've done if a pilot was alive, but I couldn't get them out of the airplane." She ran a hand through her long, blond hair, letting it fall around her shoulders.

He doubted she had done it intentionally, but it made Kyle more conscious of her sensual looks. He pulled her to him and buried his head in her hair, breathing in the scent of lilacs. He wrapped his arms around her thin waist, hooking a thumb in the waistband.

Karen leaned against him while the steak sizzled.

He nibbled her ear and began working kisses down her throat.

Karen cocked her head, exposing more of her neck, and let out a moan until the fat from the steak flared the grill into a fire. She broke away and doused it with a bottle of water. "I think this is done." She speared it and dropped it onto a plate.

Kyle let out a silent sigh and followed her into the house.

"Would you open the wine?" She pointed to a bottle of merlot on the counter.

Kyle popped the cork, taking the bottle to the table and filling two glasses.

He didn't know if it was the alcohol or his sudden wealth making Karen the woman he had married. Whatever the reason, he didn't care. Eventually, they would have to talk about what had driven them apart, but not now. Not tonight.

They talked all through dinner. "The landscaping you had done looks nice," he said.

Karen beamed. "Thanks. I like it, too." She refilled their wine glasses, leaned back, and rested her toned legs on his thighs. "On the drive home from school today," she laughed, "Travis asked me," she changed her voice to imitate their son's, "'Mom, why do girls play with their hair so much?'"

Kyle laughed at her imitation while massaging her feet. "What'd you tell him?"

"I told him I didn't know." They laughed. She told him about other things Travis had said or did that week that brought a smile. Yeah, this was how he always visualized their marriage.

They cleaned the table together. When Karen turned from the sink to put a plate in the dishwasher, Kyle took it from her, set it on the counter, and enveloped her in an embrace.

Their lips met. Their kisses became more passionate, making him run his hands over her back and into the waist of her shorts. He wanted to make love to her here and now. He couldn't wait to take her to their bedroom. The kitchen counter would do.

Karen had other ideas. She guided them into the family room just off the kitchen while continuing to kiss him. There, she broke the embrace to pull her tee over her head.

Kyle's heart rate increased, taking in her sculpted abs and pert breasts. Being a workout fanatic gave her a beautiful body.

She grabbed the hem of his polo shirt, yanked it over his head, and tossed it aside.

Khakis, shorts, and underwear were a blur of fabric as they frantically undressed each other. They collapsed onto the leather couch, touching, groping, and kissing.

Kyle wanted to make this moment last, but it had been months. Urgency overwhelmed him, shoving aside the slow, passionate lovemaking he had visualized whenever he thought of them having sex again.

Karen's wild rhythm atop him drove him on, making him lose all control.

They collapsed in each other's arms, lying intertwined, not saying a word. Kyle caressed her round, firm butt and ran his hands up her slender back and through her hair. He wondered what had happened that caused them to lose the love they had just shown each other.

Karen stood and walked naked down the hall. She came back, holding two towels under her arm. She bent and kissed him. "Let's go swimming."

It was dusk, not full dark yet. He had tried to get Karen to go skinny dipping several times in their pool, as it was hidden from the neighbors. Each time, she had turned him down. It had become a point of contention between them that no doubt contributed to growing distant. "Who are you and what've you done with my wife?"

She laughed and led him to the glass doors leading to the patio. Her gaze swept the fence bordering their lot and stepped out, hurrying to the pool. She dropped the towels and dove in. Kyle stood with his toes curled around the lip, watching her tread water. Her nudity simmered under the water, making him smile.

"You coming in?"

He dove in and swam up next to her. They hugged and kissed, then separated, splashing, and pulling the other under.

After several minutes of acting like teenagers, Karen rested her head on his shoulder.

Kyle stood in shoulder-deep water, holding onto her, hoping to capture this moment so it wouldn't pass, and they could become who they had been as a couple. He turned them back and forth, letting the water swirl around their naked bodies. "You're a beautiful woman. I'm so glad you're my wife."

Karen pulled her head back with a stunned look on her face.

Had he said the wrong thing?

She kissed him, quieting his fears of ruining this brief moment of bliss. Her tongue flicked. She wrapped her legs around his waist, squeezing.

He moved his hips, rubbing his erection between her legs.

"Let's go inside. It'll be hard to face the neighbors if we do this out here." She smiled before meeting his lips again.

Kyle walked them to the steps of the pool. They hurried into the house and to their bedroom.

Sometime later, they fell asleep, wrapped in each other's arms. He hoped in the morning, they would still be the couple they were tonight. That what they had recaptured tonight hadn't been based entirely on his new salary and position.

Chapter Twenty-Five

Saturday, June 19 7:12 a.m.

Kyle woke and found Karen staring at him as if she were studying something new and strange. "Anything wrong?"

The corners of her mouth turned up. "No." She rose from the bed and walked into the bathroom.

Kyle closed his eyes. Without Travis home, he looked forward to sleeping in with her. The toilet flushed and the shower came on. He looked at the clock and walked into the bathroom just as she stepped into the shower.

"What are you doing?" he asked.

"I'm going to go work out." No doubt the shower was to wash off the smell of last night's activities.

"Come back to bed. Let's sleep in. I'll make it worth your while." Kyle knew he sounded selfish and regretted it. He wasn't considering her wishes. But shouldn't more intimacy be what she wanted as well, after they had finally connected again?

"If I start early, I can work off the alcohol from last night."

He opened the glass door, stepped up behind her and wrapped his arms around her, rubbing his hands over her soapy body.

She pulled his hands away. "I don't have time for that."

He stepped back and watched her.

Karen usually met Rachael and a few other girlfriends at the gym after they had dropped their children off at school. Weekends, Karen didn't go to the gym but went for a run from home. He wondered if he was reading too much into this since she had followed this morning workout routine for years now.

The soap slid down her sculpted body, making him fight the urge to reach out and follow its path with his hand. He wanted to give her something to think about while running on the treadmill, but obviously that wasn't going to happen. Would it hurt her to change her routine for one day?

She finished rinsing. "Are you staying in or do you want me to shut this off?" Karen must have noticed the disappointment on his face, since she moved up against him and gave him a quick kiss and a stroke of his erection. "I didn't know you'd be home today. I made plans. We can do what you have in mind tonight after Travis has gone to bed." She kissed him again and left the shower.

He was still disappointed, but what she suggested was better than how they had been prior to last night. He moved under the water.

After showering and dressing in shorts and a t-shirt, he found her in the kitchen, gathering her purse and keys. Usually, she made a fruit smoothie to drink on the way to the gym. The blender was clean.

"Aren't you going to eat?"

"I'll get something on the way." She picked up a duffel bag.

"I guess you're not coming home after your workout." He didn't care if he sounded suspicious.

"Ah... no. I've some errands to run." Karen opened the door to the garage but stopped as if she realized she missed something. Stepping back, she gave him a quick peck. "I'll call you later."

Looking through the dining room windows, he watched her car back out into the street and drive off. She had shown no interest in what he had planned, nor revealed where she was going after her workout. He blew out an exasperated sigh, puffing out his cheeks. Life seemed back to the way it had been when he left for New York.

He put coffee on to brew and stood staring out at the pool. Did he read too much into how Karen had acted this morning?

After cleaning up last night's dinner, he carried a bowl of cereal and a cup of coffee to the study. When he checked his email, the last one he received early that morning was from a tscalone72.

Scraping the last of the Harvest Grain and Nuts cereal from the bowl, Kyle tried to jar his memory for recognition of this address, but couldn't think of anyone with the name of Scalone or Calone or any combination of those letters. The subject line was blank, but there was a PDF attachment.

Kyle opened the email. There was one line in the body that said, "I hope this helps." No name was typed under this line. He held his pointer over the attachment without clicking. He didn't want to allow a virus or malware to poison his hard drive.

He was about to delete the email, but the one line kept going through his mind. "Hope this helps." *Helps what?*

Closing the email, he downloaded the latest update to the virus software, rebooted the computer, and opened the attachment from the suspicious email.

When he read the name at the top of the pages, his eyebrows shot up. It was Ernest Norman's employment record with the FAA.

Kyle found himself leaning forward while skimming through it. He leaned back, rolled his shoulders, sipped his coffee, and read it again.

Listed in the application were six airlines Norman had previously worked for. The application didn't say why he had left any of them. He had stayed at the first airline the longest, six years. The others had progressively shorter periods of employment until the final one, where he lasted only five months.

It was not uncommon for pilots to have worked for several airlines in their careers. Most left one for another because the airline went out of business or, as they became more experienced, they moved up to a more prestigious carrier. The airlines Norman listed were still in business. None were the major airlines most pilots aspired to be employed by. Why did Norman move from one regional or low-budget carrier to another?

He had been with the FAA eight years. Listed throughout his personnel file were numerous remedial training sessions after reprimands.

While at the FAA, Norman went through United's initial pilot training and became type rated in the Airbus A-319 and A-320. That was typical training for an FAA inspector assigned to oversee an airline. He also received training in the Boeing 737, 757, and 767 as well as the Canadair CRJ. Norman had spent most of his eight years at the FAA in training. His productivity as an inspector had to be dismal.

Was that intentional, to keep him from inspecting airlines and causing trouble?

Kyle walked to the kitchen and refilled his mug. Who sent this to him, and why? He thought about forwarding it to Kevin Hays, the instructor Kyle had selected to replace him on the investigation. But Steele had informed him Hays was busy teaching in the simulator all next week and wouldn't be joining the investigative team just yet.

The address bar confirmed he was the only recipient. If someone thought it important enough for Kyle to have, shouldn't the NTSB also have it? Their address would be easy to get if this person could get Kyle's.

He typed a reply to the email. "Thank you for the information. I'll see what I can do with it. Do I know you?"

Who at the NTSB should have this? Lori would know. Pulling his cell phone off his belt, he thought about her parting hug and questioned why he would think about that when he had a wonderful evening and incredible sex with his beautiful wife.

He punched in her number.

"Kyle? How are you?"

"Hi. Good. I hope I didn't wake you."

"No, I was up."

Kyle realized he'd been silent for several seconds when she asked, "So, what can I do for you?"

"I was thinking about some things." He continued to grasp at the thoughts swirling in his head.

"Yes?"

He detected the impatient tone. He focused. "I'm sorry. My mind is going places it probably shouldn't."

She sighed. "Look, I was inappropriate when we parted. I shouldn't have been so forward. Please forgive me."

He smiled and attempted to sound angry. "What, you think I was calling about that? God, you're so full of yourself."

A pause, then she said, "Oh, funny. Didn't your mother tell you it's not nice to mock people?"

"Probably. I didn't always listen to her."

"I've gathered that."

He slouched in his chair. His thoughts aligned so he could ask what had been bugging him. "Did you notice that within an hour, you were pulled off the investigation and I was promoted?"

"I considered it but didn't know the reasons behind your promotion."

"Were you doing as good a job as assistant IIC, as others have in the past?"

"Yeah."

Picking a pen off the desk, he clicked it several times. "Did it matter when the fire and rescue personnel were interviewed, or is there an order to when they'd be questioned?"

"Not really. I guess Evans is a control freak and doesn't like those under him carrying on parts of the investigation without him assigning them."

"It would seem so." *Or he's being manipulated.*

"Where are you going with this?"

Resting a foot on the desk, he asked, "Who's left that heard the CVR recording?"

"You, me, what's his name the ALPA guy, and Skaggs and Chavette."

"I didn't see Leo Brandish at the progress meeting." He tried to visualize who had been there. "Did you?"

"No."

"So, that leaves you and me, who are no longer involved in the investigation, Brandish who might be, but hasn't been seen in a while, and the two FAA investigators."

"As the fleet manager of the accident type for your airline, aren't you still involved?"

"You would think so. Yesterday while discussing my promotion, my boss made it known I was not to involve myself in the investigation. He informed me your organization would interview me in the future about the pilots' training and how the airline trains for rejected takeoffs. But I was to stay away from the investigation and concentrate on my new job. At the time, I thought I was being relieved of the accident's burden so I could get up to speed. Since then, I've wondered if I was promoted to take me away from the investigation."

"Were you a likely candidate for the position?"

"Yes." He tried to make his voice sound confident and cocky. "I was the best candidate."

Lori snorted.

He smiled, visualizing her rolling her eyes. "Before I left for the accident, I was under the impression the airline was going to wait awhile to fill the position. Four days later, they decide they have to immediately."

"Maybe something's come up and they need someone in that position. Or, could they be worried it won't look good in our report if the position goes unfilled for a period of time?"

"Yeah, maybe, but there's something else. I got an email today from someone with Ernie Norman's FAA employment record attached. In the eight years he worked there, he's had six reprimands and remedial training after each."

"For what?" Her voice was full of suspicion.

"Ethics and culture, human interactions, observer guidelines, and anger management," he read off the computer screen.

"Who sent it to you?" she asked.

"I don't know. I don't recognize the address, and no one signed it." He smiled. "Are you pacing?"

"No." Her answer came out rushed.

He heard a squeak like she'd sat. "Bullshit."

"So, you're thinking the FAA influenced my boss and Omega to not mention Norman's involvement in the accident?"

"If they didn't, why hasn't Omega mentioned it in their press briefings? That would be something to relieve the beating we're taking. We look like the most careless airline flying. Why did your boss order you to distance yourself from us, then take you off the investigation?"

"Why are you discussing this with me?" she asked. "You should be discussing this with your superiors, or the IIC, Mark Evans."

"What if my superiors have made some deal with the FAA? The FAA wants me silenced, and what better way to do so than take me off the investigation and promote me. That leaves you who heard the CVR, and now you're not involved, either."

"That still doesn't explain why you're talking to me about this."

"I was thinking of flying to Chicago and seeing if Norman is home. His address is in his personnel file. Want to go? He might not talk to me, but would to an NTSB investigator."

"I can't pick up and fly to Chicago." Her voice was full of agitation. "My daughters and I are going on vacation we almost missed."

"Have a good time, then."

She sighed. "I don't know how I'd explain going there. My daughters will be pissed again."

"I understand. I'll forward this email to you. Could you pass it along to whoever could use it? I'm getting on a flight to Chicago and will be there about three central time. I'll talk to you some other time."

"Kyle," she sighed. "Hang on a sec."

Chapter Twenty-Six

Saturday, June 19 2:48 p.m.
While Kyle's flight taxied to the gate in Chicago, he turned on his phone and noticed he had voice mail. He worried Lori might have called to tell him she had changed her mind and wasn't coming, or Karen had called in response to the message he had left her before boarding. Either call wasn't one he looked forward to hearing.

"I don't understand why you've gone off to investigate the accident," Karen said. She sounded exasperated. "I thought you wouldn't have to investigate this anymore. I rearranged my schedule so I could be with you. Please come home. Last night was wonderful. I've been thinking about it all day. I'm sorry I left so abruptly this morning. Come home and I'll make it up to you. Call as soon as you get this."

While waiting to get off the airplane, he wondered what had caused her to have this change of attitude. Did last night's memories make her realize how unapproachable she had been this morning?

Under the guilt of leaving when he might have misread Karen's behavior this morning, was gratitude the message wasn't from Lori. Without her the trip to Chicago was probably wasted and he would have set back the progress he and Karen had made.

While walking to Lori's gate, he called Karen.

"Why are you in Chicago?"

He had explained to her why on the message he'd left her. The old Kyle would have lashed out and said, *I've already told you why.* Instead, he again explained the email. Although he tried to keep his tone friendly, having to explain himself was something new. Kyle wasn't sure if he liked it. If it would make Karen return to the woman she was last night, he'd learn to like it.

"Did Steele send you there?"

"No."

"So why did you go? I thought you were through with the accident. Won't you be in trouble for going without approval?"

"There's no one else to do it, and I'm the most up-to-date on the investigation. Besides, if I get this inspector to talk, the FAA will have to share the blame for the accident." *What's with this twenty-question routine? You haven't been interested in my job for some time, or worried about how my actions will be judged.*

"After I left this morning, I changed my plans so I could be with you."

He rolled his eyes. *Like you had a lot to change. Let's see, I can cancel shopping and lunch with my girlfriends to be with my husband, I suppose.* He tried to sound sincere. "Well, thank you, but this morning you made it seem you were too busy and didn't want anything to do with me." He was glad he spoke that last thought, hoping it made Karen realize how her inattention affected him.

She sighed. "I'm sorry. I wasn't expecting you to be home. Get on a flight and get back here. We'll send Travis to a friend's house or drop him off at an arcade. We can lay out by the pool. *Nude.*"

Visions of Karen's sculpted body glistening in sweat made Kyle's heart race. It brought a grin to his face. Nonetheless, this was out of character for her. "Why would you do that now, when you never would before?"

There was a pause which she broke by saying, "I've been doing a lot of thinking lately. I know this is something you've always wanted to do, so it should be something I should want, too."

Kyle tried to wrap his mind around this phone conversation. "There seems to be more to it than that."

"I don't know what you mean."

"A couple of days ago, you told Travis we were getting a divorce. Then last night, we did things we've never done before. I'm not complaining. The sex and skinny dipping were incredible. But then this morning... well... I don't need to keep rubbing that in your face. Now you want to spend time with me in ways you never would have before. I can't help but feel there's more to this change than what you're saying."

Again, there was another pause. "I know. I know. I shouldn't have mentioned the possibility of a divorce before we'd decided together." She sighed. "I'm sorry. I'll apologize to Travis and tell him we aren't divorcing. The... the reason I might've been different last night, and will be in the future, the thought of not being with you has made me realize I still love you. I think what we have is worth working on. I know you wish I was as... as adventurous as you. I need to change that about myself."

Although he liked what he heard, only time would prove if her words were true. There was also the thought his raise had something to do with her change of attitude. But now was not the time or place to discuss that. "I have changes to make, too. We'll discuss this more when I get home. I'll be there either late tonight, or first thing tomorrow morning. Okay?"

"Why is finding this guy more important than being with me?" Her voice rose.

Lori's flight was pulling up to the gate. "I need to find out why he urged the crew to reject the takeoff and cause the accident. He has to come forward and talk to the NTSB."

"You're not a private investigator." Her voice was harsh. "How are you going to find him and get him to do that?"

"I used to watch Magnum P.I." Karen didn't respond. Obviously, the woman he had married hadn't fully returned. "I have to try. No one else seems to want to. Please understand."

"This is one of the things about you we have to work on. You're always running off doing what you want without considering Travis and me."

Kyle visualized her glaring at him. He thought about justifying his actions, but there was some truth to what she said. Although the extra hours and effort he had put in as an instructor had paid off, training in Kung Fu, cycling, and the occasional golf game were things he did without her.

"I know this is important to you," she lowered her voice to conversational level, "but sometimes I think I take second place to your desires."

Kyle took a deep breath. *How can I make her understand?* "Karen, you're very important to me. You're more important to me than anything or anyone else except maybe Travis. This is something I have to do. Please understand. I'll be home tomorrow at the latest, and we can talk about this more. Okay?"

"Fine!" She lowered her voice. "I'm sorry. It's disappointing. Let me know when you'll be here, and I'll be waiting."

Chapter Twenty-Seven

Saturday, June 19 3:22 p.m.
Kyle stopped in front of the house matching the address on Ernest Norman's FAA employment record. "I wish I could live here." A rundown, single story home in Elwood Park west of Chicago faced Lori and him.

Lori stared at Norman's house and the others along the street, pulling her purse closer.

Kyle parked along the curb several houses down. He glanced up and down the street. The shiny new rental stood out. "I hope the car doesn't get stolen." He gave Lori a crooked grin. "Maybe you should stay and guard it."

Lori narrowed her eyes at him. "Is that a joke?"

"Yeah."

"It wasn't funny." Some of the stress in her face drained away.

Kyle smiled. "I hear that a lot."

Lori rolled her eyes.

They walked back to Norman's house. Most of the houses on the street had been maintained. Paint peeled from the lap siding on Norman's. His front porch sagged. There were shingles missing from the roof.

"How are we going to get him to talk to us?" Lori asked.

"I thought you'd show him your credentials and threaten to kick the door down if he didn't let us in."

She frowned. "You watch too much TV."

He cocked an eyebrow. "You mean you can't kick a door down?"

"I could if I needed to. If I did, he'd have us arrested."

"Could you get a subpoena and make him to talk to us?"

Lori glanced at the house. "I could if I were still part of the investigation and we felt his testimony was vital."

"When do you kick the door down?"

"Are you always this juvenile?" She'd narrowed her eyes, yet her mouth twitched as if fighting to smile.

"No."

"So, I ask again, how do we get him to talk to us?" Lori asked.

"We wing it." Kyle climbed the steps to the porch, hoping he didn't fall through.

The screen door squeaked when Kyle pulled it open and knocked.

Inside, a TV was muted, then steps accompanied by a thump, thump came toward the door. A curtain on the small side window was pulled back.

A thin, craggy face peered out. "Go away." The curtain fell back into place.

Kyle motioned with his head toward the door.

She frowned and mouthed. "What?"

"Say something," he mouthed.

"What do you want me to say?" she whispered.

Kyle shook his head. "Mr. Norman, I'm here with Lori Almond from the NTSB. She needs to talk to you about the Omega Airlines accident."

Lori glared at him before saying, "Mr. Norman, it would be better if you talked to us now, otherwise we'll issue a subpoena to get your account of the accident."

The footsteps didn't retreat. "Mr. Norman, we know you were on Omega Airlines Flight 918," Lori said. "You will be interviewed. You might as well talk to us now."

The door remained closed.

Kyle glanced out at the street. "Mr. Norman, if you don't let us in, I'll call every major TV news station and tell them the FAA inspector responsible for Omega Airline's accident is inside this house. I'm sure they'll camp out in the street, waiting for you to leave, so they can interview you."

The dead bolt clicked, and a safety chain rattled. The door opened, and Kyle's hope of getting some answers from Norman soared.

A thin man stood at the threshold, an arm in a sling, leaning on a crutch. Black stitches lined his hairline near his right temple. "I wasn't responsible for that accident." His nostrils flared. "The captain should've aborted the takeoff when they blew a tire."

Kyle wrinkled his nose at the overpowering smell of alcohol. Norman's eyes were bloodshot.

Kyle stuck his foot in the doorjamb. "That's not Omega Airlines policy."

"It should be. If he had rejected the takeoff when I told him to, the accident wouldn't have happened."

"You don't know that. If they had continued the takeoff, they would've become airborne, burned off fuel to become lighter and landed at Newark or JFK on a longer runway. They would've had a much better chance of stopping."

Norman lowered his eyes and shook his head. "You don't know they would've gotten airborne."

"No, but I bet the flight data recorder will show they were close to V1 when they rejected. They were already close to flying speed."

Norman scowled. "Get off my porch!" He attempted to shut the door.

Kyle was glad he wore shoes with a wide sole, saving his foot from taking too much of a beating.

Lori held up her credentials. "Mr. Norman, we will interview you. You might as well get it over with now."

"I've been ordered not to talk to you." His eyes widened.

Lori's eyebrows rose. "By whom?"

"I've said too much already. Get off my porch or I'll call the police."

"Let us in or I'll call the media." Kyle kept his eyes locked on Norman's.

"You son of a bitch! You don't know what that'll do to me."

Anger coursed through Kyle. This man was responsible for the death of their two pilots, ten passengers, and sixty-eight injuries, and he was worried about what talking to them would do to him? Lori's hand on his arm made him soften his stance. "Your choice."

"I could lose my job. My pension." His face broke. "Look at me. I'm too old to start anywhere else. If I get fired by the FAA, who would hire me? Flying is all I know."

"You can't hide from the NTSB forever." Lori gave him a sympathetic smile. "It might do you some good to tell us what happened. You look like you could use some relief."

When Norman made no move to let them in, Kyle pulled his phone from its holster. He punched in four-one-one and put the phone to his ear. "Chicago. CNN."

"All right." Norman stepped back. "Hang up and come in."

The door opened, revealing a small living room with a sagging sofa, a scarred coffee table, recliner, and a large TV. Newspapers and magazines were scattered about. Grit was visible in the worn carpet. There were no pictures on the wall or personal items.

On the end table beside the recliner was a half-full fifth of Canadian Mist whiskey. A glass full of an amber liquid sat beside it. On the floor, several Budweiser cans sat on their sides, the tops open.

"Nice place," Kyle said.

Lori elbowed him in the ribs.

Norman bent down and gathered up some newspapers from the couch.

"Let me do that." Lori took the papers from his hands.

Norman grimaced as he lowered himself into the recliner. He pointed the remote at the TV, and the screen went dead.

Kyle and Lori sat on each end of the couch.

Lori dug out a notebook and her glasses from her purse. She held up a digital recorder and stated the date, time, where they were, and who was there before setting it on the coffee table. "What injuries did you sustain in the accident?" Her voice was sincere.

Norman stared at the recorder before looking away. "I broke my shoulder bone and have a hairline fracture on my hip. I got a concussion." He pointed to the areas he had injured. "What were your names again?"

They handed cards to him.

"Omega Airlines. What the hell are you doing with the NTSB?"

"We're part of the investigative team looking into the accident just like the FAA is supposed to be doing," Kyle said.

Norman took a deep breath, letting it out slowly. "The accident wasn't my fault."

"We heard you the first time." Kyle said. He received another elbow in the ribs and a school-teacher-worthy glare. He knew his dislike for this guy was getting them nowhere. He shut up and let Lori lead the questioning.

"Mr. Norman, the NTSB isn't looking to blame anyone for the accident," Lori said. "We report the circumstances that caused the accident, so we can recommend ways to prevent another in the future."

Norman turned away from them. "I was told I wouldn't have to do this."

"By whom?" Lori asked.

Norman stared straight ahead, not saying anything.

She inched forward on the couch. "Mr. Norman, whoever told you that lied. We'll subpoena you if we have to."

Norman ran a hand through his thinning hair. "My boss, at the FAA."

Lori narrowed her eyes. "Who's that?"

"Pierre Chavette. He said it would be handled."

Kyle and Lori glanced at each other. Her eyes brightened, making Kyle smile even though he tried not to. He had known all along the French asshole had something to do with this.

"Didn't you feel as an employee of the FAA who was involved in an accident, you should come forward and tell the facts that led up to it?" Lori asked. "I know you've had the accident investigation course taught at the FAA."

Norman glared at Lori. "I was just following orders."

A couple of seconds passed before Lori broke the silence. "Talk us through what you observed from the time you boarded the flight."

Norman took a gulp from the glass on the end table, grimaced, and told them about boarding the flight just before push back.

"There seemed to be a problem with the webperf during the pushback," Lori asked. "What can you tell us about that?"

Norman shook a finger at Lori. "I'm glad you asked. This was an example of how incompetent this crew was. They missed the calculation for the children. If I hadn't pointed this out, they'd have never corrected it."

Kyle leaned forward. "You realize, making this correction—"

"Kyle." Lori put her hand on his arm. She'd raised her eyebrows.

He had been fidgeting and sighing while Norman spoke in his arrogant demeanor about claiming to be helping the crew. He held his hands up, palms out.

Lori continued to pepper Norman with questions which he answered as if it were beneath him to do so. She took a breath. "When the crew began the takeoff, who was flying?"

"The woman."

Lori jolted as if slapped. "You mean First Officer, Cheryl Wells?" She spoke through clenched teeth.

"Yeah."

Lori took a deep breath. "So they began the takeoff. Walk us through it. Try to remember everything you saw, heard, smell, and felt. Even if it seems unimportant."

Norman gulped from the glass. "The takeoff was normal until we felt this vibration and heard something hitting the airplane. The captain said, 'continue.'" Norman looked at Lori, shaking his head. "I couldn't believe it! What an idiot. What was he thinking? He had something wrong with his airplane and was below V1 and was going to continue the takeoff! So I yelled 'Abort,' hoping he'd realize the seriousness of the matter. I'd flown on one of his flights before and found him to be lackadaisical about procedures."

Lori made some notes. "What happened then?"

"I thought he hadn't heard me. So I yelled it two more times before he finally got around to doing something." Norman blew out a loud sigh. "By then, it was too late. We didn't have enough runway to stop on. If he had aborted when we first felt the vibration, or when I told them to, the accident wouldn't have happened. Jesus! Why didn't he stop earlier?" He drained the glass and poured more from the bottle.

Kyle wondered if Norman hadn't read the studies of when to reject a takeoff. Years ago, it was considered standard procedure for crews to reject for anything below V1. Several accidents resulting from crews doing so close to V1 proved it wasn't always safer than continuing the takeoff. There were some pilots who didn't agree. Norman must be one of them.

"What was the airspeed when the captain rejected the takeoff?" Lori asked.

Norman stared at his lap. "I don't know."

"What was the last airspeed you saw before the captain rejected?"

"Around one twenty."

"What was their V1 speed?" She held her pen poised ready to write his answer.

Norman scratched his head. "I don't remember. Maybe one fifty-four."

"How long was it from the time you saw one twenty until the captain rejected?" she asked.

"A few seconds."

"So could they have been close to V1?"

It impressed Kyle that she asked her questions in a non-threatening manner, making Norman want to answer them.

Norman shrugged and grimaced. "I suppose."

"But you don't know for sure."

"I'm pretty sure they were below V1." Norman's voice rose.

"Okay, tell us what happened after the airplane went off the end of the runway."

He told them about hitting the first approach light stanchion and crashing into the second one. "The cockpit crunched in and shoved the yoke into the captain's chest. He didn't make a sound or move after that." Norman shook his head. "Jesus, there was a lot of blood. It was squirting out his chest. The first officer was crying out. Her legs were crushed under the instrument panel. I was hurt. I knew I had to get out of there before the airplane exploded or something. I unhooked my seatbelt and left." He took a big gulp from the glass.

"When you went into the cabin, what did you see?"

It amazed Kyle that Lori had kept her tone as even tempered as it had been throughout her questions. He wanted to yell, "How could you leave everyone behind?"

Norman rubbed his jeans. "There were people screaming and yelling. Everyone was fighting to get to the front of the airplane. I knew if I stayed around, I'd get trampled. So when there was a chance, I jumped down the slide and swam to shore." He emptied the glass and poured more in.

Kyle had enough. "Are you sure you didn't freak out and get off as quickly as you could?" He tried to say this in the same non-threatening tone Lori used, but thought the underlying tension rolling off him in waves had to be evident.

Norman turned to him with narrowed eyes, his face crimson. "You don't know what it was like! It was pandemonium. I was hurt." He pointed to his shoulder in the sling. "I couldn't do any good."

Bullshit! He freaked out and didn't give any consideration to the crew and passengers. If Lori hadn't rested a hand on Kyle's arm, he might have vocalized his thoughts on Norman's cowardice.

Norman gulped from his glass. He was already slurring his words.

"What happened after you swam to shore?" Lori's asked.

"Paramedics put my arm in a sling, bandaged my cut," he pointed to the stitches, "and sent me to the hospital in an ambulance."

Blood pounded in Kyle's ears. He stood and glared down at Norman before turning away.

"We heard there might have been more seriously injured passengers that needed to go before you." Lori said.

It impressed Kyle she could remain so calm when Norman chose to blatantly lie.

"I needed to report the crash." Norman stared at his lap. "My cell phone got wet and wouldn't work. I had to get to a phone."

Kyle shook his head.

"When you got to the hospital, who'd you call?" Lori asked.

"Pierre Chavette."

"What did you tell him?"

Norman stared into the distance. "That there had been an accident and I was injured."

"Did you tell him you'd tried to get the crew to reject the takeoff?"

Norman sipped from the glass. "Yes."

Kyle returned to sitting on the couch. He thought they were about to hear why the FAA had been so manipulative.

"What did he say?" she asked.

Norman turned the glass around in his hand. "He told me not say a word to anyone. He'd handle it."

"Have you talked to him since then?"

Norman ran a hand through his hair. "Yeah, a couple of times, I guess. He told me the situation was under control and I had nothing to worry about."

Lori glanced at Kyle. Her eyes gleamed. Her expression said what Kyle thought. We've got them.

"We'll have to notify the FBI about this," she said.

Norman turned to her, fear written all over him. "Jesus! The FBI? Why?"

"You're a witness to a serious aviation accident. From what you've told us, you and the FAA are trying to cover up your involvement in it. That's interfering with a federal investigation."

"The fucking FBI?" Norman slumped, blinked, then stared at the recorder. He grabbed his crutch and lifted it in the air.

Kyle snatched the tape recorder off the coffee table just before the crutch came crashing down with a loud crack.

Lori and Kyle shot to their feet. Lori's eyes were wide.

Norman slid forward in the chair and stood.

Kyle shoved Lori behind him. "Sit down," he said to Norman.

"Get out of my house!" Norman swung the crutch.

Kyle deflected it and stepped back, centering himself.

Lori grabbed her purse and notebook and hurried to the door.

When she opened it, Kyle backed away from Norman, who threw his crutch at Kyle.

Kyle sidestepped it as it sailed past him, crashing to the floor with a rattle. He slammed the door behind him.

Hurrying to the car, Kyle glanced over his shoulder. Norman hadn't left the house. They sped away with Kyle driving. When a block away, he slowed and started laughing. "Why am I driving so fast? Like that drunk cripple is going to chase us down and club us to death with his crutch?"

Lori laughed, and the sound was enough to make Kyle's tension drain away. She dug around in her purse. "Do you have my recorder?"

Kyle raised his eyebrows and attempted to look worried. When Lori's mouth gaped, he held out the device.

She shoved him. "We need to call the FBI."

"Do you want to, or should I?"

Chapter Twenty-Eight

Saturday, June 19 4:42 p.m.
While driving their rental from Norman's house, Kyle ruminated about how incriminating the recording of Norman's interview would be to the FAA. "Before we call the FBI, I want to make a copy of that recording. I don't want this one disappearing like the CVR did."

"I have no way of copying it here. I could at our office, but we can't wait that long. We need to call the FBI. Now."

"Let's find an electronics store and buy what we need."

Thirty minutes later, they left a store with a micro SD chip reader that Lori plugged into her laptop. She copied the microchip from her recorder onto a thumb drive while Kyle drove.

A silver sedan pulled in behind them, following them for several blocks.

Pulling the drive from her computer, Lori held it out to him. "Why did you want four copies?" She glanced at Kyle, then out the rear window. "Everything okay?"

The sedan put on its blinker and pulled up a side street.

Kyle sighed. "Yeah." He didn't tell her about the sedan, fearing she would think he was paranoid. Maybe he was.

He pocketed the drive. "We'll each keep one and give a copy to the FBI. I'm going to mail one to my brother."

Two parallel lines creased the bridge of her nose. "Why your brother?"

"It'll take a couple of days to get there. I'll tell him once he receives it to mail it to my office."

Lori raised an eyebrow. "So it'll be lost in the mail for several days so no one can get it. Do you really think that's necessary?"

"Probably not. But I don't want to take any chances." He grinned. "Besides, I like bugging my brother."

Lori rolled her eyes.

After dropping the thumb drive in a mail box, Lori dug in her purse. "I have a card from the agent in charge of investigating the break-in of our offices."

"Do you trust him?"

Lori placed the card on the car's console. "It's a woman. Why, do you think whoever is behind this has someone in the FBI?"

"Norman wasn't on vacation, as we'd been told," he said. "Someone had the resources to steal the CVR and have you and me removed from the investigation. It's certainly possible they could influence the FBI."

The expression on Lori's face became vacant. Her eyes moved back and forth before focusing on Kyle. "This agent seemed professional. I trust her. Do you have anyone else you'd rather call?"

He valued Lori's judgment. If they called the FBI switchboard and were assigned someone with no knowledge of the accident or NTSB break-in, they might not be taken seriously. Kyle shook his head. "Let's keep an eye on her. If it seems she's only digging for what we know and not trying to figure out who's behind this, I'm bailing."

Lori turned her phone over and over in her hand. "What'll we do then?"

Her comment reassured him she was behind him. "Go to the media, I guess."

She punched in the number and put the phone on speaker.

"Agent Rankin."

Lori identified them and told her about interviewing Norman and what he had said. Rankin asked several questions through Lori's narration.

Kyle listened, trying to decide if Rankin could be trusted.

"You really think the FAA is trying to cover up this inspector's involvement in the accident, and would commit robbery and murder to that?" Rankin asked.

Ever hear of Watergate, Iran-Contra, or Monica Lewinsky? Still, the skepticism he detected in her voice made Kyle feel she was not hiding anything. She might be someone they could trust. Or, she could just be acting sincere. For now, he would trust her. "I do," Kyle said, and explained how the media would crucify the FAA, which would lead to congressional hearings.

"Ms. Almond, do you agree with this assessment?"

"It's hard to believe, but they've been less forthcoming during this investigation than they have in others. Normally, we would've already interviewed all the pertinent FAA personal involved in this accident. The fact they're deliberately hiding one is suspicious."

Rankin was silent a moment. "Stay there. I'll be on the next flight."

✈✈✈

Kyle parked in the Sheraton Hotel's lot near O'Hare and lifted their bags from the trunk. An Omega Airline 737 approached the airport, its gear and flaps down. He smiled at the familiar site and pointed to the airplane. "Do you miss flying?"

Lori watched the airplane, with longing on her face. "Yeah, I do."

Her phone rang. She studied the screen and her shoulders rose and fell. "It's the Chairman." She lifted the phone to her ear. "Almond."

That was fast. Kyle continued inside. His phone vibrated in its holster on his belt.

"Where are you?" Steele asked. His voice was more gruff than usual.

Kyle glanced around the opulent lobby to see if anyone was near in case their argument became heated. "Chicago."

"The FAA just called and is very upset. They said you harassed one of their inspectors at his home. This is no way to start your new job."

"Sir, did they tell you this inspector is the one who jump seated on nine-eighteen? The one who's been missing since the accident."

"That's not the point. You were relieved of the responsibilities of investigating the accident. That was not a request. It was an order." Steele's voice rose. "Get back here. Monday morning, I want to see you first thing."

"I can't do that, sir."

"What!"

Outside, Lori paced with the phone to her ear. She threw out a hand as if making a point.

"I'm here with the NTSB," Kyle said. "Norman admitted he coerced the crew to reject the takeoff, and his bosses ordered him to remain silent. His words to this were, 'I was told I wouldn't have to talk about the accident. It'd be taken care of.'"

Pausing so Steele could comment resulted in silence on the phone. "We've called the FBI about the FAA's attempt to cover up their involvement in the accident. An agent is flying here to interview us."

The silence continued for several seconds. When Steele spoke, it seemed he weighed his words. "You should have discussed this with me."

Would you have approved of me coming here? "If it had been a weekday, I would have." Kyle didn't feel too guilty saying this. He *might* have, so it wasn't an outright lie.

"How'd you know where to find this inspector?"

Kyle told him about the email.

Steele was always a deep thinker, but the silence after Kyle's comments was longer than normal.

"Call me after you've talked to the FBI."

What's up with him? He stepped outside to see how Lori's call was going.

"Sir, that's not the point," Lori said. "This interview has direct insight into the cause of the accident. It needed to be done." She paused. "I can't fly back tonight. We've called the FBI, and they are interviewing us here tomorrow morning."

From that point on, Lori's tone was less aggressive. She hung up shortly afterward.

"The FAA called our bosses and threatened them somehow," Kyle said.

"You think?"

✈✈✈

They checked in and rode the elevator to their respective floors. At Lori's, Kyle said, "Do you want to have dinner?"

"Sure."

"Give me half an hour. I have to call home and try to make some peace for leaving today."

Lori's expression suggested her call would not be any less tense. "I should, too."

In his room, Kyle dropped his bag on the bed and paused a moment before calling home.

"Hey, Dad. How'd the questioning go?"

His son's light banter eased the tension in Kyle's shoulders. Obviously, Karen had upheld her promise and told him they weren't getting divorced. Kyle hoped his and Karen's failures would be worked out and Travis wouldn't suffer any further. "About as good as questioning a moron would go."

"Was this moron you, or the FAA dude?"

Kyle chuckled. "Ha, ha, ha. Very funny."

When their conversation was over, Travis called out, "Mom, Dad's on the phone." The glow of the pleasant talk faded while Kyle waited.

"You couldn't make it back?" she asked.

"No. I found the inspector and interviewed him. It was very revealing. The FBI has been called into the investigation." He almost said *we've called in the FBI* but didn't want to explain he was there with a female investigator to avoid any tension that would hinder the progress he and Karen had made. "They want to talk to me tomorrow morning."

"It would have been nice to have you home tonight." She truly sounded disappointed.

"Yeah, it would. Thanks for understanding. I know it's hard to comprehend why I'd come here instead of being there with you and Travis. It's important for the truth to come out."

She paused long enough for him to wonder if she was considering what he said—or holding in her disagreement. "I guess so. What time do you think you'll be home tomorrow?"

"I'm not sure. The FBI might take most of the morning. I'll try to get an early afternoon flight and be home in time for dinner."

Her voice lowered and became alluring. "After Travis goes to bed, we can make up for the last couple of months."

The memory of the previous night's lovemaking flashed into his head. "That'd be nice." He hoped they could continue to mend their relationship.

At the appointed time, Kyle met Lori at the hotel's restaurant. Following the hostess to their table, he asked, "How'd your daughters take the news you'd be away another day?"

She sighed. "They acted upset, but I think—"

Kyle pulled out his vibrating phone. He studied the screen. "Excuse me." He stepped out into the hall. "Hi, Karen."

"Where are you staying?"

Her lack of a greeting or small talk puzzled him. "The Sheraton by the airport."

"What room?"

He frowned. "Nine twenty-three. Why? You can always call my cell phone. Obviously it works."

"Oh... oh, you know how cell phones can be sometime. I was just thinking about you and realized I didn't have this information. That's all. Sleep tight."

"Karen, what's going on? You've never needed my hotel information before. You've always been able to call my cell phone unless I'm out of the country, and then I gave you the hotel's phone number."

"I... ah... have just thought of the mistakes we've made over the last several months and realized I need to stay in touch better. That's all. I don't mean anything by it."

After glancing at Lori inside the restaurant his face warmed. "Do you think I'm having an affair?"

She was silent a moment before asking, "Are you?"

"No! Why would you think that?"

"That's good to hear. I didn't think so, but had to wonder because of how distant we've become. I'm sorry I'm letting my insecurities get the best of me. I'll see you tomorrow."

When sitting across from Lori, she must have seen the inquisitive look on his face. "Everything okay?"

He shrugged. "Yeah. I guess."

After their meal and in their separate rooms, Kyle checked his email. There was another one from tscalone72. It said, *No, you don't know me. Keep doing what you're doing.*

There was an attachment. He opened it, and Pierre Chavette's employee file opened. He read through it then called Lori. "Are you still up? I've got something to show you."

Lori answered the door wearing gym shorts and a t-shirt. He could hear a newscast on the TV. "Come in."

"I just got this from my mystery emailer." He handed her his phone, sat on the desk chair, and watched her face while she read.

She frowned and scrolled the screen up. Her eyebrows lifted several times.

When she had finished, she swiped back to the beginning. "What does this person mean, 'Keep doing what you're doing?' How did he know you came to Chicago and interviewed Norman?"

"I don't know."

"This has to be from someone who works for the FAA. How else did he get Norman's and now Chavette's files?"

"Must be."

She swiped a finger on the phone's screen. "Did you see every one of Chavette's last seven recurrent training sessions was signed off by Norman?"

"Yes. That would explain why Chavette tried so hard to protect him. If the accident was blamed on Norman and the FAA fired him, he might claim Chavette couldn't maintain his currency. The airlines Chavette oversees might raise hell."

Lori looked skeptical. "You think Chavette couldn't pass his recurrent training?"

Kyle shrugged. "I'm trying to not let my dislike for the guy cloud my judgment, but, yeah, I do. It'd explain a lot." He sat up. "If an airline uses a pilot who hasn't completed the required training, they'll get fined eleven thousand dollars for each flight that pilot flies. What would happen if the FAA allowed an inspector to continue overseeing an airline they weren't qualified to supervise? They're required to maintain the same recurrent standards airline pilots are."

Knowing he might be giving her information she already knew, he added, "I know you know this, but if an inspector couldn't pass the recurrent check-ride they expect pilots to pass, the airlines could claim the FAA held their pilots to a higher standard than they themselves could maintain. Look at the first date Norman signed off Chavette's training."

Lori found the date. "Seven years ago."

"Now look at Norman's file. The date of his first reprimand was a few days before that. Norman was a few days shy of having been at the FAA for a year when he received his first remedial training. If they have probation periods like airlines do, Norman should've been let go. But Chavette had just failed training for the Airbus."

On the muted TV was a reporter standing before a building with police lights flashing on it. The story appeared to be a local crime scene. "That'd be pretty embarrassing for an FAA inspector.

Lucky for him, a new inspector in the office gets in trouble and will be fired—unless he'll sign off Chavette's training. This sets in motion the event that happens over the next seven years. Norman gets in trouble and Chavette saves him, providing he signs off his training."

Lori's expression suggesting she was giving his statements some thought. "That would explain why Chavette, an inspector from Chicago, was involved in your accident investigation. That's bothered me all along. Omega's certificate isn't with the Chicago fisdo."

Kyle nodded. "Yeah, it's with Houston."

"Normally, the FAA is represented by the Office of Investigations and Prevention, who Skaggs and his team work for. Even if an inspector outside that group was interested in the accident, they wouldn't have been at the CVR hearing."

"I wondered about that. How'd they get permission to have more than one investigator there?"

Lori shrugged. "Ed told me the Chairman had approved two FAA inspectors to review the recording."

Kyle leaned forward in his chair. "Maybe now that the FBI is looking into this, the FAA might be a little more forthcoming."

Chapter Twenty-Nine

Saturday, June 19 9:08 p.m.
Kyle left Lori's room and took the elevator up to his floor.

When the doors slid open, a broad-shouldered man wearing a blue ball cap stood as if waiting to board. His gaze followed Kyle as he exited.

"Hi. How's it going?" Kyle asked.

The man simply nodded.

Kyle left the short elevator hall and turned toward his room, thinking about the ramifications of Chavette covering for Norman.

Being engrossed in thought, he didn't notice the other broad-shouldered man who wore a black cap standing at a door four down from Kyle's room until he was almost upon him.

Black Cap stuck a keycard in a lock which failed to unlock the door. He glanced at Kyle, shrugged, and walked toward him as if going to the front desk to get his key re-programmed.

Footsteps behind Kyle made him turn. Blue Cap followed him, looking down when Kyle glanced over his shoulder.

When Kyle returned his gaze forward, Black Cap continued toward him, seeming to study the keycard.

Where are you staying? What room? He didn't want to believe Karen was responsible for these men being in the vicinity of his room. Unless she had been coerced into revealing where he stayed. Each beat of his heart shook him.

Black Cap scrutinized him. It wasn't a typical once over a hotel guest gave another, but the look of someone assessing a threat.

Kyle slowed his pace and patted his pockets with hands that shook. Blue Cap was the closer of the two. "Shit! Forgot my key." He whirled around, locked eyes with Blue Cap, and watched the man's hands and hips in his peripheral vision.

When Blue Caps hips twisted and a hand rose, Kyle kicked him in the stomach, thankful for his Kung Fu training.

Blue Cap let out an oomph, stumbling back a step.

The fact Blue Cap didn't end up on the floor told Kyle what he suspected. He was the target of professional thugs.

He palm struck the man in the nose, knocking his head into the wall with a bang.

"Hotel security," Black Cap yelled from behind him. "Stay where you are."

For a fleeting moment, Kyle thought he had made a mistake. Except both men wore jeans, blazers, and polo shirts. In the thousands of hotels Kyle had stayed in during his airline career, he had never seen hotel security dressed this way.

He bolted down the hall.

The pounding of feet followed him.

Kyle passed the hall to the elevator, continuing for the stairway, where he yanked open the door. Black Cap was several rooms away, still in pursuit. Blue Cap turned down the hall to the elevators.

Taking the steps down two at a time, Kyle passed Lori's floor. Black Cap was two flights behind him.

Kyle dug out his cell phone and hit the send button, putting the phone to his ear while still rushing down the stairs.

"Yeess?" Lori asked, amused.

"Don't let anybody in your room. I'm being chased by two guys." His words came out rushed.

"What?"

"Call nine-one-one and don't let anyone in your room." He shoved the phone back in its holster on his hip.

Black Cap was half a flight behind him.

Disappointed with himself for not maintaining his lead, Kyle exited the stairs two floors below Lori's, spun around behind the door and tried to catch his breath.

When it flung open, Kyle caught it and slammed the door against Black Cap.

A grunt escaped him.

Kyle slammed it in him again.

The man grabbed the edge and held on.

Kyle stepped around and palm struck Black Cap in the solar plexus. It felt like he'd hit an oak tree. He followed this with a strike to his neck that hit Black Cap's jaw.

Black Cap shot a fist out.

Kyle attempted to sidestep it, but the blow glanced off the side of his stomach. He swallowed the bile that rose in his throat. Pain radiated across his middle, but he held it together and struck at the man's nose.

A raised arm deflected Kyle's punch so that his hand grazed his opponent's cheek.

Self-doubt erupted. This wasn't sparring in a gym. If he did not defend himself, he would be hurt badly, or killed.

Black Cap shot out a leg.

Kyle blocked it with a heel, shoving his assailant's leg to the side.

Black Cap stumbled while reaching under his coat.

Suspecting he was going for a weapon, Kyle drove his foot into the man's knee, visualizing he was driving his foot through the wall.

The man cried out and thumped onto the floor, an automatic pistol in his hand.

Kyle stomped on the hand until the pistol lay free of his grasp. He kicked it, sending it skittering down the hall.

His assailant's ribs cracked when he kicked him. Grabbing a hand, he lifted and twisted it to the breaking point. "Who sent you after me?"

"Fuck you," the man hissed.

Kyle stepped down on Black Cap's neck.

"Ahh!"

"Tell me!" Blood pounded in Kyle's ears. Sweat ran down his face. Down the hall, the elevator dinged. He glanced behind him.

Blue Cap came out of the elevator hall. Blood from his nose trailed down his face. When he spotted Kyle, he reached under his jacket.

Kyle leapt over Black Cap, yanking the stairway door open. Two bullets impacted it where he had stood a split second before. The report made his ears ring.

He flew down the stairs as if the building would collapse on him.

On the ground floor, the door banged against the wall from his shove. The hall was empty.

He raced for the lobby. Halfway there, he realized he would have to pass the elevator bank. The other assailant might emerge as he passed. He took a chance, hoping there would be people around, preventing the attackers from shooting with witnesses present.

At the front desk, the receptionist was pale and wide eyed. She said into the phone, "Yes, a gunshot."

Two people stood at the counter, glancing around as if they didn't know whether to stay where they were or flee.

If Lori hadn't called the police, he hoped they were on the way now.

He ran outside and sought out the to the darkest cover he could find, dropping between two parked cars. Police sirens wailed in the distance.

The rapid pounding of his heart made Kyle wonder if it would fail him. His breathing came in ragged breaths.

The side door to the hotel opened, and the two attackers emerged. One helped the other hop along. They loaded up in a sedan and raced off.

Police sirens grew louder, and red and blue lit up the parking lot. Two cop cars pulled into the hotel and parked in front of the lobby door.

Kyle pulled out his phone and saw he was still connected to Lori. "Are you still there?"

"Are you all right?" Her voice shook.

"Yeah, I'm okay. I'm outside the hotel." Several deep breaths didn't slow his heart rate and breathing. "The guys that attacked me have left. The police are here. I'm coming back inside in a sec. I have to call home. My family might be in trouble."

His hands trembled while selecting his home number.

Karen answered on the first ring. "Kyle?" It came out rushed.

"Are you all right?"

There was a pause that worried him. "Yes, why wouldn't we be?" Her voice was edgy.

"Someone just tried to abduct me and shot at me."

"What?" she screamed.

"Is there anyone there preventing you from talking to me freely?"

"No."

"If there is, tell me the wrong answer to this question. Where was the first place we had sex?"

"Kyle, are you okay?"

"Where was the first place?" he yelled.

"The aft lav on an airplane." She was hysterical.

Some of the tension making him rigid drained away. "Has there been someone there looking for me?"

There was just enough of a pause to give him concern. "No," she said.

"Is there anything going on I need to know about?"

Another pause, and then she asked, "Like what?"

He closed his eyes and sagged against the car he stood beside. "I was just attacked and shot at. Tell me why you needed my room number!"

"I... I was just worried. I... I thought it would save me time if I had to call the hotel." Her voice shook, her speech hurried.

"Worried? Why were you worried?"

"This... this investigation you're on just... just seemed... you know... dangerous, running off at the last minute and all. I just thought I... I should have your hotel room number in case your cell phone didn't work." Her voice alternated between pausing and stumbling over her words.

Kyle frowned. "Why did you think this investigation was dangerous?" It hadn't been until just now. He had never alluded to concern over his wellbeing.

She sobbed.

Kyle closed his eyes, bracing himself for what he might hear. "Karen, our lives and Travis' might be in danger. Tell me, goddamnit!"

She sobbed for several seconds, which drove knives into Kyle's heart. Eventually she choked out between sobs, "I... I had an affair."

"Oh God!" Tears filled his eyes and ran down his cheeks. "Fuck!" How much more would be thrown at him tonight?

"It's over. He didn't mean anything to me. I promise, it's over."

Isn't that what the cheating spouse always says when caught? So much made sense now. Karen's insecurity would prevent her from divorcing him. She would only do so if she had someone else. "Why?"

She said nothing, crying for several seconds. "It doesn't matter. It was a big mistake. After last night I realized how stupid I was. I'm still in love with *you,* Kyle. I'm sorry."

The lump in his throat made speaking difficult. He choked out, "So you tried to have me killed?"

"What? No!" She blew her nose. "Two days ago, a guy approached me. He knew about the affair. He told me he'd tell you unless I kept you away from the accident investigation. Tonight, he called and said you were in danger, and I had to give him your hotel and room number so he could protect you. I didn't want to, Kyle, but I was afraid of what might happen if I didn't." She spoke so fast it was hard to understand her.

Kyle wiped tears off his cheeks. "So you just gave it to him to protect your affair?"

"He said you had something his enemies wanted. He needed to collect it from you to protect you."

The realization of just how desperate the FAA was turned Kyle's blood to ice water. He hurried to the hotel lobby, scanning around him as he walked. "Get Travis and leave! Stop at an ATM and get as much cash as it will give you. Go to Austin, San Antonio, *anywhere,* and don't tell anyone where you're going. Anyone! Don't use any credit cards. The people after me didn't get what they wanted. They may come to the house and hold you and Travis hostage to force me to give them what they want."

"Oh, God!" She was hysterical again. "This is all my fault. I'm so sorry. I was at a really low spot in my life—"

"Karen. Karen! Get yourself together. That doesn't matter right now. Get out of the house. Now! Call me when you're on the road."

Chapter Thirty

Saturday, June 19 10:52 p.m.

Kyle's face was hot, and his fists balled. "As I said the previous four times, I think they wanted the recording I have of an FAA Inspector admitting he had something to do with our accident five days ago." He rocked in his chair, fighting the urge to flee.

"You don't really expect me to believe the FAA hired two hit-men to murder you, do you?" Tinoco, the Chicago detective who stood no taller than Kyle's nose, smirked and shook his head. "Can you believe this guy?" He looked at his partner, who also shook his head.

"Why don't you tell us why they were really here?" Tinoco leaned so his face was inches from Kyle's. He could use a stick of gum. "Might this have something to do with the hot little number I see pacing out in the hall?" Tinoco smiled.

Since Karen's revelation, Kyle's stomach had been in knots. Over the last hour those knots had tightened. Kyle shot to his feet and stared down at Tinoco. "This is getting us nowhere. I'm out of here."

Tinoco glared up at him. "Sit. Down."

The other detective hurried to block Kyle's exit.

The doors to the conference room opened. A slender woman in her early forties with dark hair pulled back in a ponytail walked in, followed by a slightly younger man with a short haircut. Both were dressed in casual business attire.

"You'll have to leave." Tinoco pointed at the door. "This is police business." He puffed out his chest.

The woman opened up a black wallet. "I'm Special Agent Sam Rankin." She gestured to the man with her. "This is Special Agent Bryant Taber."

Tinoco narrowed his eyes. "I don't give a shit who you are, lady. We're conducting an interview here. You'll have to leave."

Rankin, who was as tall as Tinoco, looked him in the eye. "We'll take over questioning Mr. Masters. This is now a federal investigation."

"Agent, in case you haven't noticed, this hotel isn't federal jurisdiction. Go back to bed and get your beauty sleep."

Rankin didn't look annoyed or insulted. In the same steady gaze, she said, "You should call your Lieutenant. I'm sure he's finishing a phone call with my superior in D.C."

Tinoco threw out his hands. He pointed at Kyle. "Stay put. We'll be right back." He motioned with his head to his partner, and they left the room.

"Ms. Almond," Rankin said, turning to the door, "if you'd join us and close the door, please."

Lori attempted a smile at Kyle before shutting the door and sitting beside him.

"I'm sorry you had to experience Chicago's finest's hospitality," Rankin said. "Agent Taber and I just arrived, or I'd have been involved sooner." She sat at the table, across from Kyle.

He wasn't sure if it was the woman's warm brown eyes or that her demeanor was the complete opposite of Tinoco's, but he would have told her where the buried bodies were if he had any in his past.

She flipped open a notebook. "Why don't you tell me what happened from the time we talked earlier."

Kyle told her about Karen's phone call, the emails, discussing them with Lori, and running into the two. Rankin and Taber interrupted now and then to get clarification. While he told them about Karen's revelations after the attack, he stared at the table.

While he spoke, Lori squirmed in her seat as if she realized how dangerous this had been. At the mention of Karen's affair, her arm lifted as if to touch him, but dropped before making contact.

"We have agents reviewing the hotel security video." Rankin made a note on her pad. "Hopefully, the quality of it will be good enough so we can get a clear picture of their faces. We'll dust the stairway doors for fingerprints." She looked at her watch. "Why don't we take a break while I make some phone calls?"

Kyle went to the men's room. When he exited, Lori paced in the hall.

She stopped before him. "You okay?"

"Great. Never better." He looked down when she flinched as if he'd slapped her. "I'm sorry. That was uncalled for. No wonder Karen had an affair. I can certainly be an ass."

She rested her hand on his arm. "I'm sure it's more complicated than that."

Was it? He didn't know. He had been shot at, might have been murdered if he hadn't run, and found out his wife had strayed, all within minutes of each other. Could feel any lower.

Lori pulled him into a hug.

He closed his eyes and encircled her with his arms, savoring her warm embrace. A sob wracked his body, but he choked it down. He wouldn't cry now. Not in front of her.

Lori must have felt his shudder as she rubbed his back. "It's okay. It's okay."

The temptation to give in to his grief grew, but he shoved it down until he could be alone.

He pulled away and held his hand to her cheek before realizing how intimate this gesture was, then dropped his hand to his side. "Thanks."

"Anytime." She tentatively touched her cheek where his hand had just been.

Kyle's phone rang. It was Karen. He wanted to ignore her, except he needed to know Travis was safe. "Excuse me, please." He stepped down the hall and answered.

"Hi," Karen said. Her voice was cautious. "We've checked into the only place that would let us without using a credit card."

"Good. Don't let Travis out of your sight. Can I talk to him?"

"Kyle, I... I'm sorry." She spoke softly. He imagined she was in the hotel room's bathroom so Travis wouldn't hear. "I'd like to explain what I was going through when it happened."

It happened. She made stomping on his heart equivalent to overdrawing the checking account. He didn't want to hear her excuse now. "Not now. Can I please talk to Travis?"

She said nothing for a moment and then sighed. "Fine." There was a squeak of possibly a door and what sounded like a TV became louder. "It's Dad."

"Hey, Dad. You okay?"

The sound of his son's concern lifted him out of his doldrums. "I'm better now, buddy. You all right?"

"Yeah, I guess. How long will we have to stay here?"

Good question. "I don't know yet. Maybe a day or two. Mom explained what's going on?"

"Yeah." The TV faded and the same squeak came over the phone. Travis' voice lowered to a whisper. "She cried a lot on the drive here. Are you guys fighting again?"

Kyle sighed. "I guess you could say that. You don't need to worry about that."

Travis said nothing, making him wonder if he was worried. Kyle leaned against the wall. They were dragging Travis through emotional hell, and now he had also put his son in danger. He said the first thing he thought of. "Take care of her for me, will ya buddy?"

"Yeah, sure."

Kyle put enthusiasm in his voice. "Hey, think of this as an unplanned vacation. I'm sorry I can't be there to enjoy it with you."

"Okay if we go to Sea World tomorrow?"

A public place with lots of people around. It was probably as good a place as any for them to hide. "Yeah. Go have a blast."

"Cool."

"I'll call tomorrow."

Lori stood where he had left her. It dawned on him her family was in as much danger as his. "Have you taken precautions to protect your family?"

"Yes. Agent Rankin had a D.C. police car assigned to watch my ex-husband's house where my daughters are."

"Good."

Rankin approached them. "Agents have found the video of you leaving your room. Will you come watch it to identify the two who attacked you?"

They followed her into an office, where a bank of monitors showed various views of the hotel. On one was a frozen picture of Kyle leaving his room and wearing a faraway look. This had been after he had talked to Karen the first time, and she had told him what they could do after Travis went to bed the next night. At the time, he had looked forward to getting home.

Now he didn't know if he ever wanted to go home. Had Karen screwed whoever she had slept with in their bed? Had she suggesting they go skinning-dipping when she wouldn't before because she had already done so to please someone else?

He shook his head and watched himself walk down the hall, wanting to yell at his picture, "You were a fool."

They fast forwarded through an hour of video until Blue Cap and Black Cap stepped into the hall from the elevator.

Kyle pointed. "That's them."

Both men on the screen glanced up and down the hall as they made their way to Kyle's door. They checked the hall again before knocking.

They knocked again.

"That must have been while Lori and I were having dinner," Kyle said.

The two had a conversation before Blue Cap walked back to the elevator.

"Freeze that," Rankin said.

The image of the man's face was straight on, but the cap he wore put his face in a shadow.

"Make a copy of that, and send it to Quantico," Rankin said. "See if they can remove the shadow and get an ID. Have copies posted at O'Hare, Midway, and Milwaukee airports, and all bus and train stations."

Several minutes later, Black Cap pushed off from the wall a couple doors down from Kyle's room, and inserted a keycard into a lock. Kyle came strolling down the hall a moment later.

They watched Kyle's brief altercation with Blue Cap before he fled down the stairs. The agent manning the video monitors selected the floor where Kyle fought Black Cap.

Kyle studied his form and technique, looking for ways to improve it, like he would a pilot's performance in the simulator. Although he was proud of his escape, he realized he should have restrained Black Cap's arm from going for the gun instead of kicking him. If Black Cap had been quicker, he might have gotten a shot off that could have wounded him—or worse.

"I don't think he'll be walking without crutches for some time." Rankin gave Kyle an appraising look.

He glowed in her admiration.

"Back up to when Mr. Masters hit him in the neck," Rankin said. "His hat fell off."

The images of the man's face during the remainder of the fight were never straight on. They selected one with the best view. "Send this one to Quantico, too, and all the area hospitals," Rankin said. "He'll need medical attention."

They watched Blue Cap appear, shoot, and run down the hall and into the stairway.

Lori hugged herself.

Kyle was glad it had been him the thugs had gone after and not Lori. If they had found her first and come to his room with a gun to her head, both of them would probably be dead now.

"These guys were pros," Agent Taber said. "They knew to wear caps and never looked up enough for a camera to record their face. When they left, they picked up the injured man's hat so they wouldn't leave DNA behind, and parked where their license plate wouldn't be recorded."

Rankin turned from the security monitors to Taber. "Do they look similar to the two who broke into the NTSB building?"

Taber shrugged. "Possibly."

"Follow me, please." Rankin gestured to Kyle and Lori and went back to the conference room.

Rankin booted up a laptop. She brought up a video and clicked on it to play. "Watch this, Mr. Masters, and see if the men in the hotel tonight were the same two who broke into the NTSB."

"That's Ed," Lori said, holding a hand to her mouth as two men came into view, guiding the bound CVR Investigator.

Kyle realized they were watching the last minutes of her co-worker's life.

The two men cleaned out the CVR vault, threw several computers in a rolling garbage can, loaded it and Ed into a van, and drove away. Rankin stopped the recording.

Kyle scratched his head. "The one on the tape who guided Ed Holstrom was his height. Ed and I were about the same height. The guy I fought was as tall as I am. The other was shorter and had a cleft chin like the guy on that video. Both men tonight seemed to have the same muscular build as the two at the NTSB."

"I agree. I think it's the same two men." Rankin tapped a finger on her lips. "What can you tell me about this person who's emailing you?"

Kyle shrugged. "Other than we think he's an FAA employee, not much."

Rankin logged into the hotel Wi-Fi. She stepped back from the computer. "Log onto your email account. I'd like to read them."

The keys of the computer clicked as he logged in, then stepped away.

Rankin read the emails and viewed the attachments before forwarding both emails to her FBI address. "You received one this morning at six-thirty and the second one at eight p.m. If this was someone within the FAA, it would appear they're sending these to you before or after work." Rankin looked at her watch. "Will you reply to the last one?"

"Sure. Why?"

"We're going to trace the computer that's sending these. Once we find the computer, we'll question its owner."

Kyle typed: *How are you getting this information? It's been informative. You also said for me to keep doing what I'm doing. What would you recommend I do next?*

Lori and Rankin watched over his shoulder while he typed.

He lifted his fingers from the keys. "Good enough?"

"Hang on." Rankin called Quantico and had them locate the hotel's Wi-Fi so they could trace the email after it was sent. "Okay, send it," she said to Kyle.

After disconnecting the call, Rankin said to Lori and Kyle, "Why don't you two get some sleep? I have to put out an APB for these two men. I'm getting a search warrant for Mr. Norman's home. I'd like you two to go with us when we look through it. You've seen him and your knowledge of the accident will help us search his home for any pertinent evidence linking him to the flight." She glanced at Taber. "Have the hotel give Mr. Masters another room while his is being dusted for prints."

"I'll post an agent outside both of your rooms," Rankin said.

Kyle followed an agent to his new room like a zombie. After the agent confirmed no one else was in the room and left, Kyle shed his shoes, pulled the comforter back, and crawled under it in his clothes. He was strung out like he had just flown a red-eye flight craving sleep, but his mind could not be quieted.

Chapter Thirty-One

Sunday, June 20 8:02 a.m.

The phone woke Kyle from a deep sleep. Before the cobwebs parted and the memories of the previous night assaulted him, he tried to figure out why a phone would be ringing. He closed his eyes, hoping sleep would return and he could escape from his memories. The shrill ring prevented any hopes of that. He groped for the annoying device.

"Mr. Masters, Agent Rankin. You'll want to watch the news. Your airline is having a press conference. We have a search warrant for Mr. Norman's house. Meet us in the conference room in thirty minutes." The line went dead.

Good morning to you too. Kyle fumbled to cradle the phone, amused at Rankin's abruptness. He sat up, rubbed his face, and found the TV remote.

John Wagner, Omega's Executive VP, stood behind a podium.

"It has come to our attention that on Flight 918, our 737 that attempted to reject its takeoff at LaGuardia airport six days ago, that there was an FAA safety inspector, a Mr. Ernest Norman, riding on the flight deck jump seat. Mr. Norman has been unavailable for questioning until yesterday, when a member of our investigative team and an NTSB investigator located and interviewed him."

The last remnants of sleep were gone now. *The FAA is not going to like this.*

He watched for several minutes, glanced at his watch, and hurried to take a shower.

When he left his room, the agent sitting outside his door stood and fell in step behind him.

"You probably could've thought of a thousand things you'd rather do than sitting outside my room all night," Kyle said.

The agent's face remained neutral. "Part of the job, sir."

Kyle smiled. A pilot would have bitched about how it had been a waste of time.

In the conference room, Lori watched the news. "Have you seen this?" Her hair was wet and combed. She wore no eyeliner or makeup.

"Yeah." Kyle wondered if she had received the phone call this morning when he had. Was she as aghast she didn't have time to put on makeup as Karen would have been?

Karen. Each time he thought of her, his stomach did a little twist.

"There's coffee over there." Lori pointed to a set-up at the side of the room.

Agents Rankin and Taber talked on their phones. They glanced at him with bloodshot eyes, continuing their conversations. Four agents typed into laptops or talked on the phone.

Kyle poured a cup of coffee and glanced at the TV.

Mark Evans, the NTSB Investigator In Charge, stood behind the podium outside the hangar in LaGuardia. "We've, ah... we've known for several days there... ah, there was an FAA inspector on board Omega Flight 918." He rubbed the sides of the podium. "The FAA requested that we not disclose this information until they had a chance to interview the, ah... inspector. We, ah... were informed he'd left on vacation and could not be located."

Kyle frowned. Normally, Evans was very articulate. Was he uncomfortable admitting almost a week later they knew of Norman's presence during the takeoff?

Lori turned to him. "Did you see your airline's news conference?"

He nodded, sipping from his cup. "Part of it."

"Why would they come out and say that now? They've known Norman was on the flight all along."

"They must've taken seriously the FAA's threat to shut us down if we reported it. When they realized the FBI was involved, they didn't want to get caught covering up the FAA's complicity."

On the TV, Evans listened to a reporter ask a question. He adjusted one of the numerous microphones, hardly moving it. "Ah... at this point, we aren't sure if the inspector's presence on the flight deck influenced the crew. As reported a couple of days ago, the cockpit voice recording was taken when our offices were burglarized. Without that recording, or the two pilots' testimonies, the FAA inspector's statements will be the only way to determine why the crew rejected the takeoff."

Gesturing to the TV, Kyle said, "Your organization must have realized the same thing and are trying to get ahead of the FAA in spinning this."

Lori frowned while nodding.

Rankin finished her call. "So far, there's been no sign of the two who tried to abduct you last night. They haven't tried to get on a flight out of here. It's possible they drove from the area. We're widening our search. We've lifted fingerprints from the doors, but there are numerous ones that'll take time to narrow down. We just got a search warrant for Ernest Norman's home and are going there now. You ready?"

Taking a gulp of coffee, Kyle stood. "Do you have a biohazard suit I could use?"

Lori rolled her eyes and turned to a confused Rankin. "Ignore him. Mr. Norman's housekeeping skills are questionable."

"Oh." Rankin smiled.

Leaving the conference room, Lori's cell phone rang. Checking the caller ID, she sighed. "Good morning, sir." She listened, smiled. "Thank you, sir. I appreciate that. I'm with the FBI now, and we're on our way to the FAA inspector's house. I'll get back to LaGuardia after we're through there." She listened more. "Thank you, sir. I'll call you when we're through at Norman's house." She disconnected.

Kyle put his arm around her and gave her a quick hug. "You're back on the investigation."

"Yeah." She beamed.

"I guess the NTSB is going to quit tiptoeing around the FAA."

"It appears that way," Lori said.

Lori and Kyle followed Rankin and Taber to a silver four-door Chevrolet Impala. Kyle opened a rear door. "I thought you guys only drove black Suburbans."

Rankin shook her head. "You watch too much TV."

"I've told him that," Lori said.

✈✈✈

Parking in front of Ernie Norman's house, Kyle smiled, anticipating the look on Norman's arrogant face when they served him the subpoena.

A black Suburban parked behind them, and two agents exited it.

Glancing out the back window, Kyle said, "See, you do drive Suburbans."

Rankin looked over the front seat, suppressing a smile, before getting serious. "Stay in the car until we serve the subpoena."

Rankin and Taber climbed the steps to the porch. The other two agents circled around behind the house.

"I hope they don't fall through," Kyle said.

Lori shook her head.

Rankin knocked on the door and yelled, "FBI! Mr. Norman, we have a warrant to search your house!" She knocked again and repeated herself.

Taber peered in the windows off the porch and shook his head.

Rankin scanned the street. "Check the street for his car." She brought a radio to her lips. "Any movement back there?"

The radio squawked, but Kyle couldn't hear what was said.

"Okay, hold your position."

She knocked on the door again.

Taber came back a moment later and pointed several houses down. "That's his Jeep Cherokee."

"He hasn't gone out the back. We'll bust the door down," Rankin said over the radio while Taber made his way to the Suburban.

He opened the tailgate and brought out a ram, hoisted it to his shoulder and lugged it back up the porch.

"You should have offered to kick it down for them," Kyle said.

Lori shook her head again and looked at him out of the corner of her eye. "You're obviously feeling better this morning."

His smile dissolved. "I'm compartmentalizing. This is the only way I know how to deal with what I'm going through. When this is over, I'll fly home and deal with my other problems."

The corners of her mouth turned up in a sympathetic smile.

Rankin un-holstered her weapon and brought the radio to her lips. "Going in now."

Taber slammed the ram into the door. It swung open with a bang. He stepped aside, dropped the ram, and un-holstered his pistol, following Rankin into the house.

Rankin yelled, "FBI! We have a warrant to search your house!"

A couple of minutes later, Taber came out and holstered his pistol as he walked to the car. He opened Lori's door. "He's deceased."

Lori's face showed the shock Kyle felt. His hands began to tremble.

"We'd like you to see if anything is different from when you were here yesterday."

Kyle's heart thumped against his chest as they climbed the steps to the porch.

They stopped just inside the door. Norman lay in the recliner. He appeared to be staring at the ceiling, contemplating life, except for the blank look and the slackness of his face.

A stench of excrement made Kyle wrinkle his nose and wonder if Norman had lost control of his bowels.

The only dead people Kyle had seen were at funeral homes—after they had been made up to look their best. He wondered if he would ever shake the image of how empty of life Norman's body looked.

Lori held a hand over her mouth and nose.

Rankin stood near the body, talking on the phone.

"Okay, look around and tell me if anything looks different than it did yesterday," Taber said.

They scanned the room, standing where they were. "The whiskey bottle was half full yesterday," Lori said. It lay on its side with the cap off. "There might be a few more beer cans beside the recliner than yesterday."

Taber wrote this down. "Good. Anything else?"

Lori shook her head.

"I don't remember that pill bottle." Kyle pointed to the side table beside the recliner.

"Come to think of it, I don't either," Lori said. "I remember thinking he shouldn't be drinking if he was taking pain medication. But since I didn't see any evidence of medication, I didn't question him about it."

"Good. Anything else?"

They shook their heads.

"Were you in any other room yesterday?" Taber asked.

"No," Lori said.

"Wait outside, then."

Kyle and Lori leaned against the Impala, taking in the fresh air, not saying a word.

Kyle had no love for Norman but wondered if he'd still be alive if they hadn't questioned him.

After some time, Kyle asked, "How well do you know Skaggs?"

"We've worked several accidents together. We only discussed information pertinent to the investigation, nothing personal. Why?"

"You realize with Norman dead, the only people who've heard the CVR and can testify to what happened during the takeoff roll are you, me, Leo Brandish, Skaggs, and Chavette. I'm sure Leo will stand up for the pilots, if we can locate him. We know Chavette will say whatever is needed to absolve the FAA of blame. Which makes me wonder what Skaggs will say."

"I hope he'll say what really happened."

He gestured toward the house. "What if he was killed so he couldn't say anything? Don't you think this will weigh on Skaggs' mind, even if he wanted to say Norman coerced the crew to reject the takeoff?"

"Norman probably died of alcohol poisoning. You saw how much he was drinking yesterday. He might have supplemented the whiskey with beer. If he also took pain medication, maybe he overdosed accidentally." She pushed off from the car and paced. "He might've overdosed on purpose. Maybe after reliving the accident yesterday, the burden of what he caused became too much for him." She shrugged. "He took the rest of his medication and swallowed it with the booze."

Although her justification for what happened sounded legitimate, her concerned expression told Kyle she thought the same thing he did. "Our lives are in danger. Last night proved that. You also realize we were probably the last people to see him alive."

Taber came out of the house with the two agents from the Suburban and walked up to them. He opened the back door to the Impala. "Ms. Almond, if I could get you to wait in the car. Mr.

Masters, I'll need you to wait in the Suburban. I need your cell phones, too."

Chapter Thirty-Two

Sunday, June 20 10:33 a.m.

Karen Masters stared out the hotel room window, not seeing the view of the parking lot or surrounding buildings. Behind her, Travis lay on one of the beds, watching TV.

So far, she hadn't told anyone where they were. The urge to call her friend Rachael about the mess she was in made her understand an alcoholic's need for a drink. But Kyle's warning not to tell anyone where they were kept her from punching in Rachael's number. *What the hell has Kyle gotten us mixed up in?*

If he had only paid a little more attention to her needs, Rolland, the man who had approached her with the knowledge of her affair, would not have had any leverage to hold against her. She wouldn't have put Kyle in the danger he was in. Of course, if Kyle hadn't gone to Chicago playing private detective, they might be spending a lazy morning at their house, and Kyle never would have known about her affair.

She made her bed, then gathered their dirty clothes off the hotel room floor, folded them, and put them in their suitcases.

"Mom," Travis said from his bed.

"Yes."

"You're driving me crazy. Let's go to Sea World. Dad said we could."

Every day, he looked a little more like Kyle, but with her thin nose. What had her affair done to him? She hadn't considered Travis when she fell into another man's arms.

At Sea World, they would stand in long lines for a short ride. The sea life exhibits would be interesting, but Travis would be bored with them quickly. She glanced around the room and knew staying there would drive them both crazy. "Okay. Let's go."

Travis smiled and hopped off the bed in one graceful move. "Cool."

She wished she could find the same enthusiasm. For months, she had thought her marriage was over. They couldn't talk without arguing. She was convinced Kyle only valued her as a housekeeper and babysitter for their child.

Then she met Chris Kelty, a wealthy guy a few years older than Kyle, at the gym. His flirting made her feel appreciated. Their affair started innocently enough. First, they discussed exercise over coffee, then an occasional lunch, then met at a hotel, thinking it would only be the one time. After that, meeting someone secretly to have sex was like a drug she couldn't get enough of. The boring humdrum life she lived became exciting, and she felt appreciated and understood for the first time in months.

In the bathroom, when she peeled off her top to put on a clean tee shirt, Kyle's expression two nights ago came back to her when she had removed her shirt before they made love. Memories of that evening made her lean against the bathroom countertop, longing for that time. That evening made her remember why she had married him. He could act like a little boy, softening her, making her laugh and become a more carefree person. He had always given her the freedom to be who she wanted without any conditions, and she always admired his strong values and substance.

Would Kyle ever forgive her? Could she forgive him for the danger he had put them in?

They left the hotel and drove to Sea World. She went on a couple of rides with Travis, and then sat nearby while he waited in line for another. Her cell phone rang with a number she didn't recognize, and she questioned if answering was wise. What if Kyle was calling on the hotel's phone? "Hello?"

"It's Rolland. Where are you?"

How did he get her number? She hadn't given it to him. "That's none of your business. Don't ever call me again."

"If you don't want Kyle to die, you'll listen to me."

Her hands shook. "W-what do you want?"

"I need to know where you are so we can meet."

"I'm not going to tell you. After we talked last night, Kyle was attacked."

He sighed. "I'm sorry about that. My opposition was in place before I could react. Right now, I'm your best friend. Kyle's life is in danger, but not from me. He has something the people after him want. If I can get it from him before they do, he'll be safe."

Karen didn't want to believe him, but what he said sounded true. Kyle mentioned the people who had attacked him didn't get want they wanted.

"Maybe you think this would end your problems if you let my enemies kill Kyle. You'd be a single woman and could marry Mr. Kelty. Do you want Kyle's death on your conscience, Karen, when you could prevent it?"

Tears tickled her cheeks. "No," she whispered.

"I didn't think so."

Karen wiped her face and glanced around. No one seemed to watch her. "How do I know I can trust you?"

"Karen, if I wanted to hurt you or Travis, I would have gone to your home last night."

This too made sense. If Rolland could get her phone number, he certainly could find out where they lived. She glanced at Travis and saw he neared the front of the line.

"The people who attempted to capture Kyle last night are regrouping and will make another attempt. To protect him, I need him to give me the recording of the interview he had with the FAA Inspector. Kyle doesn't know me and will think I'm part of the same group trying to cover all this up."

Karen's heart pounded. She wasn't cut out for this. She wasn't a negotiator trained to save people's lives. "I don't know."

"Kyle has his secrets, too."

"What secrets?" She sat up.

"Did you know Kyle met an attractive NTSB investigator in Chicago?"

Karen's heart dropped. A fresh batch of tears wet her cheeks.

Beside her, three excited children begged an adult to go on another ride. Their caretaker playfully refused them.

"From your lack of a response," Rolland said, "I'll take that as a no. She stayed at the Sheraton, too."

Why hadn't Kyle told her? She thought about their phone calls yesterday. During the first one, she hated to admit, she had sounded uptight. Later, she had been disappointed he wasn't coming home. Did he not want to upset her more, or was going to

Chicago to find this inspector an excuse to meet this woman? "How do I know you're not just saying that to get me to do what you want?" She hated the shake in her voice.

"Because this woman was with Kyle when he questioned the FAA inspector yesterday."

Karen's mouth was dry. Her hands shook so bad, the phone threatened to slip from her grasp.

"I know you're upset with Kyle right now. His inattention was probably why you became involved with Mr. Kelty. What I'm seeing, Karen, is a couple who've allowed their relationship to drift apart. I don't think either of you intended it to go in the direction it has. You've both made your mistakes. If it were me, I'd try to salvage what you have."

Before this call, that was all Karen wanted. Now, she wasn't so sure.

"There's a lot about Mr. Kelty you don't know. Has he told you he'd divorce his wife?"

Karen wrapped her free arm around her waist. She thought about all the conversations she had with Chris.

"I didn't think so," Rolland said. "He urged you to get a divorce, so you'd be available anytime he wanted. Yet he never mentioned he'd get one."

How did Rolland know all this? Chris had begun pressuring her to get divorced, and Karen had assumed he would naturally do the same. How could she have been so stupid?

"Don't beat yourself up over this. A lot of married men do that. You and Kyle have your difficulties, but I think you both have made some honest mistakes. Mistakes you'll regret if you don't correct them now. If you don't help me convince Kyle to meet me, you'll end up a widow. Is that what you want, Karen?"

She closed her eyes. "No."

"Then meet me so we can discuss how you'll convince him to give me the recording."

Should she? What if Rolland's people were the ones who attacked Kyle last night? "I don't know."

"Karen, if my enemies get to Kyle first, they'll kill him. Do you want Travis to lose his father?"

Karen looked at Travis standing in line. He would board the ride at any moment. A grin plastered his face while he talked to some other kids. Would her happy-go-lucky son stay that way if Kyle was murdered? "No."

"Then we need to meet. Where are you? I'll come to you."

Karen rested her head in her hand. "San Antonio."

"Where?"

She sat up and glanced around. "I don't want to tell you that."

"Karen, we can't discuss this over the phone."

"Let's…let's meet someplace public." She searched her mind for where an appropriate place would be. "A restaurant."

He sighed. "Where?"

Karen thought quickly for someplace she had seen. She remembered seeing a place she could get a salad and Travis a burger. "There's a Chili's near the airport on Broadway."

"I'll be there at three. And Karen, if you talk to Kyle, don't mention we're meeting. He'll be suspicious and might turn the recording over to the people who shouldn't have it. If he does, they'll kill him."

Chapter Thirty-Three

Sunday, June 20 11:19 p.m.

Sitting in the back seat of the Suburban with a guard in the front seat, Kyle could see the top of Lori's head in the back of the Impala parked ahead. He went from gritting his teeth that the FBI thought either of them had something to do with Norman's death to holding his hands together to calm their shaking. Was the FBI part of the cover-up? Would he and Lori be arrested? If detained in jail and made to empty his pockets, would the thumb drive with a copy of Norman's interview disappear?

If charged with murder, any statements they made to the press afterward that Norman coerced the crew would be dismissed as two troubled individuals trying to fabricate a story for their fifteen minutes of fame. With the CVR stolen and both pilots dead—and now Norman silenced—the FAA could say whatever they wanted to explain Norman's involvement in the accident.

Luckily, they made that copy he mailed to his brother.

Maybe he did watch too much TV as Lori joked, because the vision of bail being denied and being shanked in prison made him shake. Even if none of these things happened, what kind of hell would they be put through while they tried to prove their innocence?

When given his one phone call, could he trust Karen to get him an experienced lawyer? Could he trust Steele to do so? Or, should he consult the yellow pages?

He rocked in his seat.

Rankin and Taber approached. Taber squatted down next to Lori's door.

Rankin stopped at Kyle's open window. She studied the screen on his phone. "I see you made and received several calls to your home or your wife's cell phone yesterday. What was discussed?"

Kyle weighed whether to answer her question without an attorney present. He watched enough crime dramas where people attempting to explain their innocence gave information that was used to convict them. Yet if he requested an attorney, he'd be treated as a suspect.

Rankin studied him, her expression neutral.

His gut told him she wasn't trying to frame him. Yet, she had obviously been doing her job for years and had a lot of experience practicing this disarming look.

"Earlier in the day, my wife was upset I came to Chicago." His voice quivered. "The first two calls were to explain why it was important we find Norman and get him to explain what happened. The next call was to tell her we'd called you and I couldn't come home last night. The last call was when she'd been pressured to call and find out where I was staying."

Rankin's face remained neutral. "You received a call from a Morgan Steele yesterday afternoon. Who's he?"

"My boss."

"Why did he call you?"

Did he want to admit his suspicion the FAA and Omega worked together to cover up Norman's involvement? If he did, and this got him off the hook with the FBI, would it get him fired? "The FAA must have called him after we left here." He gestured to Norman's house. "They claimed I'd harassed one of their inspectors."

"Did you?"

"No." *I wanted to slap the shit out of him.*

"What'd you tell him?"

"I explained who this inspector was and what he admitted."

"What was his reaction?"

It was odd. "He said I should have run this interview by him before coming here. Then requested I fill him in after I met with you this morning."

Rankin made a note.

Kyle wondered if this was something she would verify later, or if she suspected Omega and the FAA were in cahoots.

"You called a Bill Masters before this call. Who's he?"

Kyle's heart hammered. "My brother."

"What does he do?"

"He's a home builder in Maine." Kyle fought the urge to dismiss the call, explaining it was simply two brothers catching up. He knew the more he talked, the more he would give away.

The cocking of one of her eyebrows made him worry she knew about the thumb drive. He stuck his hands under his legs to conceal their shaking.

"A pilot and a builder. I expected you to tell me he was a pilot, too." She handed him his phone. "The medical examiner estimates Norman's time of death between nine and eleven last night. Obviously, you were too busy defending your life to be taking someone else's."

Kyle took a deep breath and let it out silently. His tension drained away.

"If you don't mind sticking around a while longer, we'll give you a ride back to the hotel."

The weight being lifted from him made him wonder if this was how prisoners felt when released. "Whatever you need."

At the Impala, Taber handed Lori her phone and walked off.

Kyle slid out of the Suburban and stood on shaky legs. He stooped down by Lori's door. "You okay?"

The pallor of her skin told him she'd been worried too.

She nodded and opened the door.

Offering her his hand, he helped her from the car.

"I have to call my daughters." She stepped away.

Leaning against the car, he took a couple of deep breaths. He smelled freshly mowed grass and asphalt. He hadn't noticed these scents earlier.

Norman's neighbors stood in groups, watching the scene. More vehicles had arrived, full of people carrying tool boxes and dangling cameras.

Kyle watched the comings and goings but couldn't find any enthusiasm for what they were doing. Normally, he would love to see if an actual crime scene investigation was run the way they were portrayed on TV.

Could he make the FAA accountable for their actions? If he could, what would it cost him? His only consolation was the involvement of the FBI, providing they weren't corrupt.

Calling Karen's cell phone, he counted the rings. *Please be okay.*

"Hi." Her voice lacked warmth. There were children squealing in the background.

"Are you guys okay?"

"Yes."

"You must've gone to Sea World."

She sighed. "Yeah."

The strain in her voice and one-word sentences told him she felt the stress of her affair and his putting them in danger. The tension of the last half hour made him want to forgive her, open up, and tell her what he had just been through and the fear he experienced. How he just wanted to come home, hold her, and talk through their problems. Why was it that when his life became distorted, he sought out what had been important but neglected?

I had an affair. The memories of her words shut him up. Who could he trust now?

"How's... how's it going there?" she asked, pulling him from his thoughts.

Was she interested? Or coming up with something to talk about to avoid the issue making them distant? "The Inspector we talked to yesterday is dead." He regretted saying we.

Karen gasped. "What... what happened to him?"

"They don't know yet."

"You... you said *we*. Who's there with you?"

Lori paced behind the car on the phone. "The FBI and NTSB."

"Oh. You're with the NTSB?"

The accusation in her voice pushed aside the regret and fear. "Well, yeah." He realized how harsh it sounded. She had no way of knowing the NTSB would be there. Was he trying to hide Lori's presence? If so, wasn't he as guilty of secrets as she was? "Since this inspector was on our jump seat, and a factor in the accident, they'd naturally be part of the investigation."

"Oh."

Every married man in the world knew that one word carried underlying tones.

"Is this NTSB person a man or a woman?"

Kyle frowned. Why would she assume there would be only one investigator? "What the hell does that matter?"

"Just curious. You flying off to Chicago seemed... awfully secretive. And last minute."

His face warmed. If she hadn't brushed him off yesterday morning, he might not have come. Besides, it didn't matter if Lori was a woman. He hadn't run off to have an affair with her. "I've explained why I came to Chicago."

"I can't help feel there's more to it than finding this inspector and discovering what happened during the takeoff."

"Like what?"

"Like whether this NTSB person you're with is a man or woman. You avoided that question."

Why would she be suspicious of him working with a woman? Was she trying to find reasons to blame him for her sleeping around? If she wanted to be suspicious, he decided to give her something to think about. "The Investigator is a very attractive woman." Saying this made more vindictiveness surface. "Do you think I'm having an affair with her? Maybe I should, to even the score. How many guys have you slept with since we've been married? Maybe I have some catching up to do. One of the FBI agents here is pretty hot. Maybe I'll sleep with her too."

"How do I know you haven't already slept with someone?" Her voice grew enraged.

This fueled his anger. He started forming words he wanted to blast her with, but a glance at Lori's concerned face calmed him. "I don't want to get into this now. I called to make sure you guys are okay. I'll call later."

When he pulled the phone away, he heard her say, "I love you."

Pacing, he kicked at things in the street before sitting on the rear bumper of the Suburban out of sight of Lori. Why did he let Karen rile him up so easily? Her parting words puzzled him. How could she have an affair, accuse him of having one, and then say she loved him? For centuries, men had been saying women were complicated. He was never more aware of this than he was now.

When he calmed down, he returned to the Impala, sitting beside Lori.

She looked at him out of the corner of her eye.

"Do you get the feeling we're being held here so they can keep an eye on us?" He nodded toward Norman's house where Rankin and Taber conversed.

"It would be logical. They might also be keeping us close so they can protect us."

"Yeah, let's hope so." Guilt overwhelmed him because he had allowed Karen to anger him when he should have been checking on what kind of security precautions she was taking.

Rankin took a call on her phone, nodded a few times, and approached the car. Sitting in the front seat, she booted up a laptop and passed it back to Kyle. "Would you check your email again?"

Typing in his password, Kyle wondered if there was keystroke capture software installed on this computer that would allow the FBI to monitor his email. He needed to close out this account and open a new one.

"There's no new email from tscalone72. There's only junk and newsletters." He passed the computer back so Rankin could see.

She tapped a finger against her lips.

Her roaming eyes made him feel she had dropped any suspicion they were involved in Norman's death and was simply trying to solve who was behind all this. "Do you suppose he knows you're involved and won't write anymore?" he asked.

"It's a possibility. We've had a team staking out the coffee shop from which the last two messages were sent. He or she might have spotted the team and been spooked off. Are you sure you don't know anyone named T. Scalone, or some combination of those letters?"

Kyle shook his head. "This person said I didn't know them."

"They might've said that to protect themselves. Maybe T something S something Calone. Or some combinations like that."

Kyle closed his eyes, trying to recall anyone with a name or nickname similar. "I can't come up with anyone. If I could borrow a pad of paper, I'll work on it." He turned to Lori. "Were any of the NTSB or FAA guys involved in the accident investigation named Scalone or Calone, or something close?"

Tugging on an earring, she shook her head. "No. I'm drawing a blank on this name too."

"What about something that happened in 1972?" Rankin asked.

Kyle shrugged. "I was a sophomore in high school. The only thing significant I remember was Donna Humphrey breaking my heart."

The corners of Rankin's mouth turned up. "Think about that year to see if anything else comes to mind. When did you start flying?"

"I soloed in 75, my first year in college. I know what you're thinking. I don't remember any of my instructors, examiners, or other pilots with that name."

Rankin's phone rang. "Keep thinking about it." She walked back to Norman's house with her phone held to her ear.

Kyle liked the way her mind worked. It was easy to assume that since he was a pilot and the mystery emailer had sent him FAA employee records, it might be someone from his aviation past. He began jotting down any combination of names he could think of that might make tscalone but came up with nothing.

In '72, he had lost his virginity. The Vietnam War ended. The Beatles broke up. There was another moon landing. He knew very few people involved with aviation in '72. His most memorable aviation dates were July fifth in 1975 when he soloed, and then October twenty-fifth, when he got his private pilot license. His following ratings and licenses all came later. In 1982, he began his career, when he started flying for Bar Harbor Airlines in the northeast.

The only significant event he remembered was in '78. Two pilots had a midair collision near the airport where he was a flight instructor. What if the event wasn't an important event in his life, but to the informant's life? He started thinking out loud. "When you set up an email address, you try to use your name, or some combination of your name so the people you write to know it's you."

"Duh." Lori shook her head with a smirk.

"If you wanted to set up a bogus email account no one would know was you, you wouldn't?"

"Duh, again."

Visualizing a keyboard, he gave his idea more thought. "You could use the ampersand, the pound sign, and other characters with a combination of letters and numbers to come up with one, but it would be difficult to remember unless you wrote it down somewhere."

Lori rolled her eyes.

"If you wanted your identity secret because it might jeopardize your job, you wouldn't want to write it down where it might be discovered. So, you'd have to come up with an address you'd remember."

Lori patted his arm. "This is brilliant. I can see why you're as successful as you are." Her expression said she thought just the opposite.

If nothing else, Kyle was grateful he was able to make her forget how worried she was for a minute. "So, what if this T. Scalone is someone our mystery emailer knows, but we wouldn't suspect. So, let's assume it was someone significant in this person's life. Removing the family members or past or present lovers from the mix, who were some of the most significant people in your life?"

Lori's derisive expression fell away. "Some childhood friends, teachers and professors, flight instructors, or pilots I've flown with."

"That's what I was thinking. Now we're getting somewhere." He rubbed his hands together.

She chuckled. "How are we getting somewhere?"

"Instead of looking for a needle in a haystack, we're looking for a pile of needles in the haystack."

Lori shook her head.

Reaching over the front seat, he picked up Rankin's computer, went to the NTSB web site, and looked up accidents that happened in 1972. There were 27. "Why couldn't pilots have been more careful that year? Why can't I pull up these accidents?"

Lori glanced at the screen. "Accidents before nineteen-ninety-three are not on the website."

"How do we get these reports?"

"I could call tomorrow and have someone pull them. Why?"

Kyle sighed. "Since we assume the informant might work for the FAA, what if there was an aviation life-changing event that year?"

Wrinkles furrowed on her forehead. "It'll take a couple of days to pull those files and go through them looking for a name similar to tscalone."

"Well, if nothing more, we have something we can show them." Kyle gestured toward Norman's house. "We tried to come up with my mystery emailer's identity. Hopefully, that'll lower us on the suspect list for Norman's murder."

The ringing of Lori's phone made her fumble in her purse. "Almond." She listened. "Thanks for calling on a Sunday." She dug out her notebook and pen. "Just the summary now, and email the full report." She made some notes. "Okay. Thanks for calling. I'll get back to you if we have any questions." She disconnected. "First Officer Cheryl Wells' autopsy report is in. They're ruling her death as trauma resulting from the injuries she sustained in the accident."

Kyle frowned. "Are they sure?"

"No, Kyle. They're guessing." She blew out an exasperated sigh. "Of course they're sure."

Two men pulled a stretcher out of Norman's house. On it sat a man-sized lump in a black bag. Rankin trailed behind them.

Lori followed his gaze. "I know what you're thinking. They're pretty big coincidences, her dying when she did, and now his death." She faced Kyle. "She was severely injured. He might have committed suicide."

"Then who were those guys in the hotel last night?"

Lori watched the body being loaded into a coroner's van. "I don't know."

After the doors to the van slammed shut, Rankin sat in the car.

"The first officer's autopsy is in." Kyle realized blurting this out before Lori made him seem eager to be the one to give this information. As if this would make him appear less guilty of Norman's death. "Lori has the details."

"She died from the injuries she sustained in the accident," Lori said. "I can forward the report to you."

"Do that. Any luck identifying the mystery emailer?" Her question was directed at Kyle.

Kyle told her what he'd come up with.

"I'll have some people look into it."

Taber approached the car.

"We're through here. Since we haven't found the men who attempted to abduct you last night, we could guard you at the hotel. But I've sent two agents to Pierre Chavette's home to escort him to the FAA office. Why don't you accompany us? Your knowledge of the accident may be valuable when we question him."

Kyle had a sneaking suspicion they were keeping them close so they could keep an eye on them and monitor who they talked to.

He tried to hide his doubt. "I've been dying to see ol' Pierre again."

"Maybe we should leave him in the car," Lori said.

Rankin frowned.

"Let's just say, he and Kyle don't get along very well."

Chapter Thirty-Four

Sunday, June 20 1:54 p.m.

A Dodge Charger pulled into the FAA's Flight Standards District Office in Des Plains, just outside of Chicago, in front of the Impala Kyle and Lori rode in. Kyle thought he recognized Pierre Chavette's bald pate in the back of the Charger. He smiled as he anticipated how the arrogant prick would behave with the FBI.

After they parked, Chavette exited the car with a scowl on his face. It dissolved when Lori and Kyle climbed from the Impala. He turned to the two agents who'd driven him there. "What're they doing here?"

Rankin approached with a hand held out and her credentials in the other. "You must be Mr. Chavette. I'm FBI Special Agent Sam Rankin."

Chavette shook her hand, then stuffed both of his in his pants pockets.

Kyle waved. "Hi, Pierre. Good to see you." *Asshole.*

"I believe you know Ms. Almond and Mr. Masters?" Rankin asked. When Chavette said nothing, she introduced Agent Taber. "Why don't we go inside?"

Chavette started for the door, then stopped. "Why am I here? I wasn't informed and I demand to know!"

Kyle smirked at Chavette's attempt to control the situation.

Taking his elbow, Rankin urged him forward. "Why don't we go inside out of this heat, and we'll discuss that."

Keys jangled in Chavette's hand as he twisted the lock and stepped inside. Once everyone had entered, he locked the door behind them.

Straight ahead was a raised receptionist counter. Several vacant chairs and a coffee table covered with aviation magazines sat off to the side. A hallway led to the cubicles beyond.

"I regret to inform you that one of your Inspectors, Ernest Norman, was found dead this morning in his home," Rankin said.

Chavette stared at her a moment, then at the floor. His chest rose and fell. "Mon Dieu. I...I didn't know."

Kyle tried to detect a softening in his eyes or a slackening of his jaw. He realized his lack of respect for the man might be clouding his opinion when he thought what he saw was panic.

Chavette jingled change in his pockets. "So... so why do you need me?" He didn't meet anyone's eyes.

"According to Ms. Almond and Mr. Masters, you've been unable to locate Mr. Norman the last several days. You don't seem surprised he was home."

The widening of Chavette's eyes made Kyle want to smile. He did his best to hide it.

"I ... just became aware he ah...returned home." Chavette's accent had become very pronounced.

Studying him, Rankin asked, "You aren't curious how he died?"

Chavette squeezed his eyes shut. "Yes. Yes, of course. I... I was so preoccupied, I didn't think to ask."

Rankin seemed cordial in her manner, but Kyle wonder if she enjoyed seeing Chavette squirm as much as he did.

"The cause is undetermined at this time." Rankin gestured toward the cubicles. "Why don't you show us his workspace?"

Chavette shuffled from foot to foot. "Uh... um, don't you need a search warrant?"

Rankin raised her eyebrows. "One of your employees died under suspicious circumstances. I'd think you'd want to do all you could to find out how and why."

"Yes. I... I definitely want to help. But, we... um, have procedures and protocol we have to adhere to." His glance at her was brief. "I'm sure you understand."

"If we need to obtain a warrant, Mr. Chavette, we will. In the meantime, we'll post agents at the door and prevent anyone from entering or leaving, and escort you to our office downtown where we'll question you until we get one. Being a Sunday, it may take a while."

Wiping sweat from his forehead, Chavette said, "Uh, maybe... maybe I should... should talk to my superiors."

The arrogant prick who had tried to tell the NTSB how to run the investigation was gone.

When Kyle was a first officer, he'd flown with captains who exhibited Chavette's behavior. When an authority figure was not present, they put up a façade of toughness and arrogance. But when put under pressure and questioned by someone of influence, they fell apart.

Chavette must have noticed Kyle enjoying himself because he glared at him. "I still don't know why they're here." He pointed at Lori and Kyle.

"I don't think he likes us," Kyle whispered to Lori.

Lori narrowed her eyes at him, but her mouth pursed as if hiding a smile.

"They're here at the FBI's request to assist us in finding the cause of Mr. Norman's death."

"Well, he isn't a federal employee. I'm not sure he'd be cleared to view any material that might be seen at Norman's workspace."

Kyle had visited numerous FAA Inspectors at their offices and knew all they would find were manuals from airlines that explained their procedures. Though this might have been considered confidential information, Kyle could have called any of the airlines whose manuals they discovered and requested a copy. The industry as a whole tried to help each other make flying safer.

Rankin put on a thoughtful look. "That's a good point. Mr. Masters will only sit in during our questioning of you about Mr. Norman's presence on their flight deck on the day of the accident. Now, may we see his workspace?"

Chavette sighed and started toward the cubicles. "This way."

A few of the fifty or more cubicles were occupied. Kyle guessed those there on a Sunday were inspectors catching up on paperwork. He knew many inspectors avoided the office during the week to stay out of sight of their superiors and came in on weekends to drop off paperwork.

Passing a glassed-wall conference room, Chavette pointed to it. "Masters should wait in there."

Kyle stepped into the room, not feeling left out. He doubted they'd find anything of any importance at Norman's desk.

Rankin, Taber, Lori, and Chavette returned a moment later.

"Why don't we sit and discuss what Mr. Norman was working on, what kind of employee he was, and the purpose of his presence on Omega's flight?" She took a seat at the head of the table.

To the two agents who had driven Chavette there, she said, "Search his work area for anything mentioning Omega Airlines."

Lori and Kyle sat across from Chavette. Taber sat so Chavette was between him and Rankin. Kyle guessed it was to make Chavette feel pressured from all sides.

Chavette stared at the table.

"How was Mr. Norman's health?" Rankin's tone was warm and engaging.

Chavette never looked up. "He seemed okay. He was able to pass his medicals."

"I'm going to let Ms. Almond ask questions concerning Mr. Norman's involvement with Omega Airlines. Then I'll have a few." Rankin extended a hand toward Lori.

Pressing record, Lori stated her name and the name of those in the room, the date, and time. "What is your relationship with Ernest Norman?"

"I was his supervisor."

"What's your title?" Lori made a note.

"I'm de manager of de Des Plains Flight Standards District Office."

Lori lowered her head in an attempt to meet Chavette's eyes, which were fixed on the table. "When were you made aware Inspector Norman was on Omega Airlines Flight 918?"

Chavette sighed. "Shortly after de accident."

"What was the purpose of his presence on the flight?"

"I assume it was a routine route check."

Or was it to harass Captain Musgrave since Norman had been unable to bring a violation against him six months ago? Kyle wondered.

"How would you rate Mr. Norman's job performance?" Lori asked.

"Okay."

"Okay, in what way? Was his job performance about average to the other inspectors? Better, or not as good?"

"Average."

When Lori seemed frustrated, Kyle noticed she pulled on an earring, distorting the shape of her ear.

"Someone has been kind enough to forward us his and your employee records."

That lifted Chavette's head. Worry etched his features.

"Mr. Norman had six reprimands and remedial training in the seven years he's been with the FAA. Is that about average for the employees in this office?"

Chavette held his head in his hands. "Uh." He cleared his throat. "Mr. Norman, uh, he had some difficulties." He looked up with some determination on his face. "This is de FAA. We just don't fire people because dey have a few problems. We help them with their deficiencies. Our employees have extensive backgrounds in aviation, and it is to de FAA's advantage to tap into that knowledge."

Even if they're assholes, Kyle thought.

Lori cocked an eyebrow. "So, six reprimands in seven years are only a few problems?"

Chavette slumped. "That might be a few more than normal."

"How was his relationship with the other workers of this office?"

"He tended to stay to himself." He licked his lips.

In other words, no one liked Norman. Although Kyle enjoyed seeing Chavette squirm, he had some sympathy for the guy. He doubted his decisions and the actions that led to this point had been made with indifference.

"How was his relationship with the airlines he oversaw?"

Sighing, Chavette said, "We... ah, had a few complaints."

Shaking her head, Lori asked, "You have an employee that has six reprimands and generates complaints from the industry, but you kept him around? Why?"

Chavette wiped his hands on the legs of his pants.

Lori frowned. "Is there any other reason why you'd retain this inspector?"

"He had abilities that were useful."

"Such as?" Lori asked.

"He was very analytical," Chavette blurted out as if this was the first thing that came to mind.

"Would his staying employed at this office have anything to do with signing off your recurrent training for the last six years?"

The shock that filled Chavette's face made Kyle cover his mouth to hide his smile.

"No," Chavette said.

"Why was he the only inspector to sign off your training?"

"He was available?"

"I would think being the FSDO manager, you'd want to have other inspectors observe your training so you could monitor how they conducted themselves."

Lori asked these questions in an even manner, Kyle assumed, in an attempt to get Chavette to open up.

"I thought I just explained that. No one else was available!" Chavette ran a hand through his hair, disheveling it.

"Really? In seven years, *no one* was available?"

The frustration in Lori's voice made Kyle sit up. "May I ask a question?" He hoped he sounded sincere.

"Yes."

He couldn't determine if the look Lori gave him was a suspicious one or a warning to not be demeaning. "What would happen to an FAA inspector if he couldn't pass their recurrent training?"

Directing his answer to Lori, Chavette said, "They'd be given additional training."

"And if after extensive training, this inspector still couldn't pass satisfactorily?" Lori asked.

He swallowed and cleared his throat. "We'd have to... let them go."

Putting on his best, ol'-buddy tone of voice, Kyle said, "That must have put a few inspectors under a lot of pressure every year. I know that feeling. It's more of a struggle for me now that I don't fly regularly, compared to the line pilots who fly every day."

The relaxing of Chavette's shoulders made Kyle hope he had softened him. "Did you have difficulties completing your training?" he asked.

"I don't see what this has to do with Mr. Norman's death," Chavette said to Rankin.

"I'm sure the NTSB has a reason for asking their questions," Rankin said. "I'd appreciate an answer."

"The NTSB didn't ask it. *He* did, and I don't like what he's implying."

"I'll ask it, then," Lori said. "I need to know the answer. Did you have any trouble passing your recurrent training?"

After some time, Chavette said, "Because of my position and my extensive responsibilities, it was difficult to schedule sufficient training needed to complete it in a timely fashion."

This was a bullshit answer if Kyle had ever heard one. Didn't he realize he was talking to the NTSB and FBI? Lying to them could be career ending.

Tugging on her ear, Lori asked, "Would you say the other inspectors in your office had the same problem as you?"

"The other inspectors don't have as demanding a schedule as I do."

"So is that a yes or no?" she asked.

"Is that a yes or no to what?" He threw his hands up. "Your questions are all over de place. I'm having a hard time following them."

"Did the other inspectors in your office, because of their schedules, have a difficult time passing their recurrent training, as it appears you did?"

Chavette glared at Lori. "I always completed my training. If you have my record, you would've seen that."

A sigh escaped Lori. "You claim the first you knew of Mr. Norman being onboard Omega Airline's Flight 918 was shortly after the accident. What did he say when he called to report this?"

Chavette fidgeted in his chair. "I'll need to talk to my supervisors before I answer any more questions." He pushed his chair back.

Rankin narrowed her eyes. "We're not through, Mr. Chavette."

When Chavette stood, so did Rankin and Taber. Chavette looked from one to the other.

"Where were you last night?" Rankin asked.

Chavette frowned. "What does that have to do with this accident investigation?"

"It appears Mr. Norman was murdered. There's bruising around his mouth, nose, and arms like someone held him there. An autopsy will verify this. So, I ask again, where were you last night?"

This information brought back gnawing tension in Kyle's stomach.

Beside him, Lori swiveled her chair back and forth. Worry etched on her face.

Kyle reached out and grasped her hand under the table.

Lori squeezed back.

"I was home, with my wife." Chavette's voice shook. His accent became very pronounced. "You think I murdered him?"

"Did you?"

"No!"

"You had motive. You have a problem employee you've kept employed, who might've been blackmailing you. This employee was a contributing factor in an airline accident. After the accident, he is unavailable for questioning, like he was purposely hidden. I can make a case you wanted him dead to silence his involvement in the accident and to hide your inability to pass your training."

"I didn't murder him!"

"Then who did?"

Grabbing two fistfuls of his hair, Chavette pulled.

"Did Mr. Norman call you yesterday after Ms. Almond and Mr. Masters paid him a visit?" Rankin asked.

Chavette collapsed into his chair. "I... I refuse to answer any more questions until I have a lawyer."

"Mr. Chavette," Rankin said with an edge to her voice, "We'll be pulling the phone records for this office and any phones in your name. I'll find out who you called after Mr. Norman called you yesterday, and after Omega's accident. If you've committed a crime, it will be better if you come clean now. If you're trying to protect someone, I can assure you they won't hesitate to make a deal."

Chavette rested his head in his hands. "I called my superior in Washington."

"Who is that?" Rankin asked.

"Jerri Krubsack."

"What was discussed?"

Chavette shook his head. "I can't... I can't answer any more questions without a lawyer."

Rankin stood and slid the phone sitting in the center of the table to him. "Make the call. Tell them to meet you at the FBI office downtown." She motioned with her head, and the others followed her out the room, closing the door behind them. "Don't let him leave," she said to Taber. She turned to Lori. "I guess we've got phone calls to make."

Lori took a deep breath. "Yes, I guess so."

A chime made Kyle pull his phone from its holster. He had a video message from Karen. After their last conversation, he doubted she would have sent him anything. Travis must have used her phone since his didn't have the capability. A smile touched Kyle's face as he wondered what his son found interesting enough to share with him. He opened the message.

Kyle's smile disappeared.

Chapter Thirty-Five

Sunday, June 20 2:52 p.m.

Numbness spread through Kyle as he stared at his phone's screen. He squeezed his eyes shut, hoping that when he opened them, he would have been seeing things. Hitting play again, the fifteen-second video was the same as the first time he viewed it. "Oh God!"

Holding the phone in both hands didn't stop it from shaking. Travis and Karen lay slumped against what looked like a van sidewall, bound, gagged, and blindfolded. Karen was shuddering as if crying. There were abrasions on her face. Travis' nose bled.

From across the aisle in the FAA office, Rankin studied him with her phone to her ear.

"What is it?" Lori asked from beside him.

His phone chimed again. A text message from Karen's phone, said, *if you don't want them to die, you and Almond will be outside Omega Airlines baggage claim 9p at Dulles airport tonight. Bring the recording. Don't tell anyone.*

Kyle reread the message to make sure he wasn't reading it wrong. Each time, a paralysis made him have a hard time moving past the words, *if you don't want them to die.*

He dropped the phone to his side. How did they find them? How did they get them? Was Karen so upset she didn't notice men following them?

No. This was his fault. He had put them in trouble by coming to Chicago.

The logistics of getting to Dulles by nine seemed overwhelming. How long was that? He glanced at his watch. It took him several tries before he realized it was almost three. How long did that give them? With some effort, he came up with seven, no six hours. Or was it five? There was a time zone change, wasn't there?

They had to get to the airport. Would there be a flight that would get them there on time?

"What's the matter?" Rankin had walked up beside him.

Don't tell anyone. How would he explain the sudden need for him and Lori to get to the airport? Where would he say they were going? He blurted out, "Lori and I have to get to the airport."

Lori frowned, her phone at her ear.

Rankin narrowed her eyes. "We'll need you to observe the questioning of Mr. Chavette to verify what he's telling us is true."

His heart hammered in his chest. "We can't. We have to go. Now!" He knew he looked and sounded crazy. He took a deep breath. Somehow, he had to get his act together, or the clever FBI agent would get suspicious.

How was he going to get Lori to go with him?

"Okay. Sure." She gestured to the two agents who had driven Chavette to the FAA office.

Kyle's gaze followed where she pointed.

"They can—" Rankin snatched the phone out of his hand and turned away from him.

"Give me that!" He leaned around her, trying to get his phone. Anger and panic fought to be the dominant emotion.

Rankin held the phone in front of her, punching the on-screen buttons with one hand. With the other, she blocked Kyle's stabs at grabbing the phone.

"Is this your family?" Rankin asked.

Don't tell anyone.

"Is this your family in this video?" Her voice was firm.

Fuck. Fuck. Fuck. Fuck! For a moment he considered lying, but then said, "Yes."

"We have a hostage situation." Rankin stared at the screen. "Where are they?"

An image similar to the one on his phone flashed in his mind. In this one, Karen and Travis lay slumped with a bullet hole in each of their heads. Every nerve in his body vibrated. He collapsed into the nearest chair. "San Antonio."

"Where in San Antonio?"

Since the FBI now knew, he might as well have their help. "They were staying at the motel near the airport. They went to Sea World."

"Did your wife's phone send this?"

"Yes."

"I'm sending this to my phone." She handed Kyle his phone, then lifted her own and punched in a number. "This is Rankin. I have a hostage situation. I need the location of a cell phone." She read off Karen's number. "Pull up the call history."

While she waited, she faced Kyle. "This is the right thing to do, Mr. Masters. If you had done what they said, they would have killed both you and your family. They must not know you've already given us a copy of the recording. That will be to our advantage."

He hoped so.

Lori touched his arm. "What's going on?"

He set the video to play and handed her his phone.

Her eyes widened while she viewed it.

When she began to hand him his phone back, he said, "There's a text, too."

She read it. The phone shook when she held it out to him. The color had drained from her face. She hugged herself and stepped down the corridor.

Rankin listened to the person on her phone, made some notes, and ended the call. "Your wife's phone is stationary right now. We're sending police units to its location. They'll call me if it moves. Do you recognize this number?" She read it off.

Kyle shook his head.

"A call from this number this morning lasted ten minutes. It's a D.C. area code and not registered to anyone. It must be a prepaid cell phone." To Taber, she said, "We need to get to the airport. If they were kidnapped in San Antonio, why do they want to meet in D.C.?"

"It must be home base," Taber said. "They'll have other assets there,"

To the other two agents, she pointed at the conference room. "Read Mr. Chavette his Miranda rights, take him to our offices, and hold him. Lock this building down."

While she gave orders, Kyle approached Lori, who paced. He had planned to drag her into their trap however he could. Would she have gone willingly if he had asked? No, he was sure she would have told him to let the FBI handle it.

He knew he should apologize for his attempted deception, but the image of Karen and Travis in the video made words choke in his throat. Hopefully, the FBI planned on having him meet the kidnappers at nine. Without Lori, they might kill his family. If she wasn't willing to endanger her life, he couldn't blame her. He was asking a lot from her.

"Masters, Almond, let's go," Rankin said from the end of the corridor.

He put a pleading expression on his face.

Lori grasped his arm and pulled him down the hall. "The FBI is the best hostage rescue organization in the world. They'll get them back."

Kyle wanted to believe her but couldn't help noticing Rankin hadn't made any assurances.

Chapter Thirty-Six

Sunday, June 20 3:04 p.m.

The ride to O'Hare went by in a blur. The video of Travis and Karen played over and over in his head as if on a continuous loop. His hands wouldn't stop shaking.

They parked at the general aviation terminal. "We have an FBI jet here that'll take us to Dulles," Rankin said as they hurried inside.

Out on the ramp, a Cessna Citation awaited them. One of its two engines began to whine as the start sequence commenced. Kyle, Lori, Rankin, and Taber boarded, and a pilot closed the door. Before they were in their seats, the other engine came to life.

Seeing the pilots expediting the preparations for flight eased some of the urgency Kyle felt to get to D.C. Until he held Travis and Karen, he doubted he would feel completely sane.

Rankin and Taber stayed on their phones while they taxied. After they climbed a couple of thousand feet in the air, Rankin pulled hers away from her ear, frowned, and dropped it in her jacket pocket.

She must have lost the signal.

"Your wife's phone was found on the side of a road." Rankin sat opposite Kyle in the club seating.

He closed his eyes, bracing himself for more bad news.

"San Antonio police received a report of a woman and young male being abducted at a restaurant near the airport. They put out an APB for the van seen racing from the parking lot. We're searching for any flight plans from San Antonio to D.C."

Knowing the FBI was working this case so aggressively gave Kyle hope, but they didn't know where Karen and Travis were or who had kidnapped them. What would happen to his family if the kidnappers found out the FBI was involved?

"What can you tell us about this man who approached your wife a couple of days ago?"

He shook his head. "Nothing. All she said was a man approached her and knew of her affair. He'd tell me about it unless she kept me away from the investigation." He hit the armrest with his fist. "Damn it! I let myself become too upset."

"Under the circumstances, I can't say I blame you."

Kyle stared out the window. Where were they? Were they all right? Why did he have to come to Chicago thinking he could uncover the truth behind the accident?

Several years ago, he had been a passenger on a flight that had an engine failure. He had felt helpless sitting in the cabin and not at the controls. He attributed this to being a typical pilot control freak. That same feeling overwhelmed him now. He felt trapped on this airplane for the next two hours, unable to do a thing to help get his wife and son back.

"It'll be all right," Lori said from the seat beside him.

Will it? Three people had already been murdered. What if Travis and Karen were next?

✈✈✈

In D.C., Jerry Krubsack, Chavette's superior, received a call from a hysterical Chavette.

"The FBI is arresting me! I've called a lawyer."

"Why are they arresting you?" Krubsack asked.

"Dey think I murdered Norman and I'm obstructing a federal investigation."

Fuck! Murdered. Krubsack's hands trembled. "Why... why do they think you killed Norman?"

"Dey think I have motive. I'm not going to go down for dis. I had nothing to do with his death and was following orders to cover up his contribution to de accident."

Krubsack searched the street in front of his house, expecting to see an FBI surveillance team. "Where are you? Can the FBI hear you?"

"I'm at de office. No, they can't hear me. I won't go down for dis alone."

Krubsack went into his study and closed the door. He glanced at the wall of shelves with family photos, plaques, and books. He admired the wainscoting on the walls and his cherry desk. Would he be able to see these things tomorrow? "Don't say anything more until you get a lawyer. This call might be recorded." He disconnected and collapsed into the chair behind his desk. Why had he gone along with trying to cover up this mess?

He called the Deputy Administrator, Stewart Halloren. His call went to voicemail. "Call me immediately!"

Krubsack paced, pulled at his hair, and tried to think of what he should do next.

Halloren called back fifteen minutes later.

Krubsack answered before the first ring had finished. "Ernest Norman has been found dead. The FBI just arrested Chavette for his murder and obstruction of a federal investigation."

Halloren was silent a moment, then in a steady voice, said, "Tell me everything he told you." When Krubsack finished, Halloren asked, "First off, how the hell did the FBI get involved?"

"Chavette said Almond and Masters were with them. They must have called them."

"Does the FBI have any doubt Norman wasn't murdered?"

Krubsack frowned. "Why would they arrest Chavette if he wasn't murdered?"

"The FBI might be grasping at straws. I need to find out who the agent in charge of the investigation is. We can't have someone looking to forward their career by building a case against the first person they can pin something on. Omega Airlines coming out this morning and trying to spread the blame for their accident has heightened the media coverage. This is just the thing an overzealous FBI agent looking for a corner office in the Hoover Building would latch onto."

Krubsack hoped Halloren was right.

"Meet me at the office. We have to contain this."

Krubsack couldn't understand how Halloren could remain so calm. The FBI could be knocking on their doors at any moment, and he acted as if he had been informed of a budget overrun. "How can we possibly contain this?"

"Whatever misdeeds the FAA is responsible for, Chavette will have to take the fall for them. If he had fired Norman years ago, we wouldn't have this problem."

Krubsack had no admiration for Chavette. At best, he was an average FSDO manager. Regardless, he worked for Krubsack, who felt the need to protect one of his own. "I doubt Chavette had anything to do with Norman's death. He's not confident enough to murder someone. What we have to worry about is what he'll tell the FBI. He talked to me yesterday after Masters and Almond left Norman's house, and after Omega's accident. Both times, I told him we'd handle it. When the FBI asks who I talked to after these calls, I'll have to tell them you. They'll want to talk to both of us."

"So, let them. They'll have no proof we've done anything wrong. Unless you had Norman killed?"

Krubsack recoiled as if slapped. "What? Hell no!"

"Then what do you have to worry about?" Halloren's voice became soothing. "When they question you, tell them the truth. We discussed the situation after Masters and Almond visited Norman. We were glad Norman had been located and were going to notify the NTSB first thing Monday morning that he was available. We were shocked to hear of his death this morning."

Krubsack wanted to believe it was that simple. He doubted the FBI could be so easily convinced.

"Relax, Jerry," Halloren continued. "Telling the truth is always for the best." Then, as if reading Krubsack's mind, he said, "If you have a lawyer present when the FBI questions you, it'll look like you're hiding something. They'll dig deeper. I have a lot of unanswered questions about how the CVR recording went missing—and Norman's involvement in the accident—I haven't asked, fearing I don't want to know the answers. I'm sure the FBI won't be as trusting."

Krubsack tried to read between the lines of that statement. Did Halloren think he was responsible for the CVR being stolen? Or did he think someone else was responsible? There was only one other person who could benefit from its disappearance: the Administrator. "The FBI might believe we had nothing to do with Norman's death. But the NTSB won't buy the story of Norman's disappearance after the accident. They'll crucify us in the media."

"Jerry, we have the NTSB Chairman on our side. I'll let you in on a little secret. He's aiming for the Administrator's position once she leaves it. A scandal will ruin his chances of holding that position. He's had our back until this morning, when Omega

Airlines made their announcement. I'll talk to him and swing him back around to our side. Don't worry about this."

"I'd feel better if I talked to an attorney and got their advice."

"Jerry. Trust me. Attorneys only complicate matters. I saw that when I was the aide to Senator Rusklin. Save yourself that misery. I know what's best here." Halloren used a good-ol'-boy tone.

Krubsack couldn't believe Halloren's nerve. "I'm talking to an attorney. Afterward, I'll decide whether to have one present when questioned by the FBI."

"If you do that," Halloren's soothing voice became firm again, "I'll have to re-examine the events that led up to this situation. When I'm questioned, I'll remember after Omega's accident, it was *you* who recommended we hide Norman and try to alleviate any role he might've had in its cause."

Krubsack's grip on the phone tightened. "You'll never prove that."

"Don't doubt me. I'm a Senate-confirmed Deputy Administrator. I have a handful of Senators on speed dial that'll call the FBI and tell them to ease off on their investigation of me. You're a bureaucratic manager trying to cover your ass. Do you have that kind of clout?"

"Jesus!"

"Jerry," Halloren's voice softened. "If we stick together, everything will work out. Chavette will have to take the fall for this."

Krubsack rested his head in his hand.

"I've got to call Senator Rusklin and use his contacts to find out who the lead agent in the investigation of Norman's death is. I'll brief the Administrator. Meet me at the office in an hour."

✈✈✈

Nathan Kaufman, CEO of Global Security, received a call from his FAA source. "I need you to pull back on the operation I asked for your help with."

"We can't," Kaufman said. "My operatives have already set the play in motion."

"We have to. The FBI is involved. It will be just a matter of time before they're questioning me. They've already arrested one of my inspectors."

Kaufman ground his teeth together. "This complicates things. Masters' wife and child are being held." The caller's lack of reaction to this news impressed him.

"That's unfortunate."

Kaufman wanted to laugh. That was an understatement. "You told me to silence Masters and Almond and get that recording, no matter how we did it. An unfortunate event prevented us from completing the mission last night. We had to revert to plan B."

"You have to let them go. Masters is working with the FBI." The caller's voice had pleading tone to it.

"We can't do that. Mrs. Masters has seen one of my men. If we let them go, she'll be questioned. I doubt they'll find my man, but I can't take that chance."

"Then let her son go."

"You're going soft. You should have known something like this would happen when you set things in motion. If I see any Feds getting close to me, your family will suffer the same fate as the Masters."

"You have nothing to worry about."

Chapter Thirty-Seven

Sunday, June 20 4:52 p.m.
On the flight to Dulles, Kyle watched Rankin cradle the airplane's satellite phone. He leaned forward, hoping for good news.

"Two business jets left from two different airports in the San Antonio area." She looked up from her notes. "One was a Gulfstream that flew out of New Braunfels Municipal. The other was a Cessna Citation that flew out of San Antonio International. The Gulfstream's destination is Ruston Regional, Louisiana. We've ruled out that one. The Citation's destination is Baltimore. We're landing there and meeting a hostage rescue team."

Although this was good news, the knot in Kyle's stomach did not ease. What would happen to Karen and Travis at Baltimore? Would there be a gunfight? Would either one of them be shot? If their abductors evaded the HRT team, would his family be killed afterward?

Visions of shootouts he had seen in movies played in his head. In his mind, the blood splattering from his loved ones was real, not Hollywood special effects. He hugged himself and breathed deeply.

Across the aisle, Lori gave him a sympathetic smile.

He laid his head against the sidewall of the Citation and closed his eyes, wishing he could go to sleep and wake up to find this was only a nightmare. Why did he have to go to Chicago? If he hadn't, he and Karen might have reconnected. If the affair was over, as she claimed, he never would have known about it, and they could once again become the couple they had been.

He wondered if they could mend their family. Could he forgive her for having an affair? Would she forgive him for the danger he had put her and their son in?

Trying to distance himself from these gloomy thoughts, he concentrated on one that had been bugging him. He turned to Lori. "How far a drive is it from Baltimore to Dulles?"

"An hour in good traffic. Why?"

"Why would they fly into Baltimore? Why not Dulles?"

"It would be hard to transfer your wife and son to cars," she said. "There would be too many people—and security guards and cameras."

"Baltimore would have the same problems. Why wouldn't they fly into an airport nearby? An uncontrolled airport." Uncontrolled airports had no control towers and did not have the security that controlled airports like Dulles and Baltimore had. "I don't know the area, but there must be several airports close to Dulles they could land a Citation on."

Lori raised her eyebrows. "Yeah, there are several that wouldn't have the problem with security."

"So the Citation is not the right airplane."

Rankin was engaged in a conversation on the sat phone.

Kyle waved to her. "You've got the wrong airplane!"

She frowned at him. "Hang on a sec," she said into the phone. "Why?"

She listened to his explanation and said, "Witnesses in San Antonio saw a woman, a young man, and two other men board the Citation."

Kyle slumped back. "Oh." After thinking about it for a moment, this explanation seemed too easy. What if they were a family?

Rankin went back to her phone call with a subtle shake of her head.

Obviously, this bugged Lori, too. Her eyes searched the cabin, not stopping on anything. "The time doesn't add up. They were kidnapped at three Central time, right?"

"Yeah."

"Let's say they were airborne at three-thirty. It's about a three-hour flight. That puts them in Baltimore at seven-thirty, taking into account for the time zone change. An hour drive puts them at Dulles at eight-thirty."

"Which leaves them very little leeway." He got Rankin's attention again and explained.

She sighed. "They're probably taking them to a secure location to hold them until they get the two of you. They don't need to be there at nine."

"What if I refuse to go with them until I have proof they're safe?" Kyle asked.

"They must feel you wouldn't risk their lives that way. No other jets have left San Antonio bound for the D.C. area. Your family could be held in San Antonio until you arrive in Dulles. Once they have you and the recording, they'll kill all of you."

The ease at which Rankin spoke the last part of her sentence made Kyle flinch. Then he realized that in the environment she worked, this was a normal conversation. This was no different than Kyle telling pilots he trained that they would have died from the emergency they botched in the simulator.

"We're searching San Antonio for where they might be held." She glared at him with a look that said, *We're the professionals here.*

Kyle held up his hands in a surrender gesture. "Okay, okay." He could understand her irritation. If she ever came to the cockpit and tried to tell him how to fly the airplane, he would be pissed, too.

A moment after Rankin returned to her call, Kyle shook her knee.

She let out a sigh. "Yes?"

"Have any other Gulfstreams taken off from Ruston Regional after the Gulfstream landed?"

"Why?"

"The Citation might be a ruse to get your team to Baltimore, and my family is in the Gulfstream. They land in Ruston, cancel their flight plan, taxi to the end of the runway and open up another one with a different identifier and take off bound for D.C."

She rolled her eyes. "We'll look into it." Her tone and expression suggested it wouldn't be a high priority.

Anger made him sit back and glare at her. How could she dismiss so easily what he said? Unless she knew Ruston Regional was a busy airport, using it as a fake destination would seem unlikely. There was one way to find out.

He walked to the cockpit. The two pilots turned when he knelt between their seats.

"Hi, Kyle Masters from Omega Airlines. Can I see the low altitude chart for Louisiana?"

The First Officer poked around beside his seat and handed the appropriate chart to Kyle.

Kyle unfolded it and scanned it, finding Ruston Regional in the north central part of the state. He studied the map, nodding when his hunch materialized to be correct, and handed the chart back. "Thanks."

He returned to his seat across from Rankin. "Ruston Regional is an uncontrolled airport in the middle of nowhere. Probably no one would see a Gulfstream land and then take off immediately afterward without stopping to drop anyone off."

Recognition dawned on her face. "Search for any flight plans from Ruston Regional to D.C.," she said into the phone. A few moments later, "Shit!" She looked at Kyle with an apology on her face. "A Gulfstream took off from there five minutes after the other one landed. Its destination is Manassas, Virginia. That's just south of Dulles."

To the person on the phone, she said, "Send HRT to Manassas. We're on our way there, too." To Taber, she said, "Tell the pilots we need to land at Manassas. Get an ETA." To the person on the phone, she said, "Standby for our ETA. What's the Gulfstream's?"

Taber returned from the cockpit. "ETA Manassas, twenty minutes." They all looked at their watches. It was five-fifteen.

"ETA Manassas, seventeen-thirty-five," Rankin said into the phone. She looked at Kyle. "The Gulfstream's ETA is eighteen-forty-five."

Sitting back, some of the tension in his stomach abated. It felt good to be doing something. If he was right, they would land in Manassas over an hour before the kidnappers. He hoped he hadn't led the FBI astray.

Chapter Thirty-Eight

Sunday, June 20 5:38 p.m.
After they landed in Manassas, Kyle turned on his phone. There were no new messages from Karen and Travis' kidnappers. But he had a new email from tscalone72. *This will be my last email. The person responsible for your troubles is at the top of the FAA.*

He showed this to Rankin. She punched in a number on her cell phone. "Find the FAA Administrator, Deputy Administrator, and the department heads under them, and take them to the Hoover Building." She explained why.

The Citation parked at the general aviation terminal, and several Suburbans and Chargers pulled up next to it. After they stepped out of the airplane, a man a couple of inches shorter than Kyle, but built like a tank, approached them. He wore black fatigues and a bullet-proof vest with HRT stenciled on it.

"Agent Rankin," the man said, "Gary Lampe, team leader. We arrived just a few minutes ago. I've got men securing the perimeter of the airport. What more can you tell us?"

"The Gulfstream is registered to Global Security. They do contract security for the DOD and other friendly nations. Their personnel are former military. They have a hangar here." She looked at one of the agents that'd met them. "Go to airport operations and find out which hangar is theirs. Get us an airport map." She looked back at Lampe. "It is unknown how many people are on the aircraft. We know of two hostages and possibly three assailants." She pulled out her phone and showed Lampe the video sent to Kyle.

While this was being discussed, Kyle asked Lori, "Is your family okay?"

"Yes. I just called. Both of my daughters are at their father's. There's a police car parked in the street."

Kyle attempted a look to express he was glad for her. He wouldn't want anyone to experience the gut-wrenching horror that threatened to paralyze his thoughts and actions. The terror Travis and Karen were experiencing was unconceivable.

When the agent returned with the airport map, they spread it out on the hood of a Suburban. The HRT team, Rankin, and Taber huddled around it. Kyle stood behind Rankin, looking over her shoulder.

Lampe put a finger over a hangar diagram next to the one someone had written an X over in ink with the words *Global Security* printed above it. "Schemonia, set up your sniper post on the roof of this hangar. Backers, I want you on this one."

The two snipers glanced in the direction of the hangars and hurried off.

"Jalomo, Sitzies, find concealment here and here." Lampe pointed to spots in front and to the sides of the hangar. "Percell, your team will approach the aircraft with a Suburban from the south side of the hangar and park here, blocking the aircraft. Rankin, you and your partner will follow them onto the ramp and park here." He pointed to a spot behind where Kyle estimated the Gulfstream would park in front of the hangar. "My team will drive onto the ramp from the north side of the hangar and block the aircraft's exit here."

Lampe looked at the other agents. "I want two of you in the helicopter circling the area. Any suggestions?"

Rankin looked toward Global Security's hangar. "We should send a couple of agents inside to assure there's no one that might aid their team members on the airplane."

"Good idea." Lampe pointed to four agents. "Clear that hangar and hold positions inside."

The four hustled to cars and sped off.

Rankin pulled Kyle and Lori to the side. "You two wait here. I'll send someone to pick you up later." She and Taber hurried to a Suburban and drove off.

Lori gestured to the terminal. "Do you want to go inside?"

Kyle shook his head. He leaned against the Citation and searched the western sky for the approaching Gulfstream.

Lori sat on the steps of the airplane.

Airplanes with propellers landed and taxied to the ramp. The noise from their props, normally a welcome sound to Kyle, blocked any chance of hearing an approaching jet. Kyle realized he sighed repeatedly when the pilots seemed to take longer than he thought necessary to shut down.

He glanced at his watch for the hundredth time. At six-thirty-five, the roar of an approaching jet made him push off the Citation and take a couple of steps toward the runway. Every nerve in his body hummed. When the landing jet came into view, his shoulders sagged. It was a Learjet. He leaned against the Citation again.

"It'll be here any minute now," Lori said.

No shit, Sherlock. He knew she was trying to be supportive and regretted he couldn't be grateful for her support. But many unpleasant scenarios ran through his head as to what might happen after the Gulfstream landed.

The noise of another approaching jet made him take his spot at the Citation's wingtip again.

The roar became progressively louder, and Kyle spotted the long-winged Gulfstream. It continued its approach until over the end of the runway. Then, its engines accelerated and the nose of the aircraft rose.

"No! It's going around!" Kyle staggered to the Citation's wing, leaning on it for support.

Lori arrived at his side, shielding her eyes against the setting sun. "Maybe it's another Gulfstream doing training," she yelled over the noise.

Kyle wanted to believe that. But when the Gulfstream leveled off several hundred feet off the ground and disappeared, typical of an aircraft attempting to evade detection, he knew Lori's suggestion was wrong. He kept looking in that direction, hoping to see it reappear. An approaching vehicle accelerated toward them.

A Suburban with Taber driving stopped beside them.

"Hop in," Taber said.

Kyle flung the door open and slid across the back seat.

Lori followed him and slammed the door as they sped off.

"What the hell happened?" Kyle yelled.

"They must've spotted us, or landing here was a bluff," Rankin said.

Or did you or your superiors warn them? Kyle wanted to discount Rankin or Taber as the person who might have. They seemed to act promptly at the news of Karen and Travis' abduction. But their superiors could have called Global Security and warned them directly.

Kyle studied Lori. She'd supposedly called home, but what if she called someone at the NTSB, who then called Global Security? Was she even on his side?

He shook his head at the absurdity of this thought. She had flown to Chicago and interviewed Norman. The interview she conducted was a legitimate questioning of someone trying to discover why an airline had an accident. She was genuinely concerned when he had been attacked, and when his family was kidnapped.

He didn't trust her superiors though.

"We have air traffic control tracking the airplane," Rankin said. "The helicopter is following it."

Kyle knew that was useless. The Gulfstream was capable of going 350 knots. The best the helicopter could fly was 140. "What other airports in the area might they go to?" he asked Lori.

"Dulles is just to the north. Quantico is to the southeast. Reagan is to the northeast of here."

"They can't go to Reagan." Since 9-11, Reagan had become off-limits except to scheduled airlines. Only recently had private jets been allowed to fly there if they had a prearranged reservation and submitted a list of everyone on board so Transportation Security Administration could compare their names against a terrorist watch list. A jet being watched by the FBI would not be allowed to land there.

"There's Upperville to the west of Dulles," Lori said. "Leesburg Executive is just to the north of Dulles."

"If you were those pilots, which would you use?"

"Leesburg. It has major roads going by and is not in the middle of nowhere. Vehicles that met the airplane could get lost among the traffic and buildings nearby."

"They're going to Leesburg!" Kyle said to Rankin.

"I've been listening. Their direction of flight suggests that, too." She reported this over the HRT frequency. "We'll dispatch police there."

"Ten-four," Lampe's voice radioed back.

Another voice broke over the radio. There was a distinctive whine and whap, whap of a helicopter in the background. "En route to Leesburg. ETA fifteen minutes."

Taber pulled out of the airport and raced down the road. They followed several other vehicles, all with police lights flashing.

Several more followed them. Would they be too late?

Chapter Thirty-Nine

Sunday, June 20 6:52 p.m.

FAA Administrator Connie Broten sat at her home computer in Chevy Chase, Maryland. She frowned when someone knocked on her front door. She was expecting a call, not a visit. Walking to the door, she hoped it wasn't a reporter who expected a comment on the announcement Omega Airlines had made that morning. Pausing with her hand on the door knob, she prepared herself to send the reporter on their way with a bland statement promising more in the morning.

Two men dressed in suits stood on her step.

"Administrator Broten?" one of them asked.

"Yes." She swallowed.

Both men looked around her, into the townhouse. Holding their credentials up, the one in front said, "I'm FBI special agent Austin. This is special agent Murphy. May we come in? We'd like to discuss the Omega Airlines accident in LaGuardia last week."

Taking a silent, deep breath, she willed her voice not to shake. "Why is the FBI involved?"

Austin raised his eyebrows. "May we come in, ma'am?"

With trepidation, Broten stepped back. "Yes, come in."

She escorted them to the living room just inside the door. Both agents looked around before sitting. Broten didn't get the feeling they were admiring the decor. "Can I get you anything to drink?"

"No, thank you, ma'am," they both said.

"Is there anyone else here?" Murphy asked.

Did they want to discuss confidential matters, or were they concerned for other reasons? "No. You still haven't told me why the FBI is involved in an aviation accident." She hoped the edge in her voice announced her displeasure. Not anyone could interrupt a

Senate-appointed bureau head on a Sunday evening. They needed to show her more reverence.

"As the former NTSB Chairman, you know the reason," Austin said.

She frowned, trying to read between lines of this agent's statement. "The Omega Airlines accident is considered criminal now?"

"Should it be, ma'am?" Murphy asked.

Broten would give them a couple more minutes of this demeaning behavior before throwing them out and calling their superior. "Why are you asking me?"

"What has been your involvement with the accident investigation up to this point?" Austin asked.

Her anger built at their tag-team interrogation method. "I've had no involvement. I've been getting briefings by the departments involved in the investigation. I assisted in the preparation of the statement released to the media this morning." She narrowed her eyes. "Why?"

"Who, specifically, has been briefing you?" Murphy asked.

"Gentlemen, I'd like an answer to my earlier question, or this discussion is over and I'll be talking to your superiors. Why is Omega's accident considered a criminal one?"

Austin didn't flinch or seem worried he was pissing off someone who could get him fired. "We're unable to disclose that, ma'am. Who have you been getting briefings from?"

This worried her. She decided to give them a tidbit and see what they did with it. "The Deputy Administrator, Stewart Halloren."

"Has he been actively involved in the investigation?" Austin asked.

Were they testing her? It was time to test them. She rose to her feet. "Gentlemen, I need to know the purpose of these questions, or we'll stop now and I'll talk to your superiors."

Both agents stood. "We can continue here, ma'am, or we can take you to the Hoover Building and continue there." Murphy gestured to the door.

Clasping her hands together, she hoped their trembling would stop. "Am I a suspect in this investigation?"

Neither man responded.

"Why would you consider me a suspect?"

"You have motive in covering up the cause of this accident," Austin said.

She swallowed, giving herself a moment to think. "Unless you explain yourself, I'll have to ask you to leave."

"As I said, we can continue this here or at our office." Murphy's face was firm. "It's your choice, ma'am."

"I'll not answer any more questions until you explain yourself and I talk to an attorney."

"You can have them meet you at our office." Austin moved to her side and gestured that he'd follow her.

Panic raced through her. "You've obviously been misinformed. Until you tell me why you think I'm a suspect, I'm going nowhere."

"You were appointed as the Administrator of the FAA just over a year ago," Austin said. "An accident with one of your inspectors on board the flight would make your agency look bad. If you covered up his involvement until the media lost interest, you wouldn't be put before congressional hearings and potentially lose your position. Who better than the former Chairman of the NTSB to influence the current one to withhold this from the media?"

Broten's legs trembled, making her afraid they would give out. She took a deep breath and attempted to appear stoic. "I had nothing to do with any of this. I can't believe you'd think someone at the FAA would, either."

"Ma'am, we'll read you your Miranda rights and continue at our office." Murphy pulled a card from his pocket.

She shook her raised hands as if attempting to hold them off. "Wait! Just wait! You're obviously misinformed."

"If you don't go with us peacefully, we'll handcuff you," Austin said.

Just in case reporters had discovered this visit and the reason behind it, she gave in. Anything to avoid being seen in the news in a derogatory position. She would put an end to this when they arrived at their office. Both of these agents would regret this.

Chapter Forty

Sunday, June 20 6:53 p.m.

Kyle had been told it was a forty-minute drive from Manassas to Leesburg Executive if driven at the speed limit. With the police lights and sirens and on, Taber pushed the Suburban to 100 miles per hour. The tires howled as they rounded corners, and he braked heavily to avoid hitting a slow-moving car that wouldn't pull over. Kyle wished he could make the car levitate above the trees and go to warp speed.

"Approaching Leesburg," a voice said over the two-way radio, helicopter noise in the background. "We're two miles from touchdown. The Gulfstream has parked and vehicles are approaching it."

"Whose vehicles?" Kyle asked. "Yours, or someone else?"

Rankin held up a hand silencing him.

"There are four vehicles," the agent in the helicopter reported. "An SUV, a van, and two sedans."

"ETA to landing?" Lampe asked over the radio.

"Three minutes."

Kyle clenched his fists, willing the helicopter to fly faster.

Less than three minutes later, the agent in the helicopter radioed, "The four vehicles are pulling away."

"Follow the van," Lampe ordered over the radio.

The agent in the helicopter began reporting the roads the van traveled on and in which direction. "Vehicles have split up. Van is heading north. The SUV, east. The two sedans, west."

The knot in Kyle's stomach tightened. What if they took Karen and Travis in separate vehicles?

"Suspect van is approaching the police roadblock," the agent in the helicopter reported.

A few minutes later the agent said, "Two male suspects have been taken from the van. There's no one else inside."

"Shit," Kyle yelled.

"Find and follow one of the other vehicles," Lampe ordered.

At the airport, they parked beside the Gulfstream. Its door was open and the cockpit and cabin dark. Police cars had surrounded it, but the officers stood around with their hands resting on their utility belts, conversing with each other.

Kyle opened his door before the Suburban was stopped and ran to the Gulfstream.

Two officers blocked him from running up the stairs.

"My family's in there!"

"The airplane is empty," one of the officers said.

Taber grabbed his arm. "We've got a forensic team on the way. We can't have you contaminating the scene. I understand your need to see they're not onboard, but they're not there, Mr. Masters. We're still looking for them. Go wait by the Suburban."

Staring up into the cabin windows, he wished one of their heads would bob up into view. They had to be in there. With a resigned sigh, he made his way back to the Suburban, the weight of what he had exposed Travis and Karen to making his head and shoulders droop with defeat.

Rankin was on the phone, getting updates from local police. Lori leaned against the Suburban. "I can only imagine how crazy I'd be if I were in your situation."

He knew she was trying to be supportive, yet she had no idea. Leaning against the Suburban, the uncertainty of where his family was made him push off and pace. Why wasn't something more being done?

Agents questioned people at the airport who had witnessed the Gulfstream park and offload. Five men had gotten off the airplane. Two carried a woman and a young man who were put in the trunk of one of the sedans and driven away.

Rankin ordered the police units to search the roads west of the airport for a grey Dodge Charger.

Taber donned paper booties and latex gloves and entered the Gulfstream. He exited it a few minutes later and came to where Kyle stood. "There's a good chance they were on this airplane. Two of the seat cushions are soaked in urine. Someone bound and not allowed to go to the bathroom, who is already nervous, wouldn't be able to hold it forever."

Opening a door to the Suburban, Kyle dropped into the backseat before his legs gave out. He rested his head in his hands and choked down the sob that wanted to explode out of him. How long did they have to sit scared and in misery before they gave in and wetted themselves? He smacked the front seat. Then again, and again, and would have continued doing so if Lori hadn't latched onto his arm.

"Kyle!"

Taber gave him a sympathetic grimace before walking off.

Rankin ended a phone call and walked over. Kyle tried to gauge what she had to say by her expression, but it remained neutral.

"Global Security just reported their Gulfstream stolen."

"Do you believe them?" Lori asked.

"No. They said they had flown it to New Braunfels earlier today for a meeting and left it unattended at the airport. When they returned, it was gone. Neither the pilots nor the passengers who flew there are available for questioning."

✈✈✈

The carpeted floor vibrated against Karen's back. Car exhaust filled the small space and burned her nose. Beside her, Travis' breathing was steady. Had he passed out? Blood caked her lashes, sticking them to the blindfold. The tape pulled on her lips as she swallowed despite a dry throat.

The forward movement stopped, and she her head hit the hard surface with a thunk.

She rubbed her head against what felt like Travis' chest, hoping to reassure him everything would be okay.

The only thing that kept her from crumbling into a sobbing, hysterical mess was her anger at Kyle. What had he gotten them into? Did he even know they had been kidnapped?

The doors opened, and the car rocked. The lock on the trunk clicked, and fresh air enveloped them. Her trembling became more pronounced. What were they going to do to them? Hands lifted her out of the car and set her on her bare feet. She had lost her sandals at some point. A hand on her arm steadied her, and the plastic binding around her ankles fell away.

"This way," a male voice said and shoved her forward.

Where was Travis? She struggled against the grasp on her arm. She screamed Travis' name under the tape.

"Your kid is right behind you. Stop struggling or I'll taser you."

Her first few steps were wobbly on the cool concrete—or what she thought was concrete. Walking made her aware of her wet capris that were chafing her thighs. She smelled conifer trees and heard the chirp of a bird.

Tripping over something, she would have fallen if the hand on her arm hadn't steadied her. She climbed steps and kicked something. Pain shot up her leg, making her want to hop.

The hand moved her to the side and forward.

Karen limped, smelling cooked food that made her mouth water.

"We're going down a set of stairs," the voice said.

Her lifted foot felt only air. The hand on her arm shoved her, and she thought she was falling into nothingness until her foot landed on rough wood. She would have continued forward, falling down the stairs, but the strong hand stopped her. She found the next step, and then the next, until she stumbled when her foot touched the cool concrete.

A male voice behind her said, "We're going down a set of stairs." Stumbling steps followed her. Travis? Relief flooded her; he was close. Where were they taking them?

The hand guided her forward several steps until she bumped into what she thought was a doorway. The smell of mildew made her nose wrinkle. Mixed with the mildew was the faint odor of urine.

Her hands were lifted behind her back and the handcuffs unlocked.

"Don't take that blindfold off until you hear the door close. If you do, your son will suffer. Do you understand?"

She nodded her head vigorously and rubbed her wrist. She sniffed, trying to sense Travis' scent. Or hear any noise he made. She swayed and reached out to steady herself.

A hand grabbed her and guided her sideways until her leg bumped into something soft.

"There's a bed behind you. Sit down."

Feeling behind her, she lowered herself onto a soft surface. The click of handcuffs being released made her cock her head, trying to sense what direction the sound came from. Someone sat beside her. Reaching out, she felt baggy cargo shorts and a thin leg. She wrapped her arms around Travis.

"We'll bring food and water."

Bang. Click. Footsteps climbed stairs. She lifted one corner of the blindfold, glanced around, and pulled it off. The harsh light made her squint.

She pulled the tape away from her mouth. "It's okay. You can take the blindfold off." She worked at freeing a corner of the tape over his mouth.

Travis threw his blindfold to the floor. He squinted and glanced around the room, his eyes full of fear. He shuddered.

She wrapped her arms around him, holding him tight. "It's okay. It's okay," she cooed as tears wetted her cheeks.

She wiped her face and worked at the tape over his mouth again.

Travis brushed her hands away and loosened a corner and pulled it off in a quick jerk. After wiggling his lips, he said, "Why's this happening to us?"

She could tell he was trying to act brave, but his question came out sounding small. "I don't know." She tried to hold him again, but he brushed her arms away. She ached to comfort him, yet the boy, becoming a man, didn't want that right now. "I think it has something to do with the accident Dad is investigating."

The room was the size of a small motel room. There were two single beds with folded blankets on each. In the corner were a toilet and sink.

Travis stood and turned in a circle. "Why would someone kidnap us because of an airline accident?"

Didn't Travis deserve the truth? "It has something to do with a recording Dad has about the accident."

"Do you suppose Dad knows we're kidnapped?"

"I don't know. I hope so." Even though Karen would strike Kyle if he stood in front of her, she hoped he was worried about their safety.

Travis investigated the room. "Why won't they tell us what's going on?"

"I don't know."

"How long will they keep us here?"

"Travis!" She put her head in her hands, ashamed of her outburst. She stood and hugged him. "I don't know, honey. I'm just as scared as you."

What had Kyle done?

Chapter Forty-One

Sunday, June 20 7:54 p.m.

The minute hand on Kyle's watch moved quicker than the FBI. Agents entered and exited the Gulfstream or stood at the foot of the stairs conversing as if they had all the time in the world. If they planned on him and Lori standing outside the baggage claim at Dulles on the chance the kidnappers held to the original plan, they needed to get going. Kyle approached Rankin when she ended a phone call.

She gestured to the Suburban with her hand. "Let's get you to Dulles."

Rankin, Taber, Lori, and Kyle piled into the Suburban and drove the fifteen miles to Dulles with the police lights on. They pulled into the parking lot behind a hotel, parking beside a car occupied by a man and woman, who got out when the Suburban pulled in.

"Lori Almond, Kyle Masters, these are special agents Laura Katic and Martin Sexton," Rankin said. Both were dressed in khakis and polo shirts. "Agent Sexton will be surveilling the baggage claim area to cover you while you meet the kidnappers. Agent Katic will pose as Ms. Almond."

Katic had Lori's petite build, but the top of her head came to just above Kyle's shoulder. Lori would have to stand on her toes to be that tall. Katic's hair was longer and blonder than Lori's short, sandy brown hair, and she was at least ten years younger.

"No way," Kyle said. "I'll go alone and tell them I couldn't get Lori to come."

Lori chewed on her lower lip. Kyle couldn't tell if she felt relieved she wouldn't have to risk her life or if she debated if she should volunteer to go along.

"You have no choice in the matter, Mr. Masters," Rankin said. "You're only involved in this because the kidnappers saw you last night. We're hoping they don't know what Ms. Almond looks like."

"*Hoping*. You'll risk my family's lives on an assumption."

Lori rested a hand on his shoulder. "Kyle, the FBI knows what they're doing."

"They probably won't show," Rankin said. "Since they didn't land in Manassas and diverted instead to Leesburg at the last minute, they must know we're involved."

Kyle agreed with Rankin's assessment, which most likely meant bad things for Karen and Travis.

While Rankin laid out the plan for the meeting, Katic studied Lori. When Lori ran a hand through her hair, the agent did too. When Lori rested a hand on her hip, Katic mirrored the move. Lori noticed and Kyle thought she'd tell her to cut it out, but instead she reached into her bag and brought out her NTSB cap and handed it to Katic.

The agent put it on. "Thanks."

Taber handed Kyle an earpiece to communicate through.

Kyle backed up a step and held up his trembling hands. "What if they find that? They'll know you're following us."

"Take the chance, Masters," Taber said. "We might save your family because we've gained valuable information we wouldn't have without it. We'll have two helicopters overhead and numerous cars ready to follow whoever picks you up," Taber said.

Lori gave him a shake. "Kyle, these protests are coming from emotion, not rational thought. Just like the emergencies you've trained for; the FBI procedures have been thought out."

Her words made him see the logic behind their actions and the absurdity of his thoughts. After giving himself a mental slap, he paid attention, taking in what he was supposed to do and what to expect.

Dulles airport police met them at the airport perimeter and took Kyle and Katic to Omega's gates. They boarded the people mover to the terminal as if they had just flown in on the Omega flight from Chicago. Kyle bounced his knee up and down.

Katic leaned up close to him. "Relax. Act normal."

He glared at her. "Have you ever met kidnappers that took your family?"

She cast her eyes down. "No."

"Then you don't know what I'm going through. I probably am acting normally."

On the short ride, Kyle noticed Katic looking everyone over. Two guys in their early thirties glanced at them, pinging his attention. Neither seemed interested in the others around them, or where they were in their progress to the terminal. Nor did they speak or text into cell phones. Kyle hoped they were admiring Katic's good looks and were not the kidnappers.

None of the young women, who were dressed like college students going on vacation, seemed interested in them. The middle-aged ones were dressed for traveling on business and had the anxious look of wanting to get home or to their hotel. No one seem interested in Kyle.

He discounted the elderly. Although Kyle thought none were part of the kidnap team, he was out of his element. He realized anyone could be responsible for kidnapping his family. He wouldn't have suspected Katic was an FBI agent.

At the terminal, they made their way to baggage claim. It had been a while since he had been to Dulles, so he followed the signs like the passengers. Along the way, they had to step out of the path of an electric cart carrying six passengers and their luggage, which spiked his anxiety. Those passengers didn't have a more urgent need to get where they were going than Kyle.

Katic reported their progress; it echoed in Kyle's earpiece. When they stopped at the curb outside, agents reported them in sight.

"Now what?" Kyle asked.

"We wait. Keep your eyes open."

It was difficult to stand still. Each time a car approached with two men in it, he thought it might be the kidnappers and readied himself to either get in with them or fight them. When each one stopped a distance away and picked up someone waiting nearby, relief flooded him, followed by frustration. He turned his wrist. 8:55 PM.

An SUV with two guys inside stopped in front of them. Kyle scanned the backseat and cargo area for any sign of Travis or Karen. There wasn't one. He locked his eyes on the two men. Both appeared cordial and not built like the two outside his room the night before.

The passenger window rolled down. "Hey, how was your flight?"

The dryness of Kyle's mouth and the worry he might say the wrong thing kept him from responding. His heart pounded.

A woman's voice behind him said, "Smooth, thank God. I hate flying."

An elderly woman towing a suitcase stepped around Kyle and Katic. The SUV passenger stepped out and helped her load it in the cargo compartment.

Kyle took a deep breath and paced. 8:59.

At 9:00, he scanned the curbed cars. No sign of Karen or Travis. An avalanche crashed down on hope and broke it into a thousand pieces—unless they were late. He resumed pacing. If the tension that made him jittery and leery was this agonizing, what was it like for Travis and Karen?

When they were freed, Kyle would forgive Karen and do anything to be the couple they had been. He mentally vowed to be a better father to Travis.

At 9:15, Kyle asked, "Where are they?"

"They could be watching us to see how patient we are." Katic continued scanning the incoming cars and the people around them.

At 9:28, he spit out a fingernail he had chewed off. "This is killing me."

"Try to calm down."

At 9:31, Katic's voice in his ear brought him to life. "Subject approaching from the west."

Kyle spun, searching the crowd, his heart pounding. Where? Where? He didn't see Karen or Travis.

A man in his twenties, wearing baggy jeans and a loose tee with a large backpack slung over one shoulder, walked up to them. "A dude told me to give this to you." He handed Kyle a cell phone.

"Who gave this to you?" Kyle's voice trembled. He scanned the terminal in the direction of the young man's approach.

"Just some dude back there." The young man gestured over his shoulder. He adjusted the backpack and turned to walk away.

Kyle seized his arm. "Wait. Where is he? What did he look like?"

"Hey, get your fucking hand off me!" The young man pulled against Kyle's grasp.

"My family's lives are at stake! Who gave this to you?"

"Just some dude." He continued trying to free himself.

In Kyle's ear, he heard Rankin's voice. "Let him go, Masters. Other agents will detain him."

The cell phone rang.

Kyle looked at Katic. She gave a nod, stood on her toes, and put her head close to his. Kyle pushed the green call button and put the phone to his ear, holding it so they both could hear. "Hello."

"You were told to not tell anyone," a man's voice said. "You just killed your wife and kid."

"No! Wait. Fuck!"

His hand trembled as he hit the send button. The phone rang five times, and then an automated voice said, "The voice mail box for this number has not been set up."

Kyle fell to his knees. "No!" He put his head in his hands and squeezed. "No-please-no!" Tears streamed down his cheeks. "No. God, please no."

Chapter Forty-Two

Sunday, June 20 10:28 p.m.

Kyle sat off to the side in the airport security office with his head against the wall, his eyes closed, clinging to his memories. Travis' laughing, sweat-streaked smile as they shot hoops in the driveway. Or his furrowed brow and intent eyes as he concentrated on making a shot. Alternating between these was Karen, beaming with a smile when they hiked in Yellowstone Park a year ago. Or her impassioned expressions two nights ago when they made love. Would they be pale and lifeless, lying on a morgue gurney when he saw them again?

Agents had detained the young man who handed Kyle the phone and were interviewing him.

"Can I get you some water or coffee?" Lori asked.

She sat beside Kyle, eyes red-rimmed, mouth pursed. He guessed she hurt for him. He shook his head. "Thanks."

"They might not be dead. Maybe they said that just to make you worry or make the FBI back off."

A thousand rebuttals came to mind, all of them harsh, that he didn't say. She was trying to be supportive.

"No, I never saw him before," the young man said from across the room. His voice filled with impatience. "I'd just gotten off my flight from Paris, and was, like, waiting for my backpack to come by on the carousel. Then the dude beside me handed me the phone, a fifty-dollar bill, and pointed out him—" He pointed at Kyle, "and told me to give him the phone."

Rankin stood off to the side, talking on her phone. She disconnected and sat beside Kyle. "We have agents reviewing the security footage. The guy that gave him the phone," she said, gesturing with her head to the young man, "went out a side door, and they can't find him on any other cameras. We set up roadblocks exiting the airport, but so far no one matching our suspect's description has been found."

Kyle closed his eyes in an attempt to shut out more bad news.

"I could use your help downtown at the Hoover Building," Rankin said.

A day ago, Kyle would have done anything to help. Now, he wondered if there was any point in doing anything. Finding the people who killed his family wouldn't bring them back.

"We've rounded up the FAA Administrator and top department heads," Rankin said. "So far, no one has told us anything that will lead us to your wife and son's abductors. If I let them see a distraught father and husband, it might soften them up."

What else was there to do? Go home and wander around an empty house? "Sure."

They drove to the D.C. FBI headquarters on Pennsylvania Avenue. On the way, Rankin's phone rang.

Kyle wondered what size battery she had in her phone; Karen would love to have a phone that lasted as long as Rankin's. Would have. She would have loved it. He rested his head against the window. He was already talking about her in the past tense like she would never use a phone again. So many things in his life would change if his family was dead. He didn't know if he could handle the guilt and pain. How would he live with himself?

Rankin ended the call. "We've been unable to locate the Deputy Administrator, a Stewart Halloren. Either of you know him?"

Kyle and Lori shook their heads.

They parked and took an elevator to a floor with a viewing room. On the other side of the one-way mirror two men, who Kyle assumed were agents, questioned a woman in her mid-fifties and a middle-aged man beside her.

"That's Connie Broten," Lori said. "She's the Administrator of the FAA."

Remembering the email had Kyle received when they had landed in Manassas, he wanted to rush into the room, choke the woman, and yell, *what have you done with my family?* He opened and closed his fists, breathing deeply.

"How well do you know her?" Rankin asked Lori.

"When I started at the NTSB, we worked a couple of investigations together. We never met socially, but I felt she was someone I could trust. I find it hard to believe she would have anything to do with this. She talked affectionately about her children and husband."

"She's been evasive answering our questions," Rankin said.

"She had a tendency to be confrontational to men who challenged her." Lori looked at Kyle. "That might be where I got that tendency."

If Kyle hadn't been seething, he would have made light of Lori's acknowledging her temper.

"I'd like both of you to go in there with me. A woman she knows, and the devastated face of a father and husband might open her up. Mr. Masters, can you stay cool in there?"

Kyle unclenched his fists and took a deep breath. "Yes."

Rankin opened the door to the interview room. "Take a break."

The two agents left.

Rankin closed the door behind them. "I'm Special Agent Sam Rankin. I believe you know Lori Almond."

Lori shook hands with Broten. They exchanged a brief smile.

Kyle narrowed his eyes at Lori. That woman might have had Travis and Karen killed, and Lori greeted her like an acquaintance. He sucked in a deep breath, knowing he had to get himself under control. No doubt Lori hoped being cordial to an old colleague would put her at ease.

"This is Kyle Masters from Omega Airlines," Lori said.

"I'm very sorry for the loss of your two pilots," Broten said, holding out her hand to Kyle.

The loss of our two pilots! What about my wife and son? Kyle stared at her for a long moment and shook her hand, fighting the desire to rip it from her arm and beat her with it. "Thank you."

"I'm sorry for any inconvenience you've experience this evening," Rankin said. "I'll get to why we asked you here tonight in a moment. First, I'll have Ms. Almond and Mr. Masters bring you up to date on the accident investigation."

Lori told her about the takeoff, the tire disintegrating, and the conversation on the CVR.

Broten frowned. "Our inspector told them to abort?"

Judging from her expression and tone of voice, Kyle thought she either hadn't heard this until now—or was a damn good actor.

238

"Yes. Inspector Norman had previously tried to violate this Captain. Judging by the atmosphere in the cockpit on the CVR, it's apparent Norman tried to intimidate the crew."

Broten shook her head. "I had no idea."

"Mr. Norman had six reprimands in the eight years he was at the FAA. It appears he remained employed to pass his office manager's recurrent training, a Pierre Chavette. It seems Mr. Chavette had some difficulty doing so with other inspectors."

Broten's eyes went wide.

Again, Kyle thought this was the first time she had heard this. Yet, his emotions wanted to believe otherwise. He was also losing patience with this rehashing of the accident details. To resist the urge to throw the table in the air and demand to know where his family was, he focused on another image of Travis.

"Mr. Chavette claimed Norman went on vacation after the accident and couldn't be located." Lori said.

Broten rested her head in her hands. "Oh, good God."

"The night after the CVR recording was heard," Rankin broke in, "the NTSB headquarters was burglarized and the investigator in charge of the CVR lab murdered. Ms. Almond and Mr. Masters located and interviewed Inspector Norman two nights ago recording the interview. That evening, an attempt was made on Mr. Masters' life. Since then, his wife and child have been kidnapped, and he's been instructed to turn over the recording of Mr. Norman's interview or they'll die."

Broten glanced at Kyle. Her face paled.

"Mr. Masters received emails with Mr. Norman's and Mr. Chavette's FAA employment records," Rankin said. "The last email told him the person responsible for his family's abduction was at the top of the FAA."

Recognition came to Broten's face. "I had nothing to do with this." She glanced at everyone as if this would convince them of this fact. "This is the first time I've heard most of this. Who sent you those emails?"

"We're looking into that," Rankin said.

"Someone is setting me up."

"I need a few moments with my client," Broten's lawyer said.

Broten held up a hand to him. "Lori, you know me. You know I'm not capable of doing any of this."

"You have motive," Rankin said. "An accident with one of your inspectors would make you, and your agency, look bad. The Senate might re-think your confirmation. Your replacement at the NTSB has told his investigators not to reveal your inspector's involvement in the accident. There's no one in a better position to make this request than you."

"I can't believe Michael Neal would do such a thing," Broten said. "That goes against the NTSB's charter."

"I was ordered to stop antagonizing the FAA and eventually taken off the investigation by the Chairman," Lori said.

"I wouldn't have told Neal to pressure you this way. It would eventually come out, and we'd look guilty for covering it up."

Although Kyle found this conversation very illuminating, his patience was wearing thin.

"Then why would he assist in the cover-up?" Rankin asked.

Broten's eyes roamed the room. "There were those who thought he wasn't the appropriate person to chair the NTSB."

"Why not?" Rankin asked.

"He was the investigator in charge of a train accident. Some thought the accident happened because of a malfunctioning signaling device that didn't tell the train to stop. Neal discovered the conductor was texting on his phone at the time of the accident, or so he claimed. Attorneys for those who died or were injured thought Neal was paid off by the company that manufactured the signaling device. But it was never proven."

Kyle leaned forward. Lori's hand on his arm and the subtle shake of her head stopped him from lashing out with his questions.

Rankin frowned. "Is it possible someone within your agency threatened to bring this up again if the NTSB didn't withhold the FAA's involvement in the accident?"

"I suppose anything is possible."

Rankin cocked an eyebrow. "Who do you suspect would do this?"

Broten shook her head. "Friday, one of my department heads voiced some concerns about the Deputy Administrator, Stewart Halloren. Halloren is power hungry with unlimited ambition. But I can't believe he'd do what you're suggesting."

Kyle had enough. "Why not?"

Broten leaned back as far as her chair allowed, as if to escape from his glare. "He's the former chief of staff for Senator Rusklin. His family is politically connected."

Rankin slammed her hand on the table. "Mr. Halloren can't be located. He's not home. Security tapes at the FAA headquarters show him arriving there, then leaving in a hurry just as our agents showed up. We suspect a security guard tipped him off to our arrival. Does this sound like someone who has nothing to hide?"

"We need to talk to Philip Worden. He's the department head who reported his suspicions of Stewart's behavior to me."

Rankin stood. "He's next door. Let's go."

When they entered the adjacent interview room, they broke up the questioning of a gray-haired man who looked them over, staring the longest at Kyle.

"Phil," Broten said, "why did you suspect Stewart Halloren of the allegations you brought up with me Friday?"

When Worden turned to his attorney, Kyle's patience ran out. "My wife's and son's lives are at stake."

"Jesus!" Worden ran a hand through his thinning hair. "The day after the CVR was stolen, I met with Halloren."

Rankin gripped Kyle's shoulder and pulled him away from the table.

"I told him we'd have to notify the FBI if it was discovered someone at the FAA had arranged the theft. He warned me someone with the ability to steal a recording from the NTSB would be a dangerous person to threaten. This gave me the impression Halloren didn't want the FBI involved in the accident investigation and might go to great lengths to prevent that. After that, I noticed the manager of flight standards, Jerry Krubsack, going around me and meeting with Halloren privately."

This was the confirmation of what Kyle had suspected all along. Someone in the FAA had tried to cover up Norman's involvement in the accident. His suspicions hadn't been from watching too much TV as Lori joked.

"Do either of you know how Mr. Halloren would be acquainted with a Nathan Kaufman?" Rankin looked at Worden and then Broten.

Both shook their heads.

"Has the FAA ever hired Global Security?" Rankin asked.

The two frowned before shaking their heads again.

"I have some phone calls to make." Rankin turned to leave. "Mr. Masters, would you join me, please?"

Kyle glared at Worden. "You knew this man was guilty of these crimes and you did *nothing*? My son and wife may be dead because of your silence!"

Rankin grabbed his arm and shoved him toward the door. "Let's go."

"I'm sorry. I tried to help," Worden pleaded, as Kyle was forced from the room.

Chapter Forty-Three

Sunday, June 20 10:44 p.m.

Stewart Halloren's mind traveled in a thousand directions, trying to figure out how to get out of the mess he was in. What had been a simple attempt to cover up an FAA inspector's stupidity had turned into a government conspiracy that might ruin his chances of more powerful positions, if not land him in jail.

He narrowly escaped the FBI at the office, and no doubt they would be parked in front of his house, waiting for him. It was time to leave the country for a while, until his powerful friends could help him out. He would arrange for his family to meet him once he was free of extradition.

Before he left, he had one more task he needed to verify. He parked in a dark corner of Tyson's Corner mall, turned his phone on, and made a call.

"Yes?" Kaufmann said.

"Is what we discussed completed?"

"We need to talk about that."

Had the FBI picked up Kaufman? "Why?"

"I need you to realize the pile of shit you've mired me in."

Halloren tried to read between the lines. "You think I don't know that already? If it'll make you feel better, talk away."

"Not over the phone."

If the FBI had Kaufman, this could be a trap to lure him into their custody. Without Kaufman, all the evidence they had were conversations he had with others. It was hearsay that couldn't prove him guilty of anything. But if Kaufman was cutting a deal, he could turn over records of the wire transfers from the FAA accounts Halloren controlled.

Halloren rubbed his forehead. There had to be a way out of this. With anyone else, he would simply plant evidence that would prove them guilty of the crimes committed. Kaufman wouldn't be so easy to manipulate. He left the military when he saw the money he could make from the war on terrorism. He quickly made connections with many of the powerful figures within the D.C. Beltway, who now owed him favors.

"Why not over the phone?" Halloren put on an air of impatience. "I'm busy covering up your botched retrieval of the recording in Chicago last night."

Kaufman chuckled. "That's so like you civilian types to blame mission complications on someone else. You'll meet me, or I'll leave Masters' dead wife and kid on your doorstep."

Halloren gasped, regretting showing this weakness.

"That'd be quite a sight for your wife and children," Kaufman said. "How would you explain that to the FBI?"

Were the hostages already dead? He knew better than to ask. It was time to turn the tables. "I'll tell them a rogue security expert the FAA hired framed me for something he did on the side. A couple of phone calls to the appropriate people, and the FBI will back off investigating me. You, on the other hand, won't be working in this country again."

"So you think your contacts are more powerful than mine?" Kaufman's voice took on an amusing lilt. "Is that the game you want to play, Mr. Deputy Administrator?"

Being unable to intimidate the former Colonel made Halloren clench his teeth. Kaufman must know Halloren stood on thin ice. He decided to try a softer approach. "How's talking about what's transpired going to improve the situation? Will getting together and having a few beers make this mess any better?"

"You'll meet me, Mr. Deputy Administrator, or I'll email our phone conversations to the FBI, along with the wire transfer records, before I disappear overseas. My career has allowed me to make friends all over the world who will shelter me in exchange for my services. Can you say the same?"

Halloren rested his head against the steering wheel of his Mercedes. "When and where?"

"In forty-five minutes. Get on the Custis Memorial Parkway and head west. Get off on Vaden and go south. You'll end up at a construction site."

"No. No construction sites. Let's make this someplace more public."

"I'm not going to let you choose the place so you can lead the FBI there. Be there in thirty minutes or I hit send on my computer. Oh, and Mr. Deputy Administrator, if I catch a whiff of a fed or any kind of ambush, remember what happened to the Masters. I'd hate to see the same thing happen to your family."

Halloren threw the phone down. How did he get in this mess? The only glimmer of hope was Kaufman's warning about the FBI. He doubted Kaufman would say that if he was already in their custody.

✈✈✈

Halloren drove to the edge of the construction site, stopping by a sign announcing it would eventually be an office complex. In the center of the bare dirt lot, a black civilian Hummer flashed its lights. Halloren's heart thumped as he eased toward the vehicle over the uneven ground. There didn't appear to be any other vehicles or people hiding behind the construction equipment.

Nearing the Hummer, he spotted a Dodge Charger parked behind it. Just as he considered speeding away the Hummer's driver's side door opened, lighting the interior. Kaufman, the only occupant, exited and shut the door.

Halloren eased up beside him and buzzed his window down. "Explain why I've had to go out of my way to meet you here?"

Two men exited the Charger.

Kaufman shoved a pistol against Halloren's head. "Get out."

Halloren's heart pounded so hard, he thought it might give out. If he stomped on the gas could he pull away before Kaufman shot him?

The two men from the Charger aimed their pistols at him preventing any escape without driving through a cascade of bullets.

"Let's go." Kaufman used a voice no doubt practiced from intimidating enemy combatants.

"What's the meaning of this? Have you forgotten who you're dealing with?"

Kaufman smirked and pulled the door open.

Halloren shoved the car in park and stepped out.

The two men approached and stood on either side of him. One grabbed his sport coat, peeling it over his shoulders and pinning his arms behind his back.

Kaufman ripped Halloren's shirt open, exposing his bare chest.

"What the fuck are you doing?" Halloren struggled to free his arms, but the two beside him gripped his wrists like a vise.

Kaufman unbuckled Halloren's belt, unfastened his pants, and let them drop to his ankles.

"You fuckers! Get your hands off me. You're through in this country!" Halloren panted from his efforts to free himself.

"Don't piss on me, Stewie." Kaufman shoved Halloren's boxers over his hips. "Good. You're not wearing a wire."

"Of course I'm not fucking wearing a wire!" The guy on his left spun him so he faced his car, making him trip over his pants.

Hands as strong as clamps gripped his arms preventing him from falling over. His coat and shirt were yanked from him and thrown to the ground. Something was wrapped around his wrists and ankles and pulled tight.

Blood pounded in Halloren's ears. "Help!"

A dry rag was shoved into his mouth when he opened it to yell again. Duct tape was wrapped around his head, holding it in place.

While they carried him to the back of the Charger, he squirmed, but the two men held fast.

The trunk clicked and rose. They dropped him in, knocking the wind out of him. The plastic-sheet-lined trunk crinkled as he struggled to breathe. When the lid slammed shut, it ruffled his hair.

The car bounced over the uneven ground as they drove from the lot. His head alternated banging on the trunk lid and floor. Pure terror made him piss, creating a puddle he had to lay in. Where were they taking him? Didn't they know who they were dealing with?

The car stopped after what seemed like hours but might have been less than one. The trunk lid opened, with Kaufman standing behind the car. The Hummer was parked beside the Charger with its lights illuminating the gravel, tree-lined road. There were no other lights.

Halloren tried to slow his breathing through his nose. Dread knotted his stomach, making him want to vomit. He would choke on his bile if he did.

The two men lifted him out of the trunk and stood him up. Halloren swayed from his bound ankles, but one of the two steadied him before stepping away. The night air cooled the sweat on his naked body.

"I'm very disappointed in you, Stewart." Kaufman poked him in the chest with the pistol. "I did the favors you asked of me, and you bring me a shitload of trouble." He leaned in close. "Do you realize the difficulties my men and I face because of you?"

One of the two abductors unwound the tape without any regard for how much it pulled his hair or skin.

Halloren spit out the rag and swallowed. "I tried to contain the situation." His voice came out hoarse from his dry throat and mouth. "If you'd gotten that recording and killed Masters and Almond, we wouldn't be in this situation."

"You should've warned us Masters wouldn't be easy to take down."

Sweat ran down Halloren's face and into his eyes. He attempted to rub his brow with his shoulder, causing him to lose his balance and fall on his side. The gravel poked into his skin. He clenched his teeth. "I had no idea."

"You should have realized how resourceful Masters and Almond would be." Kaufman pointed with the pistol for emphasis. "How could you be so stupid to leave Norman at his home? Why didn't you put out an ad telling the world where he was?"

"I didn't think he'd be found."

Kaufman shook his head. "You didn't think? How did you become Deputy Administrator?" Kaufman kicked gravel into his face.

He blinked, trying to wash the grit from his eyes.

"The FBI has impounded my jet. They are in the process of running the fingerprints of my pilots and men. It won't be long before they are knocking on all our doors because *you* didn't think, Mr. Deputy Administrator." Kaufman's voice rose.

"You and your men should leave the country." Halloren talked fast, hoping to make them see he was in control of the situation. "I'll talk to Senator Rusklin and get him to use his influence to have the charges against you dropped. You can return and resume business afterward."

"How long before *you* and Senator Rusklin get our names cleared?"

"I don't know. I'll call him as soon as we're done with our discussion."

"Discussion?" Kaufman's voice became a roar. "Are we having a discussion? You obviously don't understand. We're not discussing anything. I'm making you understand the situation you've created. This is a lesson!"

A flicker of hope raced through Halloren. He just might be alive after this. "Okay! Okay."

"When you called and asked me to break into the NTSB and steal a recording, did I tell you I didn't know if I could?"

"No."

"Damn right I didn't. I made it happen. So why, when I ask how long it will take you to get our names cleared, would you tell me, 'I don't know.'" When Kaufman said these last three words, he made his voice high pitched, as if imitating a woman.

"This is different. We can't just call the FBI and tell them to drop the charges against you. We'll have to find something that will help them, or some secret they don't want revealed. Then we'll make a trade."

"Meanwhile, my men and I are living in some shit hole, waiting for you to make your trade. Do you see my frustration here?"

"Yes. I promise." He locked his eyes on Kaufman's, hoping he'd see how serious he was. "I'll do everything I can to get you cleared. I'll call in every favor owed to me."

"Well, tell me this. How are you going to clear us when you're in jail?"

"They have no proof I've done anything wrong. We'll stick to the plan: the FAA hired you for consulting on security matters."

"The FAA Administrator and other department heads are at the FBI right now, trying to keep themselves out of prison. Don't you think they're remembering conversations they had with you that would indicate you're behind the events this past week?"

Spittle from Kaufman's outburst landed on Halloren's face. "That still doesn't prove I had anything to do with this."

"When everyone else who's trying to save their ass points the FBI in your direction, don't you think they'll dig deep into your life? They'll review your calls. They'll find everywhere you've been the last year and talk to the people you've had conversations with. They'll hear about us meeting at the party for Senator Rusklin."

Halloren realized this but hoped his powerful connections would make the FBI back off. If it came to it, he would sell Kaufman out. Obviously, Kaufman knew this. "I'll leave the country. They'll never find me."

Crossing his arms, Kaufman asked, "How will you do that, Mr. Deputy Administrator? Order up an FAA jet to fly you to some tropical island?"

Kaufman's demeaning attitude ignited the anger he'd been holding back. "Don't worry about it. I'll do it." Halloren ignored the gravel grinding into his hip and sat up. He hoped it would show them he wasn't the wimp they considered him to be.

Kaufman took a deep breath, paused, as if considering what Halloren said. "All right. No one knows you hired me?"

He locked his eyes on Kaufman. "No."

"And there's no record of the transactions to my Swiss account?"

"No." Halloren put emphasis behind this word.

Kaufman took a couple of steps back. "Good."

The tension making Halloren shake ebbed away. He was going to live.

Kaufman aimed a pistol at him.

He ducked, not believing what he saw. "Wait! They won't know about our arrangement." A sharp pain spread across the top of his head. Then blackness took over.

Chapter Forty-Four

Sunday, June 20 11:16 p.m.

Kyle broke from Rankin's grasp that dug into his bicep as they left the interview room. He didn't need to be escorted like a disobedient child to the principal's office.

He worked at tamping down the tension that threatened to make him strike out at something. He didn't understand how Worden could do nothing about his suspicions the Deputy Administrator was responsible for the actions that resulted in Karen and Travis being kidnapped. Kyle suspected his face was crimson.

To calm himself, he brought up the memory of teaching Travis to drive on a back-country road and the smile that was plastered on his son's face.

Rankin urged Lori and him into a break room.

"Don't leave this room unless it's to go to the bathroom across the hall." Rankin pointed to the agent that had followed them. "He's under orders to arrest you if you do."

"You should be arresting those two back there." Kyle pointed in the direction of the interview rooms.

"Mr. Masters, we're building a case against them. Do you want them to get away with their crimes because you couldn't control your temper?"

"If you were interrogating them instead of reprimanding me, we might find my family." Rankin did not wither from his defiant stare.

"Calm him down if that's possible," Rankin said to Lori before closing the door.

He wondered if his comment hit home and she left to do her job, or she tired of his anger. Although he didn't like to be rude or condescending, it was hard to remain calm.

Lori watched Kyle pace. After a few moments, she stepped over to the coffee pot. "Do you want a cup?"

He plopped down in a chair at a table. "No."

Filling a Styrofoam cup, she set it in front of him.

If anyone else had done so, he'd swipe it away.

She rested a hand on his shoulder. "You've got to get a hold of yourself. It'll be all right." Her tone of voice, no doubt was to soothe him.

Yet, he couldn't help himself from standing and glowering down at her. "How the hell do you know?"

"I'm only trying to help."

"Well, then, quit trying to fill me with false hope." Saying this, the holds on his emotions began to loosen. Deep down, whether he liked it or not, he was preparing himself to hear they had been found dead.

"You've got to stay positive. Think the best. The FBI is really good at what they do."

"Well, Dr. Phil, have you noticed the FBI hasn't given me the same pep talk?"

She threw up her hands, her eyes filled with anger. "You know, Kyle, I'm trying to be a friend here, but you're making it very hard to be one. If you want to yell at someone, go find someone else." She turned away.

Her comment shattered his anger. In his mind, a dark pit formed, one he wanted to crawl into and never come out of. He thought he cried himself out at Dulles, but his vision blurred from his tears. Losing control of himself in front of her after he had been so vile would embarrass him further.

Hurrying across the hall to the men's room, he shoved the door open, slamming it against the wall. He sat on a toilet in a stall, rested his head in his hands, and let go.

He didn't want to believe they were dead, but denial was a stage of grief. He didn't look forward to when the acceptance stage replaced it, because he would have seen their lifeless bodies. Hope was the only thing keeping him from giving up on living.

Regret fought for dominance of his emotions. Lori had been by his side since being shot at and learning of Karen's affair. She had been more than a friend. Yet she was the one he chose to take his frustrations out on. A part of him wanted to justify his actions; he would have understood if she treated him the same way if her family was the one kidnaped. That still didn't excuse his behavior.

When he thought he had himself under control, he splashed cool water on his face. Patting it dry with a paper towel, he examined the dark circles under his red eyes in the mirror. Were they from exhaustion, or grief?

Back in the break room, Lori sat facing a wall. This added to his regret. Leaning against the sink, he said, "I'm sorry. I know you're trying to help and be a friend. I appreciate your being here for me. It means a lot to me. I shouldn't have yelled at you." She didn't face him. Her shoulders trembled "Lori?"

When she faced him, her eyes were red-rimmed, her cheeks wet. "I shouldn't have met you in Chicago. If I hadn't, Norman might not have talked to you. Your family would be—" She swallowed, "would be okay."

He knelt in front of her and took her hand. "This isn't your fault. I'm the one who talked you into going. If I hadn't been so arrogant and hell-bent on making the FAA admit their contribution to the accident, you'd be home in bed, and I'd be wondering when I'd get laid again."

She snorted and gave him a shove. "Typical guy."

He wiggled her hand. "This wasn't your fault."

"It's not all yours, either."

Rankin walked in, cocked an eyebrow, and cleared her throat.

Kyle shot to his feet knowing how inappropriate their positions looked.

"I have a contact at the DOD. He gave us the location of Global Security's office and training facility. The HRT team is meeting us there. I'll call you after we've raided the premises."

Kyle stood. "Are Karen and Travis there?"

Her shoulders rose and fell. A flash of annoyance crossed her face. "We won't know that until we raid the place."

"I'm coming with you."

"I can't allow that."

"My family has been kidnapped and held as prisoners." He said this in a conversational tone hoping all his arrogance was gone. "No doubt your raid will scare the shit out of them. If I'm one of the first people they see, it'll be a calming influence, and they'll know they can trust you."

"I understand your need to be there, but your safety is as important as your family's." Rankin turned to leave the room.

"Put yourself in my place. Wouldn't you want to be there?" When she paused, he added, "Please."

"Her face softened for just a moment, before becoming determined. "No. I can't allow it."

The closing of the break room door made Kyle wonder if the closing of a jail cell on you felt the same. Through the window, he watched Rankin have a brief discussion with the agent posted there before walking off. The agent remained outside the door.

With his hands on his hips he paced before dropping into a chair across the table from Lori. "Maybe they'll rescue them." He attempted a smile hoping she would see he had taken her advice.

"Let's hope so."

Chapter Forty-Five

Sunday, June 20 11:26 p.m.

Kaufman slide open the view port on the door to the cell the Masters woman and kid were in.

Mrs. Masters sat on her son's bed, staring at the door, her eyes wide. Her son sat up and glanced from the door to his mother.

Kaufman nodded and Yackel slid the bolt back and shoved the door open. Both Yackel and Montes rushed through the door.

Mrs. Masters stood, putting her son behind her. "No!" She took a swing at Yackel's throat.

He deflected the blow and drove a fist into her stomach.

She expelled her breath and doubled over.

Yackel spun her around and wrenched her arm behind her back. "If you don't want your son to be tortured, stop struggling."

What little fight the woman had drained away.

The boy had distanced himself from the bed. He held his hands up in a martial art defensive stance.

Kaufman admired the kid's courage.

"Do as they say, Travis," Mrs. Masters said.

"Hands behind your back, kid," Montes said.

The son glanced at his mother, saw her nod, and lowered his hands. Montes stepped in striking him in the solar plexuses. "Oomph!" The son doubled over.

Mrs. Masters struggled to free herself, grimacing as Yackel twisted her arm. "You said he wouldn't be hurt."

Montes grabbed the boy's arm and spun him around.

Kaufman stepped up, wrapped a zip-tie around the kid's wrists, and pulled it tight. He stepped over and did the same to Mrs. Masters.

"I don't know why you're doing this to us." Mrs. Masters' voice trembled with hysteria. "We know nothing about the accident. If we did, we wouldn't tell anyone."

They escorted them out of the room and up the stairs.

"Please, let my son go. He knows nothing. He won't tell anyone what he's seen." Mrs. Masters struggled to free herself, glancing over her shoulder at her son, her face wet with tears.

The son attempted to kick Montes in the knee.

Kaufman pulled a black bag out of his pocket and yanked it over Mrs. Masters' head.

"No! Don't do this." Her struggling increased.

"Mom!" The son lashed out with another kick at Montes.

"Shit." They didn't have time for this. Kaufman held the stun gun to the son's stomach and pulled the trigger.

The boy collapsed and lay quivering on the floor.

Kaufman pulled another bag over the kid's head.

Mrs. Masters stopped struggling, lifted her covered head and twisted it as if trying to sense her son. "Travis?"

Kaufman tasered the woman, who followed her son to the floor.

Yackel and Montes picked them up, tossing them over their shoulders. They carried them to the garage and loaded them into the back of the Hummer.

Kaufman grabbed a 9 mm pistol from the armory. They had confiscated this one, and the one used to murder the imbecile Halloren, off some drug dealers in Marshall Heights. If the FBI recovered the bullets that would end the Masters' lives, they would match other drug-related crimes.

In the garage, he nodded to Montes. "Come with me." To Yackel, he said, "I'll meet you in Kuwait in twenty-four hours."

Yackel nodded and hurried off.

Kaufman and Montes climbed in the Hummer and backed out the garage.

Once on Route 15, Kaufman glanced at Montes. "What's on your mind, Sergeant?"

It took a moment before Montes turned to Kaufman. "This goes against everything we stand for. These aren't people who've aided enemy combatants and might turn a weapon on us. This is the innocent wife and son of a guy trying to do the right thing."

His words drove straight to the nagging reservation Kaufman had suppressed when he accepted this contract. His organization wasn't as established as some of his competition, like Blackwater, so that he could pick and choose his missions. This assignment would have shown that Global Security was capable of doing what was required of them here at home.

Although he didn't like the morally corrupt places this job had taken them, he couldn't let his unease show. It would be disruptive of his command. Besides, to become soft now would put them in prison for the rest of their lives. "You knew when you signed on there'd be assignments such as this."

Montes ran a hand over his short hair. "I know. The reality of it sucks though. It's easy to put myself in Masters' position knowing how I'd feel if someone did to my ex-wife and children what we're about to do."

Taking his eyes off the road to glance at Montes, Kaufman had to agree with his employee. But this was a business now. If he and his organization didn't do these jobs, another one would. He would have to keep an eye on Montes. It might be time to terminate his employment. Permanently.

Chapter Forty-Six

Monday, June 21 2:12 a.m.

Kyle alternated from sitting across the table from Lori in the FBI break room, to pacing.

Lori sat slumped in a chair sipping coffee with bloodshot, droopy eyelids.

After several back and forth lengths of the room, he chuckled to himself at how their habits had flipped. Throughout the investigation, she was the one who paced. He found it endearing she had a hard time harnessing her fiery determination. Now, it was he who could not remain still.

Dropping into his chair, he fought the urge to reach across the table and take her hand. It would be inappropriate, and he didn't doubt that Lori's compassion for what he was going through would prevent her from pulling away. Yet, her earlier admission of guilt over the situation Kyle's family was in, made him want to comfort her. "Thank you for being here for me."

She gave him a sympathetic smile. "You'd do the same for me."

It warmed him she thought of him as a comforting friend, when he had been harsh to her several times since Karen and Travis had been kidnapped. "Nah. I'd pat you on the back and check into a hotel."

She rolled her eyes.

How long had it been since he and Karen enjoyed the companionable relationship he enjoyed with Lori?

Outside the room, the agent guarding them took a call on his cell phone and turned away. Kyle's brief moment of indulgence evaporated. Was Rankin calling to say they found Travis and Karen? Or that they hadn't? Or, they found them but... He stood and tried to read the agent's body language so he could prepare himself for the news that might be delivered.

Lori came to his side.

The agent pocketed his phone. He glanced up and down the hall, his shoulders lifted and fell before he turned to face them.

The gesture knotted Kyle's stomach.

With a blank expression, the agent opened the door. "I'm to escort you to the scene."

The pounding of Kyle's heart made his body shudder with each thud. "Did...did..." He swallowed.

"Did they find his family?" Lori asked.

"I don't know. Let's go."

No news seemed better than bad news, but it didn't ease the humming of every nerve in Kyle's body. They preceded the agent down the hall to the elevators. When they began descending, Kyle asked, "Did she say anything?"

The agent frowned, momentarily, before recognition came to his face. "No. I was just told to drive you there," he said, watching the digital readout of the floors they passed.

Was this agent pissed he was excluded from a raid, or was he naturally cold and unresponsive?

In the parking garage, the agent escorted them to a sedan and held a rear door open for them.

They headed east through an eerily quiet D.C., crossing the Anacostia River on Benning Road. The city was almost always humming, bursting at the seams with politicians, lobbyists, and government workers. Seeing the city this late at night, dark and empty, made Kyle feel even more alone.

"Global Security's training facility is in Marshall Heights?" Lori asked the agent.

He glanced at them in the mirror for a second. "This is where I was told to bring you."

The name meant something to Kyle, but he couldn't recall where he had heard it. Lori seemed to shrink into herself. "Why does Marshall Heights bother you?"

Her gaze moved from the side windows to windshield and back. "This is where Ed Holstrom was murdered."

The homes on this side of the river were close together. Some, even though lights illuminated their windows, looked like they should be torn down. The cars parked along the street had driven off the dealers' lots years ago. Kyle was glad they were riding with an armed agent.

Several pieces of the puzzle fell into place. The NTSB was broken into by what appeared to be professionals. What better place to have a training facility where there would be practice shooting, than near a neighborhood where shootings were probably a common occurrence?

The agent pulled into a lot littered with junk cars and trucks. They weaved their way around piles of building refuse and garbage to a rundown garage at the back. Approaching the building, the agent flashed his lights.

Kyle had expected the area to be awash with police lights. Instead of the numerous Suburbans, vans, and government sedans he expected, the only operable vehicle was a civilian Hummer.

Even though his mouth was dry, Kyle swallowed.

Lori had squeezed her hands together in her lap. Her arms were tight along her body.

"This is their training facility?" Kyle asked.

The agent said nothing as he parked and killed the engine.

When he opened his door, Kyle attempted to do the same, except it was locked.

The agent paused outside Kyle's door before pulling back his coat and yanking open the door. He jammed his pistol into the side of Kyle's head.

His suspicion already on high alert reached denotation. Instinct took over.

Kyle shot one arm up and out, shoving the pistol off his head. His other hand grabbed the agent's arm holding the pistol back.

Twisting and dropping he kicked the agent in the knee.

Glass shattered. The seat exploded where his head had been a second ago.

Lori lifted her hand in front of her eyes. A red dot from a laser was centered over her shaking palm.

"Another move and that sniper will splatter her head all over you," the agent said through clenched teeth. He yanked his hand out of Kyle's grasp, stepping out of reach.

"Out of the car. Hands on the back of your head, asshole." The agent limp back a step.

Confusion must have been etched on Kyle's face.

"Rankin screwed up," the Agent said. "If she had checked, she would have seen the agent she assigned to guard you worked in the Special Forces Unit commanded by Colonel Kaufman, now head of Global Security. I've just resigned from the FBI. Get out."

In slow motion, Kyle swung around and stood on trembling legs. Despite his fear, he vocalized his disgust. "Traitor."

The agent's eyes narrowed. His nostrils flared. "Turn around. Lean against the car. Almond, get out. Nice and easy or you'll be the first one the sniper shoots."

The agent handed her handcuffs. "Put those on him. Hands behind his back."

While she handcuffed him, Kyle tried to spot where the sniper might be. He could not determine the origin of the laser. The laser on Lori's head suggested it was in front of the car.

Lori was shoved up beside him. Her hands yanked behind her. Handcuffs snapped on her wrists.

While the agent was not focused on him, Kyle glanced the way they came. There were numerous places he could run and hide, but he doubted he would make it to any of them before the sniper put a bullet in his back. Even if he escaped, his actions would get Lori killed.

The door to the building the agent escorted them to opened with a squeak. Motor oil and grease scented the air. The empty vehicle service bays were dimly lit.

Sitting on the stained concrete floor in the center were two people, hands fastened behind their backs and black bags covered their heads.

A man with close cropped gray hair, khakis with a sharp crease down the legs, and a sport coat stood by them with an automatic pistol in his hand.

Disbelief made Kyle's legs threaten to give out on him. When his shock passed, he attempted to rush to Travis and Karen.

The agent grabbed his shirt collar and jabbed the gun into the back of his head. "Easy. Nice and slow." He and Lori were escorted across from Karen and Travis. "On your knees."

"I'm glad you took my offer for employment, Cavanah," Sport Coat said to the agent.

"Jesus."

Sport coat waved his pistol. "Oh, don't worry about them knowing your name. They'll be dead once our client arrives."

Beside him, Lori flinched.

Dread raced through Kyle, then resolve took over.

"They better arrive soon, Colonel Kaufman. Any time now these two will be missed and the FBI will close this city down looking for them."

The Colonel glanced at his watch. "Anytime now." Sport Coat pulled the bags off first Travis,' then Karen's head."

They both squinted, then recognition came to their faces.

"Dad!"

"Kyle!"

Tears blurred his vision before he blinked them away and tried to gain composure by straightening to as full a height as he could muster on his knees.

Travis attempted to stand.

Placing a restraining hand on Travis' shoulder, Kaufman said, "That's enough, kid."

Travis shuddered and blinked several times. Tears wetted his cheeks.

"How was Sea World?"

This seemed to have the desired effect. Travis sniffed, and settled back on his heels, never taking his eyes off Kyle.

Turning to Karen, Kyle tried to show her the remorse he carried. "Sorry I got you guys into this."

Karen's repentant expression hardened when she glanced at Lori.

"Lori Almond, my wife, Karen, and my son, Travis."

"Hi." Lori's voice quivered.

Karen's cold stare didn't soften when she turned it back to Kyle.

"Vehicle pulling into the lot," a voice said over the two-way radio clipped to the Colonel's belt. "Silver Lexus."

Putting the radio to his lips, Kaufman said, "That's who we're expecting."

Kaufman held his gun to Travis' head. "Cavanah, make sure no one else is with our guest."

His limping steps echoed across the empty building. The door squeaked. Lights through a window swept across a wall. The engine shut off and the lights went out.

A car door closed. "Driver is alone," the radio squawked.

The door to the garage squeaked and two sets of footsteps came closer. One was the clopping of woman's heels.

"I don't see why I had to be here," Administrator Connie Broten said when she stopped beside Kyle.

Chapter Forty-Seven

Monday, June 21 2:48 a.m.

Agent Rankin examined the room in the basement of Global Security's headquarters in Haymarket, a town to the west of Manassas. There were two beds with rumpled blankets, a toilet, and sink. Judging by the deadbolts on the outside of the door, this room appeared to be a holding cell. Had the Masters family been held here?

The raid on the building had found it to be empty. The coffee pot in the break room was warmer than room temperature, as if turned off some time ago.

Holstering her Glock, she sighed, not looking forward to calling Kyle Masters and telling him his family hadn't been found. "Let's get the crime scene techs to go over this place," she said to Taber.

She climbed the stairs and stepped outside where she could make the call without interruptions. Her call to Kyle's cell phone rang five times and then his voice told her to leave a message. Maybe he was in the bathroom. "Mr. Masters, Agent Rankin. Return my call when you can."

She punched in Lori Almond's cell. She might know why Kyle wasn't answering. This too went to voicemail. Strange.

She pulled up the number of the agent guarding them at the break room. It too, went to voicemail.

Now she was suspicious. She called the security office for the Hoover Building. "Bring up the camera showing the fifth-floor break room and hallway outside it."

"Break room is empty," the man's voice said. "Hall is clear."

"Agent Cavanah is supposed to be standing outside that break room. Rewind until you see him leave his post."

Computer keys clicked, then the security agent said, "Okay he's leaning against the wall. He gets a call. He hangs up and opens the door to the break room. He follows a man and a woman down the hall and they board the elevator."

"Describe the man and woman."

"The man is average height but looks to be in shape. He's wearing khaki pants and a blue polo shirt. The woman is short and petite wearing khakis and a short sleeve red blouse."

Rankin frowned. That was Masters and Almond. "Tell me where they got off the elevator."

More clicking, and then the security agent said, "The parking garage. Agent Cavanah escorts them to a Toyota Camry and they drive away."

Where the hell were they going in his personal car? "Does it appear they're being escorted under duress?"

"No."

Why would they leave? "Pull up the view outside of the parking garage. Which direction did they go?"

"East."

East? Haymarket was west of D.C. Prior to hearing they had gone in the opposite direction, she suspected Masters had convinced Cavanah to find out where the raid on Global Security was taking place and drive them there. Obviously, that wasn't the reason. "Thanks. Transfer me to Agent Matuszek."

When her supervisor came on, Rankin said, "Sir, I believe Kyle Masters and Lori Almond have been convinced they are being taken to my location to meet Masters' family, but have been kidnapped by Agent Cavanah. I'd like agents using traffic surveillance cameras to track where Agent Cavanah has taken them."

✈✈✈

Beside Kyle, Lori stiffened at the appearance of the FAA Administrator.

Glaring at her, Kyle said, "You? It was you covering up your inspector's negligence?"

Broten smirked down at him. "It was Stuart Halloren's idea to bury our inspector's contribution to your accident. He was so eager to prove himself I did nothing to discourage him. When things began to unravel, thanks to you two, I knew he'd be skipping town and leaving a trail of evidence pointing in my direction. It was time to take matters into my own hands."

"I thought you were being questioned by the FBI?" Kyle had believed her performance in the interrogation room.

"The FBI is so afraid of taking away the rights of a Senate appointed Administrator. They released me until tomorrow morning when I'm to be questioned again. Where's the recording of Norman's interview?"

"How could you do this?" Lori asked. "This goes against everything you worked for at the NTSB."

Broten shook her head. "Grow up, Lori. The NTSB charter is reassuring to the public. Omega Airlines and the FAA would have implemented the corrective actions your report would have suggested. Norman and Chavette would have been fired. We can't have these changes forced on us by a Senate hearing. I wasn't going to lose my appointment because of some incompetent inspector. That would ruin my chances at more lucrative positions after I leave government service. Where's the recording?"

When Lori's shoulders sagged and her gaze went to the floor, Kyle spoke up. "We gave it to the FBI."

Broten kicked him just below his ribs. The point of her shoe drove a spike of pain through him, but there wasn't any power behind her kick.

"Ahh! You and your meddling," Broten said. She paced a couple of steps. She glanced at Lori who still stared at the floor and then at Kyle's defiant look. "No doubt you did. After your CVR went missing, I doubt you'd keep only one copy of that recording. Where are the copies?"

To save giving anything away by giving Lori a warning shake of his head, Kyle took in Travis' worried expression, and Karen's frightened one. "Let my family go and I'll tell you."

Broten glanced at Karen and Travis. Her face brightened. "Okay, we'll let them go as soon as we have the other copies of the recording."

"No way. You've already shown you'll lie to get what you want."

"You're right, Mr. Masters." Broten turned to Kaufman. "Kill the kid."

Kaufman backed up two steps and lifted his pistol.

Panic surged through Kyle. "Wait! I have it here in my pocket."

Broten smiled. "I thought as much."

Kaufman lowered his weapon and nodded at Kyle. "Cavanah."

The agent bent and patted Kyle's pockets. He shoved his hand roughly in the front left one, pulled out the thumb drive, and handed it to the Administrator.

She dropped it to the floor and smashed it with the heel of her shoe several times.

"The FBI does have a copy of that," Kyle said. "How will you get it? Bribe another agent?" He directed his glare at Cavanah.

"Without you two or Norman to verify what's on this recording, I'll be able to dismiss it as a fabrication." Broten studied Lori. "Check her pockets. If it isn't on her, check her purse."

When Cavanah bent to search Lori, she glowered at Broten. "It's in my purse. Out in the car."

Kaufman nodded at Cavanah who limped out of the garage.

"You have your recordings, let my family go."

When Broten turned to Travis then Karen, and her expression softened, Kyle said, "Lori said you have children. Would you want them in this position for something you did?"

Karen inched to Travis' side. "He's only fourteen. Please. Let him go."

Her quivering voice replaced Kyle's anger with the remorse or what he had done to them. "They won't tell anyone what happened here, I promise." Kyle didn't have to work at sounding sincere. His voice broke on its own.

Cavanah returned with Lori's purse and handed it to Broten.

She dumped it out on the floor and poked through Lori's wallet, cell phone, lipstick, brush, and notebook. She picked up the digital recorder and removed the micro SD card and snapped it in half.

Kyle was beginning to think she wouldn't find the thumb drive until Broten opened Lori's wallet and found it in a pocket.

"D.C. police car pulling in," a voice from the radio on Kaufman's belt said.

Light through a window illuminated a back wall.

Kaufman brought the radio to his lips. "Take it out."

✈✈✈

Lying atop a rusted-out van, Montes sighted through the scope of his rifle.

The D.C. police car inched ahead, and the spotlight on the top swept across the lot. At any moment, the beam would cross over the van.

Montes placed the crosshairs between the eyes of driver and took up the slack in the trigger.

Inside the garage a woman and child would be murdered very soon. This had been eating at him since they kidnapped them in San Antonio. If the two had done something illegal he might be able to justify their deaths. On top of this, he was being ordered to kill a police officer.

Squeezing his eyes shut, Montes took a deep breath, letting it out slowly. When he opened his eyes, the spotlight beam swept his way. He adjusted his aim, exhaled, and squeezed the trigger. The suppressor on the rifle made a cough like noise and the slide rattled as it ejected the spent cartridge.

✈✈✈

The FBI Bell Long Ranger helicopter that had been circling Global Security's headquarters during the raid, landed in the parking lot, and picked up Rankin, Lampe and four members of the HRT team. It lifted off and turned east, back to D.C.

Rankin donned a headset.

"D.C. police are reporting the unit you requested sent to the address in Marshall Heights has been fired at," the copilot said over the intercom. "They're dispatching other units to the scene."

"What's our ETA?"

"Eighteen minutes."

Rankin glanced out the side window of the helicopter. Even though the helicopter was flying at 120 knots the lights below seemed to pass by in slow motion. She understood what Kyle was going through on the drive from Manassas Airport to Leesburg earlier. The people she was charged with protecting could be dead well inside the eighteen minutes it would take to reach them.

✈✈✈

Inside the garage, Kyle heard the roar of a car's engine fade as the light on the back wall swept across the wall and disappeared.

Kaufman's eyes narrowed as he brought the radio to his lips. "Status?"

The radio was silent.

"Montes. Report."

In the distance, police sirens wailed.

Broten stepped over to Kaufman. "You told me we wouldn't be discovered here." Her voice was enraged. She hurried to the door.

Kaufman looked at Cavanah and nodded in Broten's direction. "Stop her." To Broten, he said, "You'll drive right into their ambush."

"It'll be better than being caught with hostages," Broten yelled over her shoulder.

Behind him, Kyle heard Cavanah hurry to the door. Kaufman seemed occupied with the retreating Administrator. Kyle tried to judge if he could leap to his feet and deliver a kick to Kaufman's gun hand and then another that would disable him before Kaufman noticed him rise.

As if reading his mind, Kaufman's eyes swept over his four hostages. He stepped closer to Travis and held his pistol against Travis head, before glancing back to the door.

The sirens grew closer.

"Let go of me," Broten yelled.

"Bring her back here," Kaufman said.

The Colonel's gaze moved from his four hostages, to the door, back to his hostages. He looked over his shoulder to the back of the garage to another door.

Kyle was about to leap when Cavanah arrived at his side with the struggling Broten. He kicked her in the back of the knee and forced her to kneel on the floor.

"Let go of me, asshole," Broten yelled, shrugging from his grasp.

Red and blue police lights flashed on the wall.

Cavanah glanced towards the window and back at Kaufman. "Colonel, we need to get out of here."

"Watch them," Kaufman said, as he stepped around them and hurried to the window.

Cavanah held his pistol against Broten's head. His gaze followed Kaufman.

If Kyle was in Cavanah's position, he would be worried Kaufman was leaving him here with the hostages. "I bet you wish you hadn't become a traitor to the FBI now," Kyle said.

Cavanah aimed his pistol at Kyle. "Shut the fuck up."

"Or what? You'll shoot me? Go ahead. I'm sure the SWAT team out there will storm this place as soon as you pull the trigger." Kyle cringed, waiting for the pain from the bullet, but didn't lower his defiant stare. Then, he realized how stupid his comment was. If Cavanah shot him, would he then turn the gun on everyone else?

When Cavanah lifted his gaze to Kaufman, relief swept over Kyle.

"Colonel?" Cavanah said.

"Hang on!" Kaufman hurried to the door in the back.

"He's leaving you with the hostages," Kyle said.

"Don't let him get away," Lori yelled.

Cavanah glanced back at Kyle and Lori, then Kaufman. He aimed his pistol at Kaufman. "Where are you going, Colonel?"

Kaufman had reached the door. "Just hang on for a fucking second."

Out of the corner of Kyle's eye, he saw Karen move.

Cavanah twisted and fired at her as she fell on top of Travis.

"Ahh," Karen screamed.

Fear paralyzed Kyle as he saw blood blooming across Karen's t-shirt. She writhed in pain.

Under her, Travis yelled, "Mom!"

Broten jumped to her feet and ran to the door at the front.

Cavanah aimed his gun at her. "Stop!"

A squeak announced the back door being opened.

Cavanah turned to the noise as Kaufman started to step through it. "Colonel!"

While he was distracted, Kyle could spin and kick Cavanah's legs out from under him.

Before he could act on this thought, the front door squeaked. Turning towards Broten, Cavanah's gaze swept over Kyle and seemed to read his eyes. He backed up a step, out of striking distance.

At the back of the garage Kaufman disappeared out the door.

Cavanah's head swiveled to both doors several times.

From the front, Broten was yelling. "Don't shoot. I'm a hostage. Don't shoot."

"On your knees," someone said over a loudspeaker from the front. "Hands on your head."

Cavanah sprinted for the back door and disappeared through it.

"Mom!"

Kyle crawled to Karen's side on his knees.

Travis squirmed out from under Karen's shuddering form, his shirt soaked in blood.

From beside him, Lori yelled, "Help! Someone please!"

"Dad, do something!"

Twisting so his back was to Karen, Kyle attempted to hold pressure on the wound. He couldn't apply much pressure in this backward position. He fell to his side and attempted to slide his cuffed hands over his butt. The cuffs cut into his wrists making his hands throb. His arms weren't long enough to make it around his rear.

Karen had stopped squirming and lay shivering. Her face drained of any color.

"We need medical attention in here," Lori yelled. "The kidnappers have gone!"

Kyle violently shoved and wiggled. His hands inched over his butt. He pulled his legs through the loop of his wrists. Bending over Karen, he shoved a finger in the bullet hole, her blood warming his finger.

A helicopter approached.

The back door remained open. There was no sign of Kaufman or Cavanah.

"Help," Lori yelled. "The kidnappers have gone! We need medical attention!"

"Dad, is Mom okay?"

I don't know. Kyle didn't dare remove his finger from the bullet hole to feel for a pulse.

Lori ran to the front door. "I'm a hostage! I'm coming out! Don't shoot!"

Kyle had a brief moment of admiration for her, before this was replaced with fear when Karen coughed up blood.

The helicopter sounded like it was hovering just above the building.

Police officers stormed through the front door. Their weapons swept the building. Several rushed to the back door and took up positions on both sides of it. They ducked their heads out and pulled them back, before disappearing out the door.

"Clear," officers yelled as they swept the corners and side rooms.

Two officers dropped beside Karen. One put his hand over her carotid artery. "She has a pulse." Twisting his head, he spoke into the microphone clipped to his shoulder. "We need paramedics. Now!"

"Paramedics are en route," a male voice over the radio said.

Kyle had hoped they were just outside. Could Karen make it until they arrived?

The slowing of the helicopter's rotor told Kyle it had landed. A moment later Rankin rushed through the front door, her gun held out in front of her in both hands. She stopped beside Kyle. When her gaze swept over Karen and Travis' tear streaked face, her face twisted up. She took a deep breath, righting her face into the professional one she'd exhibited since Kyle had met her. "Let's get her on the helicopter. Now!" She lifted her wrist to her mouth and began issuing orders.

An officer took the cuffs off Kyle. When Travis was released, he took his son in his arms, squeezed him, and followed the officers carrying Karen to the door.

Chapter Forty-Eight

A year and a half later.

Kyle walked into the conference room of the Marriott hotel in Washington D.C. wearing a new charcoal gray suit with chalk pinstripes. He had other suits he could have worn, but he wanted to impress Lori.

He stayed at this hotel when he had flown here on an FAA jet to listen to the cockpit voice recorder. Today, he was here as an interested party to hear the NTSB's issuance of the final accident report on Flight 918.

Some of the same people from the initial investigation stood in small groups. The mood in the room was less tense than the previous time they had been together. Rows of chairs faced a platform with a podium next to a large white screen with the NTSB logo projected on it. He shook hands with several NTSB investigators, then stood alone off to the side, watching Lori at the front of the room. She spoke with a group from Boeing.

Clasping his hands together behind his back, he immediately let his arms fall to his side, thinking he looked too stiff and formal.

Shortly after they had been rescued at the abandoned garage, Lori had been appointed the Investigator in Charge. This, Kyle assumed, was a political move. The previous investigator, Mark Evans, had admitted to helping withhold Norman's presence in the cockpit from the media. He had been fired.

Kyle had not talked to Lori since they were liberated.

She had grown her hair, wearing it in a bob that hung below her ears. It looked good on her. Her navy-blue suit and cream silk blouse accented her petite body. Although he had grown accustomed to the casual dress she wore during the investigation, he enjoyed seeing her in a business suit.

In the last year and a half, Kyle hoped they would see each other when they testified at the numerous depositions and trials for the men from Global Security, the FAA, or during the Senate hearing.

Unfortunately, Lori had always testified on different days. Each time, Kyle left disappointed he hadn't seen her smile or heard her laugh. Another NTSB investigator had come to Houston and conducted the investigation of Omega's training for rejected takeoffs and how well the simulator represented takeoffs—and rejected ones—with a blown tire. He explained Lori was occupied with other aspects of the investigation.

Kyle wondered then if this was true, or if she was giving him space.

Agent Rankin stepped up to him and offered her hand. "Mr. Masters, it's good to see you." Her eyes were warm, her smile genuine.

"Thank you. You too. I didn't think you'd be here. Rumor has it you've been promoted."

Her eyes twinkled. "Yes. I'm the assistant agent in charge of the Louisville field office."

"That's good. You deserve it. How's Agent Taber?"

"He's good. I'll send your regards. I never thanked you for your help with this case."

Kyle shrugged. "Any word on who killed Kaufman and Cavanah?"

"Our assumption is the sniper at the front of the building had a change of heart. When the first police unit arrived, he shot out the spotlight, hoping they would call in backup, then waited to see what would happen. When he saw Kaufman and Cavanah escaping, he couldn't let them go. We're still looking for him."

Kyle felt no remorse for the two criminals who had been involved in their kidnappings. He wondered what that said about his morals. Had they changed because of this experience?

Lori glanced at them and broke into a smile. She shook hands with the men she talked to and walked toward them.

"I've already said hello to Ms. Almond," Rankin said. "I'll let you two catch up." She stepped away as Lori stopped in front of Kyle.

"Hi. I hoped you'd be here." Lori's brown eyes were bright. He had forgotten how brilliant they could be.

"I... I wouldn't have missed it." The glow of life that had been missing for some time snapped on. "You look great. How are you? How are your daughters?"

"We're all good. Brooke is in her second year of college, and Drewe has picked out the one she wants to go to." She shook her head. "I hope I can afford two tuitions. How's your family?"

His smiled dissolved. "Travis is doing okay, now. We had some trouble with him afterward." He paused, gathering his courage. "I'll tell you about it if you'll have dinner with me tonight."

She met his eyes. "Would your wife approve of us dining together?"

Kyle remembered the disdain Karen showed Lori at the garage. "We're divorced."

The brilliance of Lori's eyes dimmed as a sigh escaped her. "I'm sorry for you." She glanced at her watch. "I need to start this hearing."

"Have dinner with me, Lori. Let's catch up. I've missed our conversations."

She glanced around the room, nodding at several people.

In those few moments, Kyle's heart began to crumble. She might have begun dating someone or gotten married. He should have called one of the many times he had the phone in his hand and considered doing so. Why hadn't he?

She turned back to him. "Okay."

Yes! Though he tried not to, he broke into a smile. "I knew you would."

She shook her head, chuckled, and patted him on the chest. "Oh, I've forgotten how you're so full of yourself."

Walking to the front of the room, she kept shaking her head, a smile plastered on her face.

At the podium, she clipped a microphone onto her lapel. Her smile fell away. "If everyone could take a seat, we'll get this hearing started." Her voice wavered as it came out of the overhead speakers. Her hands rubbed the side of the podium. Conversation slowly died down as everyone sat.

Kyle sat in the center of the front row.

"Hello, everyone. My name is Lori Almond from the NTSB. I was the Investigator In Charge of the investigation of Omega Airlines Boeing 737, Flight 918, which rejected its takeoff from

LaGuardia Airport on June 14th of last year and came to rest in Flushing Bay."

While she spoke, a copy of the inch-thick accident report was handed out. Although the report was being released today, someone had overnighted a copy of it to Kyle. He had read it on the flight to D.C., wondering if Lori had been the one who sent it.

The display of the NTSB logo on the white screen behind her changed to a picture of the airplane where it had come to rest on the approach light stanchions.

The memory of standing on the end of the runway staring at the wrecked airplane the first night of the investigation came to Kyle. Then, a disconcerted feeling overwhelmed him that one of Omega's crews had caused the destruction he saw before him.

Now, it comforted him that the accident wasn't totally the crew's fault. That First Officer Cheryl Wells had performed the evacuation training given to her from memory that aided the passengers in getting off the airplane.

Lori described Captain Brent Musgrave and Cheryl Wells' experience, how long they'd been on duty, and the amount of rest they had the previous night, the weather, the airplane's age, condition, and number of passengers.

"The FAA Inspector riding on the jump seat of Flight 918 had previous experience with Captain Musgrave," Lori said to the crowd. She went on to describe Norman's attempt to bring a violation against Captain Musgrave and how it might have affected the Captain's decision to reject the takeoff. She pointed out the narration of the CVR recording they had pieced together from Lori's, Kyle's, and FAA Inspector Glen Skaggs' memory, as well as Norman's interview at his home.

She went on for close to an hour, discussing various engineering aspects of tire wear, braking coefficients, how the crew was trained and how it could be improved, and the need for crew training to avoid distractions at critical phases of flight. She also emphasized the need to educate FAA Inspectors from distracting or coercing crews from performing their duties.

"In conclusion, the NTSB ruling on the cause of the accident was the crew's decision to reject the takeoff with insufficient runway remaining," Lori said. "Contributing to this cause was an FAA Inspector's interference with the crew at a critical time on the takeoff roll. Also contributing was the condition of the tire and the wet runway conditions."

Lori stared at Kyle from the podium and said to the crowd, "I'd personally like to thank Kyle Masters of Omega Airlines for his assistance in the investigation. Mr. Masters and his family suffered a terrible ordeal because of his participation. Without him, the true outcome of this accident might not have been revealed. Thank you, Kyle."

People patted him on the shoulder. The crowd applauded, making him wish he could hide. He gave Lori a devious look.

She unclipped her microphone and stepped off the platform. Several people surrounded her with questions. Kyle went to the back of the room and poured a glass of water from a pitcher. Water droplets clung to its sides.

Philip Worden approached him.

The contempt Kyle felt for the man in the FBI interview room after Worden revealed his suspicions of Halloren resurfaced, making him consider walking off.

Worden's expression was cautious. "Mr. Masters, I hope your family is well?" He held out his hand.

"They've been better."

Worden turned away from Kyle's glare. "I realize now I should have reported to the FBI what I knew instead of sending you emails with the records attached."

Kyle frowned. Then it dawned on him. "You were tscalone72?"

"Yes."

Some of his condescension left him. "Thank you for your help." He knew he should be grateful, but when he thought about Travis and Karen's needless kidnapping his blood pressure spiked. "If you had, you could have prevented a lot of people from being traumatized."

"I know." Worden sighed. "It will be something I'll have to live with."

"Why didn't you come forward if you suspected Halloren?"

He studied the floor. "I truly feared I might be murdered. My reluctance almost cost you your family. I'm very sorry."

Kyle sighed. He could understand the man's reasoning. Prior to this experience, he wasn't sure he would have the courage to go to the authorities and report something suspicious with no real proof if it might get him murdered. "Why tscalone72?"

"Tony Scalone was a close friend who flew a last-minute charter for me so I could keep a date with the woman who became my wife of thirty-five years. He got careless and crashed into a mountain." He was silent a moment. "I've thought of his death almost every day since then. I'll now have your family's experience and the deaths of others to think about, because of actions I should have taken. I retired shortly after your ordeal. Good luck, Mr. Masters."

Kyle watched him walk away. He tried to find some satisfaction that he had figured out the email name tscalone72 had something to do with aviation, but none came.

Chapter Forty-Nine

That evening, Kyle and Lori sat at a long, dark wood bar waiting for their table. Kyle ordered a scotch and water, Lori a glass of Merlot.

While waiting for their drinks, he flipped the cocktail napkin over and over. During the time they worked together, he had never had a problem talking to her. He cleared his throat. "I never thanked you for the risk you took rushing out of the garage to get help for Karen. Thank you."

Lori's eyes became vacant as if remembering that night. She blinked her thoughts away. "You would have done the same for me."

When she placed her hands on the bar, Kyle noticed a silver band with diamonds and rubies on the ring finger of her left hand. His heart lodged in his throat. He turned away, pretending to study the other patrons so his disappointment would not show.

"I'm glad that's over with," she said. "It's part of the job of the IIC, but I hate standing up in front of so many people and trying to sound intelligent."

What did he expect? She was an attractive, engaging woman who thought he was married. Could they be friends? He put on what he hoped was an amused look. "Yeah, that must be tough for you."

She narrowed her eyes. "What, the standing up in front of everyone, or sounding intelligent?"

"Well, obviously, you stood up in front of everyone." When her eyes turned to fire, he chuckled.

She swatted his arm, then shook her head. "Why did I agree to meet you?"

"I thought you did great. You sounded very intelligent and everyone thought you knew what you were talking about. And you looked hot, too." Her cocked eyebrow made him close his eyes, regretting what he said. His face warmed.

"So... I looked hot?"

He sipped his drink. "Ah... well, yeah."

He squirmed under her scrutiny. It was time to change the subject or he would embarrass himself further. He told her about the conversation with Worden.

"That solves that mystery." She sipped her wine. "What kind of trouble did you have with Travis?"

He smiled that she remembered his son's name, but it faded. "For a while, he seemed okay. After Karen's and my problems started coming to a head, he became distant, rebellious, and didn't come home when he was supposed to. Karen found marijuana in his room."

Either the scotch or talking about it eased the tension in his shoulders. "I'd moved out by then, so we scheduled a family meeting one evening, and we discussed what we'd experienced and how it affected us now." He studied her, looking for any sign of, *why'd I ask?* "You sure you want to hear this? I don't want to dump my problems on you."

Her eyes brightened. "No, I'd like to hear."

Lifting his hand to pat hers, he stopped it midair and grabbed his glass. "Surprisingly, the trauma of being kidnapped didn't bother him as much as Karen and I separating. After we were rescued, he thought Karen and I would work out our problems. When we didn't, he blamed himself for our failures." Kyle shrugged. "We convinced him it wasn't his fault. It's taken some time, but he's himself again."

"Why did you get divorced?" Lori swirled the wine, then lifted her eyes over the glass to him.

Laughter came from a table behind him. Kyle turned away, pretending to see what was so funny. He blew out his cheeks. "I tried to get past Karen's affair and forgive her. It made me distant. Karen couldn't forgive me for putting them in danger." He turned back and studied her a moment, wondering how she might take what he said next. "One of the guys that kidnapped them convinced Karen you and I were having an affair."

"What?" Her jaw dropped. "Why would she think that?"

"It was how they convinced her to meet them when they were kidnapped." Lori's eyes remained narrowed. "No matter how much I denied it, Karen wouldn't believe me."

She gulped down the rest of her wine and flagged the bartender. "Can I have another, please?"

"I tried to look at it from her perspective and could see why she might think that was true. Our marriage was on the rocks. I worked with an attractive woman away from home for almost a week. Being insecure, it was easy for her to think I might be attracted to you." He sipped his drink, wondering if he should tell her Karen probably didn't believe him because of how weak his denials of his attraction to Lori were. "So, we had trust issues."

The barstool squeaked as she swiveled it back and forth.

He glanced at her ring and would have loved to ask if she was married, but now didn't seem the time. "Enough about me. How's your last year and a half been?"

The colors of her cheeks faded. She stopped swiveling and sipped her wine. "During Brooke's fall break, I managed to get some time off, and we took the vacation we'd planned. You were right, Cape Cod was nice."

The hostess approached them. "Your table is ready."

After paying their bar bill, they sat at the table and fell into an easy conversation through dinner and over coffee afterward. He didn't hear about a man in her life. Typical of Lori, she probably wouldn't mention a new love when he had recently fallen out of it.

She wrapped both hands around her mug.

He pointed to her ring. "That's beautiful."

She lifted her hand and examined the ring with a smile. "Yes. I think so, too." Her hand plopped onto the table, and she seemed to work at washing the smile away. "Any vacation plans coming up?"

He tried to mask his frustration in not knowing her marital status. "I'd like to go skiing with Travis during his winter break. This summer, we might go to Vermont and take soaring lessons. He's shown interest in it and is old enough to solo. What about you?"

"I'm hoping the girls and *I* can get away together for a week this summer. Although they wouldn't be interested in soaring lessons, if they could find something to occupy themselves, I, too, would love to get my glider rating."

Did she emphasis I? What's with this making the same plans?

She spun her band round and round her finger. Her eyes sparkled and her lips drew into a thin line.

He rolled his eyes and gave an exaggerated sigh. "I think I'm being taunted, and you know I'm dying to know if you're seeing anyone?"

Lori's laugh was infectious, her smile brilliant. "You've been eyeing this ring all evening and I loved watching you squirm. It was a gift from my daughters. No, I'm not involved with anyone."

Kyle threw his napkin at her, shaking his head.

She used it to wipe the tears from her eyes. "Oh, that was so much fun."

"I'm glad you had a good time at my expense." Although he pretended to sound sarcastic, he knew his smile betrayed him.

"Oh, I did."

He paid their check and followed her to the hostess stand. This had been the most fun he had had in a long time, and he didn't want the evening to end. "Want to go have a nightcap?"

That amused look she wore earlier spread across her face. "A nightcap? I think you have more in mind than a nightcap."

"Well, as you're well aware, a good pilot should be prepared for any contingency."

Lori subtly shook her head. She grabbed his tie, pulling his face until their lips were an inch apart. "Your place or mine?"

THE END

Author's Note

Thank you for reading The Cover-Up. I hope you enjoyed it.

While trying to come up with an idea for an airline thriller, I looked back over my twenty-five years of pretty routine flying and considered some of the situations I'd encountered. I've had to divert from the intended destination because of weather, sick passengers, airport closings, and mechanical issues. Luckily, I've never had to divert because of rowdy passengers like some of my brethren have. It would be a stretch to dramatize what is a pilot's typical day to make into an exciting plot.

I gave some thought to having a terrorist problem but decided against it for several reasons. I didn't want anything I dreamed up to be something terrorist might try. I would also give away some of the security procedures that have been implemented since the attacks on nine-eleven.

During this brainstorming I remembered a few years prior a routine line-check, what the FAA calls a route check, by an FAA inspector who didn't say much during the flight.

Unlike Ernest Norman in this book, almost all of the FAA Inspectors I've encountered are good people doing what is often an unrewarding job. It must be frustrating working around aviation but seldom being able to sit at the controls of an aircraft. There are a few who like to exert their authority by making airlines, mechanics, or pilots feel their licenses are on the line.

Most of the time the inspectors giving the line-checks will interact with the crews easing the tension that always rises when pilots feel they're being watched. The feeling is similar to when a police officer follows the car you're driving. When I get a quiet one who doesn't attempt to converse with us, I question if they're trying to be out-of-sight-out of-mind so we can do our jobs as we would without them there? Or, scrutinizing our every move and word hoping we'll do something wrong so they can issue a violation.

My line-check went fine with no issues for the inspector to discuss after we had parked at the gate. But during the flight, I wondered if a situation arose and I made a decision the inspector disagreed with and thought the safety of the flight was in question, what might he do?

I ruminated on that thought for some time and asked myself: What would happen if I followed the inspector's advice and it caused an accident? What would the FAA do to prevent the lashing they would take in the media? I had to have the crew in my story follow the inspector's recommendation during a critical phase of flight when there wasn't time to discuss the safest course of action. A blown tire on takeoff from a short runway that ended with the aircraft departing the runway fit my needs.

As mentioned in the story, blown tires on takeoff are very rare and seldom cause accidents. Intimidating inspectors are also extremely rare.

If you enjoyed the book, I would appreciate it if you would leave a review on Amazon, GoodReads, or your online retailer of choice so that other readers considering the novel will get an idea if it's worth a read.

Dana Griffin
January 2015

Acknowledgements

Thank you for reading The Cover-Up. This book wouldn't have been written without the help from many.

Many thanks to:

Public Affairs Coordinator Keith Holloway of the National Transportation Safety Board for arranging a phone interview with Investigator In Charge Lorenda Ward. Ms. Ward patiently answered my questions on what it's like to investigate an airline accident. The talented people who work at the NTSB truly do make the transportation industry much safer.

The following authors from critiquecircle.com helped make this novel so much better, R. D. Brady, Carla, H. C. Elliston, Pam Godwin, Barbara Humphrey, C. K. Raggio, Chuck Robertson, and Katie Salidas. You have taught me so much about writing. This story would be a rambling wordy mess if it weren't for you.

This book was initially edited by Susan H. Gottfried: https://westofmars.com, a talented author in her own right. A later edition of this book was edited by Erin Greenwell of Bourbon City Editing: https://bourboncityediting.com. Both put the commas in the proper places and corrected all my many grammatical goofs, as well as helped characterization and the plot.

David C. Cassidy formatted the manuscript and created the incredible cover art: http://davidccassidy.com. David manages to take my vague thoughts and turn them into art that always lifts my brow and makes me smile. If you're a fan of novels with good people who have bad things happen to them, treat yourself to one of his books.

I can't thank my wonderful, beautiful wife Becky enough for allowing me the freedom and encouragement to write this novel. You spent hours alone without complaint while I pursued this dream of becoming a novelist. This story floating around in my head wouldn't have become a book without you listening to my many hours of strategizing.

Author Bio

Dana Griffin is a Boeing 737 pilot for a U.S. Airline. He lives in Kentucky with his wife and two four legged children some people call dogs. When not flying, he's working on another Kyle and Lori story that follows *The Cover-Up*.

Turn the page to read the first chapter of, *Coerced*. The next Kyle Masters/Lori Almond airline thriller.

COERCED

DANA GRIFFIN

Chapter One

Omega Airlines flight 1194 would land at New Orleans International just as the approaching thunderstorm moved over the airport.

Air traffic controller Jacob Crispen looked out the airport's control tower windows and observed the black line of clouds two miles to the west continuing eastward toward the airport. Every few seconds, lightning shot out.

If Omega 1194 didn't land in the next few minutes, the storm would close the airport. Any other traffic inbound would have to hold or fly to their alternate airport.

Omega was three miles from the airport and several thousand feet higher than other flights would normally be that far away. It seemed impossible they would lose their excess altitude and make a normal landing.

Crispen considered giving Omega the option of flying a three-sixty-degree turn to give them more time, but that would have them landing after the storm hit. He brought the microphone to his lips and keyed the transmit button. "Omega 1194, winds two one zero at fifteen, gusting to twenty-five. You're still cleared to land." His foot tapped a steady beat.

"Omega 1194," one of the two pilots radioed back.

The 737's wings rocked. They were two miles from landing, but their altitude readout on Crispen's radar showed them at three thousand feet. Most aircraft would be at eight hundred feet. He couldn't believe they were continuing the approach.

"Omega 1194, wind one eight zero at twenty gusting to thirty." Crosswind gusts in excess of twenty-five knots made landing difficult.

The plane continued toward the airport.

The wind howled as it rounded the control tower windows. Crispen considered evacuating the tower and seeking the safety of the offices at ground level in case the wind toppled the tower, or blew out its windows. After Omega landed, or aborted their approach, he'd scramble down the stairs.

Omega was a mile from the airport and a thousand feet above it. They should be less than five hundred. The plane's wings continued to rock from the thunderstorm half a mile away. "Omega 1194, wind one seven zero at two two. We just had a gust of forty." Crispen stood and stepped from foot to foot in time with the plane.

The flight crossed the end of the runway two hundred feet in the air. Most aircraft would've been at fifty feet. It continued descending, the wings rolling left and right.

"Go around. Go around," Crispen said without keying the microphone. He could only order the flight to do so if the runway wasn't clear of traffic.

Over halfway down the runway and twenty feet off the ground, Omega's nose aligned with the runway. The aircraft descended fast, hitting the runway in what must've been a jolt. It bounced ten feet into the air and hovered while continuing on its path, before dropping to the concrete once more.

Do they have enough runway to get stopped?

The spoilers on top of the wings lifted, and the slots in the side of the engine opened, signaling the pilots had selected reverse thrust.

The aircraft swerved back and forth.

Crispen's mouth gaped when Omega went off the right side of the runway. Pieces of smashed runway edge lights flew into the air.

The thunderstorm swallowed Omega in the heavy rain. Visibility dropped, making it difficult for Crispen to observe Omega's roll out.

Without taking his gaze off the ghost-like shape of the plane continuing down the side of the runway, he lifted the phone with a trembling hand and speed dialed a number.

"Fire and Rescue," a male voice said.

"This is the tower." Crispen's voice was louder than necessary. "Omega Airlines 737 went off the side of the runway and may need assistance."

"Location, damage, and souls onboard?"

"They just came to a stop at the west end of runway two-eight. Aircraft appears intact. Souls onboard unknown."

"We're rolling."

He hung up. "Omega 1194, tower. Rescue equipment is on their way. Do you require assistance?"

No one answered.

THE END

List of Characters by Position

Omega Airlines

John Wagner – Executive VP of operations.
Morgan Steele - Vice president of Flight Standards and Training.
Earl Dorsey - Vice president of Flight Operations.
Kyle Masters – Boeing 737 Assistant Fleet Manager.
Richard Ryan - Boeing 737 Assistant Fleet Manager. He and Kyle share this position.
Troy Kircher - Newark Chief Pilot. One of five.
Brent Musgrave – Captain of flight 918.
Cheryl Wells – First Officer of flight 918.
Brandon Spikol - Maintenance Investigator.
Leo Brandish – Omega Airlines Pilot, who is also an investigator for the Airline Pilots Association (ALPA).
Sherri Logsdon - Lead Flight Attendant for flight 918.
Demisha Melton – Forward Flight Attendant on flight 918.
Luther Stoess and Laurinda Cowan – Flight 918 aft Flight Attendants.
Kaydrain Gognat – LaGuardia Airport Gate Agent.

National Transportation Safety Board (NTSB)

Michael Neal - Chairman of the NTSB.
Mark Evans – Investigator In Charge (IIC) of Flight 918's accident.
Lori Almond – Assistant IIC.
Benjamin Caulk – Investigator who accompanies Kyle and Lori into the airplane.
Ed Holstrom - CVR Analyst.

Federal Aviation Administration (FAA)

Connie Broten - Administrator.
Stewart Halloren - Deputy Administrator

Phillip Worden - Associate Administrator of Aviation Safety.

Jerry Krubsack - Manager of the Flight Standards Service. Chavette's Superior.

Chris Emerson - Manager of the Office of Accident Investigation and Prevention. Skaggs Superior.

Glenn Skaggs - Head of the FAA investigative team of flight 918.

Pierre Chavette – Manager of the Chicago Flight Standards District Office. Norman's superior.

George Niemeier – Principal Operations Inspector in Houston. In charge of overseeing Omega Airlines.

Ernie Norman - Inspector on flight 918.

Federal Bureau Of Investigation

Special Agent Samatha (Sam) Rankin – Agent in charge of investigating the NTSB break in.

Special Agent Bryant Taber – Rankin's partner.

FBI Special agent Austin – Lead agent who goes to FAA Administrators house.

FBI Special agent Murphy - Austin's partner.

Special Agents Laura Katic and Martin Sexton – Agents at Dulles airport.

Gary Lampe – Commander of the Hostage Rescue Team (HRT).

Agent Cavanah – Agent that guarded Kyle and Lori at the Hoover building.

Global Security

Nathan Kaufman - CEO
Yackel and Montes – Operatives.

List of Acronyms

ALPA – Airline Pilot's Association. The Union that represents Omega Airlines pilots. This is acronyms is pronounced al-pa.

CVR – Cockpit Voice Recorder

FAA – Federal Aviation Administration. The government agency that regulates aviation.

FSDO – Flight Standards District Office. This is pronounced fis-do.

FO – First Officer. The copilot.

IIC – Investigator In Charge. The lead NTSB investigator for an accident.

ILS – Instrument Landing System. A navigation system that guides an airplane vertically and horizontally to a runway.

MEL – Minimum Equipment List. The handbook that lists whether a component on an aircraft can be inoperative.

NTSB – National Transportation Safety Board. The government agency that investigates transportation accidents and promoting transportation safety.

POI – Principal Operations Inspector. The chief FAA Inspector responsible for overseeing an airlines operation.

QRH – Quick Reference Handbook. The handbook in the cockpit listing emergency and abnormal procedures.

RTO – Rejected Take Off. A setting on the autobrake system of the 737.

V1 – The speed a crew decides to either continue a takeoff, or reject it.

Webperf – Omega Airlines weight and balance and performance sheet that is printed before each flight.

Made in United States
Troutdale, OR
08/20/2023